the
note

zoë folbigg

First published as an ebook in 2017 by Aria,
an imprint of Head of Zeus Ltd

First published in print in the UK in 2017 by Aria

9 7 5 6 8

A catalogue record for this book is available
from the British Library.

ISBN (PB): 9781788543606
ISBN (E): 9781786698070

Typeset by Adrian McLaughlin

Printed and bound by
CPI Group (UK) Ltd, Croydon, CRO 4YY

Head of Zeus Ltd
First Floor East
5–8 Hardwick Street
London ECIR 4RG

WWW.HEADOFZEUS.COM

the note

Zoë Folbigg is a magazine journalist and digital editor, starting at *Cosmopolitan* in 2001 and since freelancing for titles including *Glamour*, *Fabulous*, *Daily Mail*, *Healthy*, *LOOK*, *Top Santé*, *Mother & Baby*, *ELLE*, *Sunday Times Style*, and Style.com. In 2008 she had a weekly column in *Fabulous* magazine documenting her year-long round-the-world trip with 'Train Man' – a man she had met on her daily commute. She since married Train Man and lives in Hertfordshire with him and their two young sons. This is her debut novel.

"You know I dreamed about you...
I missed you, for 29 years"

The National, 'Slow Show'

Part One

I

Maya has done it. She has delivered three sentences and a friendly sign-off, and now it is out of her hands. She struggles to walk the incline of the seemingly uphill train carriage because her legs are shaking, her mouth is dry, and putting one foot in front of the other takes effort and focus her racing heart isn't capable of at the moment.

Her legs buckle as Maya slumps into a seat on the other side of a grubby internal door. Which is just as well because she wanted to linger with the last straggles of bedraggled Train People disembarking reluctantly; to make herself invisible to all the commuters she just embarrassed herself in front of. So, Maya lies low with the sleepy people. The people who can't stand their jobs. The people who are lost in someone else's life, frantically turning or swiping pages to find out if the girl got the guy, the adventurer made it back to London or the heretic was burned at the stake.

Train Man isn't a straggler. Every day Maya sees him stand up confidently at the same point on the track, somewhere between the football stadium and the tunnel, as the train snakes towards a new day and a new terminus. Equine legs, strong arms. He throws a grey backpack with two thin brown leather straps onto his back, stands in the doorway and, as the train comes to a stop and orange lights ding, he steps off with pace and purpose. Maya usually walks a healthy distance behind Train Man, tiny sparks flying from her heels, down the platform and through the barriers under the canopy of a reverse waterfall bubbling white and bright above them. The intimate huddle of a metal umbrella for thousands of people who don't even look up. Train Man always walks straight through the station and Maya wonders what he's listening to, trying to guess from his gait, not realizing he was at four of the six gigs she went to in the past year. Every day she sees him turn right out of the station and walk swiftly, resolutely, into a mist of people down the road. Until she can't keep up with his long stride, he in Converse, she in heels – or ballerina flats if she needs to be nimble and get to a meeting – and Maya tends to lose him around the big crossroads at the artery by the hospital. But not today. Today Train Man has long gone.

When Maya's legs buckled and she fell into a dusty seat, she put distance between where Train Man had been sitting, where she had awkwardly stood over him, and into this sanctuary of a cringe-free carriage. Catching her breath, she waits for three minutes until she, Maya Flowers, is the last of the stragglers. Hot face. Thumping heart.

I did it!

In the empty carriage, Maya's legs stop shaking and she flattens her wavy hair in an attempt to regain composure for no one's benefit. She takes long deep breaths and calms herself by putting her fingertips against her ribcage to feel her lungs fill slowly.

A tall man in a bright blue short-sleeved shirt that sits pleasingly against Somali skin steps on and starts to throw newspapers into a sack before passengers board the train that will take them north.

Maya stands and tries to stride with Train Man's purpose. She knows she won't catch him up today, to see whether he is clutching her note to his heart, whether it's crumpled in his pocket, or whether he tossed it into a bin. It doesn't matter for now. What matters is she did it.

Spring sunshine looks down gently and tempers rise noisily in the gridlock of an underpass, but all Maya can hear among the birds and the horns are the words of an American woman in her head.

'*What's the worst that can happen?*'

Maya smiles proudly as she passes a bin and gives a cursory glance into it.

2

Nipping across traffic lights and weaving between cyclists at the junction where nine babies were born last night in the hospital on the corner, Maya skips over towards Marylebone Road and wonders what today will bring her. She can't wait to tell her eight-hour friends that she only went and bloody did it. Maya finally gave Train Man the note.

But first, there is another announcement to be made. At 9.30 a.m., the new site editor will be revealed to the marketing team and all the heads of department. It's a big deal at FASH, the clothing giant where Maya works. For a moment, Maya forgets her heart and remembers that, a fortnight ago, she stood nervously in front of five members of the board, including her boss, content director Lucy, who had advised Maya to go for the job of site editor – and was definitely the most encouraging pair of eyes in that room. Maya delivered a presentation on how she sees the future of the FASH website, how FASH can keep engaging with style-savvy girls around the world who want fast fashion in just three swipes and a tap of their phone, and how Maya would play her part in keeping the content compelling. Maya was dreading it. Her voice wobbles a bit when she talks to groups of more than four people and she didn't really want to go for the job, she likes being chief copy editor at FASH. It's fun. It's frivolous. And she gets to look at clothes all day and write sparkling descriptions of them. As if a metallic silver midi skirt in camo jacquard isn't enough, Maya gets to give it a name – that was the Lupita. Then Maya hands Lupita over to the writers on the team, Alex and Liz, who fashion a story around selling the skirt – in the Lupita's case it was 'Dazzle On Date Night' – which Maya then edits and, boom, FASH's millions of customers around the world are inspired to buy it. You know when you buy a dress or a skirt or a top and see it's called something like Hepburn or Elissia and wonder who came up with that name? Well, at FASH that's Maya's job. Clothing names. Campaign names. What to call the trends. What to say about them on the site. 'Ten ways to rock Baroque' and 'Nineties normal' were two of FASH's most clicked looks in the past year and Maya was the star wordsmith behind them. But editing the site? That's a proper grown-up job dealing with finance and staff appraisals and negotiating with brand managers and heads of department vying to have their clothes placed most prominently on site. Maya likes to be the confidante on the team, not the commander. Although the money would be handy. Just last December Maya bought her first home, a Victorian first-floor maisonette, with high ceilings and mouldy window frames, and it needs a bit of investment and love. Maya is happy living on her own for the first time ever. She doused the whole flat in shades of white and grey so she could get to know it before she goes full-on lime green and gunmetal, but yes, it's a home that needs money and love.

And Maya didn't want to look unambitious and ungrateful. Lucy was behind her, egging her on, and that's a big deal.

Lucy is one of FASH founder Rich Robinson's chief advisors, and she is always championing Maya because Maya is smart, she works hard, she's never a diva and she just gets on with it. Plus Lucy thinks Maya's little crush on the stranger on the train is just adorable.

Lucy first heard about Maya Flowers when Maya worked for FASH's biggest rival, Walk In Wardrobe. Maya joined Walk In Wardrobe straight from university. Maya had already bitten the travelling bug when she was eighteen and wanted to get on the career ladder. She didn't plan to work in fashion but did want to work with words, so when she landed her first proper job at Walk In Wardrobe she was over the moon. At Walk In Wardrobe, Maya was diligent and friendly, which was rare among the Sloane Rangers, but she quietly worked her way up from junior copywriter to chief copy editor in less than four years before Lucy poached her for the role at FASH when Maya was twenty-five. Two years later Maya thinks perhaps she does deserve a promotion.

Gosh, my fate will be revealed on many levels today. Good job I wore nice shoes.

Maya marvels at the queues of people at the Planetarium and crosses the busy road to avoid the packs on the backs of continental schoolkids, while also noting that their pastel drainpipes would fit nicely in a 'Fondant Fancies' collection she's putting together. Maya skips left onto Baker Street and two thirds of the way down is FASH HQ. An art deco Egyptian Revival building with an ornate colonnade of twelve decorative columns proudly lining the front. Two glass ramps jut out between four of the columns in opposing directions, converging at the same point on the pavement. Maya often wonders which arm to choose as both lead to the same set of glass doors and through to a modern atrium, so today she chooses the nearside catwalk, her hair waving a little as she darts through the doors past three bald and bored security guards. Maya swipes her pass, goes through a second set of glass doors and heads up the metallic silver staircase.

The entrance to FASH sums up all it is about. Excitement! Colour! Fun! Pride! On the left of reception, giddy interns sit on the low-backed curve of two colour-clashing sofas, nervously awaiting the start of a brilliant career in fashion. To the right, glass-fronted meeting rooms showcase the early risers, coffees in hand, as they look over samples and swatches of what you will be wearing next year. Models saunter past in dressing gowns, waiting to be shot wearing the thousands of new pieces that landed that day from factories in far-off lands. In the middle of the space, a receptionist sits at a silver desk with blonde ambition, her headpiece in place ready to answer the phone while she scrolls through pages and pages of clothes, deciding what to buy with her forty per cent staff discount. A huge video screen sits behind the reception desk, leading from the floor all the way up to the top of the staircase showcasing FASH's key looks of the season: the happy redhead in the yellow and white shift dress with the peplum skirt and two-tone strappy sandals. The brunette in the black dressy dungarees over a simple black bandeau top and skate shoes.

Maya hops up the stairs in her bow heels to the open-plan canteen at the top. This ceiling is lower than the atrium of the reception and achingly cool, deliberately exposed metal pipes sit above a collection of multicoloured chairs and distressed wooden tables. Maya looks ahead. A cooked breakfast station to her left. Porridge in front. Croissants to her right. Which to choose from this confection of free food? FASH *is* the most fun place to work in fashion retail. The food is free, the clothes come at forty per cent off and its epic summer and Christmas parties are the stuff of legend. Everyone who works there has a feeling of pride, of being looked after, of being at the forefront of a digital fashion revolution.

After what Maya just did on the 8.21, she can't really face food, plus you can't exactly take a fry-up to a heads of department meeting for a big announcement. So she bypasses the cooked food and heads for the pastries.

'Hey Maya!' says Sam, grabbing a pain au chocolat from over her shoulder. Tall limbs knock into small shoulders and Sam blushes. 'Sorry mate, bit of crumb on your top.' Sam goes to brush it off Maya's blouse but stops himself.

'Don't worry, it's flaky pastry,' Maya says with a soft flick, hoping the butter doesn't leave a grease mark on her silk blouse. Maya is wearing a green and white silk blouse tucked into grey 'awkward-length' culottes (Maya came up with that term too) and green shoe boots with a bow on each ankle. She is dressed smartly this morning for two reasons: 1) to wow Train Man, and 2) in case she has to stand up in front of all the heads of department in the next half hour and humbly smile when she's appointed site editor.

'Psyched about the big announcement?' asks Sam.

Maya gives a fake smile.

'Grinning not winning,' she says.

Sam is a developer – head of the tech team in fact, and has been rooting for Maya to get this promotion since she confided in him that Lucy had asked her to go for it.

'You'll be great!' he says.

A few weeks ago, just before Maya gave her presentation, Sam left a mixtape on her desk of clichéd go-get-'em songs to help her get in the zone.

'I can't play it! I don't have a tape recorder!' laughed Maya.

'Yeah but it's the thought that counts,' said Sam, who emailed Maya the track list so she could listen to it through her computer headphones as she worked on the finishing touches of the presentation.

Maya wraps her pain au chocolat in a white tissue and looks up at Sam.

'The site needs a figurehead to lead it forward, and there's no one better than you Maya, you'll be perfect. People respect your opinion, you're authoritative, but crucially, you're not a dick.' Eloquent as ever. Like most developers at FASH, Sam isn't interested in fashion. He works there because it is one of the world's most visited websites, and with that comes some techie kudos. He wears old rock T-shirts with holes in, faded jeans ripped at the bottom and flip-flops even in winter. He is tall with Tintin hair and has a round face with crinkly eyes that look like he's laughing even when he's stopped.

'Never mind that announcement,' says Maya. 'I have one of my own.'

Sam looks at her, narrow eyes as expectant as they can be.

'I gave Train Man the note!' she squeaks, waiting for a fanfare.

Sam's round face turns pink. 'You did? Wow! Well done! What did he say?'

Sam knows how Maya feels about Train Man, his desk sits back-to-back with Maya's and he is the only guy on the two islands of desks they occupy. He has listened to Maya talk about Train Man for the past ten months. What he wears. What he reads. Whether he looked up that day.

Maya knows what Sam thinks about her crush and rudimentary stalking. At Christmas, when Maya asked Sam how he would feel if a girl he didn't know, gave him a home-made mince pie and a Christmas card with her number written on it on his commute from Brighton, he said, 'I'd chuck it in the bin and think she was a nutjob.' Which was enough to squash that idea.

'Well he didn't say anything this morning, he was a bit flustered, and I didn't give him a chance to, I walked away, but I haven't checked my email yet, there might be something there...' Maya says with a hopeful heart, as she pulls her phone out of her pocket. It is 9.28 a.m. 'Shit, we'd better go downstairs.'

3

In the biggest meeting room there is a huge space with a wooden floor, a bar and colourful patchwork pouffes like rectangular bales of hay where all the big events and company announcements are held. It's also the place Maya goes once a week for her Monday morning inventory of new stock, so she can rummage amongst scarves, shoes, dresses, skirts, hairbands, tops, trousers and bags to come up with names for each and every one of them before they are shot in the studio on a schedule run with military precision. If the clothes are really good, they'll then be packed up into enormous suitcases to be photographed in glamorous locations by the fashion team led by Zara. Maya goes through every item to make it something more than a SKU number. Sometimes Maya is inspired straight away. The Nena skirt was easy. Multicoloured like a Frida Kahlo-inspired creation. It screamed of her best friend Nena. The beige bag that was shaped like a square and Maya called Boxy was a little less inspiring. When Zara talks Maya through a collection that's about to be shot in Miami or LA or Cape Town, Maya has to come up with a name for that collection, a tone, a trend, and the writers will write stories for the website based around it. When the pictures are back from the retouchers, the clothes are at the warehouse and the collection is ready to drop, Maya's words bring the whole look together. The lace dresses and high-neck blouses of 'Ten Ways To Rock Baroque' all started in that room. Perhaps Maya's new managerial career is about to as well.

Sam and Maya pull up a patchwork bale and perch on it. Maya wonders if Lucy ought to have warned her in case she has to prep a speech. Why leave it to a big reveal in front of most of the department heads? She looks around the room. It's a daunting collection of FASH's most senior people. Maya's legs feel weak for the second time today. In the two years Maya has worked at FASH she has come to recognize these powerful faces, even if they wouldn't recognize hers. There's the executive team, five of whom she presented to last week: the CEO Rich Robinson, dressed like Bobby Ewing in a blazer, white shirt and jeans; CFO Rich True who is tall and stringy like a green bean, but he does actually count beans for a living; editorial director Lucy; head of customer experience, Geri, a pint-sized powerhouse of a woman; head of legal, Andy, with a high dome-shaped bald head, reminiscent of the Planetarium Maya walks past twice a day; head of the international sites, Sarah, who always looks like she's asleep, probably because she crosses the International Date Line at least once a week; head of womenswear, Zara, whose jet-black hair and gap-toothed smile make her look like a seventies rock chick, and head of tech, Sam. They're joined by the other six members of Maya's editorial team, who have all been invited to find out who their new boss is.

At the front sit Rich and Rich, who founded FASH as the Fast Accessible Style Hub at the dawn of a new millennium, when everyone said online shopping wouldn't take off. Within ten years FASH was selling all over the world. Mums might have stuck to the high street so they could see, feel and try on clothes in poorly lit dressing rooms, but their style-savvy daughters cottoned on fast and now twenty-somethings from Milan to Paris, Madrid to Moscow, New York to Sydney turn to FASH for their outfits. Women's clothes have made Rich and Rich *very* rich.

Lucy got on board soon after FASH launched, when Rich and Rich realised that forty-something men dressed as oil tycoons know more about retailing than they do about style. And Lucy is the most stylish woman at FASH.

She stands up ready for the big reveal; her black halter top exposes Pilates-perfect arms on a sinewy, powerful body. Her shiny butter-blonde bob falls into place to frame brown eyes, and she dusts down her immaculately ironed silk palazzo pants. You would never guess Lucy has two preschoolers.

'Thanks for coming, I'll keep it brief because you're all super busy,' says Lucy, north-west lilt still there despite years of living in London. That's what Maya admires about Lucy. She could so easily have got caught up in an overblown fashion bubble that comes with her style nous and her salary, but she's a fiercely proud Lancashire girl at heart. 'But I'm delighted and honoured to reveal our new site editor to you this morning and want you to congratulate her on this amazing role.' Eyes dart around the room. 'We interviewed some of fashion's editorial elite but when it came to the crunch, this person stood out for her brilliant word wizardry, her knack for spotting the next big trend, and her ability to translate that to millions of customers around the world – while also having the people skills to keep an overworked team working happily and passionately.'

Maya's face flushes. Sam gives her a gentle nudge with his forearm as he leans into her ribs.

'She is such a bright spark, I couldn't resist poaching her from Walk In Wardrobe...'

Oh my god.

Maya pictures replacement double-glazed wooden sash windows shining bright in the gleaming sunlight on her first-floor maisonette.

'So please put your hands together for Cressida Blaise-Snellman!' Lucy cranes her head towards the door. 'We're so happy to welcome you to the FASH fold, Cressida, come on in!' Hands clap. Cressida, a blushing willow of a woman, walks in with a coquettish pout. Razor-cut cheekbones, long, thin honey-blonde hair tucked behind her ears, and the exact same outfit the model in the smart black dungarees and bandeau bra top wears on the big screen behind reception, only Cressida styles hers up with a neat black blazer resting on her shoulders like a cape.

'*Cressida?*' Maya says, aghast, a faintly freckled nose crumpling. Fortunately no one hears among the applause because FASH is a place where triumphs are to be celebrated. Maya worked with Cressida at Walk In Wardrobe and she definitely doesn't remember her for her people skills.

'Bad luck mate,' says Sam apologetically, although his crinkled eyes make him look like he's laughing. 'Back to work.'

4

Maya and the rest of the editorial team snake back through reception and up the stairs with a little less vim than their descent, as they head to their two islands of desks.

'Well, that sucks,' says picture editor Olivia flatly, as she slumps into her window seat in the chair next to Maya's. Olivia is as loud as she is big and her wild orange corkscrew-curled hair is like a sunburst of sunshine and warmth whatever the weather.

Social media manager Emma sits facing Olivia on the other side of the desk next to the window. Blue, flower fairy eyes sparkle in the sunshine and jump out against dark brown shoulder-length hair. She is Maya's oldest friend at FASH and is online day and night, responding to tweets, searching for what's trending, advising the team on what the customers are rating and hating, and is too lovely to work in fashion. She sits next to Lucy, who is opposite Maya, making up the fourth terminal, so she can keep Lucy up to date on breaking fashion news. When Lucy's at her desk that is. She's been so busy lately. For months, she's needed a new site editor to support her and take a load of work off her hands while she moves into her more strategic role.

On the bank of desks behind Lucy and Emma sit the other four members of the FASH editorial team. Senior writer Alex and his junior Liz. Between them they translate the looks into shareable, clickable and – most importantly – shoppable articles, so that the FASH visitor will see exactly why she must have the new must-have bomber. And then buy it. Liz is a meek and mousy girl with an encyclopaedic knowledge of every item of clothing any major fashion house ever sent down the runway. Liz is so nice, even Lucy feels guilty asking her to get her a bread-free sandwich from the deli café over the road at lunchtime. Alex is a carefully coiffed, softly spoken fashion powerhouse. His experience in fashion writing is vast and he has tried every trend going since he was clumsily clipping Grolsch beer bottles to his shoes in the eighties.

Opposite Liz and Alex giggle Chloe and Holly, the youngest and most fun members of the team. If you want to know who snogged who at the summer party, Chloe and Holly will tell you. All those fancy graphics flashing on the home page? They're designed by Chloe, and Holly is a picture researcher, who, when she's not scrolling through Instagram or braiding her long dip-dyed hair, is focused on the shots from the hundreds taken in the FASH studio every day.

So, these are Maya's eight-hour friends, but she is also their confidante. Most of the team at some point have asked Maya for 'a quick word in the canteen' and usually it's about a family dilemma, boyfriend issue, or party outfit advice. All of them, apart from Lucy evidently, wish Maya had got the site editor job rather than the willowy woman they were just presented with downstairs.

*

Maya sits at her computer in the big open-plan office. Refresh refresh refresh. Not a single email from anyone who could be Train Man. Maya ponders Cressida Blaise-Snellman but doesn't glance up at her as she moves into her new desk opposite, filling Lucy's empty magazine box files with her copies of *Vogue*, *Vanity Fair* and *The New Yorker*. Maya knows that Cressida recognises her; they crossed over at Walk In Wardrobe for a year before Lucy poached Maya. But as Cressida introduces herself to the editorial team, she pretends she doesn't.

'Gather round my desk everyone!' she beckons. Chloe and Holly walk over while Liz, Alex and Emma swing their chairs around. Maya and Olivia stand at their desks. 'Super excited to be here obvs,' she says in a cut-glass Chelsea accent. 'I will learn your names in due course, promise. But let's just say that I'm better with faces than names,' she says, holding up a Models 1 directory and filing it alongside her magazines.

There are only seven of us to remember.

Perhaps Cressida doesn't remember Maya, perhaps Maya is that insignificant. Train Man has barely noticed her in almost a year of sitting *almost* opposite him, every single morning. Maybe Cressida is embarrassed. She is now working with someone who might remember how she bullied an intern so badly that one lunchtime the intern left her desk and didn't come back. When Cressida finally got through to her mobile and demanded she come back from lunch, the intern pretended she'd been run over by a bus and couldn't return. Ever. Maya saw the intern in a pub in Soho the next night, not a single bone broken nor a limb in plaster. Sheepishly, the intern confessed she had to get away from Cressida. Maya didn't tell Cressida about it at the time, she didn't want to embarrass her, but the whole team suspected that Cressida had pushed a young and once enthusiastic intern to make up such a drastic lie.

'I will of course arrange one-to-ones with each of you, my BF owns a chi-chi bar on Marylebone High Street, so we can do them there.' A pause for effect. 'For now, back to work, chop chop.'

Olivia sits back down in her chair and sends Maya and Emma an email.

Did she just say 'chop chop'?!

Before Emma has a chance to read Olivia's message, Cressida asks her if she would kindly switch desks so she can have Emma's window seat.

'Cressie is just a *nightmare* if she doesn't have optimum daylight,' she says in the third person.

Maya tries to get lost in 'Varsity Chic', a new trend from the autumn/winter lookbook that is all about collegiate jackets, PE socks and prep-school stripes, and it's all a bit nauseatingly reminiscent of Cressida's style. Refresh refresh refresh. She can't concentrate. Cressida Blaise-Snellman's arrival is making Maya's freckles wilt. But more upsettingly, Train Man is making Maya's heart crumple. It is gone 11 a.m. and she hasn't heard anything.

5

As the spring afternoon draws to a close and the sun on Marylebone's rooftops bathes London in a magical glow, the communication Maya craved since the first moment she saw Train Man almost a year ago finally appears on her screen, sitting in her email inbox like a hand grenade. 5.08 p.m. Subject matter: The Guy From The Train.

'God, he's emailed me,' Maya says flatly, betraying the flip, kick, stab, she can feel in her stomach. After Cressida's appointment this morning heralded a new, quiet office order, Maya didn't feel it was the right time to blurt out to Emma and Olivia, or anyone else for that matter, how she'd finally given Train Man the note.

'Who's emailed you?' asks Emma, her canny intuition knowing this blurting out might be something important.

'Hush, I'm on a call,' waves Cressida dismissively.

'Did Train Man reply?' Sam swings around in his chair.

'Train Man?' shouts Olivia gleefully, clapping her hands together.

Damn.

If Maya had just stayed quiet, opened the email, read it and digested it in silence, she could have coped with whatever was written with gentle dignity. Now she's blown it. At least Chloe and Holly didn't hear, lost as they are in instagossip.

Alex stands up, smooths his hand delicately up his ice-cream-perfect quiff of hair and pushes circular horn-rimmed glasses down his nose inquisitively.

'Erm, Maya, do we have news?' he asks over his spectacles.

Cressida, phone in one hand, furrows a fair brow and puts an index finger to her pout with the other hand, to tell the team to shush again.

'Shit man,' whispers Sam. 'What does he say?'

Maya,

Thanks for the note – sorry if I seemed dazed on the train, I was battling hay fever.

It was really sweet of you but unfortunately I have a girlfriend, and I don't think she'd be impressed if I went for a drink with you.

What you did wasn't silly though, it takes a lot of guts – I'd never have the courage to do something like that.

Happy birthday!
James

He's called James. *James*, Maya thinks to herself. Nice reliable name. Three sentences and a friendly sign-off. Underneath, it says James Miller, Account Director, MFDD – whatever that means.

Four eager faces look at Maya hopefully. She reads it again, surrounded by people she wants to disappear but feeling bad that she's about to let them down. Maya's like that you see, worried about disappointing her friends, even though she is devastated herself.

I have a girlfriend.

'What does he say?' badgers Sam, pretending not to read the screen.

I don't think she'd be impressed.

Maya wants to cry. There's another woman Train Man wants to impress. A woman he loves. Maya's face is hot. She knew this would happen. Life never works out as it should.

I have a girlfriend.

It would have been too good to be true otherwise.

I don't think she'd be impressed.

'He has a girlfriend,' Maya casually waves.

A collective moan rises up into the strip lighting of the fading day, but Emma is silent, she can tell how much the email is hurting Maya.

'Fuck him,' says Olivia, bringing her brash brilliance to diffuse a clearly awkward situation. 'You're gorgeous, his loss.'

Cressida puts her palm over the mouthpiece of the phone that's still clamped to her ear and looks across the desk at Olivia crossly.

'Guys, can you keep it down please? I'm on the phone to HR for my staff discount code.'

Everyone gets back to work. Maya rises out of her chair and walks through the glass doors to the canteen and straight past the food stations that had long stopped serving cooked breakfasts, lunches and snacks. Her face is burning hot, her heart shrinks with every step she takes. As Maya crosses the canteen, the low silver pipes of a hip industrial ceiling make her feel like she can't breathe. She swipes her pass and goes through the identical glass doors on the other side and walks in a daze until she gets to the ladies' toilet. Maya opens the door and walks in. She looks down at her feet so people won't notice her eyes welling up, even though the bathroom is empty. They are nice shoes, her favourite pair in fact. Maya made an extra effort today, as she has for the past eleven days. She should feel as gorgeous now as she did when she bought the shoes three weeks ago, with her forty per cent staff discount, but every step that distances her from Train Man's words makes Maya feel smaller, weaker, more hopeless. Maya turned twenty-eight eleven days ago. It's not even her birthday.

Maya looks in the mirror and puts a damp paper towel over her red face to calm it. Her friends probably think she's crying, so she fights it. Maya is always the calm one. The controlled one. And really, no one died. Not today anyway.

I suspected this might be the outcome.

Although Maya can't explain why, she's still surprised by it. Maybe it serves her right for thinking she had a chance.

Of course Train Man has a girlfriend, he's too beautiful.

But part of Maya is surprised because she could see herself with Train Man, together in a happy future. Not a Hollywood future either. A real one, where hair greys, smiles thin, but lovers still hold hands, despite having seen the worst of each other. Her intuition was wrong, it has failed her.

Maya used to have great intuition and Seeing The Future skills. Like the time in her early twenties when she won a weekend trip to Paris. As Maya took the coin out of her purse to buy the raffle ticket, she had a vision, a flash of her sister Clara giggling with her along the edge of the Seine, smiles smattered with ice cream, as they were just six weeks later. Or the time someone burst into the back garden of the Flowers' family home when Maya was eight. She was making perfume under the old elder tree, grinding rose petals with water. The perfume would never smell like the beautiful rose-shaped soap on her mother's dressing table, but Maya tried for a whole summer to nail the elixir, and sometimes splashed it on her face while she sat looking in Dolores Flowers' triptych mirror. Maya ground rose petals in solitude as the skinny man with the beard ran down the side of the house and burst through the garden gate at the back of their Georgian house on the hill. Before the man opened his mouth to speak, Maya knew that Clara was lying in a heap in the middle of a road three streets away.

I must have got this one wrong.

Maya concludes that her Seeing The Future skills can only fully function where Clara is concerned. After all, Maya's Seeing The Future skills had already failed her catastrophically in her twenties, the time her hair turned wavy.

Part Two

6

Ten months earlier – July 2013

Maya stands on the steaming tarmac of the London-bound platform. Bumpy grey paving is trimmed by a bright yellow safety line, giving her the uncomfortable sensation of walking on Lego. It is Platform 2 and Maya had to dash from Platform 1, down some stairs and through the tunnel that smells of urine to get there. Every time Maya walks the subterranean gauntlet, she worries that this twenty-second necessity will coincide with a high-speed train passing on the tracks above, and that today will be the day the rickety tunnel roof finally gives in.

It's an overcast, oppressively warm kind of day but Maya isn't sad to be waiting for her train again. Soon she will be with her friends and they will have fun. They'll talk about ideas for autumn/winter even though it is high summer, they'll laugh about last night's TV and they'll help frame the future of affordable fashion (while also having a good laugh about the Christmas tree onesie that just arrived in the office).

Sometimes they go quiet for a few hours. Maya is very good at going quiet for a few hours, and getting lost in her world. When she was seven, Maya used to sit staring at a bookshelf in her parents' bedroom. A dusty structure about two metres wide with four levels of shelves packed too tightly with books, as was her father Herbert Flowers' storage solution. On the shelves Maya would place little wooden figures, about the length of her longest finger. The wooden figures had the same simple face with the same simple features, two black dots for eyes and a red curve for a smile, but they were dressed differently to give them their characteristics. One had long black wool hair and a red body, another wore a grass skirt, another looked like a policeman in blue. Maya's mother had bought them as stocking fillers for each of the Flowers children the Christmas before and Maya was transfixed by the dolls, creating rooms and antechambers in this dusty makeshift dolls' house by pulling out books at strategic points. Then she would place the dolls in the various rooms or corridors, and sit and stare. As still as a wooden doll herself. Creamy skin, shiny poker-straight golden brown hair, delicate freckles that came out in summer. For hours Maya would stare and envisage whole scenarios and relationships between these unlikely associates. Herbert Flowers would wonder where Maya was amid the commotion of her siblings, but she was quiet upstairs, staring at the dolls, listening to imagined conversation, immersed in another world for an entire morning.

This morning is wet, but the rain has a mugginess about it, even at 8.16 a.m. Long ago, while working in a bakery in Mexico, Maya learned that such rain was called 'chipi-chipi', a misty humid fizz of rain that does nothing but make souls wilt and hair rise. She stands on the platform reading the new-season lookbook, trying to come up with words to go with the pictures, but she can't seem to concentrate.

Same routine, same two-minute train delay on the platform departures board. Same glib faces.

Shall I make chilli tonight? she thinks while rereading the words 'Aztec print' three times. Not knowing why she can't concentrate, Maya looks up across four tracks to the steamy smeared glass of the crowded ticket hall on the other side of the expanse. She can't see that the person she's been looking for all her life is in there.

Tardy commuters run the underpass from the ticket hall to the platform with a different kind of urgency. As the train approaches, Maya focuses on the lookbook. She could board this train and sit down with her eyes closed. She even knows without looking up that today the train is a Superior Train with green and red seats, more kindly spaced apart. Not one of the clapped-out blue trains with too many seats, packed together and stained. Matted gum with skin particles stuck to it, burrowing itself into the stale faux-velveteen upholstery. Inferior Trains have carriage-to-carriage doors you have to open by turning a greasy circular handle, too small for any normal person's hand. The sound of this train alone is enough for Maya to know that it's a Superior Train. Smoother, more solid, more buoyant. Automatic internal doors and carpet. A Superior Train gives Maya's day an edge. Still she doesn't look up and flips through the lookbook and circles keywords.

For a reason she doesn't yet know, Maya is torn away from neon dogtooth and tartan and sees a new Train Person on the platform. Someone Maya has never seen get this train, at this time. Or any of the other trains she sometimes catches either side of it – but now won't. And she can't take her eyes off him as he hurriedly battles to close his umbrella as the train pulls in. New Train Person looks so different to the melee of men in suits or women in frumpy skirts and cheap jackets that they think make them look authoritative, with sleeves that are slightly too long so cuffs hang over their hands. The usual suspects she sees every day but never speaks to. The plain girl with the spherical head, whose facial features move so slowly she looks like an animatronic owl; the blonde woman with a tiny waist but inflatable-looking arms who anxiously pushes her way onto the train every morning, even though she'll always get a seat; the man who reads his *Metro* tucked inside a copy of the *Times Literary Supplement* and thinks no one notices.

This man is different. He is tall with slim legs and reassuring shoulders and has hair that is so dark brown it could be black, windswept to the side in the chipi-chipi, or is it meant to be like that? He has olive skin, wears black rectangular glasses, a black V-neck jumper, despite the warm air, and grey skinny jeans, the exact same shade of grey as the pair of jeans Maya is wearing today. She watches him walk past her, heading towards the front end of the platform alongside the braking train and stares, small, pillowy mouth open in wonder. Everything feels comforting, everything feels like home. It's a feeling Maya hasn't had for years and doesn't want to go away. Maya steps out from the hollow shelter of the leaking 1930s roof and walks up the platform after him.

As Maya hobbles on Lego behind this wondrous New Train Person and sees his equine legs striding out ahead of her, she has the sensation of a reassuring palm, gently pressing into the small of her back, urging her along.

In the carriage no one talks, everyone seems tense, and Maya tries not to look across the aisle at this man as he reads *One Hundred Years Of Solitude*. She can't help it.

Is he married?

Maya pictures her beautiful train fellow swimming in an infinity pool somewhere tropical with a ridiculously glamorous woman with ridiculously long legs wrapped around him. A disheartened heart gazes down.

He's not wearing a ring.

This man, Train Man, is sitting diagonally from Maya, on the opposite side of the carriage. Two seats face two seats, separated by a little table with gum stuck to its underbelly. The table in front of Train Man has crumbs on it but he has taken off his glasses to read (*ahh, short-sighted*) and puts his glasses on the crumbs. He is in the corner next to the window, not sitting in the direction of travel. Maya doesn't know that facing backwards makes Train Man feel uncomfortable – it doesn't even cross her mind. Maya is facing forwards in her set of four seats, and she leans her head in towards the window but doesn't touch it.

I wish I were sitting opposite him to see if his soul is as lovely from that angle.

Maya wants to look at Train Man's unbespectacled eyes but instead she hides her head in the lookbook. Maya crosses a tightly clothed leg and doesn't realise the toe of her orange Converse boot points to him.

The train stops at its one stop before the final destination and the unfortunate commuters get on. Unfortunate because they live in this unfortunate town. Unfortunate because the remaining few seats have gone now. Unfortunate that, although their fare is seventy-six pounds cheaper a month, they live in a less attractive, more thoughtlessly built modern town and they will have to stand. Maya wishes she wasn't such a snob. Her Clause IV parents wish she wasn't such a snob, but they try to see the funny side.

What's his name? He looks like he has a nice name. Bookish but sexy. Perhaps Seth or Milo, yes, I like Milo. What do you do, Milo?

Maya's imagination starts galloping with the horse in the field under the viaduct and flies along the track past swathes of red poppies jutting out of the cornfields. Maya thinks that Train Man must have started this job recently, perhaps today, as he's new on the train and she would definitely have spotted him before.

He must work for a record company or maybe he's an architect or a literary agent or something equally creative and cool.

He looks cool and Maya, looking down at her thin marl sweatshirt with a cartoon of a rainbow on it, grey jeans and Converse, suddenly feels in need of improvement. She thinks of her wardrobe packed with cute vintage dresses and fulsome skirts she saves For Special, knowing that they're being neglected while she puts her life on hold. She feels a pang of guilt.

I should treat every day as if it is special.

With the sound of a horn, the train enters a tunnel and makes the top window above Train Man blow open. Wavy hair flies across Maya's face, which she peels away and tames by tucking it behind her ear and smoothing it down.

I need to up my game and revisit my wardrobe. Maybe actually brush my hair in the morning. I should make more of an effort for work anyway, Lucy always looks so polished.

The sudden clatter of the open window pulls Train Man away from his novel and he looks up at the unfortunate commuters who have had to stand up. His gaze around the carriage, familiarising himself with newness, gives Maya her first proper insight into Train Man's eyes. Wide, lovely eyes of the darkest brown, separated by a straight nose – a nose Maya thinks is the most beautiful nose she has ever seen. She can see his eyes clearly as he looks up without his glasses on. Big and inquisitive. She's seen that shade of brown before. The seventy per cent cocoa solids that bring together the two shells of a Plantation Paineiras chocolate macaron that she saw in a shop window in Paris.

Maya hopes Train Man isn't feeling nervous about his new job, if it is a new job; there's a slight sadness about his gaze.

Did he see me look?

Maya looks away, closes her eyes and tries to fall asleep so she can free herself. The imprint of those beautiful eyes shines behind flecked eyelids as Maya starts to drift off. Eyes Maya has sought all her life and which finally arrived, two minutes late, nineteen minutes ago.

I hope I don't dribble.

7

Maya races from the Egyptian columns of FASH HQ and turns left onto Oxford Street to the Ionic columns of Selfridges' façade, where a familiar face is waiting under the black and white canopy. It's a good job Maya has runner's legs because she was already late, but now her nose, with its smattering of summer freckles, is beading and she looks even more dishevelled. You wouldn't know from the now streaming sun that this morning was so dreary. Maya's grey skinny jeans seem a little wintry for the way the day turned out, but she raided the fashion cupboard at lunchtime and changed out of her rainbow sweatshirt into a cropped T-shirt with illustrations of beetles and butterflies all over it.

'Nice bugs,' says her best friend Nena, looking at Maya's chest and her widening enormous, feline eyes.

'Thanks,' Maya replies with a wink and kisses her friend's cheek, wiping a smudge of white face paint off it as she draws away.

Nena is wearing her trademark black vest top over skin-tight leather-look leggings and ballet flats. The blank canvas for whatever incarnation she has been today, which from the remnants of white face paint Maya is guessing was a clown.

They pause to let shoppers out of heavy brass and glass doors and enter the sweet and heady scented world of the perfume hall. They snake through the beauty department, where gurus from Henriksen to Hauschka promise skin salvation, bypassing Hermès for Hermé in the confectionary hall. This is what they do when they meet after Maya has finished work for the day, before Nena starts her evening's graft. They will choose four macarons from the counter at Pierre Hermé, which they will take carefully up four escalators to the food hall on the top floor, where they will enjoy them with an unsullying sparkling water to clear the palette between flavours and a sullying gossip. When Maya and Nena first began this tradition, they would each buy the other four flavours, a different combination every time, but now they do away with that and choose their own at the counter with orange, grey, fuchsia and lime stripes above it to colour-match the confections sitting under climate-controlled glass.

'So what's new?' asks Nena. Black, mischievous eyes, sparkling brightly despite their darkness.

Everything about Nena sparkles brightly.

Maya looks around the confectionary hall, bursting with women weighed down with designer shopping bags after a day of frivolity and she feels as unsophisticated as she did on the first sweet treat outing she made with Nena, who would become her last best friend, eating ice cream together on a south coast pier.

The friends met on their first night at university, freshly arrived cohabiters in the same halls of residence. That sorry Sunday evening, when teary parents had long since headed back up the A3 and Maya's mother Dolores had done her best to make breeze-block walls look homely, and the warden, a mature Scottish student in an Australian cork hat, read an unnecessarily unfriendly riot act on the rules and regulations of this cell-block style accommodation. Maya looked at the strangers packed into the windowless TV room to gauge faces: did anyone else find this approach a little heavy? There were, after all, 188 scared teens in the room. But as Maya looked around, only Nena's face stood out. Bored at the back. Twirling a strand of long shiny black hair from the artwork piled high on her head and woven intricately in fabrics of turquoise, red and yellow. Dark skin that made it impossible to detect her ethnicity: was she Latin or Indian or Caribbean? Her huge eyes had whites around the edges like a lion pup but looked as though they were painted in thick eyeliner; her plump lips were raspberry red, even though she wasn't wearing a scrap of make-up. She wore a loose black off-the-shoulder top over a black vest and leggings and delicate dusty-pink ballerina flats on small feet. Small but strong, a body like an acrobat's. The sort of girl who stands out in a crowd, as she had earlier in the week when Maya noticed her and her tower of hair, not falling out of place while she jumped up and down to 'Last Nite' at Brixton Academy. They hadn't spoken that serendipitous night; Nena hadn't noticed Maya, but it was enough of a coincidence to be a conversation starter for Maya six days later.

After the introductory sermon, Maya went over to Nena and said hello. Nena smiled and they never looked back.

Almost a decade later, they are still the best of friends, as silly as each other, with strange hang-ups or ways of thinking that only the other would understand. Nena is scared of stickers and won't ever eat fruit in case a gluey Cape, Enza or Del Monte logo touches her. Maya lines her home with conkers every September to keep the spiders out. It has

38

worked for the two autumns she has rented a room in her brother Jacob's house. Last year, Maya collected seventy-six conkers from the common near their parents' home on the hill, lined them up along windowsills and doorways, and by the time they'd shrivelled up that December, Maya realised she hadn't seen a single house spider all season. Jacob finds it somewhat annoying in autumn when he walks in from work, slips and almost breaks his leg on a conker, but ever since his big sister came to live with him, when her hair turned wavy, he let the small stuff slide. Plus he's not that fond of spiders either.

'Let's get the macarons, I'll explain upstairs,' says Maya.

At the counter Nena chooses the most colourful concoction she can: pistachio and raspberry compote; yoghurt and grapefruit; rose and lychee; passion fruit and rhubarb. As the French woman serving them hands Nena her cellophane bag she passes it straight to Maya to remove the sticker seal for her. Maya then chooses, following today's high-summer leanings, and opts for lemon; jasmine flower; orange and basil flower; carrot and pistachio.

'Oh my god, AMAZING,' says Nena, sinking white teeth into passion fruit and rhubarb as they rise on the first escalator from leather into denim.

Maya can't wait for the fourth floor before she tells her friend the news.

'I got it back. I got The Feeling!' she bursts, clasping Nena's bare brown shoulder.

Nena chokes on crispy, powdery shell as she takes in a deep gasp.

'THE feeling? Like Leonardo DiCaprio through a fish tank kinda feeling?'

'Yep... Although the guy I'm in love with wasn't looking

at me like that. Or looking at me at all for that matter. But it was proper butterflies I haven't had in, well, you know...'

'Bloody hell, what does he look like?'

Maya ponders. How can she describe those eyes, that beautiful full reading mouth, or the solid V at the base of his neck? How can she explain falling in love after nineteen minutes without sounding crazy?

'He's got that cool nerdy rock star thing. Dark. Hipster glasses. Mysterious. Beautiful. Oh my god, Nena, he shines. But quietly, unassumingly. He looked lovely. And he gets my train!' Maya says with glee, as if this means they're in a relationship. 'Or at least I hope he will tomorrow. And the day after. Oh god, what if he's a tourist?' she says, running desperate fingers through her scalp.

Nena has never seen her best friend behave so strangely, Maya is usually more measured and thoughtful than this. In fact, it's usually the other way around. But Maya's eyes look so bright, Nena can see orange blossom shards floating among praline pools.

'A Monday morning commuter train? He's not a tourist,' says Nena with authority. 'Is he married?'

'No ring.'

'Did he give any signs of having a Special Someone?'

'Well he's very handsome and looks nice, so I guess he must. And he's reading *One Hundred Years Of Solitude*, so he's a romantic. And cerebral. He'd be in demand.' Maya's heart sinks a little at the prospect.

'Let's face it, any hot guy in London is in demand,' shrugs Nena, taking the rose and lychee macaron out of the bag and raising an exasperated eyebrow. As if she's ever had to make an effort for someone to fall for her. Nena has never had trouble finding love in London, no matter how much she pretends she and Maya are in the same single sisterhood. Nena is one of those people who is so vivacious, she could go to a party on her own, which she often does, and come home with five people's numbers in her phone: men wanting to date her, women wanting to go for coffee with her, parents wanting to book her. She is a swashbuckler by day and a dancer by night. When the sun is up, Nena is a children's entertainer, making kids marvel at how she can turn a balloon into a cutlass at pirate parties or how she can throw sparkles up in the air and make them land perfectly on her eyelids for little princesses. When the sun goes down, Nena wows the West End. She can't hold a tune, but you know that dancer in the ensemble who you can't take your eyes off when the leading lady is desperately vying for your attention? That's Nena. Her father is a retired Brazilian dancer who joined the English National Ballet and fell in love with Nena's principal dancer mother. That's why when Nena walks she glides, and when she shakes her head with fierce attitude, her thick long black hair seems to move independently, falling gently into place of its own accord. Nena always has at least three boyfriends on the go. At the moment she is seeing Tony, the leading man in the West End's biggest show; Darius, a waiter from her favourite Camden coffee shop around the corner from her flat-share; and Pete, the plumber who just did a great job in fixing her pipework.

'These are amazing!' Nena says, rising past wool and cashmere into lace with a full inelegant mouth that would probably break Pierre Hermé's heart. Maya knows the love that goes into making those bad boys, so she always waits until she is in the food hall to give the macaron her total appreciation. When Maya's hair turned wavy and she moved out of London and in with her brother Jacob in Hazelworth, she bought herself a KitchenAid as a consolation present, and has been working hard to crack the secret of making the perfect macaron for the three years since. So far it's evaded her.

Maya and Nena reach the fourth-floor food hall and weave through white square tables and red and black chairs to their favourite spot in the corner that overlooks Oxford Street and Duke Street at rush hour; to the window where they can best see the top arc of the London Eye beyond the cranes and rooftops glimmering in the warm light of a summer evening.

Nena grabs two sparkling waters so she doesn't have to watch Maya unpeeling her own sticker seal and squirrel it onto the cover of a notebook safely out of Nena's sight. Maya then unwraps the cellophane bag with care and precision, takes out the jasmine flower macaron and looks at it, misty-eyed.

'Nena, I love him.'

'What the fuck?'

'I know. But I can see myself with him. He looked so... right, I just wanted to bury my head in his neck and close my eyes. I've never felt like that about anyone.'

'Not Jon?'

'Nope.'

'Not even Leo?'

'Not even Leo.'

'God you have to take a photo of this guy and show me what you mean.'

Maya suddenly feels protective and changes the subject. 'How's it going with West End Boy?'

Nena twists her straight shiny hair with one finger then ties it expertly in a bun on top of her head. Without her usual flowers or hair adornments, Nena looks naked. A blank canvas ready for Act II tonight.

'Oh, he's hot. We're having a LOT of fun. Although it's a bit annoying waiting for all the girls at the stage door to bugger off before he can bugger me.'

Maya chokes on ground almonds and icing sugar, takes a sip of water to compose herself and gives Nena a mock disapproving look.

'How long will he be here for?'

'His visa runs to the end of the year and I think he's booked until Christmas, which is cool. We both know it isn't anything heavy.'

Maya marvels at how Nena can be so casual about someone she has given her body to, someone so in demand, and washes down her fourth and final bite of the jasmine flower macaron with another sip of water. She folds the cellophane back over the remaining three.

'I can't eat the others, I've lost my appetite. I'll report back on them later, but the jasmine flower gets a thumbs up,' she says, tucking them carefully into her lilac scalloped-edge satchel.

'Well rose and lychee is the mutt's nuts. You should try recreating it, Maya.'

Maya daydreams about one day finding patisserie alchemy, while Nena eats her remaining two macarons and talks Maya through the rest of the cast she's working with.

'Your life is so much fun!' exclaims Maya.

'Well maybe yours is about to get interesting, if you can get it on with Train Man.'

Maya looks at her watch. 'I'd better go.'

'Already?'

'I have a class tonight, last one of the year,' she says standing.

'OK Sugartits, I'm going down to the beauty hall. Gotta

43

get me some more paint. Gimme a hug. And text me if he is on the train tomorrow,' Nena says, slinging her large holdall of tricks and costume changes over her shoulder.

Tomorrow? Maya doesn't know if she can wait that long to see him again. Her heart feels tight in her chest but her runner's feet take her back down four escalators past lace, wool, denim and leather, and she skips onto a number 390 bus. All Maya can think about is how she hopes Train Man will be on her train home this evening.

8

James walks through the door of an unhomely home and dumps his backpack on top of a cardboard box that's bursting at its parcel-taped seams. James had a lot of boxes to choose from but he slid his grey backpack from his shoulders down his back and onto the nearest box, marked 'Air ➤ Leonard Cohen'. Dark terracotta rectangles and circles on the walls tell tales of where pictures and plates once hung; a paler, sun-bleached hue envelops the rest of the room on a light summer's evening as rays pour through dusty wooden blinds. The room is dominated by brown. The two-tone terracotta walls, the heart-wrenchingly dull boxes, the thin veil of beige dust on each slat of the pale brown blinds, all underscored by a dark brown carpet that highlights flecks in need of a vacuum. James makes a mental note to ask the landlord if they can paint the walls before autumn, so he and Kitty don't feel like they're living in a molehill.

Clearing the boxes would be a good place to start.

The boxes mostly contain books, vinyl and photo albums. Mementoes that punctuate their journey to this point.

'It all takes up so much space,' Kitty complained yesterday. 'Why don't you go digital?'

It's a question Kitty often asks and James just doesn't answer. He silently plods on. The sentimental collector, even though it is quite difficult for him to open the front door amid his boxes of things. But this is his life, laid out before him in a small front room.

James pushes his glasses back up the bridge of his smooth straight nose and looks at the shapes on the walls. He wonders what artwork might have watched the lives of others, then he sees the mantelpiece above the fireplace and realises that along with all the other brown cardboard in the room, Kitty won't notice a tube lying along it until he's ready to tell her about it.

James can't hear any noise from inside the house, just the sound, via televisions, of tennis balls bouncing, coming through open windows along the street.

'Kitty?' he calls, as he walks to a middle room starved of natural light, tripping over a box marked 'Primitives ➤ The Streets' as he goes. 'Kit?'

Still no answer.

It's 8 p.m. James has just got home from his first commute from Charlotte Street to the suburbs on the rainy morning that turned out good. The commute home went pretty smoothly, better than this morning's journey when James almost missed the train because the woman at the ticket desk moved at the pace of a sloth. But tonight he left his friend Dominic in the Fitzroy Tavern at 6.30 p.m. and still made it home by eight.

As James got off the train, turned right out of the station, across two roads and a park lined with copper beeches, he drank in his new surroundings. At the end of the park, he came to what felt like *his* neighbourhood and crossed two more roads into the quiet street of Victorian terraces. Open windows and blaring televisions revealed the state of play as

James walked to 73 Sandringham Road, and the rhythmical knock of felt and rubber on polyester strings gave him a feeling of the familiar in an unfamiliar place. James even took off his headphones to see if he could gauge who was winning.

In the windowless middle room housing nothing but a dining table and two chairs, James calls up a flight of stairs. A toilet beyond the kitchen at the back has recently been flushed.

'Oh. You're home,' says a tall woman with short white-blonde hair as she tiptoes barefoot down the stairs and walks past James into the kitchen. Her limbs are almost as long as his. 'I was in the attic room. How was the journey?' She rummages in a box in the kitchen for food, like a hungry greyhound, and pulls out some cheese crackers.

'It was OK. Took the same time, door to door, as it did from Tooting, I couldn't believe it. I even had a quick pint after work.'

'All right for some.'

Kitty takes another cracker.

'What are we having for dinner?' she says with a full, dry mouth.

'I dunno. Did you make it to the shops?'

Wheaten lips tense. 'No James, I've been busy unpacking upstairs. All day.'

Wide, lovely eyes react quickly to diffuse a bomb. 'That's OK, I saw a chip shop on the way home, I'll get us dinner from there. Gives us a chance to check out the local catch of the day.'

'Hazelworth is no nearer the sea than London, you know?' Kitty says flatly.

'It was a joke.'

James and Kitty moved to Hazelworth yesterday in time for Kitty to start her new job at Cambridge University.

'Such a cliché!' joked their London friends about them moving to the Shire as they approach thirty. Although, a family home proved hard to find in the time they had before Kitty's new job started, so they're renting for now. And they can't even think about kids until Kitty has been in her new job long enough to qualify for maternity leave. But Hazelworth would be a great place to raise kids, they could see that from the coffee shops and playparks and the market square when they did their recce and looked at some rentals. Kitty stumbled upon Hazelworth before she knew it was family-friendly. When she dropped a pin in an old road atlas to work out which town was equidistant from London and Cambridge, Hazelworth was slap bang in the middle. The decision was made. And the nice estate agent who showed them five Victorian terraces that day said that Hazelworth is full of London and Cambridge commuters, so that seemed perfect for them. It's just a coincidence that Hazelworth might also be a nice place to raise kids.

'I bought you a present,' says James proudly, hoping for complete disarmament.

'Why did you do that?' she snaps.

'As a good luck for next week – come here.'

James takes Kitty by the hand and into the front room and presents her with the tube sitting on the mantelpiece.

'Ta-da!' he says quietly.

Kitty can't remember the last time her hand was in his. It feels strange, even though it's a hand she first held when she was sixteen and she knows its shape, its contours, its smoothness better than she knows her own. This evening James's hand feels strange, but it is soft and comforting because Kitty has been using her hands to unpack boxes, remove dust, hang clothes, and pull out rusty nails from crumbling walls. She is surprised by how nice it feels. Kitty is a scientist and works in a lab, where her dry hands infect mice with viruses to see if three days later they will wilt or rise from the ashes. She has just won a post in Cambridge and starts next week. Another lab. Further research into the genetics of memory T cells. Hoping to save the world thanks to mutant mice.

Her hands needed some tenderness, but the unfamiliarity of someone so familiar makes her let go.

'I need some cream,' she says. 'I hope you bought me hand cream.'

'No, it's this. Here.'

James hands Kitty the cardboard tube. Her face flushes with self-consciousness. She doesn't like being put on the spot. She pops open a white disc at one end and pulls out a poster, then starts to unravel it. As paper unfurls, it reveals monochromatic dystopian chaos in lino cut. Cars sink into waves under a shower of meteors under the Hollywood hills. She examines it with an unmoved gaze in her cement-grey eyes. She doesn't like it.

'We don't need any more artwork, this house won't have enough walls.'

'It's Stanley Donwood.'

'It's hideous, James, it makes me feel really stressed,' Kitty says, dropping the print on the floor and walking out of the room and back upstairs.

James listens to the thud of footsteps overhead and looks down as the ends scroll back together, leaving a little bit of chaos peeping out from the living-room floor.

9

It is twenty-three hours and fifty minutes since Maya first saw Seth or Milo or Train Man.

Please please please let him be a commuter and not a tourist.

Maya has got to the train station early so as not to look flustered or dewy, and is already standing at the front end of the platform, where the first carriages will stop. It's a sunnier, fresher morning than yesterday, reflecting the optimism burning inside her. Gone are the sweatshirt, jeans and Converse in favour of a soft black T-shirt tucked into a large fulsome skirt in a black and white graphic print that swings into swathes at her calves. Red wedges with a raffia heel give Maya the oomph her average-height legs need.

The clock ticks. 8.16 a.m.

There's still time.

Maya rummages in her satchel.

8.17 a.m.

Please come.

She starts to feel ridiculous but still she reapplies lip balm.

8.19 a.m.

Shit. What if he's further back and I never know. I committed too soon.

Hang on. Did Maya just see Train Man coming through the ticket barrier on the other side of the tracks?

Not sure from this far up. If it was, he probably won't make it.

8.20 a.m., an Inferior Train pulls in.

I could cry.

The train departs at 8.21 a.m., on time for once. Maya feels small, hope squashed like the flies the train driver is trying to look through on the windscreen in front of him.

Maya sinks into the seat of the Inferior Train and a puff of grey dust hovers in the space between the top of her head and the luggage rack. She swipes a bare arm in front of her face to clear the dust cloud and sees a figure through the thin glass rectangle of the internal door beyond it. Train Man turns a door handle and bows a little so he can walk through the too-small carriage door and into Maya's life.

Not a tourist. A commuter.

Happy day.

Black rectangles slip a little down his beautiful nose as he ducks his head. Maya is facing backwards today, and can see wide, lovely eyes look around the carriage, searching for a seat.

Please sit near me...

That's the trouble with Britain. No one talks on public transport. In Mexico City, Maya couldn't hear herself think on the train while women shouted exuberantly across her. In San Salvador, people chatted on buses so loudly that Maya didn't even bother to listen to her iPod, although probably best she kept it out of sight. But this uptight British train carriage is so quiet, Maya can hear the sound of people clenching in their seat. Buttocks on polyester on dirty blue gum-stained seats. How is Train Man supposed to make a connection and fall in love with Maya when she can't say a word to him? She wants to tell him she won a game show recently. That always makes people a) impressed, b) laugh and c) want to talk to her more. It's the best chat-up line she's ever had, but she's not been able to use it.

Train Man sits down across the aisle from Maya, also facing backwards, and Maya's heart soars so high, even an Inferior Train can't quash the wonderful feeling.

If I were to raise my arm a little, I would be able to hold his hand.

Maya can sense that Train Man is having a bad day. Nearly late. Flustered. Glasses not sitting properly on his nose. And now she gets the impression he doesn't like having to sit backwards. But that's not the thing that's making him feel most uncomfortable today. Maya doesn't know that this morning, as James walked along Sandringham Road, it didn't feel like the happy kingdom he knew last night. The open windows of the terraced houses blaring out a British victory in the tennis were shut; the bright evening full of bounce and excitement at the prospect of giving a gift had turned flat; the *really good* fish 'n' chips from his new local chip shop gave him a knot in his stomach. And the four hundred pound art print was still scrunched up on the floor where Kitty dropped it. Maya doesn't know any of that.

To make matters worse, as James sat down in his seat on a train he nearly missed, he remembered he should be preparing for a pitch he and Dominic have to deliver later in the week but all he wants to do is get lost in a book.

He opens the backpack he only just placed on the floor between his legs and takes out his book.

Maya tries to glance into Train Man's bag for more clues by only moving her eyes and not turning her head.

Calm, methodical, gentle. Words tumble onto James's lap. He forgets the Donwood, he forgets the fact he should be reading up on depilatory products and enters another world, oblivious to everyone around him. Oblivious to the girl he didn't notice yesterday even though she was dressed almost identically to him. Oblivious to the effort she has made today in a fifties-style tight tee and swirly skirt. Oblivious to her soft chestnut-brown hair with caramel-tinged tips, her faint freckles, her small waist and her strong, if not spectacular, legs. James gets lost in *One Hundred Years Of Solitude*, in Macondo and a world away from Maya.

Did he even notice me?

Maya strokes her straightened hair, today's more polished version of herself that Jacob laughed at as she left home this morning.

'Sucking up to the boss?' he teased.

Of course he didn't notice, he was looking for a seat, he's not looking for me.

10

'Excuse me, you dropped this,' says the girl with the *Girl With A Pearl Earring* in her hand.

Simon knows he dropped it. In fact he did it on purpose because he wanted to talk to her, and he thought he'd be much more interesting to her than that tedious-looking historical book. So Simon engineered it so that *The Times* would fall off his lap and onto the girl's feet. He pretended to be listening to music on his iPhone so that he might not have heard it drop, if he hadn't already known that it had.

Simon takes a headphone out of his right ear.

'Excuse me?'

'You dropped your newspaper.'

The elfin-looking girl hands Simon his newspaper. He rolls his eyes and puts a palm to his forehead, as if to call himself a name.

'It's 6.18 a.m., I'm always a clutz at 6.18 a.m., this train is brutal!' he endeavours.

The girl smiles a knowing smile, looks back at her book, then glances up again fleetingly at the man with the crumpled newspaper. His silvery hair looks like he just ran his fingers

54

through it and it stayed there. Floppy but back off his face, kissing his collar at the nape of his neck. His big nose gives him a look of cocksure confidence, as do the strong thighs that open outwards, as if waiting to snare her like a Venus flytrap.

Without speaking a word, the girl returns to her book.

Simon delves into his manbag, perched on the floor between sturdy feet. He lost her attention and wants it back again. Rummage, delve, search.

'Polo?' he proffers.

The girl giggles and puts a thin delicate hand to a small mouth, knowing what he's trying to do. Ordinarily this would annoy her: the spread legs, the faux fumbling bumbling Englishman, the arrogance. But this morning he is making her laugh. Maybe she just needs a laugh.

'No thanks, I don't eat sweets at 6 a.m.,' she smiles politely.

'Beats cleaning your teeth!' he jokes.

'Eww.'

'So what's your secret to looking so fresh-faced and minty at this time of day then?' he asks, admiring her small opalescent features.

Ears prick up across the aisle. The half-asleep students leaning against the windows next to them listen through closed eyes.

'Oh I don't know about that, I must just love my job.'

'What do you do?' he asks.

'What do *you* do?' she answers, raising a pale, perfectly arched eyebrow.

Flirtatious, I like it.

'Techie start-up, Silicon Fen,' he says.

'I don't understand what you just said!' she laughs, a husky laugh belying her fragile face.

'Sorry, let's start from the beginning,' he says, blue eyes set deep behind his nose. 'I'm Simon,' this time he proffers a hand.

'I'm Catherine.'

11

Maya is winding down for the day, filing printouts of dresses, shoes, knits and jewels into box files marked by the week in which they will drop. Emma can't believe it's already the end of the day, even though she can see from her window seat that the sky is a shade of home time. LA is only just waking up and that's when a lot of the stars FASH follows are getting dressed by their stylists and posting #OOTDs.

'God I can't believe it's 5.30 already! Where did today go?' asks Emma. She stands and sees Maya looking in a mirror at her desk. 'Doing anything nice tonight?'

Maya pulls down a lower lid to examine an unenthusiastic eye. Even though she had her eight hours last night, she just wants to go home to bed.

'Oh,' she lets out a sigh. 'I'm meeting Game Show Guy for a drink,' she says, looking across at Emma while still holding the mirror in front of her left eye. 'I really can't be bothered.'

'That doesn't sound like you, Maya.'

'Well we've got this one thing in common so my sister said I should go for it, but, I dunno... I think Clara's just bored of Train Man chat.' Maya looks back to her mirror and pulls the other eye down to her cheek, as if to find an excuse in her eyeball. 'It's definitely drinks, not a date.'

Emma is as kind and as honest as usual. 'You can't force it, Maya – if you didn't fancy him the first time you met, you're not going to fancy him now, are you?'

Maya feels the feeling of compromise hug her throat.

'Did you fancy Paul when you first met him?' Maya asks, still searching. Apart from their boss Lucy, Emma is the only other married person on the editorial team, which makes her the only other proper grown-up.

'Erm, no!' she laughs, holding a sweet hand to a delicate nose. 'It was a slow burn. So yes, maybe you should go for it with Game Show Guy!'

Emma and her husband met back in the good old days of magazines. She was website editor at *HoneyBee* where Paul sold advertising space. It took three Christmas parties and two Maggie's awards – the industry's annual knees-up – before Emma finally agreed to go on a date with him, and they've been together for ten happy years, although the past four haven't been without their struggles.

'Well, you've got nothing to lose – as long as he pays.'

'I won the money, Emma, I ought to pay.' Maya looks guilty, even though she won the money fair and square.

'Well good luck, I want a full report in the morning.'

Emma flutters out of the office, along with most of the other staff, back to the lovely husband she didn't fancy from day one. Maya stays with Lucy to talk about the Christmas campaign, even though it is September. Maya doesn't mind staying late. She likes her job, she likes how her boss entrusts her with such important projects, and is grateful for the distraction from her looming evening plans.

Last year's most searched item on the FASH website was

'Christmas jumper'. That was over the *entire* year. Christmas is huge: December always has the company's biggest sales day of the year, and there is always an elaborate Christmas party for all FASH employees in a Soho nightclub. DJs spin records. Canapés and cocktails are endless. Next Big Things sing on stage. Staff pretend to be rock stars in the dress-up corner and the photo booth, and Maya is under pressure to invent a new spin on FASHmas. Which is tricky, as last year's was such a success. Maya came up with FASHmas Wonderland and Chloe and Olivia put together a magical ethereal look for the website, which went down a storm.

'We need to go one better,' says Lucy, perching on Maya's desk in her pussy-bow blouse and pencil skirt. 'And I know you're capable of it.'

Maya blushes.

'We need to reinvent the wheel, give Christmas a whole new meaning to twenty-something women. Make it *all* about the fashion. The office party outfit, the Christmas Eve down the pub with your mates outfit, the Christmas Day outfit, the sparkly New Year's Eve outfit – this has to be all we eat, sleep and breathe over the next few weeks to really nail the tone of it, right?'

'Sure thing, Lucy, I'm already working on it.'

Maya has already begun researching ideas in the evenings, but soon her nights will be taken up with marking and preparing too.

When Maya started to feel guilty for having a fun and frivolous job in fashion retail, and not saving the world as her parents would have expected her to, she started volunteering as a Spanish teacher at night school. All classes at the Hazelworth Collective College are free and all of the staff are volunteers. It's about sharing knowledge and paying back to the community. One evening a week, Maya teaches Conversational Spanish in a small classroom in the 150-year-old building next to the library. Maya has loved her evenings teaching at the college for the two academic years since she moved back to the town she was born. Last year she even tried a course herself, studying cake decorating, but realised by Christmas, when her angel Gabriel looked more like Simon Cowell, that sugarcraft wasn't her strong point and perhaps she should stick to working on macaron shells.

Teaching keeps Maya on her toes and she is a good, thoughtful teacher who listens as much as she speaks. That year she spent in Central America before university wasn't wasteful soul-searching on Herbert Flowers' credit card. Maya learned the language and worked her way from Ciudad Juarez on the Texan border down to Bogota, teaching English, learning Spanish, and doing stints as a waitress in bars and cafes along the way, so that when she returned in time to start university, and her sister and two brothers picked her up from the airport, she was ready for anything college life might throw at her. It was the bravest thing Maya had ever done, until she decided to stand up in front of a roomful of strangers and teach them.

Next week, Maya will meet her new students for the next academic year.

Maya doesn't mind working late tonight, she might not even touch up the lilting make-up on her face. It hasn't gone unnoticed that she's worn more make-up of late, in fact Sam is surprised how well Maya scrubs up compared to the wild-haired girl he has teased for a year and a half, but Maya has already made her effort for the day, for Train Man.

'Right, I have to get back for the boys,' says Lucy. 'Let's reconvene tomorrow. Have a look back over last year, look at the mood boards Chloe has put together for this season, and let's have a breakfast meeting tomorrow to brainstorm ideas, right?'

Maya wishes Lucy wanted to work even later, give her an excuse to get out of this meet-up, but now she's the last one in the office. Just the sound of the vacuum sucking up a day's fashion while the cleaner from Ecuador hums Rubén Blades salsa songs. Maya looks in her little compact mirror and steels herself.

I wish I was meeting Train Man.

12

Maya has always absorbed facts like a sponge. Like her brother Jacob. Facts and miscellany were Jacob and Maya's thing in common, their Special Memory skill, and one that led Maya to go on to develop her Excellent General Knowledge skills. Jacob, Maya's younger-but-not-youngest brother, used his Special Memory skill to plots stars and planets in the night sky. At eleven he could tell his father precisely when Swift Tuttle would be arriving in the Perseides, even though his sisters and brother didn't know whether he was even speaking English. When the four Flowers siblings were children, Clara's skill was confidence in front of a crowd. While Maya would cringe given an audience, and once broke down during a trumpet recital – which is tough given how hard it is to play a wind instrument when you're crying – Clara always shone on stage and owned every school production. Florian, the youngest but the largest of the Flowers, found his special skill in growth. Florian was so tall, unlike the other average-height Flowers children, and no one really understood why. As an adult, Maya sometimes wondered whether it was all the Weetabix Florian had eaten as a child that had made him so tall. Or was Florian always destined to be tall, and the eight Weetabix he piled into his breakfast bowl in a soup of thick creamy milk were just a necessity, feeding his fast-growing bones?

Maya and Jacob's Special Memory skill enabled them to remember all manner of bizarre facts and data. They could recount every registration plate of every car their parents had ever owned.

'Mum's Fiesta?' one would ask the other.

'A689 RMJ,' they'd shout proudly in unison, letters and digits tumbling past milk teeth in a race. Sometimes Jacob would say 'E655 FBM' out of the blue, and only Maya would know he was talking about the Volvo estate their parents had bought shortly after Florian was born. Children speaking a secret language of DVLA data.

Maya's friends at school always marvelled at how she remembered there were 206 bones in the human skeleton, that the Luddite revolution started in 1811 or that Belmopan was the capital of Belize, especially when Maya wasn't ever the cleverest girl in class.

And her magical memory came good for Maya on that day, five months ago, when she went on a game show and won five thousand pounds. Nine contestants from the usual demographic, and Maya hadn't fancied her chances at all. But she played a mean game, remembering facts she'd never even learned before.

Where did that come from?

She was stunned as she took the cheque after the grand final, smiling confidently as though it was a breeze. Gary from Edinburgh thought the smile was a wee bit conceited, and tried not to look angry while he feigned happiness. *I shouldn't have fallen for her friendly banter, I should have played hardball.*

And here Maya is, in a pub off St Christopher's Place, looking for the face she can't quite remember. Facts not faces, that's what Maya is good at. Except for the face of the beautiful man on the train. She has seen it every morning for two months and feels like she knows every line and pore, even though Maya hasn't seen him smile yet so she doesn't even know about the dimple. But Maya knows Train Man's reading face and his inquisitive face extremely well. Both are beautiful, both break her heart.

As the game show hasn't yet aired, Gary from Edinburgh is fuzzy in Maya's memory. She sits at a table peering through the smoked-glass window, tired and ready to go home. Maya circles the stirrer in her gin and tonic and looks up at the door to see a soft-waisted man with small features and round wire glasses over pale, earnest eyes enter the room.

That's him.

Gary recognises Maya instantly and walks over to kiss her awkwardly on both cheeks. Maya remembers everything now. Gary from Edinburgh looks like a chubby schoolboy who has been wronged, and for a second she feels guilty about winning. Maybe she was a little manipulative to be so friendly to the man standing next to her in the semicircle of wobbly voices.

'Hi!' Maya says, friendly again.

'Hi, how's it going?'

'Great thanks. Welcome to London!'

Gary from Edinburgh goes to the bar and buys himself a Jack Daniels and Coke before they sit at opposite sides of a dark rectangular table next to the window.

'What are you doing down here?'

Maya is friendly but absolutely not flirtatious because she doesn't fancy Gary from Edinburgh in the slightest.

'I'm here for a legal workshop in Bow, work have paid for me to come down, so that's nice. And hopefully it'll be a little more successful than my last trip down here!' Gary gives a wry smile.

Ahh yes, he was a solicitor.

'Gary, thirty, a solicitor from Edinburgh.' He'd had to say it five times into the camera because the man from Newcastle to their right was so nervous he kept fluffing his line and everyone had to repeat themselves again. And again.

'Work have paid'. Was that a barbed comment? 'More successful than my last trip'. That had a definite spike.

Maya feels restricted and defensive.

He should have known Earth's surface is seventy-one per cent water.

As Gary drinks his third Jack Daniels, the bitter tinge in his voice grows. Then he builds up the false confidence to ask Maya the question he's been aching to know the answer to since his world unravelled. 'What did you spend the winnings on?'

Maya coughs into her second (and last) gin and tonic of the evening. She wonders what she ought to say.

What's the etiquette for this situation?

Maya doesn't know what Gary would like to hear, and as a people-pleaser, she just wants to extract herself from the situation in the easiest and friendliest way possible, but she's at a loss.

'I bought myself a Vivienne Westwood dress...'

His face drops, so stubborn Maya decides not to tell him it was her first ever grown-up designer dress purchase, and came heavily reduced. 'And I put the rest into savings, I'm hoping to buy a flat soon.'

Pale, earnest eyes flicker with disdain.

I needed to buy an engagement ring more than you needed a Vivienne Whatever dress, he thinks, picturing his ex-girlfriend in the arms of his old snooker partner.

I bloody love my dress, Maya thinks, wondering if she ever got to go on a date with Train Man, whether it would be a bit much to wear it.

They talk for a not-embarrassingly short amount of time and eventually laugh about their freakish combined experience. Just after 9 p.m., Gary's friend with ginger hair whose name Maya doesn't catch shows up. Maya is mildly offended by his arrival, suspecting he must have been Gary from Edinburgh's Plan B for when he decided to downgrade this evening from a date to just drinks. Although his arrival gives her a get-out card, which she is relieved to be able to play. Especially after they laugh hungrily at Maya for having confused the Home Secretary with the Defence Secretary on the game show – laughs tinged with meanness, so she makes her exit and wishes them a happy viewing for when the game show finally airs next week.

Bitch.

He's not Train Man.

13

James looks out of the boardroom window and down onto the lights of Charlotte Street below. The restaurants are starting to fill with post-work revellers. Leaves are turning to shades of rust and dust and the air looks crisper, even though James can't actually feel it through the floor-to-ceiling window. His closest friend and partner Dominic is talking to their new clients, Sebastian and Duncan from Fisher & Whyman, two serious-looking men in three-piece suits, who are dressed far too smartly to be talking about pubic hair. Since the summer, when Dominic talked a mean pitch and James won them over with his creative vision, they can do little wrong in Sebastian and Duncan from Fisher & Whyman's eyes. They can do little wrong as far as Jeremy Laws, their boss at the MFDD global advertising agency is concerned either. Winning the Femme campaign brings Fisher & Whyman, one of the world's biggest health and well-being consumer goods producers, into the MFDD client list, and if the campaign they pitched is as successful as they promised, James and Dominic's career trajectory will soar.

James and Dominic have been a great partnership since they met at university in Leeds. Despite physical and verbal clumsiness, Dominic was always a charmer: talking the talk in the union bar, getting them out of scrapes in pubs, negotiating free drinks in the curry house, dreaming up straplines and slogans on their advertising course while James diligently sourced pictures or shot his own for them to use on undergraduate projects.

Kitty moved up from Kent to Leeds to be with James and study microbiology, not wanting to break off their fledgling high-school romance, and she warmed to Dominic as much as James had. A softly shaped swarthy boy with Hobbit-like feet but a warm honest charm to his ineloquence. A talker, a seller, a player, always true to his word. James marvelled at how Dominic believed in everything he did, how he would get as passionate about pet food as he did about the charity campaigns they worked on.

A long way from Leeds, Dominic and James are an award-winning advertising dream team, coming up with campaigns that bring a tear to any steely brand manager's eye, let alone the housewives who hoped the hungry dog found its way home, the old widow who would find love again or the priest who would be reunited with his favourite whisky. And Dominic is fiercely loyal to his art director best friend. When rival advertising agencies tried to poach Dominic, as the more vocal half of the partnership, the better networker at conferences and creative festivals, he wouldn't go anywhere without James. Quieter, more considerate, unable to bullshit.

'James?' urges Dominic. 'What do you think?'

Dominic only ever calls James 'James' in front of clients, which snaps him back into the room.

He had been lost in a daydream, looking at the effects of the light from the sinking sun over Charlotte Street. Wondering how Monet managed to capture sunset on the Thames when it was so fleeting. Wondering what the burritos taste like in the new cantina down the road. Wondering why Kitty hasn't spoken to him for fifty-two hours.

'I think we need to ask a woman,' James replies, without looking away from the window. 'What do we know about it?'

Sebastian and Duncan are taken aback.

'Well, you gave us the impression you knew a lot about what women think, how you see them connecting with Femme,' says Duncan with one eye narrower than the other. A first crack appearing in the love-in.

'Of course we do!' says Dominic. 'James just believes in authenticity. We need to consult the Femme woman at every step of the way, and that's why we have this brilliant focus group on board.' Dominic rubs his eyes to conceal his exasperation. 'I tell you what, we'll put it to them this evening and get back to you with next steps.'

'This evening? It's not your wives and mothers, is it?' winces Sebastian half-jokingly as he peels his suit jacket from the back of his chair to signal the end of the meeting.

'Of course not!' says Dominic, pulling his notebook towards him like a security blanket.

'We have a focus group, a panel of experts: consumers, mothers, students, friends, journalists, who are always keen to feed back to us when we put it to the market. We'll email the women tonight and will have feedback with you by 3 p.m. tomorrow. Sound good?'

Sebastian and Duncan stand and shake Dominic's thick hand. James, torn from an otherworldly gaze, stands and holds out his.

'Sorry,' James stumbles, pushing the bridge of his black rectangular glasses back up his nose. 'Yes, we'll put it to panel. Great to see you two again.'

Dominic walks Sebastian and Duncan to the lifts by reception and heads back to the boardroom, where James is sitting in his chair, spinning around in it for no particular reason.

'You all right, Millsy?'

'Yep.'

But James isn't all right. The glass wall onto Charlotte Street feels unusually restrictive today. He doesn't feel the passion for depilatory products that Dominic clearly does. He didn't feel as excited as Dominic did when they collected their pet food campaign award in a buzzy auditorium in Cannes back in June. Despite the pool parties and the yachts and the forums and the fun, this year's annual advertising awards frenzy just felt chaotic and exhausting and competitive and James wanted to be back in London, packing up the flat with Kitty. But Dominic is loyal to James and James is loyal to Dominic, so they both put on their tuxes and celebrated their achievement. They are a team.

'Coming for a drink with the focus group?' asks Dominic.

'Who, Josie?'

'Yeah!' laughs Dominic, a pudgy smile lighting up drooping, bear-like eyes.

James laughs. *He* almost believed in this panel of women, waiting for a call from Dominic to ask them whether hair-free armpits or a hair-free bikini line is more important to them.

'No thanks. I'm going to head back to Hazelworth, got to pick up my camera on the way.' James's beloved SLR sits in a repair shop on Tottenham Court Road. It has been there, sad and unloved and lonely, since Kitty threw it down the stairs three weeks ago. She cried. She said she was sorry. She said she didn't know why she had done it, but cement-grey eyes turned black at the point which she let go of it. 'Give Josie my love.'

14

'Hands up who liiiiikes… elephants!' shouts Nena, who has eight children sitting on the carpet in front of her, hanging on to her every word.

'Meeeeee!' shout eight big mouths as sixteen hands reach as high as the sky.

'Well I heard that Arlo LOVES elephants, so as it's his birthday, let's make an elephant for Arlo, and then the rest of you can choose your favourite animal. Sound good? We might even have enough for a zoo!'

'Hurraaaay!!!' bellow the four boys and four girls.

As quick as lightning, Nena twists a long blue tubular balloon into the shape of an elephant. Look closely and stars might shoot out of her fingers as she skilfully turns and ties. Separated parents stand separately on either side of an arch in a grandiose living room, united by wonder, over how this small woman with a clown's face and flowers in her hair has tamed their birthday boy and his best friends.

'Where did you get her?' the father mouths.

The mother smiles, bittersweetly. This has been a success.

A little boy, with a shiny light brown bowl-cut, beams a proud smile as he clutches his special birthday balloon.

His friends patiently wait in uncharacteristic silence for one of their own: a tiger for Ollie; a dog for William; a cat for Luca; a giraffe for Eva; a lion for Florence; a parrot for Tabitha and, well, Bella wanted an anteater but Nena fudges it by doing a second elephant and bending the trunk the other way.

A pirate cake is brought in. Arlo's mother's face glows as three candles soften lines carved by lies and guilt, and her new boyfriend puts his hands on her shoulders, marking his place at this landmark moment. Nena watches as Arlo's dad looks on, leaning against the arch, lost in mourning for a second before he sees Arlo's face, and his, in turn, lights up.

'Happy birthday to youuuuu...' The dad starts boldly before Arlo's mum and her boyfriend and Nena all join in. Seven lispy bumbling versions follow suit. Everyone claps, a doorbell rings, and parents start to climb the steps of this impressive townhouse, a home Arlo's dad loved, saved for, decorated and now can't live in. He can't smell Arlo's morning breath or read him a bedtime story, or help him pull up his pants when he proudly does a wee all by 'hiththelf'. Despite his breaking heart, Arlo's dad stands tall, smiling, convivial and welcoming, to answer the front door, *his* old front door, to the mums and dads coming to see how their little darlings have behaved. Impeccably under Nena's watch. One mum walks over to say hi.

'Ah Kate said she was going to book you, you did such a good job at Ollie's party!'

'Well Ollie's had fun again today,' Nena motions to a tired blond boy clutching a balloon tiger. 'I am wondering if I'll get a bit passé for them and they'll say "not you again!" next time I rock up at a party.' Spoken with the confidence of a woman who knows she will be booked again.

At two hundred pounds for two hours' work, the Islington mummies and daddies are Nena's bread and butter. In the West End you never know how long your run will last. Shows open and close, the chorus line can be replaced at the drop of a top hat, but there is a constant conveyor belt of preschoolers whose parents want good old-fashioned balloon modelling, dancing and face painting, and Nincompoop Nena is the best clown in town.

Nena starts packing up her things. Arlo's mum comes over.

'Thanks so much, Nena, you were every bit as brilliant as Elaine said and it was JUST what Arlo needed.' She squeezes Nena's arm and gives her an envelope full of cash.

'No problem, Kate, Arlo is adorable, it's been a pleasure.' Nena always says the kids are adorable, even the less than adorable ones, but in this case the child was sweeter than many of Nena's birthday boys and girls.

Arlo runs over to give Nena a cuddle and little cupid's bow lips kiss the white paint on her brown skin as she scoops him up.

'Ahhhh happy birthday, Arlo! I hope you have your best year yet,' Nena says with a big warm hug, before he slides the short distance down her body to the floor and runs back to his elephant.

Nena heads to the toilet with some baby wipes – she can walk from Canonbury to Camden but she doesn't want to do it dressed as a clown.

Eight minutes later, as she's leaving the house with a heavy Ikea bag full of tricks, Arlo's dad comes rushing to the door.

'Wait!' he says.

Nena turns around, colourful fake flowers still in her hair, blue Ikea bag hauled over her shoulder, and looks up the steps towards the tall man standing at the top. His head is mostly bald, the remaining hair shaved short. He is handsome and has deep-set but piercing eyes and a huge smile. Nena can imagine why Arlo's mum fell for him, and wonders why she's now with the awkward-looking guy wearing a bad jumper inside the house.

'Oh, do you need a hand with that?' Arlo's dad says, seeing the bag must weigh as much as Nena does.

'No, I'm fine thanks, you go back to Arlo,' Nena smiles. She can tell this is a precious moment and she doesn't want him to waste it outside with her.

'I just wanted to give you this.'

He hands her a card.

Tom Vernon, Commissioner, Children's. The BBC logo shines brightly in monogrammed raised letters on reassuringly thick paper stock. Nena is confused, bag weighing heavy on her cold bare shoulder, but makes light of it with her usual sparkle.

'Wow. "Tom Vernon, Commissioner" is *way* more impressive than "Nincompoop Nena, clown" on my business card.' They both laugh and stop.

Tom sees the whites of Nena's eyes as she looks up and takes a deep breath.

'I thought you were brilliant and I can so see you working in my field, if you're interested.'

'I don't know anything about television, I'm afraid, although I am good at watching it.' This time neither laugh.

'Just have a think. I'm looking for a vibrant, camera-friendly, kid-friendly face and you're... you're perfect,' he says, eyes gleaming.

'I'll call you,' Nena purrs, as she swings the bag onto her other, covered shoulder, and slopes off into the teatime tussle, gliding like a panther in black off-duty-dancer attire.

15

At FASH HQ, Train Man has become a regular fixture in office banter, along with which celeb is wearing what, last night's TV and tonight's dinner.

'Did you see Train Man today?' Emma tends to ask first, hoping so.

Maya does see Train Man most days, getting onto the train with his grey backpack. Lean legs that perfectly fill slim jeans. Train Man is her reliable morning ray. Always on the 8.21 a.m. Always in the front carriage.

'What banal thing did Train Man do to light up the Home Counties this morning?' mocks Sam with his crinkly eyes and acerbic tongue. Sam doesn't realise how biting he can sound – or how seriously Maya feels about Train Man. It makes Maya feel small, stupid and that perhaps she should be more professional at work and stop talking about him. But she can't.

Even Lucy knows about Train Man now, and as editorial director, she's far too important to discuss the minutiae of Maya's crush: what he's wearing, whether his black Converse suit him more than the white ones, or deciphering from the books he reads whether he is single or in a relationship, with a woman or a man. But despite her seriousness, Lucy thinks the whole notion of falling in love with a stranger on a train is wonderful.

Today a different aspect of Maya's life has the office on tenterhooks. The team can't wait for 5.15 p.m. and have been talking about it for most of the day. At 5.10 p.m. Lucy cracks open a bottle of Prosecco taken from the tall crammed fridge in the communal kitchen and asks Liz to go and get some plastic cups while her colleagues start live streaming television on their Macs. Maya looks up and sees a wall of the same thing, on Olivia's desk to her right, Liz and Alex's desks on the next island in front, and in the reflection of Lucy and Emma's eyes facing her. Sam swings round to watch it on Maya's screen.

'Put it on then!'

Maya wants to hide in the canteen but is intrigued to see how the game show turned out versus the memory of that peculiar day in her head. Sam leans in, eyes widening a little; mouth gaping open like the face of a child who is captivated by a cartoon.

Maya is embarrassed. Her freckles are matted under studio make-up and her hair is straightened to within an inch of its life.

Cosmetic cringes are overriding Maya's brilliance as she takes out her opponents one by one. Knowledge so general she's both proud and embarrassed.

Straightened hair makes me look old.

'I look awful!'

'You look great,' says Sam quietly, seriously.

'Does my voice really sound like that?'

Perhaps a silent carriage is best in the morning.

'Oh my god that's the douche you went on a date with!' cackles Olivia.

'It wasn't a date, it was drinks.'

Texts roll in to Maya's phone, a buzz of friends and family lining up to say they're watching, or how proud they are, or to ask about how the hell she came up with Norman Mailer out of thin air.

'Maya, you're brilliant!' says Lucy as she walks around to Maya's desk. 'It's so tense, even though I already know you won.'

Maya feels comforted by Lucy's sinewy maternal embrace, and wonders what are the chances of Train Man watching BBC2 right now.

James weaves carefully so as not to spill a drop, back to a tiny window table in a cafe packed with people and their coats. Beyond it, Shaftesbury Avenue is lit by billboards, buses and the orange lights of the black cabs, pinging on and off with every drop-off and pick-up they make in the heart of Theatreland. An artery of excitement being observed by indifferent grey eyes.

'Sorry, took bloody ages, too many decisions.'

'I only wanted a flat white,' mumbles Kitty, flatly.

'Yeah, but did you want soy milk or skinny? A half shot or a whole one? What about a muffin? How about I ask you so many questions you miss your film? Would you like to miss the last train home too? Jeez...' James gives a sardonic smile and places the cups on the table carefully, pushing his glasses up his nose as he squeezes into the corner.

Kitty draws away from people watching and looks at her cup. Her passive gaze flickers to aggressive. 'I didn't want a big one. I said a small one.'

James takes off his coat. The first time he's needed it in months.

He widens his eyes in quiet disbelief. 'Really? Can't you just leave what you don't want? I'll finish it.'

'I said *tall*.' Kitty sweeps her short platinum hair to the side with long fingers.

'I'm sorry, I didn't know what "tall" meant. It sounded big.' James feels the uncomfortable wrench of tension rising. 'Want me to change it?'

Arms fold, pale eyes gaze back out of the window in sullen, silent resentment.

'I'll change it,' James says, standing.

'It doesn't matter now, we'll miss the film, I'll drink it.'

Kitty strokes the ends of her hair at the nape of her neck like a sleepy child looking for comfort. She doesn't touch her drink.

James takes a sip of espresso and nods to the electric blue lights on the façade of the cinema opposite. 'I'm so pleased we're finally getting to see it,' he says, trying to lift the mood.

Thin lips feign a smile while the rest of a face stays static. Kitty says nothing.

'Maybe next time I see one of his films I won't have to read the subtitles.'

Arms unfold to raise a heavy cup reluctantly, in defeat. 'What do you mean?'

'I've signed up to learn Spanish.'

A tiny nose, so pale it is almost blue, creases.

'Spanish? Why?!' Kitty scorns.

'Why not? There's a really cool college on that little road off the town square. Run by volunteers. I went in at the weekend when you were having your eyebrows done. They had an open day.'

Kitty runs her forefinger along a thin white-blonde brow.

'They teach Spanish, Polish, Swedish, cake decoration. Raqs sharqi...'

'James what the *fuck* is racks sharkee?'

'Belly dancing apparently. I thought Spanish might be more useful. And it's free.'

'Why would you want to learn Spanish now?' Kitty asks, with dismay and pity.

'Why wouldn't I want to learn Spanish? Think of all those amazing holidays we could go on to South America without me sounding like a bumbling idiot. Remember how embarrassing it was when I took you to Venice? At least Spanish covers more countries.'

Kitty remembers, and for the first time in months James sees her totally crumble into laughter. Sharp shoulders soften. She lays her forearm low across a jutting pelvis to control herself and regain composure from a laugh stained with malice. 'Oh god that was so funny! Please don't try to speak another language. I think you have to accept that languages aren't your thing.'

Wide, lovely eyes stop laughing along.

16

An alarmingly fast intercity train brings autumn rushing behind it, and as leaves rise in a tornado, Maya decides to be uncharacteristically pushy today.

Inflatable Arms is not going to sit closer to Train Man than me.

Mind you, if there was a seat available next to him, Maya probably wouldn't take it. She'd be too scared of giving herself away. Maya won't admit that she's too much of a coward to sit next to him but quietly feels hard done by when other people do.

Today she stands firm at the spot next to the second set of double doors from the front. Train Man stands a few people back. This morning Maya wants to sit near him, not next to him. Near him. Facing him preferably. She doesn't mind if she has to sit backwards.

If he sees my face, actually sees it, he might recognise me from the TV and know that I have Excellent General Knowledge skills.

The train pulls in. A Superior Train with green and red seats and carpet on the floor, and Maya is more assertive than usual, puffing out small shoulders so her collarbone protrudes a smidge. She sits down on a seat in a set of four, next to the man with the red nose, and wills Train Man to sit opposite her. Two seats remain, Train Man must take one. Inflatable Arms looks irked but she collapses into another, sitting down breathlessly. The final seat remains vacant and Train Man sees it, gently edging up the carriage, holding the straps of his backpack to his chest like a protective embrace. It is the seat opposite Maya and her eyes widen encouragingly, shards glowing in the morning sun. Excitement floods Maya because, finally, Train Man is going to sit opposite her and she will have an excuse to look at him directly, although discreetly of course, and to get closer to him than she's ever been.

'After you,' James signals, as he holds out a palm for the man with the fold-up bike who never takes off his helmet, no matter how hot he is. Or the fact he won't need a helmet for the next thirty-five minutes. The man with the fold-up bike came down the carriage lightning quick, to rob James and Maya of their moment. As Train Man walks on and concedes to standing by the doors, Maya tries not to scowl at the man with the fold-up bike, smug and sweaty in the seat opposite her. And she knows she can't keep letting incidences like these shape her entire day.

He won't have seen the game show anyway.

Maya consoles herself with the thought that at least Train Man won't have heard her strange TV voice. Maya's never even heard Train Man speak.

I hope he doesn't have a weird voice.

A woman further down the carriage cranes her neck to have a closer look at Maya's familiar face, she's sure she saw her on the telly last night.

❤ ❤

'Hi Tom, it's Nena... Nincompoop Nena, from Arlo's party?' Nena's trademark purr is tamed today by a rare feeling of nerves.

'Nena hi! I hoped you'd call.'

'Well, here I am,' she says, twiddling Tom's business card in her brown hand as she lies on her back in a silk vest and shorts, in bed, even though it is way beyond brunch time. Her flatmate Signe's laptop balances on her taught tummy, open with tabs of children's TV programmes, all playing simultaneously on mute. If Nena hadn't been interested in a career change, she wouldn't have done this much homework.

'You were so great at Arlo's party, I just thought it would be brilliant if you could come in for a screen test. Look around the studio, see a bit about what we do and the programmes we broadcast, see if it could work out.'

Nena punches the air silently with her free hand. 'I think I could do that,' she says calmly.

'Great, when's good for you?'

Nena thinks of the days of the week song she just watched presenters in primary colours sing, knowing Tom probably made it, and she sings, badly, down the line. '"Give it up for Friday..."'

Toms laughs and Nena remembers his huge smile and twinkling deep-set eyes.

'Friday's good! Let's say 3 p.m. yeah?'

'Sure.'

'And Nena...'

'Yes?'

'There's always one clown.'

Nena hangs up, smiles, slides Signe's laptop onto the bed and kicks muscular legs in excitement as if she's dancing on the ceiling with glee.

17

Maya is standing in front of a whiteboard with a lump in her throat. She hasn't taught a class since July and suddenly the prospect of doing so again fills her with dread, even though she knows that by 9.30 p.m. she will be on a high, that feeling of having faced a challenge and overcome it. This is what Maya does. She tests herself. This is why she travelled to the jungles of Colombia at eighteen, this is why she runs distances that don't suit her legs, this is why she signed up to be a volunteer teacher at the Hazelworth Collective College. This is why she is trying, still without success, to work out the alchemy of the macaron. Jacob is getting a little fed up with icing sugar all over his cramped kitchen at the weekends, but he can see an end in sight because Maya is looking at flats to buy and soon Jacob's girlfriend Amelia will move in.

Even though Maya feels a bit sick right now, the memory of two years of hilarious, bizarre and engaging students makes Maya marvel in nervous anticipation. Who will walk through the door this year? Stab turns to tingle and Maya shuffles her notes.

In walk students who might also be feeling a little nervous to be taking the plunge, doing something they talked about doing for years. Or perhaps they signed up on a whim when they passed by on the open day last weekend. Maya looks at new faces as they enter the room and tries to look as friendly as possible. She has been told her resting face can seem a little serious.

'Wow, you look like a dream!' A big New York voice comes out of a very small woman as she shuffles in. 'How are ya?'

Maya smiles. 'Welcome. You are... ?' Maya looks down at her list of names and looks back up – or down rather – at the tiny bundle of a woman with cropped grey hair and thick bottle-end glasses.

'Velma. Velma Diamond, pleased to meet you, Miss...'

'Oh, just Maya.'

'Well Miss Oh Just Maya, that skirt is *darling*, you look like a movie star from my era! I just know we are going to have fun!' Velma Diamond clasps her veiny liver-spotted hands together.

Maya blushes and smooths down the enormous bulk of her voluminous minty green skirt. 'Pleased to meet you Velma, find a seat, it's going to be great.'

Nerves fizzle and fly out of the classroom door and Maya has a hunch that Velma Diamond makes people feel upbeat and at ease in every room she shuffles into.

A photographic scene of an Italian harbour fills much of one wall in this high-ceilinged Georgian classroom that has been ruined by eighties decor. On the opposite wall a poster in bold black capitals on light blue paper reads:

POLISH

SWEDISH

FOR BEGINNERS.

When Maya was learning cake decorating she marvelled at that poster on the wall, black and blue, lit by strip lighting that gives everything a yellow tinge. She envisaged an old white-haired carpenter like Geppetto taking his yellow duster in hand and teaching a group of amateurs how to polish miniature models of Bergman, Blix, Benny and Bjorn, buffed and brushed in a most proficient way.

More students file in, trying to look as if they've done this before.

'Hi, I'm Gareth,' says a fifty-something in guyliner, a checked shirt and DMs over rolled-up jeans as he extends a cold hand. 'This is my daughter, Cecily.'

'Ahh, I did see we have a few students with the same surname on the list. You must be the Taylors. It's great when people come to class together because then they can spur each other on with homework.' A serious face softens and smiles.

'Homework?' says Gareth. 'You didn't tell me I was signing up for homework!' he laughs as he nudges an adoring daughter, who rolls limp eyes lovingly, adorned with the same eyeliner as her dad's.

When everyone has settled, Maya welcomes the class and asks them to introduce themselves and say why they want to learn conversational Spanish.

There is Gareth and Cecily – an A Level student who joined because she couldn't fit Spanish into her timetable at school, and she's brought her dad along in the hope of him meeting a nice woman. Everyone laughs, except for the two women nearest his age bracket who look nervous and explain they are both happily married with two adorable children each thankyouverymuch. Housewife Esther Patterson has two boys who are eight and five, Doctor Helen Cruikshank's girls are twelve and nine.

'I don't fancy either of them anyway,' Gareth whispers to Cecily.

Jan and Doug Kinsella hope to open a B&B in Andalucía; Glyn Davies – a six foot seven inch giant wearing head to toe beige – just wants to get out of the house because his wife is addicted to soap operas. This is the fifth course he'll have done at Hazelworth Collective College. He also took the cake decorating course last year, despite not knowing how to bake a cake let alone cover it, so Maya recognises Glyn and it explains why he does look like he's done this before. There's Nathaniel Francis who is ludicrously handsome and looks about twenty years older than he probably is, wearing a cravat and a blazer. He's there because he thought learning Spanish would be 'jolly'; there's Ed Noy, in his early twenties, whose girlfriend Valeria lives in Argentina. Ed wants to impress Valeria and her family by learning to speak their language. And of course there's Velma Diamond, tiny but indomitable, who decided to learn Spanish because she wants to retire to Florida like a Golden Girl. 'And if I'm gonna go partying in Miami Beach, I gotta speak the lingo,' she smiles.

Maya is fascinated, and wants to know how a seventy-something New Yorker with plans to retire to Miami Beach ended up in Hazelworth. But right now she has a class to teach.

'OK, I think we've covered everyone apart from... you,' she says, looking from a man in the doorway to her list. 'You must be... James Miller?' A heavy skirt turns to the gormless-looking man with long hair hanging lankly over an undercut.

'No, I'm Keith Smith,' says a voice devoid of any character.

'Oh I don't have a Keith on the list, sorry Keith, hello – why do you want to learn Spanish?'

'Well, you could say I'm partial to an Ibero-Romance language, heavily influenced by Basque, Arabic, French and Italian,' he says in a monotone as his eyes dart under heavy, furious blinks.

Everybody stays silent.

'Ah, great. Do you speak other languages then, Keith?'

'No.'

'Wonderful, let's get started!'

Maya crosses out James Miller with her black felt-tip pen, not knowing that it will be a name she will soon yearn for, and writes Keith Smith on a new line below it.

18

December 2013

Simon's legs widen as the doors beep rapidly ten times and close. Catherine hasn't got on. Catherine hasn't *not* got on the 6.18 train since Simon first offered her a Polo mint and they started talking, travelling together, exchanging texts... and for a moment, a rare thing happens and Simon starts to doubt himself. He looks at his phone and scrolls through their most recent flirtation. Simon always ends the conversation on a text from Catherine. In business, he'll respond, look keen, be last to send a friendly note, but with women, he ensures he isn't the last to reply. That's how he works and it's never failed him before. Keep 'em hanging. Last night, Simon made one simple suggestion as he arched his phone screen towards the radiator, away from his wife Laura sitting next to him on the sofa doing online banking, while Gracie, Monty and Esmé slept upstairs, dreaming feverishly of Christmas to come: 'Meet for an after-party of our own?'

Catherine didn't answer. The conversation ended with *him* texting *her*. That made Simon feel more uncomfortable than the risk he had taken, putting the idea out there, of he and Catherine meeting after their works' Christmas parties. Now Catherine isn't on the train and Simon's face feels hot with embarrassment and rejection and he's worried he might have blown it when it felt so obvious they were going to fuck.

He looks out of the window as the train gathers speed. Over the bridge. Past the house with the two iron butterflies nailed to the render. Towards bare brown fields, ploughed into orderly lines that are gently kissed by the first frost of the season.

A phone vibrates in Simon's tight raspberry red trouser pocket. Party trousers. A little jazzier than his usual work attire. He runs a hand to push his grey hair back from forehead to crown and it perches obediently in place, as if on tenterhooks to see what communication awaits its master.

> Stuck in back half so found a seat here. But I like your style. I'll see you at the Hotel du Vin you Naughty Boy.

He replies with a wink,

> Happy fucking Christmas.

> Oh, and I'm not wearing any knickers.

Simon laughs audibly and northbound commuters look at him witheringly.

Slut. She deliberately got on the back half of the train, the tease.

Simon wonders what Catherine's beautiful pixie face will look like when they're having sex. And doesn't reply.

Jacob and Florian lift the last of the boxes over the threshold and into the hallway of Maya's new home. As with all the other boxes, trunks and suitcases they moved five streets from Jacob's terraced house to this airy Victorian maisonette, they carried them at an incline of fifteen degrees as Florian's formidable height made the contents of, well, everything, slide to Jacob's end, and stockier shoulders had to bear extra weight.

Jacob leans his back against the hallway wall and slides down it until his bottom hits the black and white checked tiles of the floor. Florian looks at him with brotherly disdain and a dry mouth.

'Jesus Christ any chance of a tea?' Florian shouts up the flight of stairs.

'Kettle's boiling!' Maya hollers back.

Maya stands in the small kitchen at the top of the stairs with Jacob's girlfriend Amelia, who is rummaging for mugs in a crate marked 'crockery'. Maya opens a box of tea bags she just picked up from the corner shop on the next street. The boys regroup.

'Watch it, bellend!' snaps Jacob as Florian nearly lets go of the last box and sends it down the stairs, flattening Jacob in its wake.

'Sorry, my bad.'

As brothers with tired arms leave the box at the top and walk into the kitchen, both are hit by the glimmering light of winter sunshine bouncing through an undressed window and onto the stainless-steel kettle. Both make a visor with their right hand to protect their eyes. Both have the same pistachio green eyes of their father, the same light brown hair, and the same acerbic wit. Clara and Maya got their mother's darker eyes, although only Maya's flash with shards of orange.

'Got any biscuits?' grumbles a disgruntled babygiant. 'I'm starving.'

'Oh yeah,' Maya says, rummaging through the red and white stripy plastic bag from the corner shop.

'Custard Creams, Jaffa Cakes, or Lindt Santas?'

'Two of each,' Florian commands.

Amelia, with her deep auburn mane plaited into a braid, hands mugs of tea out while Maya, dusting her hands down on her running sweatshirt and leggings, opens the biscuits.

'I'm really so so grateful, guys,' she says, eyebrows rising just in the middle.

'No problem,' says Jacob, ever accommodating. 'Flowers & Flowers Removals really ought to go into business.'

This weekend the brothers will move Amelia from her Nottingham flat into Jacob's house in time for their first Christmas together.

'No, we shouldn't,' Florian says flatly.

Maya gives him a grateful rub on the back.

'Got any bread?'

Maya opens a box marked 'food' and finds some pumpernickel.

'Any good?' she shrugs apologetically.

Maya's baby brothers, as reliable as ever. Clara's hands are so full with her three sons that it's always Jacob and Florian who rise to this kind of occasion. They are young, they are strong and they are around. They helped Maya out of her Finsbury Park flat three years ago, when her hair turned wavy, and brought her back home. At first, home was Flowers Towers, as their father Herbert calls it. The Georgian house at the top of the hill overlooking Hazelworth that has the perfect balance of symmetry for its orderly patriarch. Two chimneys at opposing ends of the long roof. Two long white windows on either side of the threshold, and one more with a small wrought-iron balcony perched above the grand white stone surround of the front door. Inside, pictures adorn every wall in pleasing, if dusty, alignment, and how fortuitous that Herbert and Dolores Flowers filled the house with two girls and two boys. It was healthy for Maya to be home, to be reunited with the bookcase she gazed at as a child, but when Jacob bought the terraced house near the train station, he offered Maya the spare room while she fixed her heart and found her feet. Jacob. NASA StarChild at five, Young Scientist of The Year at thirteen, first-time buyer before his big sister.

'It really is lovely, Maya,' says Amelia, looking to the high kitchen ceiling. 'And it doesn't need all that much work.'

'Oh god it does, look at those frames,' Maya motions to the kitchen window, sun still beating in. 'I could break into those windows with a toothpick! Good job my most valuable item is only a KitchenAid.'

'Bingo!' says Florian, pulling a squashed loaf of bread out of a cardboard box.

Florian stays for a sandwich while Jacob and Amelia stroll down the road arm in arm, back five streets to his house – *their* house – and an exciting future ahead of them.

19

Maya waits nervously in a buzzing reception area as big faces of big TV stars look down on her from digital walls. The Doctor incumbent points at her from the largest, most fanfare-like spot in the lobby.

She picks up a copy of the staff newspaper and flicks through. A familiar face shines on page three.

Nena Oliveira is the new face of Children's...

'Oh put that down!'

Seemingly the photo can talk.

'Look at you! All grown-up!' says Maya, turning to the figure standing over her.

They hug. The smudgings of Nena's DIY clown make-up are long gone: sleek but heavily applied gold sparkles line her eyes and her red lips have been toned down with a blush beige. The apples of her cheeks look rosier than ever. Nena is a girl who doesn't need make-up, and with so much on she looks like a cartoon caricature of herself.

'I look ridiculous! Let's get outta here.'

'Hang on, you have to take a picture of me in front of that, my nephews will go nuts.' Maya points to the blue telephone box down the hall and gives the man on the wall a quick glance to see if he's still disapproving.

'You're such a tourist,' Nena scoffs as she glides across the shiny reception floor in her Bloch ballerina flats, hair swishing independently behind her. She takes her phone out of her pocket. 'Come on then!' she whispers urgently, worried that Maya's starry eyes might embarrass the new star signing.

Maya stands in front of the Tardis and beams for her nephews.

'Want me to take one of both of you?' leans in a tall man wearing a flat cap and a superhero smile. His pale, penetrating eyes shine.

'Erm, no!' Nena snaps. 'I mean, thanks, but no, it's just my friend here seems to be a geek – I've known her almost ten years and I didn't know that.'

Is it me or is Nena flustered?

Maya didn't know Nena could look flustered in front of a man. Where is the purring girl who would have guys falling at her dancing feet while she tangoed them into a spin?

Tom extends a confident hand. 'Hi, Nena's friend, I'm Tom, her…'

'My boss.' Brown apples go rosy as Nena twists her hair into rope at the side of her cheek.

'Hi, Nena's boss, I'm Maya,' Maya says with wide, gossipy eyes.

'We were just heading out to get a bite to eat,' interjects Nena, gold eyeliner fluttering like the wings of a hummingbird.

'That's cool, I'm off to get Arlo. Maya, great to meet you – and can I say, your friend is AMAZING. Never been on camera and she just lit up the studio. Nena – the controller came to watch and she thought you were brilliant. We all did.'

'That's my girl,' beams Maya brightly.

'Thank you,' Nena smoulders modestly. She had a feeling it had gone well.

'When can I catch her on air?' asks Maya excitedly.

'January. New Year, new look, new talent.' Tom looks towards Nena proudly and pauses before remembering himself. 'Anyway, I shall leave you beautiful ladies to your dinner, I have to go. Maya, it's a pleasure,' Tom nods at Maya then cups her hands in his as an affirmation that it really was lovely to meet Nena's best friend. He then turns to Nena, gives her a nod but doesn't say anything. He walks out hastily through revolving doors, into the dark evening illuminated by the Christmas lights of Regent Street.

'Well, he's lovely,' gushes Maya as she gives Nena a knowing look.

'I know. And he's my boss. And he has a kid,' Nena sighs and a little crinkle appears in that flawless forehead of hers.

Maya offers a consolatory arm and Nena threads her hand through it. The girls head out of the revolving doors, following Tom's path down Regent Street only they're heading towards their favourite Thai restaurant, past the giant illuminated robins silently flapping over Carnaby Street.

'How's the new pad?' asks Nena, as she slides into her seat on the bench at a shared square table with the agility of a limbo dancer.

'Lovely. Quiet! I didn't realise how much background noise Jacob made. On the phone to Amelia, listening to the radio while he cooks, watching *Stargazing Live* on catch-up...' Maya pauses thoughtfully. 'The quiet's a bit weird actually, but it's nice to have my own space and not feel like I'm in the way. Even though Jacob never said I was. And I can make macarons at midnight if I want to.'

Glitter-lined eyes roll. 'Jeez Maya, is that what you get up to when the rest of the world is partying?'

Maya raises her chopsticks and stops. 'We can't all enjoy sexual gymnastics with three guys at a time.'

Fellow diners squished on corners either side of them look up. Maya takes a bite and lime leaf and chilli buzz in her mouth.

'Hang on!' protests Nena, dropping a piece of stir-fried cod. She turns her voice to a shouty whisper. 'I *never* shag more than one guy at a time!' Nena scrabbles to pincer the cod back up. 'Anyway,' she says returning to a normal volume, 'Tony's going back to New York on actual Christmas Day, so I'm not even sure if I'll see him again now I'm not doing the show. He has eight shows a week for the next two weeks. And Liam... well...'

'Liam? I thought he was called Pete!'

'Oh Pete was the plumber, Liam's the electrician. It was over with Pete ages ago.'

'What about Tom? He's gorgeous.'

'And he's my boss. And he has Arlo. Who is equally gorgeous – but no. Not going there. Anyway, what about Train Man?' Nena switches the subject as deftly as she switches the bowls around so she can try some of Maya's smoked chicken noodles.

'I love him.'

'So why don't you talk to him?' pleads a friendly face. Nena can't comprehend why Maya doesn't.

'I can't. I see him every day. I see what he reads. I glance at his beautiful face. And I'm silenced. If I wasn't too scared to talk to him, I'm not even sure I physically could, he is that mind-blowingly beautiful and perfect, I am silenced.'

'What's he reading now?'

'*I, Claudius*.'

'Well he's not that perfect,' Nena says, as she rolls her eyes and makes a bored faced.

'He's perfect.'

Maya looks at a bowl of calamari tangled up in beautiful green bubbles of peppercorn and can't eat.

'Well why don't you ask him out for a Christmas drink as you're getting off the train in the morning?'

'Mulled wine at 8.52 a.m. is excessive, even for you Nena.'

Nena sucks up a noodle.

'I thought about giving him a mince pie and a Christmas card on the train, of putting my number in the card, but Sam at work said that if a stranger on the train gave him a mince pie and a Christmas card he'd think she was a nutjob.'

'You make good mince pies.'

'Come to Hazelworth, see my new flat, I'll make some especially.' Maya feels needy.

Nena doesn't acknowledge the invitation. 'Oh fuck it, just slip him your number, girl. I do it all the time and guys do NOT think it's weird.'

20

Kitty sips a French Martini.

'Happy New Year!' says James, raising his red wine and watching it cling to the sides of his glass in desperation.

Eyes look up but don't make contact. Glasses chink.

'It's not for another three hours,' Kitty says sternly, before looking over James's shoulder at the bustling bar behind him. Bottles sit on iron shelves against an exposed brickwork wall.

What am I not giving her?

James looks at Kitty's white-blonde hair, swept sleekly in a side parting as she injects some glamour into her androgynous look. James knows all of Kitty's looks so well. White shirt buttoned up over skinny charcoal jeans and pointed navy stilettos. Muted palette. Icy complexion. Frame so thin her wrists look like they might snap. But clothes hang beautifully from her.

Kitty gazes up at the sage green vintage bicycle hanging from the ceiling above, a garland of fake flowers twisted around it and silk blooms bursting from the basket. This is the most London-style bar and restaurant they have discovered since moving to Hazelworth, so it is the only place

Kitty likes to go out. Dominic and Josie invited them to their house party in Greenwich but Kitty thought they should stay close to their new home this Christmas and New Year. She didn't even want to see their parents as they usually do. Their parents live in the same street in the same town in Kent that they lived in when James and Kitty got together when they were sixteen. In fact, James and Kitty's parents are spending New Year's Eve together tonight.

'I wonder if they've broken out the Trivial Pursuits yet,' says James desperately.

Kitty arches her body back to look up at the ceiling above them again, to look anywhere but at him. James marvels at her beauty and wonders what her laugh sounds like. He can't remember the impish cackle that used to fill a classroom. How she would tip her head back and a joyous sound would come from her belly. Everyone loved that laugh, it's what made him fall for her in Religious Education.

'Are you OK?' James whispers. Kitty doesn't hear. Raucous laughs envelop them. Diners in the space beyond the hanging bicycle, where an old ballroom used to be, chat, oblivious to the raging flames sizzling close by in the open kitchen. Anticipation fills the room.

'What are your hopes and dreams for next year?' James asks, trying to engage the girl he used to know.

Kitty's eyes well up.

'What's the matter?'

Kitty was like this all Christmas. Quiet. Tense. James was pleased that she wanted to lay some roots and stay in their new home because he hadn't even been able to decipher if she was happy to have moved there or not. She seemed to miss London. Miss something anyway. Just the two of them for Christmas wasn't fun. James made a roast dinner with

99

all the trimmings and Kitty said she wasn't hungry, she'd eaten breakfast too late. James ate as much as he could so it didn't go to waste but he missed his mum's roast potatoes. He even missed his dad and sister Francesca having their annual Christmas Day argument after one mulled cider too many. He'd wished they were spending New Year's Eve with Dominic and Josie and their mates on the meridian. But he wouldn't say any of this out loud of course.

'What are we doing in here?' Kitty pleads with a crinkled forehead.

'I thought you wanted to come, you like this place.'

In a booth just beyond the hanging bicycle, tucked around a corner against a tall oblong window topped with an arch, Maya sits with her siblings. Clara and her husband Robbie, Jacob and Amelia, Florian and his girlfriend Rose, a meek and shy flower if ever there was one. The circular table tidily hides the fact Maya is the only single person there and she already knows that at midnight, Clara will hug and kiss Maya before she hugs and kisses Robbie. She has done so for the past three New Year's Eves that Maya has been single.

'Stop it, you don't have to hug me first, I can handle it,' Maya always says.

'Get outta here, I like you more than I like him anyway,' Clara always winks.

Clara and Robbie are high-school sweethearts who were pushed together at the prom, married at twenty-three and had three sons in quick succession. And because Clara has never been on a date in her life, she has never had to sit through 100 awkward questions or the disappointment of knowing within the first five minutes that this will go nowhere.

She has never had that feeling of squash, clatter and crumple in her stomach.

Clara's stay-at-home life with Henry, Jack and Oscar is so full of laughter and love and puzzles and puddles and T-Rexes and time out, and the boys are so all-consuming, that it's hard for her to understand Maya's world at all. Her job at FASH in exotic London. Her exciting dating stories. Maya adores her nephews. Jacob and Florian do too, but none of them think they have the energy for longer than a couple of hours spent winding them up with treats and sweets and tickles and cuddles before they walk away to their peaceful homes.

A distinctive New York voice travels across the restaurant and Maya turns her head.

'Velma?' she whispers to herself.

'Who's Velma?' asks Clara, raising a mojito to her lips. Clara looks very much like Maya but older than the three years that separates them. She looks wilder, her hair is more unruly, her hips are broader and her face tells tales of a life filled with more laughter. Clara wouldn't know how to dress for a date, she can't bake a birthday cake without it looking like Henry made it, and she doesn't know the shortcut from the Victoria Line to the Bakerloo Line at Oxford Circus. But she knows how to make a robot out of a cereal box, some foil and an old egg carton, which makes her a goddess on the other side of Hazelworth.

'One of my students, she's brilliant. You'd love her, Clara! I'm just going to go and say hi.'

Maya stands up from the cream cushion of the circular booth and walks gingerly across the restaurant after two passionfruit daiquiris. Her peach shift dress with lilac flowers and a full skirt makes her look ladylike, even though she doesn't feel it as she totters to Velma's table near the open kitchen, feeling a little bit squiffy.

As his sister walks off, Florian sees the three bows fastening the dress down her spine.

'She looks like a five-year-old,' he grunts.

'Velma!'

'Oh my goodness, look at you! Maya, you look *darling*, Happy New Year!' Velma stands, although she's so small you'd barely notice. Even for a special occasion, Velma wears her wardrobe staple of a black roll-neck over black trousers and shoes that look like they might be slippers. In a nod to celebration, sparkling multicoloured earrings dangle below her short grey hair. She turns to her companions. 'Boys, this is Maya. Maya, meet my sons!'

New York giants dab their mouths with their napkins and stand heroically, a prim-looking woman with her hair twisted into a chignon stays seated and smiles waspishly.

'This is Conrad and his wonderful wife Madison, and this is Christopher.' Velma sits down, her boys bow their heads and shake Maya's hand. Suddenly she doesn't feel so out of place in her princess dress.

'Pleased to meet you,' Maya says as she wonders how someone so small birthed two such square-jawed and supreme specimens.

'Maya is my Spanish teacher!' Velma says with delight, Manhattan rasp sounding stronger for a few days spent with her family.

'In that case, *encantado*,' says Christopher, white teeth gleaming.

'Maya, who are you here with? A boyfriend?' Maya sees a twinkle in Velma's eyes, accentuated by her thick bottle-end glasses.

'Oh, my sister and brothers and their partners, over there,' she motions to the booth under the window. Jacob is refilling glasses with Malbec.

Velma strains to look.

'Are you single?'

Oh god, I can see where this is going.

'Erm, yes.'

'Well I can't believe that, you're so pretty! Isn't she pretty, boys?'

Maya's flushed face is highlighted by a flambé in the open kitchen.

'I would fix you up with my Christopher but he's got a lot of baggage right now. Haven't you, honey?'

Christopher laughs.

'Messy divorce,' Velma mouths in a half whisper.

'Thanks, Mom.' Christopher rolls his eyes and then looks at Maya and smiles.

Maya laughs.

'But didn't I make handsome boys?'

Maya looks back at Christopher. He certainly is buff.

'And Madison is expecting, I'm gonna be grandma. Finally! In the spring.'

Maya looks at Madison, whose tiny frame shows no sign of a bump. 'Wow, congratulations Madison, congratulations Velma! What an exciting year ahead of you,' Maya smiles but Velma's trained eye sees sadness behind it. Steak arrives. 'I'd better get back to my table and let you eat, it's great to meet you all. Enjoy dinner and Happy New Year. See you back in class next week, Velma.'

Conrad and Christopher stand again and nod their heads like obedient puppies.

Velma stands and takes Maya's hand in hers and cups

her other hand on top. A wedding ring and an eternity ring on liver-spotted hands encase Maya's with warmth. 'Happy New Year Miss Oh Just Maya.'

Maya nods a farewell to Velma's family and walks back to the booth, not knowing why she wants to cry.

Wine flows. Glasses smash. Jacob and Clara get noisier. Rose looks more and more terrified. Robbie and Amelia talk about the decorating Amelia has just commissioned Robbie to do in Jacob's house. Florian gets quietly drunk. And, as Maya wonders where Train Man is tonight, who *he* will be kissing as Big Ben chimes, she doesn't see him walk out of the bar area with his arm around a woman who isn't talking to him.

21

January 2014

'I had to see you, I missed you so much!'

It is a grey wintry start to a new and exciting year. Catherine tightens her legs around Simon's waist and they kiss frantically. She breaks off and looks up and around from under her hat, although it is Simon who is playing a dangerous game. He is a school governor, he runs the local triathlon club and his wife Laura has friends in most of the cafes and tea rooms in Hazelworth, none of which are open on New Year's Day.

Catherine squeezes his muscly Lycra-clad thigh, open and cocksure, lapping up her lover.

'I was so lonely without you at Christmas!' she says.

'Me too.' Frantic hands grope cold small breasts.

Catherine feels bad for Simon's children – who are all still asleep, unknowing that Daddy has gone for a run – little Esmé nestled into her mummy's back with her legs horizontal across the space where her dad lay. Catherine doesn't feel too bad though.

'What did *she* get you for Christmas?'

'Don't talk about Laura, we don't have long.'

'Well, I got you this,' Catherine says with a mischievous, competitive smile as she takes an envelope from her pocket with Eurostar written on the front in a curly script. 'I have to go to Brussels next week for work. Please say you can come with me. Two nights at the Steigenberger. Me. Naked. With a bow on if you like.'

Lycra stretches. Teeth clatter.

'Fuck, you're amazing. I'll see what I can do.'

Maya wakes to the buzz of the radio. Nick Cave. 'Get Ready For Love'. The world outside is grey and still and she wonders why she set the radio at all. She scrapes long waves back off her face and into a messy bun high on the crown of her head and walks to the tall wardrobe at the top of the tall maisonette. She sheds her thermals and drops them to the whitewashed floorboards before putting on a white sports bra, a coral pink vest and deep purple tights, then throws a grey long-sleeved top over her head and shoulders. Eyes barely open.

Maya skips down the first flight of stairs, the one that turns a corner as she goes, and into the high-ceilinged bathroom on the landing below, then down another small flight of stairs into the kitchen. She looks out of the window onto the junction and roundabout two streets away below. No cars. The gastro pub with the pretty hanging baskets is closed. Commuters don't hurry across the zebra crossing. Maya already knows how this day will pan out. The sky has a still greyness about it that will linger until it gets dark at 4.01 p.m. The sun won't burn through. Birds won't chirrup. It feels like the sort of day that, unless Maya makes any effort, she knows she will spend alone.

Maya takes a bite of honeyed toast with a dry mouth and thirst consumes her. She looks around the kitchen. The water glass she forgot to take to bed last night sits by the sink. A wire rack on the opposite counter displays the offcuts of macaron failure. Dented, blistered, cracked. Maya looks at the broken pistachio shells on the kitchen worktop, but, smiles to herself as she remembers the perfect ones she ended the year making, before going for a meal out, sitting in the freezer now.

I think I've nailed it.

Maya takes a final bite of toast before leaving the rest for her return and carefully slopes, eyes not yet fully ready for this New Year, down the longest flight of stairs to her trainers on the black and white checked floor by a stained-glass front door. As she laces up her trainers, Maya knows she will feel so much better after her run.

When Maya's hair turned wavy and Jacob and Florian brought her back to the place she was born, their father Herbert Flowers inspired her to run, citing it as a cure for all ills, but mostly a great opportunity to write haiku. Maya hated those first months of fatigue and thumping. Lump, sweat, wheeze. But on seeing her dad's upbeat silhouette through the glass in the front door of Jacob's house, and hearing his chuckles of glee as their feet hit the pavement in unison, she didn't have the heart to let him know she wasn't enjoying it. Besides, Maya couldn't give up; she is one of four children, running was rare time spent alone with her father. As the pair began to run more fluidly, Herbert started to suggest a haiku theme for each run and the two would plod silently side by side. Father hearing the sound of one hand clapping, daughter trying not to let him see her counting syllables on her fingers. Hours later, with tired but satisfied limbs, they would text each other a poem they had created.

Maya would always press send self-consciously, worried that Herbert would think it was prose rather than poetry, or that she might have miscounted the syllables. She needn't have. She couldn't see it but Herbert always loved them, kicking one leg in the air in delight as he read Maya's haikus out loud to Dolores from his armchair.

Running worked. Her father was right about its curative powers. As Herbert pencilled more and more haikus into his lined A5 notebook, Maya ran stronger, seasons changed, and she soon forgot she was ever broken.

At times, father and daughter would run side by side under an inky sky, not saying a word but breathing in the same Flowers rhythm and puff. Other times Maya would struggle, running behind her father so she could visualise him giving her a piggyback. He'd carry her home while she looked at the criss-cross lines on the back of his pineapple neck, although the comfort he brought made her feel like she was already there. Same short legs under a long lean and muscular back. Same funny flat feet that slightly opened outwards. Same wavy hair, although Maya's flowed behind her while Herbert's bounced above.

Those runs with her father were precious, but as Herbert's knees weakened and Maya's life became busier with work and teaching, they stopped running together as much. Herbert's silhouette doesn't wait through the stained glass of her new front door now and Maya doesn't run up to the symmetrical house on the hill. The house that still has the dusty bookshelf in the bedroom, although the wooden figures have disappeared to no-one-knows-where. Father and daughter don't run to the common where the Flowers children used to climb trees, past the tennis courts and rose fields and down the hill to Hazelworth's market square and back. Herbert Flowers doesn't hold out his finger for Maya to squeeze in farewell as she peels off down the road back to Jacob's house, seeing her future ahead of her. She occasionally creates haikus, but mostly forgets to send them.

Strong and alone now, Maya runs her street, her route. She runs, turning right out of the road lined with spiky bare hazel trees, onto the zebra crossing by the roundabout and left down the thoroughfare that takes you into the centre of Hazelworth and the market square. The spire of the church looks down disapprovingly at bottles and pint glasses strewn on pavements from last night's revelry. Maya runs more carefully across the cobbles and down a winding street where sparkling blue bunting crosses overhead, past the florist with slate love hearts in the window; the bridal shop with dresses that look like edible confections; the antiquated barber's shop; the French-style bakery whose metal shelves are void of rosemary bread and cinnamon swirls today.

Those first few minutes of a run are always the hardest, but Maya finds her stride as she turns left past the puddings parlour onto a road that runs along a river. Tudor buildings house solicitors' offices and hair salons and Maya passes a road sweeper heading in the other direction. Maya sees the path to a hill that overlooks the centre of the town and decides to start the year on a positive note and conquer it. Legs have awoken and funny feet feel unstoppable.

One of Herbert Flowers' many mantras flashes in her mind as she leans into the hill and up towards the site of the long-since burned-down windmill at the top.

Imagine a hand at the base of your spine, encouraging you along.

Breathing becomes more difficult at the summit as Maya winds along a path between two rolling expanses of damp grass, silent and lifeless apart from a squirrel to the left and two lovers kissing frantically on a bench in front of her. The town is behind her. Maya glances back. She wishes she could pinpoint Train Man. He turns right out of the station, she turns left. Where is he sleeping? Who might he love?

The New Year view from Primrose Hill is more resplendent, more full of hope. London's skyline looks postcard perfect, even under the grey sky there is an autumnal feel about this chilly midwinter morning and trees still show orange flare in the last dying months of winter. A little boy tries to whizz through the grass on a shiny new scooter, shades of orange and purple stalling under chubby little legs. He looks up at his dad with pleading eyes and a snotty nose.

'You need to go on the path with it, Arlimoo,' says a loud and loving voice.

'You come with meeee,' asks the boy, although it's more of an instruction.

'I'll go,' says Nena, jumping up from the bench as she twists her hair in a bun. Black hareem pants and bright trainers dart across the grass to guide the scooter with the boy surfing on it back onto the path.

Tom observes, long arms outstretched, resting on the top of the bench, huge smile on his face.

'OK, put this foot on the flat bit and your other foot on the floor...' Nena's small muscular legs provide a back support for Arlo as she surrounds him to help position him on his favourite Christmas present.

Tom watches Nena move around his son, mesmerised by the way she arches and leans. Nena moves in front of the scooter facing Arlo and crouches down, nose to nose.

'OK, ready? When I count to three you will start using this lovely strong leg to power yourself forward, OK?'

'Yeth,' nods Arlo, as enchanted as his daddy.

'One... two... three!' Nena tugs the handlebars as she glides backwards, pulling Arlo towards her, who starts to scoot as she runs even faster.

'Careful Arlimoo!' shouts Tom from the bench.

A shiny brown bowl cut becomes ruffled in the wind, as a beaming face, with a gap between two top teeth, advances towards Nena. Proud, cold, rosy.

'Arghhhh, you're so good I don't think I can keep up...' Nena laughs, still running backwards, bent down to eye level with Arlo, who is scooting with all the strength he has in his little right leg.

Arlo tires and puts both feet on the board while Nena slows him down. As he draws to a stop, she pretends to fall backwards and rolls acrobatically three times on her black leather biker jacket.

'Ouchy! You sent me spinning!'

Arlo giggles the delightful gurgles of a boy whose father's happiness is rubbing off on him.

Nena looks at his round, contended face and marvels at how she can be up and out at 9 a.m. on New Year's Day and feel so alive. 'Arghhhhh, you're so fast you knocked me over!'

Tom runs over and wraps warming arms around them both. His flat cap blows off in the wind to roars of laughter.

'Come on, let's get hot chocolate and marshmallows.'

22

'Maya, can I have a word?' Lucy stands up from the other side of the desk. Emma darts a diagonal look over to Maya from her seat by the window.

'Yes of course, Lucy.'

As senior as she is, Lucy doesn't have her own office yet, but given that she's already walking off to look for a meeting room, Maya knows this is private and not one of Lucy's usual chats or instructions from the other side of the Apple divide.

Emma watches them walk off. Alex turns around to Emma and raises an immaculately arched eyebrow over round horn-rimmed spectacles. No one says a word.

Clunk. The meeting-room door shuts.

'Maya, I didn't want to say this in front of the team because I don't want to put any noses out of joint, but...'

Maya's face feels hot.

'...your FASHmas Fairies campaign exceeded all expectations and sales are through the roof year-on-year – and we thought FASHmas Wonderland couldn't be beaten.'

Maya lets out a gasp of relief. 'Wow, that's great news, Lucy.'

Maya casts her mind back to the campaign, which featured

a team of four high-fashion fairies darting around the home page granting customers' wishes with inspiration, personal styling advice, gift ideas and discounts.

'Again you totally nailed Christmas and the tone of it for FASH: you communicated all of our key messages so expertly, I wanted to give you this by way of a thank you.'

Maya looks at the envelope in Lucy's Barbados tanned hands. It says Cypress Manor Hotel & Spa. She's never heard of it, but coming from Lucy she imagines it's very chic.

'I don't want to shout about it because staff aren't getting bonuses this year.'

Lucy casually drops the bombshell as if Maya was in the boardroom when that particular decision was made.

'Staff aren't getting bonuses? Even though we made a gazillion pounds last year?' Maya is confused. 'Rich's weekly emails always say how profits are up...'

Lucy nods but cuts Maya off.

'We're expanding so fast – outgoings are so high – soon FASH will be the world's number-one fashion brand. No bonus this year is a small price to pay when next year the rewards could be massive.'

'Yeah but for who?'

Maya has that uncomfortable sensation of a knitting needle being inserted into her stomach and feels sick for all the staff who will be relying on their annual bonus pay packet at the end of the month.

This isn't going to go down well.

Lucy frowns.

Maya realises she has to measure her face, to not look ungracious when an envelope containing the gift of a luxury getaway is being proffered in front of her by her boss.

'Well I did pull strings, Maya. I spoke to Rich and Rich

about this – about you – and they agreed that the Christmas campaign outshone the competition and helped drive sales. So they've endorsed this as an exception bonus,' Lucy says, waving the envelope still in her hands as she gesticulates. 'No one else will be getting this, Maya.'

Suddenly Maya feels ungrateful, so she smiles and takes the envelope.

'And look, while we're here, I'm trying to get sign-off for an editor on the team. I'm far too busy with executive board stuff now and I need someone at the helm of editorial every single hour of every day. Someone I can trust.'

Her eyes widen encouragingly.

'Wow, I don't know what to say.'

'Well just hold that thought because it's not going to be for a few months, but when I do have the green light, and the budget for the role, I want you to put your hat in.'

This all feels somewhat overwhelming. Editor? But Maya is flattered.

Lucy smiles and looks at her Cartier watch, signalling that Maya's time is up, and heads towards the door and opens it with a smile. Maya walks through, clutching the white envelope, keen to head back to her desk and Google Cypress Manor Hotel & Spa, wondering what she will say to her friends who will be devastated when they hear the news about the bonuses.

Maya removes her pink cocoon coat and throws it over her lap as she slumps into one of the last remaining seats on this Superior Train. Happy day. A gold star at work and a seat on the train home, when there must only be a couple left in the carriage. Doors beep furiously and a tall figure slides through just before they shut. Maya looks up. Double luck. It's a double luck day. It happens so rarely, but given that Maya seems to be blessed today, she ought to have expected this. Train Man stands strong, looking up and down the carriage.

There's one just there!

As if he could read Maya's mind, Train Man cranes his neck and sees the one remaining seat tucked in the corner. Facing each other. On opposite sides of an aisle. Three rows away. Maya most definitely doesn't mind going backwards. This is a bonus. If she didn't have a class to teach tonight she could perhaps walk his way home, see where it takes him – a safe distance behind of course, she wouldn't want him to think she was a stalker.

Maya smooths down her floral top and co-ord pencil skirt, so beautiful is the print it looks like she stood still while Seurat painted on her blank clothing canvas. Maya wriggles in her seat as she composes herself for the benefit of someone who hasn't noticed. Heart beating faster.

Train Man wears a navy peacoat and is wrapped up warm in a lighter blue cable-knit scarf. He pushes his black rectangular glasses up his nose. He looks so cosy Maya wishes she were in his pocket.

Train Man takes out this morning's free paper he hasn't got around to reading yet. Old news. Maya wants to tell him she did really well at work today and has a voucher for a romantic getaway at a luxury hotel and spa in her bag, to be taken next month if he'd like to accompany her. New news. She wants to share all the ridiculousness of her life with him. She wants to get off the train with him because this never happens, go home together, show him her new flat, sack off class, cook him something nurturing and do things to each other that two people who are meant to be together do to each other.

He folds the paper away and takes out a copy of *National Geographic*. He locks eyes with a little boy on the cover from an Amazonian tribe and wants to know all about him. He looks up. Olive cheeks turned slightly pink. Overheating in this heated carriage. Hot air blasting at his ankles. He rises slightly out of his seat to take his coat and scarf off. Train Man doesn't look up for long. Back to his magazine. Back to his train of thought.

Maya doesn't know Train Man is thinking about how he can earn money as a photographer. What would Dominic say if he left their partnership? Why didn't Kitty ask him what his hopes and dreams were for this year?

The steely noise of electric wheels gliding along track punctuates the silent carriage on the dark evening.

'Tickets please,' bellows a thuggish-looking man with a square head and stained trousers.

'Bueno clase, es todo por hoy, gracias por venir. Hasta la semana que viene.'

Even though not all the class understand what Maya just said, the fact that the clock above the poster that says **POLISH SWEDISH FOR BEGINNERS** is ticking on 9.30 p.m. and she's shuffling her papers means they know this week's class is coming to an end.

Doug helps Jan out of her chair, a chivalrous arm held out is something so normal to them they don't know how lovely they look to Maya. Glyn packs his beige notebook away into his beige manbag and stands tall in his perfectly pressed – long – beige slacks. Nathaniel stands up, bows and says, 'Enchanté' as he backs out of the classroom.

'Ponce,' Gareth mumbles to his daughter.

Velma shuffles to the front of the class and presses a piece of paper into Maya's hand. Maya blushes, confused, then goes to open it.

'Not now, honey,' Velma waves knowingly as she turns to Ed, but Maya doesn't understand what just happened.

'Now tell me, Ed, did you book your flight already?'

Eager eyes light up as Ed tells Velma that on Good Friday he will fly out to Buenos Aires to be reunited with his girlfriend, Valeria, and meet her family for the first time. Velma once lived in Buenos Aires for a spell and the two have struck up a bond based on a shared love of all things Argentine.

As Velma and Ed head out of the door at the back of the classroom, Maya puts her bottle of water and phone in her bag. Curiosity gets the better of her and she unfolds the crumpled piece of paper in her hand. An elegant scrawl fills it: *1a Market Place. Whenever you fancy tea and sympathy. Velma x*

23

'I'm so glad you came!' Spotted, happy hands clap together as Velma opens the door wider.

Maya smiles nervously.

'Well I didn't know if you meant it,' she says, as Velma beckons her into a treasure trove of clutter, where a seat isn't adorned without at least three mismatched velvet cushions and you can't see the walls for books.

Velma looks puzzled. 'Why would I say something I didn't mean?'

New York attitude meets British reserve.

'Oh, sorry.'

Maya feels bad. Firstly for imposing on a Sunday afternoon, and secondly for trying to second-guess someone who was just being nice. But something made Maya visit today, although she's not sure what. As she walks sheepishly into the apartment, she worries she might be breaking a teacher/pupil code that doesn't apply to volunteers or their septuagenarian students. Especially not two who warmed to each other so naturally.

Velma takes Maya's pink cocoon coat and throws it onto a threadbare chair piled with three plump cushions at a console table under an open window. On the other side of it window boxes tell tales of frost and neglect. *Gardeners' Question Time* blasts from the radio in the kitchen just off the living area where two mismatched camelback sofas reveal elegant wooden ankles below colourful tasselled throws and more velvet cushions.

'Cup of tea?' Velma says with affected British propriety.

Maya would never say no to such beautiful diction. 'Yes please.'

'Hang on, let me switch that off. I don't know why I listen to it, I don't even have a garden!' Velma chuckles as she kills a switch at the plug next to the kettle and the Sunday lunch bustle from the pizzeria underneath them starts to rise. 'Company, I guess.'

Maya studies the bookshelves and wraps her arms around her ribs to warm up. An arctic blast is coming through the window Velma obviously keeps open all year round.

'This is wonderful, Velma! I'm amazed you live here.'

Here is the noisiest sixty-five square metres in the entire town, above Hazelworth's most bustling Italian restaurant and next to its old corn exchange, where merchants made their money and a town was built upon the grain trade. Nowadays drunken girls tumble out of the old corn exchange in miniskirts and bra tops, onto the market square, where they might end up plying a less wholesome trade.

'Are you *kidding*? In London I lived on Old Compton Street, in Paris it was Pigalle, and you couldn't tear me away from San Telmo in Buenos Aires. This is eerily quiet.'

Maya laughs.

'But I was born on Broadway. I adore noise. Why do you think I'm moving to South Beach? I am *not* a country mouse.'

'So how did you end up here?' Maya's nose crinkles as she says it.

'In suburbia?'

A kettle rumbles in a battle against limescale Velma refuses to remove, lest it make for a quieter boil.

'Conrad and Christopher thought I should slow down. When I hit seventy, I agreed. So they came over and wheeled me out to the sticks. Actually it was prompted by my being mugged in Soho, which was particularly mean since I had lived there for so long and never once encountered a bad word or a single ruffian there, until the day a tourist snatched my purse. But the flat on Old Compton Street was pretty run-down and hard to negotiate, I needed something...' She looks around at organised chaos and waves an arm, 'Calmer. Conrad and Christopher are strapping boys – you've seen them! – but they're not much help over in New York. So I promised them I would try a quieter pace of life.' Velma raises an eyebrow above a thick lens.

'Do you hate it?' Maya winces, feeling guilty that Hazelworth – *her* Hazelworth – isn't as exciting as Soho or Manhattan.

Velma busies herself in the kitchen beyond glass doors that look like they're made of ice cubes, and are propped open with towers of books.

'I don't love it. Hence the Florida plan. It's fun there, it's warm there, I can continue my work... and it's in the same time zone as my sons.'

'And grandchild!' Maya calls, turning around from the bookshelf to a beaming old lady in the kitchen.

'And grandchild,' Velma smiles, rubbing her hands together. 'Plus Florida is where we middle-class Americans go to see out our lives in the sunshine. It's the right move for me now.'

'Oh don't say that!'

'It's true.'

'So you still work?' Maya asks, staring at the spines of the books on the shelf, as she did in her parents' bedroom as a child. *Wuthering Heights*, *Shantaram*, *Strangers On A Train*.

'I will work forever, my darling, it's all I know.' Velma carries a tray through into the living space, and perches it on the coffee table in front of the camelback sofas. She edges magazines out of the way with a shaky elbow.

'Ooh, let me help you,' says Maya, holding out two hands.

'I got it.'

'What do you do?' Maya feels bad for assuming Velma was retired. She's known her for five months now, and didn't even know that she worked. From looking around the apartment, Maya assumes Velma must be an academic, and feels somewhat embarrassed about the fact she comes up with silly names for clothes for a living.

'I'm an agony aunt.'

Maya's mouth hangs open. She's never met an agony aunt before. 'Wow!'

'Radio, magazines, books… Less radio now, as I am finding it harder to get to the studio, but that was the same when I was only travelling in from Soho. My old legs need that Florida sunshine!'

Now the tea and sympathy make sense and Maya feels a little, well, exposed.

'How do you take it?'

'White, no sugar thanks.'

Velma tilts the chipped Royal Albert teapot towards one of the mismatched china cups, then lifts a floral milk jug, pours, and stirs with a fragile hand. Clank, chink, splosh.

'Oh silly me, I forgot the cake.' Velma shuffles back to the kitchen in the same shoes-cum-slippers she wears to class.

'Do you always have cake on the go?' asks Maya, seeing something of herself in Velma. A sweet tooth and once-adventurous spirit.

'Uh-huh. In truth I don't have many visitors since I moved here – my London flat was always bustling, in fact it was hard to get any work done with all the friends I had dropping by. But I'm a creature of habit, I like to have a fresh bake on the go in case I do, and baking is wonderfully therapeutic. Although I'm a little naughty and eat all the time when I'm writing. My hips certainly know it.'

Maya doesn't think Velma could possibly have any hips under her baggy grey jumper.

'Here, lemon and poppyseed.'

Maya takes a pale green tea plate with gold trim and tiny white polka dots and inhales the citrus scent and smiles. 'Oh I totally understand that mindspace you get from baking – and the sweet reward at the end of it.'

'You bake too?'

'Yeah, I love it. I moved in on my own just before Christmas so I've upped the ante since then. I finally bought my own place,' says Maya as she lowers a brass fork into yellow crumb.

Velma laughs. 'How old are you?'

'Twenty-seven.'

'Sweetie, I have *never* owned my own place, so don't feel bad. I have lived on my own for a long time though – longer than you've been alive in fact, and I wouldn't have it any other way. Not now anyway.'

The teacher and the pupil eat cake.

'So tell me about yourself, Miss Oh Just Maya.'

Maya feels sad that she has nothing to tell. Velma can tell Maya feels sad.

'Are you dating?'

'Not really. There's no "special someone".'

'Anyone *not* special, but just a bit of fun?' Velma gives a cheeky laugh.

Zingy lemon flavours burst in Maya's mouth with the realisation that she is having afternoon tea with a kindly woman who clearly wants to know more about her – oh, and who just so happens to be an agony aunt. Her shoulders relax a little.

'Actually there *is* someone. But it might sound silly.'

Velma pushes thick glasses down her long nose and looks at Maya with unmagnified, understanding eyes. 'Honey, remember your audience. Nothing relating to matters of the heart will ever sound silly to me. I have genuinely heard it all.'

'There's a man who gets my train to work in the morning. Train Man.' Maya says his moniker as if Velma must have heard of him.

'Train Man, I like it, sounds dashing.'

'Oh Velma, he is!' Maya's face completely softens. 'He's so beautiful. Not in that square-jawed way your Christopher is – who by the way is *very* hot, well done on making him...' Maya is going for a laugh to lighten the intensity of her feelings.

Velma doesn't laugh, her listening eyes open wider. Kind, caring and tiny when not sitting behind thick lenses.

'Train Man is just the most beautiful man I have ever seen, and from the minute I saw him it was like I *knew* him, and he felt like home and he looked... *right*. He looked lovely. He was the man I had dreamed of all my life but not known what he looked like until he arrived on the platform last summer.'

'Have you spoken to him?'

'No.'

'Do you want to speak to him?'

'Yes! I want to actually know him. I want to laugh with him, I want to kiss him. It feels weird that we don't. But he doesn't even see me. How can we feel so differently when I think we're meant to be together?'

Velma's eyes narrow and she looks deep in thought. Maya takes a sip of tea to fill the pause. The punctuation of the slurp in the quiet apartment makes her realise the lunchtime rush must have ended in the pizzeria downstairs.

'You know, Maya, there's only one thing you can do and that is make contact with him. I can't promise that he'll be interested, although he'd be crazy not to be...' Velma winks and pushes her glasses back up her nose, 'But he might be in love with someone else. Or you might not be his type. Or gender.'

'I did think of that.'

'But you will never know unless you talk to him, say hi, ask him out for a drink.'

Velma lifts the cake knife to trim another few slices of the rectangular loaf. Crumbs fall onto an already speckled carpet.

'But no one talks to each other on the train, he barely looks up once he's found a seat.'

'Well you need to find a way, Maya. Use your feminine wiles. Do that thing you British people do really well and raise your eyeballs to the sky and talk about the weather. Or just tell him you think he looks like a lovely person and ask him if he'd like to go for a drink with you.'

Maya looks bewildered. 'I'm not sure I'm brave enough.'

'Oh, I bet you are.'

Silence fills the apartment but for the jingle of the bells on the wind chime by the open window.

Velma lifts the teapot once more and pours.

'Tea and sympathy, huh?' laughs Maya, as she takes the floral cup. 'How did you know, Velma?'

'I know a sad heart when I see one. Here, have another slice.' Maya holds out the polka dot plate again. 'What do your friends think?'

'My best friend thinks it's funny, just a joke really. I don't think she realises how serious I am about him. And I tell my workmates about Train Man because he's become a bit of a talking point in the office in the mornings. And my sister, well, I haven't really told her the depths of my feelings because she's got her hands full with her kids and she would think I was crazy if I said I loved a stranger.'

'And what would you say if your best friend or your sister told you what you just told me, with as much conviction and passion in her eyes?'

'I'd say she should talk to him, ask him out.'

'Well I think he sounds darling and you already know what to do. What's the worst that can happen?'

24

February 2014

James is sitting at his desk with his back to the floor-to-ceiling glass window behind it. Dominic's thick stance leans in as they scroll through the pages of a photographer's website. James isn't impressed.

'Nope, it's not strong enough. He's taken a beautiful woman and made her look dead behind the eyes. How does someone even manage that?'

'It's not her eyes we'll be focusing on,' laughs Dominic like a schoolboy.

James scowls, irritated more by frustration than his friend. Last summer he and Dominic won the biggest account the MFDD agency has ever had in its eighteen-year history, but James doesn't feel excited.

'What about Catrin?' Dominic tries to muster some enthusiasm.

'She shot for *Vanity Fair* last month,' James counters flatly.

'Bloody hell. Yes, I imagine pubic hair removal will be erm, beneath her, now.'

Dominic finally gets a laugh out of his mate.

'Look Millsy, it's hardly our dream product but look at what it means around here. Jeremy thinks we're the mutt's nuts now, Fisher & Whyman are already asking us to pitch for more business and we've not even shot Femme yet. We're flying here, mate. Why are you so down on it?'

Dominic perches a small doughy bottom onto James's desk and folds meaty arms in his blue checked shirt.

'I'm not down on it. I'm just struggling to get excited about it, I don't know why really. I guess all this chat about camellia oil and ylang-ylang isn't exactly my bag.'

'You didn't eat dog food, but you managed to get enthusiastic about that one. Mate, we just got a ten grand payrise. We're casting models in bikinis tomorrow. We're shooting in South Africa next month, Jamaica in September, this is the dream, Baby.'

James looks up at his friend. He used to find Dominic's enthusiasm infectious and feels shitty that it isn't now. He feigns a smile, dimples flash and disappear.

'Look how far we've come! All those chumps out there on Charlotte Street who would give their right bollock to work at MFDD. We're here, we worked our arses off to get here. Our boss thinks we're great. This is a good thing, Millsy. Remember the spotty oiks we were at uni. Well, I was spotty...' Dominic looks at his pockmarked face in the reflection of the glass then sees the reflection of the clock. 'Shit I'm meant to meet Josie...' he says, turning his head so he can read the time properly. 'Two minutes ago.'

James laughs to himself. His friend is vocal and vulgar and talks the talk about living the dream on shoots with models, when actually he's a pussycat, besotted with his girlfriend, who is the PA to the CEO at the first advertising agency he and James worked for, straight out of university, situated about fifty metres up the road from the one they're standing in now.

We haven't come that far.

'Oh I'll come out with you and say hi.'

'I'd say you could join us for lunch but, you know, it is Valentine's Day and all, Josie might rather you didn't.'

'Shit, Valentine's Day. I didn't realise it was the fourteenth.'

'Millsy, how could you not realise it's fucking Valentine's Day? You work in advertising. We've been ramming it down people's throats since Christmas. Jesus, you are distracted. Bad luck, Kitty's going to go mental.' Dominic lets out a little laugh.

'Well, she didn't mention it either. You go. Say hi to Josie, I'd better make a call.'

In the low light of a lab on a science park, thin fingers answer a silently flashing phone.

'I'm in the middle of something, can I call you back?'

Terseness people only save for people they know will tolerate it.

'Sure. Just wondering if you want dinner out tonight?'

'Oh. Erm, well where? Why?'

'It's Valentine's Day.'

'We never celebrate Valentine's Day.'

'We used to.'

'Well, obviously you've only just been reminded by Dominic, so it can't matter that much to you.'

A furrowed face keeps trying. 'Why don't you get the train all the way through to London tonight, don't get off at home, and I'll take you somewhere special?'

'Not Moro. Dominic is taking Josie to Moro tonight, at least be original.'

James doesn't mention that Dominic and Josie are also meeting for a sandwich right now, so they must still really like each other.

'Not Moro. Wherever you want.'

'Well let me see how long this takes, I'm in the middle of an experiment, I have thirty mice all waiting to be infected.'

'Nice,' says James sarcastically.

James marvels at how only Kitty can do something so amazing for a living as trying to eradicate a disease yet speak so indifferently about the killing that is part of the process. How her face can look so hard and so ethereal at the same time. The bones of her spine stick out so prominently she looks like she might break, yet the steely glare of her grey eyes can floor him.

'Look I have to go, I'll let you know later if I can get in, if not I'll see you at home.'

'OK, bye.'

James puts his phone on the desk and looks back at his screen, to the beautiful woman who is dead behind the eyes.

'Fancy being my lesbian lover?'

Nena's puzzled face rises up from behind her menu, starting with the colourful fake flowers in her hair. They are in their new favourite Soho eatery celebrating their least favourite night of the year. Part canteen, part deli, colourful woven bags adorn metal shelves and Middle Eastern delicacies jump out at diners, hoping to take the flavours of the meal home with them: pomegranate and orange blossom syrup, preserved lemons, sliced pink pickled turnips and Turkish delight in dusty colours stand like bright and beautiful treasures. Last year, Maya and Nena drank too many mango margaritas at the curry house up the road and the year before, they were thrown out of Soho's best veggie restaurant after Nena drunkenly demanded flank steak five times from a humourless waiter.

Valentine's Day dinner together has become something of a tradition. Even though Nena is never short of a date, she would rather be with Maya than with the barman or the handyman du jour. Usually.

'Tempting as that offer is, Maya, you're kind of lacking an appendage.' Appendage. It's a Nena word if ever there was one. 'But if I were to be a lesbian, there is no other girl I would rather be with.'

'Don't be silly, I'm far too reliable and normal for you. I'd call when I said I would. You love a lover who doesn't because he's got into some ridiculous scrape, like that acrobat guy who fell and got tangled in his safety net, stood you up, and you had to pick him up from A&E.'

Nena raises a quizzical eyebrow as if to tell her that isn't so, that she's fallen in love with someone who's very reliable in fact, and who calls every time he says he will. And when she sees his call incoming, her heart flutters and she feels... secure. And happy. But she's not sure how to say it. Telling Maya, revealing that she has left the sisterhood of the solitary, feels like it might be a great treachery. Not because Maya wouldn't be happy for her, she would. But admitting it might make it one hundred per cent real, and Nena can't quite believe it herself. So she keeps her secret as close to her chest as the menu for now.

'Why do you ask anyway?'

'It's just my boss has given me a voucher for a weekend in this luxe hotel and spa, and I have to take it before the end of the month. I have no one to go with, *obviously*, so I wondered if you fancied coming with me next weekend?'

Nena thinks through the Rolodex in her mind and sinks a little in her chair, hiding her face behind the menu so she doesn't give herself away. Next weekend is a weekend Tom will have Arlo and Nena doesn't want to miss out on a weekend with Tom and Arlo, although she can't admit that just yet either.

Maya cranes her neck. 'Are you hiding behind that menu?'

'No, it's just I'm crazy busy rehearsing through to March, so I can't take any time off now, not even weekends.'

Nena's star is soaring: her presenting has gone down brilliantly at the corporation, she's done a few glossy magazine interviews and there's talk at work of her being giving her own dance-based show for kids. Thirty and forty something parents have started saying hi to Nena in the supermarket, thinking they must know her from playgroup or Tumbletots, when actually she's the girl from the TV who their kids love and laugh along with.

'Thanks, though. I do appreciate it. Why don't you take Clara? Gawd knows she'd need some peace and tranquillity with all that running around after three boys. I don't know how she has the energy.'

Maya has never seen parental empathy in Nena before, but it's a good suggestion.

'Yeah, maybe I'll ask her. I'm not sure she's ready to leave Oscar though.'

'How come your boss gave it to you anyway? Gold star for Maya again?'

'Well, it's a bit weird. I kind of got it for something I did, but it feels like a bit of a payoff.'

'What do you mean?'

'Oh, it's too boring to go into. I've just noticed a few changes around work lately.'

Maya is conveniently interrupted by a waiter with slicked-back hair and stubble as black as his shirt.

Maya and Nena decide to share a mezze platter of baba ganoush, hummus, tabbouleh, falafel, pitta and pickles, washed down with a rose and rum daiquiri for Maya and an Arak mojito for Nena.

'Easy on the rum though,' says Maya, a private joke with Nena about the mayhem of Valentines past.

Nena suddenly feels very exposed without a menu in front of her face, and very guilty about what she's going to do later. She can't keep this secret from her best friend any more.

'Happy Valentine's Day!' Maya toasts when the drinks arrive. 'All these losers will have split up by Easter anyway.'

Nena looks down while she chinks her Moroccan tea glass against Maya's.

'Actually Maya... I may as well tell you now, otherwise I'm going to be feeling rotten all night...'

'What, what?'

'I'm going on a date later.'

'Wow!'

'Well, not really a date. More of a booty call.'

Maya can tell when Nena is playing something down.

'It's OK, you can tell me...'

'Well you know my boss,'

'Tom!' they say in unison.

'I *knew* it, Nena, he's lovely! And he so clearly had the hots for you.'

'Well I did worry that that was the only reason he hired me, but since it's taken off and other people like me too, I've relaxed about it, I've relaxed about him. He's amazing.'

'What about Liam?'

'Who's Liam?'

'Your electrician!'

Nena takes a sip from her cocktail to wash down any parsley, mint or cracked wheat that might have got stuck between her white teeth.

'Oh, him. The spark went out.'

The girls laugh. Nena relaxes.

'Wow, so you're not seeing anyone else?'

'Nope.' Nena looks proud and happy. Her face lit up with a flush of love.

'What about his kid, didn't you say he has a son?'

'Yes, and I am as in love with him as I am with Tom. He's amazing Maya. Arlo. He's so sweet. So funny. So cuddly. He lives with his mum, who has been pretty cool about us, and he stays with us – with Tom – every other weekend and a night or two in the week, depending on when Tom can get him from the childminder.'

Maya knocks back the rest of her sweet fragrant drink and feels instantly heady.

'You said the L word. Wow.' She smooths down the chiffon of her love-heart print dress – her only nod to romance this year; she couldn't bring herself to give Train Man a card. 'It takes a lot for you to shock me, Nena, I think I've seen it all – but... monogamy! Parenthood!'

Nena pauses to read Maya's familiar face, hoping that her friend is happy for her and not upset that, if she were to know the truth, she would rather be with Tom right now.

'It's amazing. I'm so happy for you.'

Maya squeezes Nena's hand and accidentally gets some hummus on it.

'Oops. Sorry.'

Relief.

'That's why I can't really go to the spa with you... thanks though lovely.'

'It's OK, I get it. But you have to help me now otherwise I'm going to be the annoying third wheel. How do I make Train Man mine? I've got to do something to initiate a conversation on an otherwise silent train. Help me out, you're the master at this.'

Eyelids painted as brightly as the flowers in her hair flash as Nena blinks slowly and thoughtfully. 'Shit, you missed a trick with Valentine's Day. You could have given him a card.'

'I did think about it, but no... too schoolgirl.'

'Well I'm assuming you've done the ticket drop,' Nena says, as if it's standard procedure.

'Ticket drop?'

'It's textbook, Maya! "Accidentally" drop your ticket on the floor – in Train Man's vicinity – and see if he picks it up. If he does, you are on his radar, so he's secretly tracking you too. If he doesn't notice and someone else picks it up, then it's curtains, game over, move on, sit in another carriage.'

Suddenly Maya feels sad.

How can she be so flippant about this?

The thought of moving to another carriage and no longer experiencing the best thing about her day is too much.

Under the fan on the high ceiling of a small kitchen, Maya is using tonight's meal as inspiration for her next attempt at macarons. The whizzing motor of the heavy white KitchenAid won't disturb anyone; it doesn't matter if a dusting of icing sugar coats the surface of her kitchen. It doesn't even matter if Maya doesn't get as much sleep as she ought to tonight.

She has too many ideas whizzing around her head. Rose and lemon and almond and orange blossom flavours whisk and blend and fold and pipe and rise and come out of the oven looking almost perfect in rows of yellow, pink and orange. The few shells that are slightly too brown on one side make a good midnight treat.

As Maya sandwiches her Valentine's gift together and stacks the finished articles in a box, she thinks of Nena. How happy she is that Nena has found love. How surprised she is that Nena wants to be a mother to a toddler. How proud she is that Nena's career is soaring and soon she will have her own TV show. But as Maya turns the oven off at 12.59 a.m. and walks the two flights of stairs to the top of the maisonette in silence, she can't help but feel sad about how, when she turned back to say one last thing to Nena as they parted, she couldn't. Nena was already running away from her down Oxford Street, desperate to be somewhere else, a rainbow of flowers darting into the distance.

25

Maya pretends to read *One Hundred Years Of Solitude* in the hope of making a connection, in case Train Man looks up and recognises that same cover of that same book. Perhaps he'll be impressed that Maya's edition is older, more dog-eared and loved. Her hot face is flushed with fear and excitement on a cold morning, her ticket lies on the train floor. Angry Man has just huffed off, marching up the train, nearly knocking the delicate box of macarons nervously resting on Maya's lap as he created a mini tornado in his wake. Stamping a heavy footprint onto Maya's ticket as he left this irksome carriage.

Well Angry Man clearly doesn't fancy me.

Maya laughs on the inside. Anticipation giving her tummy ache. After the Superior Train stopped to pick up the Unfortunate commuters from their Unfortunate town and everyone was present and correct, Maya heeded Nena's advice. Nena was right. Why hadn't Maya thought of this before? So simple! So telling! And now, she and Train Man happen to be sitting diagonally on a set of four seats, him facing backwards reading Harper Lee with nothing but a dirty little table jutting out in front of him, her facing forwards.

Maya had no choice, this seemed like too happy a happenstance. Edge, edge, drop. Off her knee, making sure she didn't throw the macarons down onto the floor too. Now the plastic wallet that contains Maya's ticket is slightly soiled by Angry Man's tread, but she hopes that won't stop Train Man from picking it up.

Maya turns down the music in her ears in preparation because if, out of the three people around her, Train Man is the one to pick up her ticket, the one to speak to her, she will need to drink in his voice. Maya puts on her best reading face while the ticket on the floor in her peripheral vision calls her; calls him. The large woman sitting opposite Maya, next to Train Man, is chewing her nails in ignorance – blissful ignorance to Maya. The small man, who Maya imagines might be a jockey in another less nine-to-five life, is asleep on her left.

The ticket has been on the floor for eleven excruciating seconds. In his peripheral vision, James saw it fall. He saw the angry man with the goatee tread on it, half deliberately, half accidentally, and he can see that its owner, the girl with the pink coat, the pink cheeks and the brown hair, hasn't yet noticed that it fell. He puts a thumb between two pages to stop Atticus Finch in his stride and leans down, uncomfortably close to the large woman chewing her nails.

'Excuse me, you dropped this,' James says, proffering the ticket.

A heart soars.

Maya is finally able to look at Train Man. Maya could melt and disappear, through the seat, through the floor, into the scorching rails on a freezing February morning. She is elated. She fumbles to take silent earphones out of her ears.

'Sorry?' Maya says, pretending she didn't hear him, so she can reabsorb his calm and cautious voice.

'You dropped your ticket.' James looks up from where he has leaned down to pick it up. Wide, lovely eyes.

'Thanks,' squeaks Maya as she takes it. And that is all that she can manage to say.

I am on his radar.

'I made these for you!'

Maya hands the pristine oblong box over the great divide of the desk. Pride fills her.

'What are they?'

'Open them and see.'

Emma unties the apricot-coloured ribbon.

'You made these?'

Maya nods.

Alex turns around from his seat back-to-back with Emma's by the window. His strawberry-blond whip bounces perkily.

'O.M.Gee. No way, Maya!' he says, looking over Emma's shoulder.

A row of six pastel yellow, pink and orange macarons alternate gleefully.

'Where are mine?!'

'You're next, Alex, one at a time though, I only just mastered them last night. While all you loved-up losers were out having fun with your special someone, I was tearing it up in the kitchen. On my own.' Maya is good at laughing at herself.

Emma looks sad.

Other members of the team start to arrive for a full-on day ahead. Chloe's corkscrew curly mane wobbles through the glass door, Liz has a red face from cycling in the cold and Sam saunters in wearing flip-flops.

Emma walks around to Maya and Olivia's desks.

'You are lovely, thank you,' she says, wrapping wispy arms around Maya. 'I needed a little pick-me-up today.'

'Are you OK?'

Eyes well up but Emma brushes it aside. 'I am now, look at these, Sam!'

Maya has a thought and lowers her voice. 'Hey, Emma, what are you doing next weekend?'

'Not sure, why?'

'Well don't tell Lucy, but how about you take this?' Maya rummages in her bag and pulls out the envelope with Cypress Manor Hotel & Spa written on the front in a frou-frou font.

'Maya it was for *you*, Lucy was really happy with your work. And you worked so hard!'

'It's wasted on me. You take Paul. You could have a dirty weekend and some pampering. A couple's massage isn't much use for one. Besides, we're a team, FASHmas wasn't just down to me.'

'Are you sure?'

'Wow,' says Sam, peeping into the box of macarons in Emma's hand and looking at Maya in awe. Sam has a bit of a sweet tooth himself. 'You made those?'

Maya smiles at Sam, who starts up his many machines, and turns back to Emma.

'I can't go anyway,' Maya lies, in hushed tones.

'Thank you.'

Emma rushes back around to her desk to grab her phone and call Paul.

Maya slinks into her chair. She's desperate to tell her friends that she spoke to Train Man this morning, but she'll save it for lunchtime; Emma is already walking out of the office with a phone clutched to a rosy face. Eyes shining like sapphires again.

Maya hears Paul's voice on the other end of Emma's mobile as she walks through the doors and tries to remember what Train Man's voice sounded like sixty-seven minutes ago.

26

March 2014

'I booked my flight, I'm actually doing it!' says the jubilant old woman.

Maya and Velma are sitting in the first-floor lounge of Maya's Victorian maisonette. Budding branches dance high in the wind outside the peeling sash windows and the room looks bright and white since Maya painted the entire flat a shade of *I'll come back to that*. The first-flutter-of-spring afternoon accentuates the fresh feeling reeling from the walls and it's nice to have a visitor. Most of Maya's friends live in London, her siblings are all in relationships and Nena has been too busy with Tom to come and see the flat yet. But afternoon tea with Velma brings as much cheer as the blossom in the sky outside, despite a sadness in the pit of her stomach that Maya is trying to ignore. It's become something of a Sunday ritual since the grey January afternoon Maya first visited Velma's town square apartment. The hostess always bakes. The agony aunt always listens. Although today she is even giddier than usual, brimming with excitement.

'Heathrow to Miami, July 22nd. Although I'm going to

take a little trip to New York before that when my grand-daughter is born.'

Velma is beyond excited about becoming a grandmother. She didn't have Conrad until she was thirty-six – 'which was practically ancient back then!' – and ever since her sons were young she had this niggling fear in the back of her head that she might not live to see her children have children.

'When is Madison due?'

'May 1st. I cannot wait.'

'Well I'll give you a pass off class to go visit the baby, but I am very glad you're not moving to Miami until the end of the academic year!' Maya jokes as she pours tea from a pot into two little handleless cups with sunbeams on them.

'Well that was a consideration, my darling, it really was! I wouldn't miss class for the world. I'm genuinely going to miss Spanish with Miss Oh Just Maya. And our afternoon tea dates and chats...' Velma rests an elbow on the cushion of Maya's brown leather sofa. 'But you know you will always have a home in South Beach if you want one.'

Words an adventurous girl like Maya likes to hear, although she hasn't been anywhere in a long time.

'Oh, just try keeping me away! I'm thrilled for you, Velma, and your Spanish is coming along really well. You'll be teaching me when I visit. Cake?'

Maya lifts the cloche off her favourite cake stand to make a big reveal.

'Honey, that's something else!'

It certainly is. The cloche almost squished the top of the cake, it's so bountiful. Four sponges create a tower of caramel in four different ombres of brown. Pale vanilla sponge with just a hint of caramel in its light muscovado sugar sits at the bottom; next up, pure caramel, made even sweeter by dark brown treacly sugar in the mix; then choco-caramel with a hint of cocoa; and sitting on top, dark chocolate sponge. All sandwiched with dulce de leche, which oozes out from between the layers, stopping at varying altitudes down the side.

'My dentist is gonna *kill* me!' Velma claps.

Maya is happy.

Ever since Maya was a little girl she loved to bake. Chubby legs would climb onto a kitchen stool and soft dimpled hands would pull down the ingredients from the cupboards, as instructed by her mother. Baking transferred Maya to a world away from the raucousness of boisterous baby brothers, a loud big sister and chaotic parents. Dolores the dressmaker, who made dresses for her girls and dungarees for her boys, but always managed to forget she had left pins in them, so they prickled little legs on the first wear. Herbert the teacher, the poet, the symmetry obsessive. But, oh, the results! Maya could make such sweet triumphs that would bring Clara, Jacob and Florian to the table and silence them for five whole minutes. Maya loved watching little faces light up for those brief moments, people-pleasing even when she was six.

By the time she was ten, Maya would get so lost in a recipe, she would forget she was in her parents' kitchen and silently pretend that there was a TV camera watching her knead, fold and smooth. As if she was one of those precocious children from the TV show only children presented. Dolores Flowers didn't know there was an imaginary camera crew and invisible studio lighting watching her and her daughter in the kitchen. She didn't know her little girl was being watched by millions, but she did know that sharing her baking knowledge was a Good Thing To Do. Dolores didn't communicate with Maya much – Maya was such a quiet little thing – and it made her feel like she was getting through to her daughter in her own imaginary world. A freckled mystery who would play entire games just by sitting, staring at the bookcase. Dolores often asked Herbert where he thought Maya went when she was sitting still.

'She's fine, my love, we all need space to meditate.'

Feeling distant from her daughter, Dolores was relieved that they were so similar looking, it aligned them.

A mini version of me.

Same almond shaped eyes with long straight lashes. Same chestnut brown hair, shiny and poker straight. Same straight nose and small round lips. They didn't know then, as the sweet smells flowed through the kitchen, that, some twenty years later, heartbreak would make Maya's hair go wavy, distancing them physically but bringing mother and daughter closer than they had ever been. Now Velma is sitting in Maya's sitting room, intrigued by the creation in front of her.

'So tell me news of Train Man. Have you seen him this week?'

Velma always raises the subject of Train Man. She likes how Maya's serious resting face lights up when she talks about him. But Velma knows that talking to Train Man is something only Maya can do. Maya told Velma about the ticket drop and was surprised when Velma said she thought pretending to drop her ticket was a bit duplicitous.

'You're wonderful enough to just be yourself, Maya, to smile and say hi.'

Maya accepted the wisdom, but she's still not sure how to strike up a conversation in a silent carriage.

Today Maya's face creases. It doesn't light up.

'I haven't seen him, Velma, and I'm worried he's moved away or changed jobs and got a different train.'

'Vacation?'

'I hope so. He wasn't on the train all this week, and I'm shocked by how much I miss him. How can I miss someone I don't know?'

'It's a pure emotion, it's how you feel, sweetie. Let's hope he's back on the train tomorrow and you haven't let the opportunity pass.'

Maya doesn't have much of an appetite as she lowers a knife through a silky tower of caramel sponge.

27

Simon runs his fingers through obedient hair and lifts his bag up and across his body. Commuters stand, eager to get off, all noticing that it is lighter than it has been when they've got off this same train recently. A little fog of optimism wafts through the carriage. Catherine presses her pelvis into Simon's bottom as she stands in the line behind him. The urgency of commuters, the urgency of lovers. Simon moves forward, away from her, in case he reveals himself. The fingertips of her right hand tickle the fingertips of his right hand, hidden low in the melee. They can't get off the train together since Simon spotted his triathlon clubmate on it a few weeks ago, whose wife is a great friend of Laura's. If they were to talk in front of anyone else they would give themselves away immediately. Too silent and it's obvious they are comfortable and intimate; polite chat would feel strange to two people in love.

Catherine texted Simon halfway through the journey, suggesting he gets off the train and goes to her house. Hope no one sees. Find an excuse to stay the night. Finally *sleep* together, in a home. Her home.

Too risky, he thought. And didn't reply.

Doors ding, buttons are pressed, and a sea of commuters

step out of the fug and into the brighter evening, keen to get home to wives, husbands, children, Champions League. Catherine knows they won't have time alone in the alleyway tonight, having got off such a packed train.

Too risky.

She feels spurned.

She wants two minutes alone with Simon, to look him in the eye, press into him and tell him she will make it so worth his while if he goes to her house and not back to Laura, his dowdy wife, and their three children. Catherine can offer him a warm bed, peace, love all night, and if he's really good she will fix them a cooked breakfast before they both head off to the station together in the morning, just so he knows how much greener the grass is.

'Please,' she says to him quietly in the alleyway, through gritted teeth.

'I so want to but people have seen me now. Lee from Kettlebells was at the station. If I say I'm stuck in Cambridge, I can't see anyone who knows me here. Tomorrow. Let's do it tomorrow. I'll find a way.'

Catherine ups her pace and peels away without saying another word. She is not used to feeling second best. All her life she has been treated like a queen, her preferences came first, she got her way, and even though she knows Simon is married and has a depth and connection with Laura and their children that she cannot yet understand, so sure is she of her power in this relationship she knows she can make Simon take bigger risks.

He watches her from behind. A black blazer over a pencil skirt. Her frame, her walk, her beautiful neck, and as the gap between them in the alleyway widens, he knows that he can't go on not waking up next to her.

Nena is in a small studio with a camera pointing towards her face as she reads birthday cards for broadcast tomorrow, which feels strange given it's her own birthday today. Yesterday she started filming her own-fronted Nena's Tiny Dancers show that will go on air in autumn, and she is glowing under the studio lights.

'Louis is three today, happy birthday from Mummy, Daddy, Alfie and your pet rabbit Tweak... Bea it's your birthday! You're two today, and here's a picture of you with your brother Elijah at the zoo. We hope you and your animal friends have a wonderful day, all our love Mummy, Daddy and Jah-Jah...'

Tom is watching from the gallery. He studies Nena's face up close. Anticipation makes his safe hands sweat. He waits for the next card. Nena opens it.

'Nena, you're twenty-eight today...'

She reads the rest of the card in silence, and looks up at the gallery with tears in her eyes.

'Yes, yes I will!' she cries softly into her mic while a giant inflatable robot reads over her shoulder. Nena brings two palms to her glistening face. 'Sorry everyone, we'll have to reshoot the birthday cards.'

Cameramen clap. The floor manager cheers so vigorously her head set slips off her ears and down her back. Tom runs down the stairs from the gallery and takes Nena in his arms. Nena Oliveira, who couldn't commit to one man just three months ago, is committing to Tom Vernon for the rest of her life.

'Will Arlo be OK with this?' she whispers.

'Oh yeah. He almost asked you himself this morning.'

Five bikini-clad models line up in front of James on the white sand of a beach 6,000 miles from Maya. Twelve Apostles watch him work, but even the spectacular sight of lush green mountains jutting out of the ground like a windbreak can't make this an easy day at the office. Everyone on the trip is going to James with their gripes, their complaints and their demands. And today, even patient James has had enough of it. Melody fell out with Tara because they both wanted to wear the coral bikini; India refused to wear anything other than the halter-neck because halter-necks make her boobs look 'real perky'; and Kim has been sniping at Anja because, last night, Anja slept with Pez the photographer and Kim said it was unprofessional and gives models a bad name. James is just shocked that Anja would want to sleep with Pez.

Pez is a stringy Mancunian with a beard as long as his straggly brown hair and he has been the biggest diva of the trip. At first his hotel room wasn't tall enough, so James arranged for him to be moved to a different hotel with rooms with higher ceilings, further down the strip. Then Pez was overheard telling his assistant Joe that he thought Tara was 'a bit fat', and when Tara was told this (helpfully by Melody), she came running to James in tears and said she wouldn't take her robe off unless Pez said sorry. Pez refused, but said Joe would say sorry for him – and did that count? Tara accepted. Pez and Dominic almost came to blows when Pez told Dominic to get out of shot and called Dominic 'a hairy fucking meatball'. James was almost punched in the face by his best friend as he jumped between Dominic and Pez to break up the fight. Fortunately, Pez's assistant, Joe, seems to be the thickest-skinned assistant on the planet and Lisa and Yoshie, the brilliant hair and make-up girls, said even Terry Richardson was less of a diva.

But given that Sebastian and Duncan from Fisher & Whyman have liked Pez's work and put his lack of charm down to him being a creative genius, Dominic and James are having to smile politely and give Pez what he wants, which right now is a tequila sunrise.

'What a cunt, I can't wait for this to wrap,' says Dominic, who can't bring himself to look at Pez since meatball-gate. 'We're not taking him to Jamaica.'

'We have to, he's signed,' says James, who after five days of art-directing the How Femme Are You? shoot is completely drained. 'Plus the kill fee is almost as much as his fee. I'm afraid we have to go through all this again in September.'

Dominic looks like an exhausted child, brown eyes melting down his face like chocolate buttons.

'At least they're happy.' James nods towards Sebastian and Duncan, as smartly dressed as they can be at the beach in 30-degree sunshine, wearing tailored shorts and polo shirts, beers awkwardly in hand, smitten by long legs, Amazonian shoulders and perky boobs. Everyone else looks altogether more casual.

'Guys, guys, what a job! This is going to look awesome!' Toothy English tumbles from Sebastian's mouth.

'We think so,' says James in his denim Bermudas and Breton striped tee, forcing his 4,009th smile of the trip. James wasn't feeling the Femme campaign before they all boarded a plane from Heathrow to Cape Town to shoot it, but given how stressful the trip has been, and how Dominic is quicker to fly off the handle than he is, going into firefighting mode has made James forget how bored he is by the entire advertising world he inhabits.

'What time's Joze arriving?' asks Sebastian, intoxicated by hops and beauty and now overly familiar.

'Joze?' snarls Dominic, forgetting Sebastian isn't Pez.

James speaks for his friend, extinguishing another fire. 'Josie. She'll be here at five. Dominic, why don't you head out to the airport now and meet her, I can finish up here.' James gives Dominic a knowing nod. Olive skin a little darker than a week ago, a freckle or two might even have come out on his nose.

The light is about to hit the golden hour, just before the sun goes down. Pez takes a sip from his tequila sunrise, hands it to Joe, and finally stops whining so he can make the most of the light. The last chance to get The Shot before the trip is over, before the bikinis and beauty products are packed into silver flight cases, before everyone will go back to their hotel for one last chance to let loose before the obligatory post-party fallout.

James and Sebastian stand on the sand, beer in hand, and look at the models working the camera while Pez shoots. James feels a first hint of calm as his mind flits to a more relaxing week ahead. He, Dominic and Josie will take a road trip along the coast, they'll visit sun-drenched vineyards and will eat the best seafood they've ever had. Josie will ask James why Kitty didn't want to come out too and tag a holiday onto the boys' work trip as they have done before, and James will answer, 'I don't know.'

28

It's the first day of the year when the words 'unseasonably' and 'mild' are bandied around. That day in spring when you can just about get away with wearing flip-flops even though only last week it was biker boots and cable tights weather. Although the stylish little worker bees at FASH already know that this summer will be all about the pool slider, some people will always wear flip-flops. And the most faithful exponent is swinging into FASH towers.

'Morning Sam, good weekend?' says Emma as Sam skips through the double glass doors and slides straight into his low seat. Emma is always there early, catching up on what's been trending across the globe overnight. Wondering which of those trends can translate into something relevant to their customers. Always eating her muesli and berries, as bursting with goodness as she is, although this morning she can't stomach breakfast.

'Emma,' Sam salutes.

Lucy races through the glass doors, plonks her coffee on her desk and doesn't even sit down on her chair, next to Emma's, before sending a quick email to Maya – who isn't there yet – to confirm the date for her to present to the executive team. Lucy doesn't have a clue Maya might have doubts about going for the site editor job, and Maya, the people-pleaser, would never want to tell her, through fear of letting her down.

Maya sits down and plugs in her earphones. She is facing backwards on an Inferior Train. Matted gum sits on matted blue faux-velveteen upholstery with white chevrons all over it, but Maya accepts that it is just one of those days. Maya wears a white Bardot top tucked into a lilac circle skirt. She has dressed up in the hope that Train Man will come back to her this morning, but she didn't see him race into the station from the other side of the sweeping approach where buses, bikes and cars pull up with brakes squeaking. She didn't see him hurry through the ticket barrier and under the subway where the train tracks rattle overhead and shake the tunnel roof. And she didn't see him walk with purpose up the platform. Maya hasn't seen Train Man for over two weeks and she feels empty. The possibility that Train Man might have moved away is something Maya doesn't want to accept.

Music starts. Maya closes her eyes and on the inside of her eyelids she sees dappled sunshine poking through the trees from yesterday's run. Worry and absence and yearning took her further into the woods beyond Hazelworth than she had gone in a long time. Music gets louder, a crescendo builds, and through closed eyes Maya remembers how tired her legs felt when she got home and started baking for another Velma visit.

As the train gathers pace, Maya is distracted by the uncomfortable feeling of an Inflatable Arm nudging into her waist, as it was a few minutes ago. Maya ignores the sensation and hugs the pale green leather bag on her lap for comfort as she is pulled back into a rhythmic doze. The quickening beat and the rising whir of the track beneath fades as PJ Harvey starts to roar.

Time and space muddle and a befuddled Maya awakens and opens her eyes after a jolt on the line. The jolt all regular commuters know, but still, every day, it catches them out. Eyes open. The man she doesn't know but loves is there sitting opposite, looking down, lost in a book. Darker skinned. His face more thoughtful looking than ever. Sad eyes. The crescendo of PJ Harvey makes Maya well up. *One day... we'll float. Take life as it comes.*

'Do you have time to grab a quick drink after class?' Maya asks, as she files her papers away into a lever arch file.

'Sure thing, honey, what's up?'

Maya pauses and waits for Gareth and Cecily to leave before she says any more. They are the last of the remaining classmates and are bickering about who's going to drive home. Cecily passed her driving test last week but had a near-miss with a post in the supermarket car park as they arrived tonight. They nod farewell mid-argument and Maya and Velma smile at them.

'I have to give a presentation in the morning at work.'

'Wow, big deal, tell me more,' says Velma as she shuffles towards the door.

'Well it's more like an interview, I've been asked to go for the site editor job. And I've prepared a presentation for it.' Last month, Lucy finally got sign-off to replace herself so she can focus on being a senior strategist at FASH, and Maya has been nervously putting together her pitch. Trouble is, she's not very good at selling herself.

'Amazing. Wanna do a run-through with me?'

'God no, I'd be too embarrassed.' Maya hasn't told Velma much about what she does for a living. When they meet they tend to talk about matters of the heart or family or their adventures overseas, and Maya feels that FASH is too trivial for a woman who answers every single one of the thousands of letters she receives a year, each with candour and kindness.

'Well how can I help?' Velma asks cheerfully, happy to extend her day and for company on a balmy evening.

Thirty minutes later they are sitting in the pizzeria beneath Velma's apartment. Bustling and busy despite it being 10 p.m. on a Tuesday in March.

'I'm just not great at standing up in front of a crowd as it is, but all of FASH's big guns will be there.' Maya takes a sip of her limoncello and smooths down the arm of her floral bomber jacket.

Velma tilts her head contemplatively. 'You stand up in front of us every week. I think you'll be just dandy. Practise tonight one more time at home straight through, then just go there. Be who you are. Make eye contact and engage.' Maya drinks in Velma's advice and nods. 'But that's you all over, Maya. You're not showy or overwhelming. You are warm, you are interesting, you look interested and you listen.' Velma turns the stem of her red wine glass as she talks. Maya looks her in the eye. 'Don't forget that even when you're presenting you need to listen. Listen to their questions and give thoughtful answers.'

Maya nods again.

'But really, being yourself is enough,' Velma says with the brush of a hand.

Maya's heard that from Velma before and still not acted on it. She wishes she had Velma's confidence.

Maya takes the last sip of zingy limoncello and changes the subject.

'How's Madison getting along?'

'Oh she's doing fine, thirty-five weeks now, still working like a donkey, but you know those New York women, they're tough.' Velma laughs. 'In fact, take some advice from a New Yorker. New York women don't question whether they're good enough for a promotion, they feel entitled to it. I suspect you're entitled to yours. Your boss urged you to go for it, so clearly she thinks you're amazing. Just believe it yourself.'

Maya blushes. 'Thanks Velma.'

'You're welcome. Now go home and get your beauty sleep. Not that you need it, you have a glow about you tonight.'

Maya's tired eyes light up as she remembers to tell Velma. 'Oh. Train Man was back on the train yesterday.'

'I thought as much.'

29

Maya stands small in front of the big screen in the boardroom, five pairs of executive eyes look her up and down. She has just finished her presentation, her vision of the evolving voice of FASH: words like STRONG, BRAVE, CONFIDENT jumped out from the screen against a backdrop of models on rollerblades that she lifted from the Miami lookbook. Catwalk footage of so-now supermodels juxtaposed with FASH models wearing similar designs. All current FASH content that Sam helped her put together in a PowerPoint presentation, but Maya's words helped make it feel 'next-season now'. She dreamed up future campaigns in the hope that Rich Robinson would rub his moneyed palms together with glee, which he almost did, but it might have been an itch. HIKER CHICK. FUTURE FRESH. The FASH girl is quite different to Maya. She is brash, bold, oozes confidence and will take risks. Maya is more measured. Measured in the art of precision baking, measured in the way she advises her friends. Although, right now, Maya wants to make the very unmeasured move of ruffling up her hair, screaming at the CEO and his closest advisors and running out of the room, out of the building and out of London, like a crazed banshee. One part relief: two parts exhaustion.

Five pairs of hands clap and bring Maya back into the moment. Lucy's palms, straight and tanned and hopeful, clap the most vigorously, her neat bob even sways as she does so.

Staff walk past the glass walls of the boardroom and pretend not to glance in. They glimpse in casually and look away, not realising how nerve-wracking and important these few minutes are to Maya.

Now it is the part Maya is most dreading. Questions. Rich Robinson holds court in the middle of the five, sitting at the long table like a TV pundit in a white shirt and black blazer. Maya can't see his legs but already knows that beneath the table he is wearing his uniform of faded denim jeans and stacked Cuban heels.

'Great presentation, er, Maya,' he says, looking down. 'Well done.' Rich Robinson oozes confidence and wealth. Maya made him a lot of money thanks to the FASHmas Fairies last Christmas, he really ought to be able to remember her name. 'I can see your clear vision for how the site should look and read, but one thing you didn't touch on is how you would manage the team to ensure they're all working towards your vision, even if they're not on board.'

Maya looks at Lucy for reassurance. 'Well, I'm a team player, so I'd never want to ruffle feathers, but I'd just stress the importance of consistency and ask everyone to get behind it.'

'And if they didn't like it?' asks head of customer experience, Geri, a pocket rocket who looks like her touchpaper has just been lit.

Maya knows how Geri would react to people who didn't agree with her, which is why she's always been relieved to have Lucy for a boss.

'Well I'd ask for their opinions and consider them, because they might come up with an even better idea, and we're all a team, so I'd value what they had to say.'

Head of womenswear, Zara, looks Maya up and down.

Geri looks down at her notebook.

Did she just shake her head?

Rich Robinson has more.

'Maya, how would you deal with difficult situations? Like, say, with the bonuses.' He makes an exaggerated awkward face, as if to mock the disappointment the staff felt. 'How would you have told staff they wouldn't be getting a bonus this year?'

The FASH models on rollerblades in South Beach, with all their effervescence and exuberance, seem a world away, as a party popper fails to go off and a tumbleweed rolls across the desk.

Maya is stumped. She doesn't understand why staff didn't get bonuses this year, especially after all the back-slapping emails about sales booming... And she couldn't help reading the story in the *Evening Standard* last week about Rich Robinson naming his new yacht Deedee after his wife Denise. Right now, with her clammy palms and dry mouth, Maya doesn't know how to answer.

'Well... to be honest... I don't know why bonuses weren't awarded. All the talk about great sales built up staff expectations. People started to plan their lives around it. Holidays. Helping out with deposits for flats. Buying a car...'

Sarah, the head of international sales, leans forward slightly and shoots Lucy a look down the table. Now it's Lucy looking down at her notebook and ever-so-slightly shaking her head. Maya realises she might have just shot herself in the foot and needs to backtrack.

'It's just that last year's bonus was so generous, maybe it raised hopes and expectations.'

'Well a bonus is just that. Never something to be expected,' interjects Geri, toeing the party line and thinking about how Rich will like that one, how she might keep her bonus this year, because all the board are still in line for theirs.

'Well if I were site editor I would take the team to one side, explain it's for the greater good, and suggest some kind of group night out or lunch to raise morale.'

Rich smiles at Maya, who can't work out if it's a smile of pity, but she suspects it's a smile he's forced many times in his career.

'I think that's all then, Maya, that was wonderful, thank you for taking the time to present.'

Rich stands up to indicate that it's time for Maya to skedaddle.

'Oh, thanks for seeing me.'

Maya clumsily collects her laptop, notebook and bottle of water, her face getting hotter with each scramble. As she shakes Rich Robinson's proffered hand, she drops her shiny silver laptop on the floor. An apple dims.

'Oh gosh!'

Zara lets out a gravelly laugh.

'Oops,' cringes Rich. 'I hope that wasn't a FASH one,' he half jokes, as he bends to pick it up. Maya bends down too and clonks her chin on Rich Robinson's head as he rises.

'Ouch.'

'Uff.'

'I'm so sorry!'

Geri shakes her head again.

Blushes abound, Maya makes her exit clutching a laptop

as dented as her pride and strides out of the glass boardroom and back to the sanctuary of her desk.

Sam swings around in his chair, leaning so far back Maya wonders how it doesn't tip backwards.

'How'd it go? Did my mix tape work its magic?'

Maya's face feels hot. 'It was awful, Sam, I have to get out of here.' Maya slings her things onto her desk and picks up her bag.

'Wanna grab a bite?'

Maya is so embarrassed she can't speak in case she cries, so she looks at Sam through watery eyes and nods a yes. Besides, when Lucy comes back to her desk after the post-mortem she knows is happening right now, she'd rather not be there sitting at the opposite computer.

Sam and Maya walk out together into the spring sunshine and across busy Baker Street to a little coffee-shop-cum-deli over the road, owned by a Venezuelan couple.

'You get a table, I'll get the drinks. Hot chocolate, yeah?'

Maya wonders how Sam knew.

Sam walks up five rickety wooden steps to the counter, Maya walks down nine to the underground seating area and slinks towards the sofa at the back. The lunch rush hasn't started yet so she gets them the comfiest seat and plays through the past forty-five minutes in her brain.

Why did I say that about the bonuses?

Maya puts one palm on her forehead.

Sam skips down the stairs and little splashes of hot chocolate and cappuccino dance out of their cups. Sam sees Maya at the back, puts the drinks down on the wooden table and falls into the leather sofa next to her.

'Oh Sam, it started so well! The presentation – your presentation – went really smoothly. Thank you so much for your help by the way. They seemed to like my new words and new direction, and they gave me a big clap at the end, BUT...'

Crinkly eyes laugh in anticipation, even though he knows there's a but.

Maya tells him about the bonuses part.

'Well it's a true fact, My, they can't deny that.'

No one calls Maya 'My'. Apart from Sam.

'Yeah but it kinda killed the moment. After that, the whole vibe changed, the Q&A bit was cut short. They probably think I'm not on song, or brand, or whatever they call it.'

As a head of department, Sam knows the executive team better than Maya.

'Or Rich might just think you're the mutt's nuts for saying it like it is, for caring about how his staff might feel. I know he looks like a bit of a tool, but he's an all right guy.'

Maya's left arm and Sam's right arm mirror each other as their elbows lean on the top of the low leather sofa, palms supporting their heads. Sam looks at Maya's face closely, trying to read her.

'Arghhhh, I can't believe I messed up!' Maya buries her head in her hands, and waves of chestnut fall forwards.

'I'm sure you didn't.'

'Oh, well,' she says, emerging from her hands and tucking her hair behind one ear. 'I'm not sure I wanted it anyway. I'd be a rubbish boss.' Maya wonders if Sam can see through her breezy change of tune, she had rather warmed to the prospect of more responsibility. And a payrise, she could really do with a payrise since having a mortgage.

'You wouldn't.' Smiling eyes turn serious. 'You'd be great.'

Maya lifts her drink to her face to break Sam's lingering eye contact and changes the subject. 'So, guess who was back on the train on Monday?'

'Gee I dunno, Maya. Mother Teresa?'

Maya places her cup back down and licks chocolate froth from the top of her rounded lips. Sweet comfort. Train Man is back. The job doesn't matter.

Sam's heart breaks.

30

April 2014

'How many bedrooms would you like?' asks the lady with a neckerchief and a Dr Seuss snout.

Catherine looks at Simon, wanting to reassure him of their fun future ahead.

'One?'

He already has three children, she doesn't want him to think she is desperate for another, which she most definitely isn't.

'I was thinking three at least, the kids will need to visit.'

'Oh, of course.'

The woman with the funny nose is surprised the couple standing in front of her didn't discuss such a fundamental decision before stepping into her immaculate office, but then again she did notice *He* was wearing a wedding ring and *She* wasn't.

'Well I have this delightful four-bedroomed apartment on the picturesque banks of the River Cam, with the city centre and leafy Midsummer Common on your doorstep, which offers a unique – and exclusive – lifestyle, for just £3,500 a month.'

Simon spits coffee back into a brown cardboard cup and Catherine shoots him a mock-disapproving look behind the estate agent's back. Catherine can't disapprove, or complain about the kids visiting. She is just happy to be with him, to tuck her nimble hands around his middle-aged washboard waist in public. This is a rare Saturday when they will spend a whole day and a whole night together after Simon told Laura he was going to a triathlon training camp. It is the first time they can truly test what their future will be like. This time they didn't go abroad for a dirty weekend wrapped in hotel sheets, away from life and distractions. They're shopping with the shoppers. They're doing what people do at the weekend together, and doing it hand in hand. Simon is still anxious about being spotted, even though he's in another town, but he's more careless now their decision is made. They just have to get the building blocks in place.

Catherine looks at the spec. It certainly looks exclusive, but she knows they won't be able to afford it, especially not on top of Simon's existing share of the mortgage and child maintenance.

'It looks beautiful, but at £3,500 a month it's not going to happen. And given that I know they've been empty for months, I think you know it's not going to happen at that price too. So, what's the best you can do for us, erm...?' A charming pixie looks at the estate agent's chest for a name tag but can't find one.

'Morag.'

'What's the best you can do for us, Morag? I'd love for us to come to an agreement.'

Morag seems to have been placed in a trance by the tall but delicate woman standing in front of her who has elfin features but a huge sway.

Catherine can be curt and demanding and aggressive and charming in equal measure, and it turns Simon on like crazy.

Maya jogs up the familiar windowless staircase to Velma's apartment and knocks on the door. She hears a shuffle of slipper shoes on the other side and Velma opens it, sending the wind chimes by the window into a frenzy as she does.

'Good afternoon Miss Oh Just Maya. Do come in.'

A book on the coffee table whirls in the wind, like a flip book revealing a trick, and Maya brings it to safety in her hands as she walks into the apartment.

'How are you, Velma?'

Velma gives a mischievous smile and heads into the kitchen, ready for her big reveal.

Maya looks at the cover of the book in her hand. Josephine Baker in pearls, a bra top and a banana skirt ready to do the *danse banane*. Maya thinks of Nena and misses her. They haven't exchanged more than a couple of vague texts since Nena's birthday last month, and Nena still hasn't been to Hazelworth to see Maya's new flat. Maya is wondering what happened to her friend. Why she's gone off grid since falling in love. She knows she's been busy with her new TV career but surely Tom would encourage her friendships?

'I'm fine but are you OK, honey?' Velma asks.

Maya snaps back into the room and looks up at her new old friend.

'Sure, I was just looking at this. Is it any good?'

'Wow, what a woman, what a life! It's the third biography I've read about her and every time I fall more and more in love. I saw her at Carnegie Hall you know, with the boys' father.'

Maya realises she knows nothing about Velma's husband. She had kept wanting to ask about him, but she's almost too scared to because she knows the answers will be sad. And Velma hasn't ever volunteered the information, so interested is she in other people. But now, as the kettle boils, Maya feels she can be candid.

'Who is Conrad and Christopher's father?'

'*Was*. Who *was* their father.' Velma pours hot water into the chipped Royal Albert teapot and smiles. 'He passed a long time ago, the boys were only nine and seven, they don't remember much about him.'

'I'm so sorry.'

'Me too. I'm sorry we only had twelve years together, we were so excited about our life ahead of us because it took us so long to find each other. But we crammed a lot into those twelve years.'

'How did you meet him?'

'We met on the subway, would you believe...' Velma gives Maya a knowing look. 'On the 6. I was going from 116th down to Spring Street and he got on at 103rd. We had from East Harlem to the East Village for him to ask me out.'

Maya looks at Velma with surprise, still standing in the middle of the room with her floral bomber jacket on.

'You wouldn't ask him?'

Velma lowers her head and looks up over her thick milk bottle lenses conspiratorially at Maya. 'I was quite traditional back then,' she whispers.

'But you'd lived all over the world!'

'I know, I was a very modern thinking journalist, but in matters of the heart, I was a traditionalist. I'd just gotten back from the Paris bureau, Parisian women are *always* asked out.'

Maya knew Velma was compassionate, but now she understands why Velma's magnified eyes are quite so empathetic when it comes to falling for a stranger on a train, and she feels a glimmer of hope.

It can happen.

There's so much she wants to know.

'What did he look like?'

'He was small like me – I have no idea how we made two such tall and handsome beefcakes!'

Maya laughs.

'And so proper-looking! He had silver hair in a side parting and bright eyes, and he was always so well turned out. Polo necks and suit jackets, even when we were going to the grocery store. We were so different! He was neat and tidy, I... well, look around you, I'm a...'

'Collector,' says Maya with a polite smile, removing her jacket and throwing it onto the folds of velvet and boucle piled on the sofa.

Velma brings a tea tray through the open doorway of the kitchen. The cake in the centre of it stands like a dome of deliciousness. Layers of vanilla sponge, jam, custard and custard cream all topped with a layer of pale green marzipan and a delicate pink rose perched on top. It doesn't look like one of Velma's usual rustic loaves or cobbled together cakes. It is precise and pretty.

'Wow!'

'Yes Maya, I think your baking style might just be rubbing off on me. I saw it in one of last Sunday's papers and thought it was very... You. Isn't it *darling*?'

'A prinsesstårta from Sweden! I've heard of them, but never had the fortune to try one.'

Maya's Excellent General Knowledge skills stretches to cakes and where they come from.

'Oh Maya, you're so clever, I'd never heard of it, but I thought you might like it.'

'It's beautiful. I can't wait to try a slice!'

Maya rubs her hands together in anticipation.

'So tell me about how he spoke to you. What was his name?'

'Duke Diamond.'

'Duke Diamond? Wow.'

'Well, when a handsome stranger extends his hand and says that name in such a gentlemanly fashion, you're kinda hooked there and then.'

A knife slices through a soft pink rose bud and into verdant marzipan. Both women stop to admire the cross-section shades of pink, green and white.

'So pretty!' marvels Maya.

Velma continues, full of pride and excitement, for her cake and her story.

'We talked all the way to the East Village, about how I had just gotten back from Paris, my time in Buenos Aires before that, about how he worked at the United Nations Secretariat, and he said he'd help me settle back into New York life. I didn't dare tell him I knew those streets like the back of my hand, I was swept up along with it. And when we got off together at Spring, we stayed together from that moment.'

'That's amazing. And it explains a lot,' Maya says, sinking teeth into custard, jam, sponge and whipped cream. 'Heaven!' a full mouth exclaims.

'Isn't it just?'

Silence sweeps across the apartment, chasing out the wind, as Velma and Maya eat.

There are so many questions Maya wants to ask, but one stands out more than all the others.

'Do you mind me asking how Duke died?'

'Not at all, darling,' says Velma, as she clumsily wipes cream off her lip with a shaky hand. 'We knew straight away that we wanted to settle down together. I wasn't getting any younger, and Duke was ten years older than me, so I happily gave up being a correspondent and took the agony aunt job so I could stay in New York where his work was. We got married, had the boys, my work fitted in nicely around motherhood, and we had this lovely life in Brooklyn. Until…'

Maya looks terrified. 'What happened?'

'One day he got in the car to go to work, drove across the Brooklyn Bridge onto FDR Drive, and had a massive heart attack at the wheel. He was only fifty-five. And when the police came to our house, I just knew it. The hardest thing I ever had to do was tell the boys. It was even worse than hearing it for myself.'

Maya's eyes are so full of tears she knows the next blink will send one tumbling. She puts her plate down on a pile of books with caution.

'I'm so very sorry, Velma.'

'Thank you,' Velma pats Maya's hand in comfort. 'Me too. Sorry for the boys mostly, he was such a wonderful father.'

Velma puts down her cake plate and pours tea.

'At first, I was angry. Marriage and kids caused me to lose my adventurous spirit and I became a bit more timid. When Duke died I felt hopeless, and I kinda resented him for that. But that passed. The boys grew up. I travelled again, went to the West Coast, back to Europe. To London.'

'You didn't ever fall in love again?'

'Nope.'

Velma stirs the tea.

'Do you think then that there really is only one person for everyone? One true love, and Duke was yours?'

'Hell no!' Velma laughs, as she brings her hands together in a clap. 'I have received enough correspondence and heard enough tales from the heart to know people can fall in love many times, sometimes as deeply and passionately as the last, sometimes even more so. There isn't just one person for everyone. That's nonsense.'

'But you travelled all around the world and met Duke on your return to New York.' Maya takes her teacup and looks down into it, feeling bad about what she's about to say. But if there's anyone she can be candid with, it's Velma. 'And there's been no one since.'

'I'm sure I could have fallen in love anywhere if he was right. But that's the thing. The connection and that feeling of everything being right is so rare and only happens a few times in life. For me it happened once, but it can happen more. I have widowed and divorced friends who have gone on to love again, and it's a very real love. I have friends who have fallen in love when they shouldn't have. But it happens. I just know that those feelings, those connections, those moments... they don't come along all that often in life. And they need to be acted upon. I didn't let suitors pass me by out of some widowly duty to Duke, I was just unlucky not to have had that feeling again. You have to make the most of it when it does come along.' Velma gives Maya another of her kind, knowing looks.

'Oh, I wish Train Man would ask me out like Duke did you. He's barely noticed me.'

'Well times are different now, honey. I might have even asked Duke had it been another day.'

The cake is so delicious their plates have almost cleaned themselves.

'Another slice?'

'No, thanks, I'm going to my sister's for a roast dinner with her family.'

'Oh, how wonderful. Why don't you take the rest of that for them when you go?' Velma says, nodding to the remaining cake. 'It won't keep. And would you like to borrow the book? I've just finished it.' Questions that come like friendly commands.

Maya picks up Josephine Baker again and looks at the cover. Carnegie Hall 1973. What must it have been like to be Velma? To only spend twelve years of a lifetime with your soulmate, although Maya feels that she would give anything for just one hour to talk to Train Man. She tucks the book into her bag.

'Oh, I have something for you!' Maya remembers, as she takes a dainty-looking rectangular box out.

'Are these what I think they are?'

'I made them!' Maya squeaks. 'My best batch yet!'

31

Nena sits on the multicoloured chaise longue of FASH reception, legs curled underneath her, black mischievous eyes eyeing the side of the staircase high in front of her to see if she can spot her friend's feet, ankles and legs before her torso lowers into view above them. It's just a little game Nena's playing with herself to while away her nerves. But Maya descends in too much of a hurry for her best friend to recognise her as quickly as she might. Or maybe Nena's not seen enough of Maya lately to recognise her by her clothes. Nena has pretty much always worn a dancer's uniform of leggings, a vest or off-the-shoulder top and then one brightly coloured piece on top. But ever since Maya went to work at Walk In Wardrobe, after they graduated from their south coast sojourn, her style has evolved. At first it was all about black separates in a killer cut. All-black everything was easier than having to think about what to wear in an office where it was all about high-fashion. When Maya moved to FASH and everyone seemed a little bit more street, a little bit more high street and a little bit more relaxed, Maya slunk into her comfort staples of jeans and Converse. But since she first saw Train Man on the platform that drizzly morning last July,

Maya decided to unleash all her dresses that are cinched in at the waist, the cute vintage twinsets and the button-down circle skirts that she was Saving For Later because Maya realised that later had arrived. Who was she saving them for if not for Train Man?

So Nena doesn't realise that the blush pink pumps with the bow on them or the stripy peach cotton dress with the big nude belt belong to Maya, until Maya's chestnut waves bounce into sight.

Nena twists the ring on her left hand nervously, uncurls her legs and stands up with her arms open.

Maya doesn't give Nena a bear hug as usual, just a gentle embrace and a quick peck on the cheek.

'Hey, hey, you OK?' Nena says.

'Yes, fine, where did you want to go? The canteen upstairs? A cafe out?'

Maya was surprised Nena wanted to come to meet her for lunch in the first place. She hasn't seen her since Valentine's Day two months ago. Nena was too busy around her birthday to meet for a cocktail and she still hasn't been to visit the flat in Hazelworth. So why the sudden urgency to meet today?

'Don't mind, as long as we get out of here, all these fashion losers are making me want to hurl,' Nena says, nodding her head towards the fresh-out-of-college intern in hot pants and Buffalo boots as she wheels a rail of clothes across reception.

Is Nena belittling what I do?

Maya tries to shake it off, she is after all happy to see Nena. It's been too long.

'How about that cafe there?' Nena asks, pointing through the gaps in the columns to the cafe run by the Venezuelan couple over the road.

'No, it's not that good,' Maya lies, thinking of their creamy fifty per cent cacao hot chocolate, wanting to keep that to herself and her 'fashion loser' friends.

'Hermé?' they both chime at the same time then laugh, relieved that a tense cloud is starting to evaporate over their heads.

Nena threads her arm through Maya's, conveniently hiding her ring as they walk south towards Oxford Street exchanging pleasantries. Like fighter planes turning at the exact same time, they curve left through an unimposing side door into the food hall where sandwich shoppers fight through the crowds. Maya and Nena weave past the slim black deco font that says DELICATESSEN and down the steps into the gilded grandeur of the chocolatiers and macaron maestros.

Lemon and hazelnut praline; rose and quince; salted caramel; candied chestnut for Nena. Rose petal; Brazilian Paineiras Plantation chocolate; jasmine; pistachio and mandarin for Maya. They file through the stationery section and to the nearest Up escalator, all the way to the top-floor food court.

The window tables that look out onto Oxford Street are all occupied. Maya points to a table in the middle of the cafe, under a large white domed lampshade, and Nena nods. It's a sunny spring day but light is needed in the middle of the department. As they sit, Maya wonders why Nena wanted to meet her, then a bright sparkle refracts from the light above.

'Is that what I think it is?'

Nena looks flustered.

The girls have only just sat down but Maya's bottom bounces straight back up off her chair.

'Oh. My. God! When? How? When? How? How exciting!'

Maya's face is hot under the light and she's glad she's

wearing just a cotton sundress. Suddenly she wonders if she's jumped the gun and Nena's ring is costume jewellery. Surely Nena, the last girl to settle down, wouldn't settle down with a guy – a dad – this quickly. But it doesn't look like costume jewellery. It's beautiful. A baguette-shaped diamond, deco and decadent, shining shyly on its new owner's finger.

Nena smiles nervously. 'Tom asked, I said yes,' she shrugs sheepishly.

Maya clutches Nena's hand then wraps her arms around small shoulders, hugging from an awkward angle across the table.

'How? When?' Maya repeats, her voice getting higher.

'My birthday, in the studio. Everyone was in on it. You know me, I don't like a fuss...' Nena flutters a huge eye and winks as she lets out a single bellow that belies her nerves.

'I wasn't in on it,' Maya blurts uncharacteristically, surprising even herself. 'Why didn't you say sooner? Your birthday was a month ago.'

'I don't really know why. I'm so happy, I guess I was worried you'd disapprove.'

'Disapprove?'

The girls look away from each other while the bubbles in their sparkling water jump and fizz. Nena is the first to speak.

'It is sudden,' she concedes.

'I don't think so,' says Maya, thinking back to the conversation she had with Velma about the moment she met Duke Diamond on the subway. 'If it's right, it's right. It doesn't matter how quickly or slowly it took you to reach this point. And Tom seems amazing. I just wish I saw you both more so I could get to know him better. You must come up to Hazelworth and see the flat.'

Nena looks down. She knows she hasn't been around for her friend lately. And looks back up.

'You're amazing, Maya. I should have known you'd be nothing but happy for me.' Nena twists the rope of her hair to one side with both hands. 'I guess I felt bad, for going off grid and spending all my time with Tom.'

'Oh, don't worry about it!' Maya casually waves a hand in the air pretending she doesn't wish Train Man was her Tom. She doesn't want to ruin Nena's moment.

'I was just trying so hard to ingratiate myself with Arlo and being around and constant for him. He needs consistency.'

Maya feels bad for feeling sorry for herself.

'Don't worry, really, it's more important you're there for them. I'm happy for you, I really am.'

'Well, it does feel weird and I have been feeling wretched for deserting the single sisterhood for Netflix and soft play.'

'What's "soft play"?'

'Hell on earth, mostly.'

Maya laughs and looks down at the shiny cellophane bag on the table in front of her: pink, brown, green and orange hues snuggled together for comfort, destined to make the people whose mouths they unravel in happy. Although it will be Maya's mouth and she hates to admit it, but sometimes she's not happy.

'I am sorry I've neglected you; that I haven't even been to visit you in your flat yet.'

'Don't feel bad. I'm OK. And besides, we have a wedding to plan!'

'Ah yes, but first this,' says Nena, taking two tickets out of her bag. 'Jack White. Hammersmith Apollo. July.'

Nena the charmer. As colourful and as full of zing as the macarons on the table.

Maya walks through her front door, kicks off her pumps and loosens the belt on her peach summer dress. Hot commuter feet are cooled by the black and white chequerboard tiles of the hallway. On the train home Maya looked for Train Man from the security of her seat and couldn't see him. She thought about Nena. She felt sad that for one whole month Maya's best friend didn't tell her something she thought she would share with her straight away. She thought about the shock that Nena, the free spirit, is getting married.

Halfway up the hall, Maya spies a postcard that must have danced through the letter box and almost reached the foot of the stairs. Maya cricks her neck, drops her keys on the console table and picks up the card on her way up the stairs. On one side is an illustration of Josephine Baker. On the back is a little drawing of a macaron and in the same pen the familiar flowery scrawl of a familiar student fills the card even though it says just four words:

Perfection! As are you x

32

'Knock knock' says Glyn, not actually knocking as he walks into class.

'Oh sorry, Glyn, I was miles away in another world, take a seat.' Maya pivots around to face incoming classmates. 'How's your week been?'

Maya *had* been in another world, an Italian small-town fishing port. As she daydreamed waiting for class, Maya had stared at the photographic scene on the wall, wondering where the little harbour actually is in the world and whether it has changed much since the eighties, when it must have been photographed and someone thought fit to turn it into wallpaper.

'Not too bad, thank you, can't complain,' Glyn answers. Glyn is always Not Too Bad. Never actually bad, never good, although he always seems quite cheery.

Jan and Doug walk in, hand in hand, and take their seats, always at the front, always next to each other. Always in harmony.

Esther and Helen walk in together, complaining about not knowing it was fancy dress day at their children's schools and how the lack of communication with the parents isn't good enough. Maya doesn't interrupt and lets their conversation peter out.

Keith walks in, doesn't say anything and sits in his usual seat in the far corner at the back, tossing his long hair like the whip of a lasso.

Ed is absent because he's still in Argentina wooing his girlfriend Valeria with his new-found vocab. Ed must have been the keenest student this year, taking to Spanish with the enthusiasm of a man in love.

Cecily walks in on her own.

'No Dad tonight, he has a gig.'

Gareth plays the fiddle in an Irish pub on the third Tuesday of the month, and right now he's warming up to 'Two Reels'.

It's a depleted class tonight. Still no Velma, still no Nathaniel. Maya decides to get started anyway so as not to lose time.

'Buenas tardes clase.'

Nathaniel walks in with a dandy flounce.

'Perdoname la hora,' he says in the most English of accents, smiling at his subjects before sashaying to his usual seat in the middle of the room.

Velma's seat, next to Jan's, at the front and in the middle, is empty, but Maya tries to focus on the class in hand and not speculate or worry. She had said she was going to record a piece for *Woman's Hour* at the BBC at some point this week, perhaps it was today.

Maya ploughs through where buildings are in relation to each other.

El cine está a la izquierda del supermercado.

La biblioteca está enfrente de la sinagoga.

'I wouldn't miss class for the world!'

Bad feelings rise and Maya's Seeing The Future skills come to the fore.

While Glyn munches on a Custard Cream during the half-time break, Maya says she has to pop out. She rushes across the road into the little antiquated arcade that leads to the town square. Maya looks up across the cobbles to the pizzeria in the corner. A light is on in Velma's apartment above it.

Relief.

Maya opens the grey door next to the red double doors of the restaurant, climbs the staircase and raises a clenched fist to knock.

Seeing The Future skills fill Maya with a sense of doom and her fist knocks noisily with four curt taps.

A man answers. Tall, shorn black hair, square-jawed, ashen-faced. The all-American smile from New Year's Eve is nowhere to be seen.

'Christopher?'

'Maya, right?' he says, knowing all about Maya, having heard so much about her over the past few months.

'Yes, is, er, everything OK?'

Maya already knows the answer is no.

'I literally got here a half hour ago, I took the first flight I could.'

Maya scans the apartment behind broad shoulders that fill the door, but there is no loud laughter emanating from the kitchen. No hands clap together in glee. Tiny feet don't shuffle in shoes that look like slippers. The radio is turned off. The wind chimes are silent. For once the window is closed. All Maya can hear is the muted noise of cutlery chinking and a muffled sing-song of 'Happy Birthday' below.

Christopher looks at Maya's panic-stricken face and realises she doesn't know. He widens the door to let her in.

'Mom died yesterday. Massive stroke, here in the apartment.'

Maya gasps for breath.

'The postman was delivering a parcel in the afternoon, a proof of her new book, and heard her crying out so he broke in, called for help.'

'Oh my god, I'm so sorry,' Maya says, slumping into Christopher's chest and putting her palms on his back to steady herself. In an unnatural situation it seems like the most natural thing to do.

Sturdy arms wrap around Maya's shoulders and Christopher puts his hand on Maya's head to hold her in while he stifles tears. He hasn't had a chance to cry yet. He was so desperate to get to England, to Hazelworth. And he doesn't have anyone to cry with anyway.

'Does Conrad know?'

'Yes, but he can't leave Madison, she's due in a couple of weeks.'

'Oh god, the baby!' Maya feels like she can't breathe.

'He really wanted to come but was torn, so I said I could sort things out alone. We both feel so awful for being so far away when Mom needed us.'

Maya sobs into Christopher's chest, the thought of Velma on her own as she left the world she lit up. She didn't ever get to be a grandmother. Maya pulls away and looks up at Christopher's blue eyes. He looks so strong and solid, standing there needing to be comforted.

'I'm so sorry,' is all Maya can say. Muffled, teary, snot-filled.

Maya composes herself, releases from Christopher's arms and goes into the mode Maya knows best.

'You're not alone. What can I do to help?'

'Nothing now. I can't face going through her things yet.'

'Oh, I totally understand. Sorry.'

'That makes it real. I guess I have to start planning a funeral, but that can wait for the morning. Right?'

'Right.'

'Right now, I need a drink.'

'I'll get you one,' says Maya, breaking away from their bubble in the middle of the chaotic living room to find a glass in the kitchen.

'Stay with me?'

Christopher gently pulls on Maya's arm and she turns back to look at him and nods reassuringly.

A classroom of eight students dust down biscuit crumbs and place empty cups of tea on the table at the edge of the room, awaiting their teacher who won't be back tonight.

Maya wakes on the sofa. Christopher lies on the floor next to her, both draped in blankets, shawls and throws that were dotted all over the room. They were up for hours, Christopher telling Maya stories about his childhood in Brooklyn; his visits to his mother on her overseas adventures; how he and Conrad felt as proud of their mother as she clearly was of her sons when she introduced them to her colourful friends.

Maya looks up at Velma's grandfather clock in the corner and sees it's already 8 a.m. She'll miss the 8.21. She'll miss Train Man.

'Shit, I left my bag at college. It has my keys and train pass in it, I'd better go.'

'Can't you stay?' says Christopher.

'I have to go to work.'

Maya looks at Christopher's forlorn face.

'I'll call my boss and see if I can take compassionate leave.'

Christopher walks through the glass doors to the kitchen and scratches his head while he looks in the cupboards for coffee. He'd hoped it was all a bad dream. That he was in New York and his mother was in England just fine. He feels sick and slams a cupboard door shut.

Maya, having slept in one of Christopher's roomy T-shirts, throws on yesterday's pink houndstooth-check capri pants and black polo neck and ties her hair into a high pony. Christopher watches her clutch the phone to her ear as she talks.

'Hi Lucy, it's Maya, I was wondering... I've had some bad news...' Maya looks towards Christopher and feels guilty for using his mother's death as a reason to skip work, even though he has asked her to.

Maya turns away and stands in front of bookshelves that line an entire wall.

'A friend of mine died on Monday and I only found out last night, I kind of need a day to get my head around it and help the family sort through things for the funeral.' As she says the word family she nods to the solitary man in the kitchen.

'OK, bye.'

Maya ends the call and unfurls the twisted polo neck around her neck that's making her feel claustrophobic.

'My boss wants me to go in. She says my company only gives compassionate leave if it's a direct relative who has died. I'm sorry, Christopher.'

Maya feels wretched. Christopher was doing OK until Maya said the word 'died' but now he's starting to cry. Maya walks over to Christopher and puts her arms around strong shoulders as he slumps over the kitchen counter, his face in giant palms. Maya rubs the expanse of Christopher's bare back as she leans into him.

'I'm so sorry.'

She kisses his warm cheek and leaves.

33

May 2014

It is the last hour of the last day that Maya will be twenty-seven and she is lying on the living-room floor. The television is on mute and she's not paying attention to the CIA agent in the asylum. Prince oozes out of speakers that are too small for this large and airy room. Maya flips open a white unlined notepad, one she's never used before, but now seems like the right time to christen it. Virgin A5 paper. In Maya's right hand is a black Stabilo OHP pen for permanence and neatness. Maya's words need strength but they should not be imposing.

In her left hand is the birth announcement card that arrived through the door this morning. Audrey Evelyn Velma Diamond was born two weeks ago, on the day her grandmother was interred. Christopher gave a heartfelt eulogy at St Anne's Church in Soho. Radio producers, book and magazine editors, journalists, politicians and key movers in the feminist movement turned out in Velma's signature black and grey and squashed into the modern-looking chapel within Wren's historical church. Maya looked around, thinking it was the perfect venue for an ageing yet thoroughly modern thinker who had spent much of her life in London, in an apartment just a stone's throw away.

Maya wasn't surprised by how revered and respected Velma was. Words such as 'passion' and 'wisdom' and 'independence' tinkled across the piano bar at the wake. Maya walked around the room, smiling at people but not knowing anyone. Except Christopher. Maya felt fraudulent being there. She had only known Velma for a few months of her long and full life. People who had known her for many years had flown in from all over the world to be there.

I'm just a girl from the suburbs.

In the church, Christopher spoke about Velma's love for his father, how their marriage had made him believe that there is one true love for everyone in the world. Maya looked down at her shoes on the cold stone floor, knowing Velma had thought otherwise, she had said so just a few weeks earlier with laughter and custard emanating from the corners of her mouth. Christopher spoke eloquently about what it was like to have a mother whose spirit you couldn't stop from soaring, even when he and Conrad thought she should settle down, be around the corner harassing them with hot dinners like a 'normal mom'. But she wasn't a normal mom and they were proud of that.

He spoke about her youth as a journalist in Paris and Buenos Aires, their childhood with her in New York, her career as an agony aunt and writer, and how she was still making new friends in her last days. He referred to his mother's afternoon tea dates with Maya, and how Velma would call Christopher or Conrad on a Sunday lunchtime in New York, full of cake and the joys of life. He looked up at Maya and gave her a smile that spoke a thousand words more.

He talked about Velma's excitement on the eve of becoming a grandmother, of her big move to Miami and how the family had been looking forward to breaks in the sunshine with her. How heartbroken he and Conrad were now that they were robbed of these.

But as Maya walked the piano bar, smiling but not knowing, she felt the atmosphere was upbeat. A room full of gratitude. And Maya met more interesting people that day than she had met in her entire life. She felt privileged to be there.

As the sun was setting over Soho, Christopher found Maya on her own on a little balcony facing a cinema on Shaftesbury Avenue, its façade lit in electric blue.

'Hey,' he said, handing Maya a glass of fizz, the knot of his tie loose around his broad neck.

'Hey.'

'Sorry we've barely had a chance to talk, I wanted to catch up with you,' Christopher said, blue eyes shining in the twilight.

'Oh god, don't worry, you must know so many people here, you've had to run it all.' Maya paused to sip her Prosecco. 'You've been amazing, Christopher, your eulogy was just beautiful.'

Maya wrapped a floral shawl around her shoulders, hugging her body and enveloping her dark grey tulip dress as the evening chill started to settle. Christopher put an enormous arm around Maya and took in the view of Soho's twilight rooftops by her side. Maya leaned in to the warmth of his body.

'Where on *earth* do these come from?' she said, nudging the side of her temple into Christopher's huge bicep. 'What *did* your mum feed you?' They both burst into laughter.

As Maya walked away from Soho and towards the train home, she knew the biggest tribute she could make to Velma would be to ask Train Man out for a drink.

Now the card with the photo of a tiny newborn on a vast fluffy cushion is in Maya's left hand and Velma's advice is ringing in her head, as it has been since she died.

'*What's the worst that can happen?*'

The pen shakes in her right hand. Maya has seen Train Man every weekday morning since the funeral but has barely been able to register him, so nervous is she at the prospect of what she knows she is going to do. How can Maya sound sexy, friendly and sane all at the same time? How can three sentences and a friendly sign-off make someone realise you are their soulmate?

Maya decided not to write the note on the train in case the chug, click, jolt made her writing look spidery or silly. She wants to give Train Man the impression of having written an off-the-cuff note, breezily penned by an über-confident yet down-to-earth goddess. This needs to be legible. So Maya casts aside six pieces of paper into crumpled balls on the floor around her before crafting the final note:

Hello,

It's my birthday today, and I think everyone should do one crazy thing on their birthday, so here's mine:

I think you look lovely, so I was wondering if you'd like to go for a drink sometime? If not, don't worry, I'll leave you in solitude and wish you happy travels.

Cheers,

Maya x

maya.flowers@fash.co.uk

Three sentences and a friendly sign-off. And a kiss. And her email address so he doesn't have to reject her by phone.

Be positive.

Maya puts Solitude in title case so Train Man gets the literary reference and realises that she too has read it. Although if they ever do go on a date, Maya will never tell Train Man that she didn't enjoy *One Hundred Years Of Solitude* as much as she thinks she ought to.

Maya examines attempt number seven. Lucky number seven. She has written clearly and with satisfactory neatness, so she tears the page away and places it back into the notepad, just to ensure the note has a clean tear but stays flat until morning. With a shaky hand, she picks up the phone to call Nena and tell her what she is going to do tomorrow.

34

Maya sits facing forward, chugging into twenty-eight. She hopes that the associated glow of her birthday teamed with the bow on her new green ankle boots will give her an air of allure and – more importantly – confidence that is lacking on this mid-May morning. She peeps into the sanctuary of her slouchy brown leather bag and opens the notepad to check that the note is still there. Still pristine. She deliberately doesn't touch it yet so clammy palms won't sully it.

Train Man sits far away from her in the carriage, also on an aisle seat but on the other side of it. Facing backwards next to the automatic Superior Train door that goes through to the next carriage. He is looking down, almost-black hair slightly shorter today, beautiful straight nose lost in a book, although she can't see what it is from this far.

Maya's phone dings with congratulatory birthday texts. One from Jacob, one from Clara, one from Herbert and Dolores, another from Nena. She reads them all and smiles, feeling loved but unloved at the same time and wondering whether Train Man might notice that her phone keeps pinging from that far away – she likes the feeling of looking popular. Still he reads. Black rectangular glasses folded on the table in front of him.

Maya likes her birthday, she is happy to have completed another year. She knows she won't always feel so strong, so appreciates that today, she is. Maya likes other people's birthdays even more than her own. She loves to bake for them, thoughtfully picks presents and cards and loves to make a fuss. She looks up the carriage at Train Man and wonders when his birthday is; how she would love to make a fuss of him, to make him happy.

With another ding of her phone – Sam this time – it occurs to Maya she has never seen Train Man send or read a text. She has never heard him talk on the phone. She has never heard him calling a special someone to tell them he's going to be late home. Or to discuss a meeting. Or to make plans for dinner. Or to just hear someone's voice. He only seems to use his phone to listen to music. If indeed that is his phone he's plugged into. Maya has never actually noticed.

Suddenly, Maya has a feeling of hope.

If he's not on the phone to a wife or a girlfriend then perhaps he doesn't have a wife or a girlfriend.

And her stomach trembles a little more, knowing that the moment is approaching, not knowing that in eleven days' time her worst fear will be confirmed and she will feel small, crumpled, rejected.

The train approaches industrial outskirts and starts to slow as Maya's heart hastens. The grand shell of Alexandra Palace is her cue to stand up. She will gather her things, slink down the carriage, hand Train Man the note, and confidently ooze into the next carriage; nonchalantly, casually, breezily, like a goddess with green bows on her shoes. She will get off the train at the station and walk as best she can at this height, weaving her way into the bookshop on her left to regain and regroup. That's the plan, anyway.

Maya stands and her legs don't feel as strong as she expected they would. Metal screeching, snaking towards the terminal. Clickety click over canals towards Camden. Other people are starting to shuffle and stand, eager to get to their coffees and their emails. Maya feels a sense of urgency in her bladder as people begin to stand between her and her beautiful target, unaware, lost in his book, totally oblivious to the turmoil Maya is going through as she approaches him from the other end of the carriage.

'Excuse me, please,' Maya murmurs to the woman blocking the aisle, moving slowly to reach up to her bag on the luggage shelf that runs along the top of the carriage.

As Maya waits for the woman to move to one side and let her pass, she takes the note out of the notepad and folds it neatly in half.

Train Man is still absorbed, unaware that the woman sitting next to him by the window is starting to gather her duffel bag from the floor between her feet.

Maya reaches the end of the carriage, just before the automatic doors that slide satisfactorily through to the next carriage, and pauses at Train Man's right knee. Hesitant, clammy, sick.

Train Man folds the top right-hand corner of the page he's reading, closes his book and leans down to open his grey backpack.

Maya presses the button on her side of the internal door with the clothed elbow of her floral bomber jacket. Her blue high-waisted circle skirt fills the aisle. Doors hiss open and Maya walks on through, as pretty and as unsure as she was on her eighth birthday in a big flouncy skirt, knees trembling. Note still shaking in her hand.

*

'I froze, it was impossible,' says Maya. 'He was totally looking into his bag, I would have had to shake him to get his attention. I'm not on his radar at all.'

'Don't be sad Birthday Girl,' pleads Nena. 'There's always tomorrow. Fuck it, give him the note then.'

'But it won't be my birthday.'

'Doesn't matter. If you end up going on a date, you can fess up then. If you don't, he'll never know. Bingo.'

Nena says 'bingo' like it's a good thing but Maya feels sad at the prospect of Train Man never knowing when her birthday isn't.

'True,' she sighs.

Maya looks at the menu but can't take in the words.

'I guess I have no choice, it's my only idea. And I owe it to Velma.'

'Well then do it. Dress as if it's your birthday tomorrow and give it another whirl. You look gorgeous by the way.'

Maya doesn't feel very gorgeous sitting in a burger bar with its metal chairs and plastic red checked tablecloth draped over her big blue skirt, although everyone did their best to make her feel special today.

Lucy took the team out for lunch at a French bistro down Baker Street, and on the walk back to FASH HQ she quietly hinted that a verdict on the site editor job would be imminent. Mid-afternoon, Chloe nipped out and bought a caterpillar cake that everyone stood around a table eating in the communal kitchen, but not before Emma and Sam made everyone sing 'Happy Birthday'. It was a good work day, but all day Maya had a feeling of failure and emptiness. She won't go home to someone who loves her, unlike Nena.

Stop feeling sorry for yourself, Flowers.

'Enough about Train Man, tell me happy news. What about the wedding? Any developments?'

Nena is bursting with excitement. 'We've set a date!'

Maya is grateful for the shift in focus.

'Amazing! When?'

'December!'

'Ahhh, I love a winter wedding! So cool, Nena. Oh hang on, that's, what, seven months?' Maya says, counting on her fingers. 'We'd better get moving. Where have you booked?' Maya unzips her floral bomber, hangs it on the back of her chair and rubs her palms. She revels in planning mode.

'Here in London. Simple, elegant, bloody expensive. The venue itself is costing a fortune so we need to keep costs down everywhere else.'

If Nena was ever going to get married, Maya thought it would be Elvis doing the honours in Vegas, or on a dreamy beach in Bahia with her Brazilian relatives. A city wedding to a TV exec is not what Maya expected. But then Nena has always managed to surprise her.

'Right, well leave the dress with me. We have *loads* of designer wedding dresses at work, and I have a forty per cent discount.'

'Bingo.'

'I could sort Tom out with a nice suit too.'

'I love you.'

Two Coke floats arrive, and as Maya takes a pen and the spiral ring-bound notepad out of her bag and opens it carefully so as not to reveal Train Man's note, her Brilliant Imagination skills help her float out of the burger bar and away on a sea of tulle.

35

James sits at a small dining table, leaning against the wall in a room with little natural light. A large orange lampshade made of glass illuminates muesli and cornflakes, which James raises to his mouth slowly and rhythmically. The sound of James eating makes Kitty place her coffee cup on the table with an agitated bang. She scrunches her face semi-apologetically, mostly revealing surprise at her own force, but doesn't say anything.

James stares into the space of the front room and the front door ahead of him, unfazed by the thump, then puts his hand over his mouth to stifle a springtime sneeze.

Kitty scowls.

'How about a career change?' James says, breaking the silence with a bombshell – to see if Kitty is listening, more than anything else.

Pale brows furrow.

'I love my job.'

'Not you, me.'

'James, I'm late. I really need to get my train. What are you talking about – and why the bloody hell bring it up now?'

James shrugs and raises his breakfast to his lips with a lacklustre spoon.

Kitty ruffles her hair in exasperation before slicking it back down with a pang of guilt. 'What do you *want* to do?'

'I was thinking of retraining, becoming a photographer.'

'What? Are you crazy? Be some diva photographer's bitch like that guy you went to South Africa with? Work for peanuts for five years until you realise you gave up a good salary for *nothing*?'

'I don't care about the money, I'd rather do something I loved.'

'Yes, but little hobbies don't pay the rent.'

'Thanks for the vote of confidence.'

'Get real, James.'

James watches as Kitty slings a large canvas bag bursting with folders and files, angles protruding, over her shoulder blade.

'I have to go.' She turns on a low heel and opens the front door.

James tries to finish his mouthful of breakfast to say goodbye but he's not quick enough. The door slams.

'Bye,' James says, to no one.

Doors ding, lights illuminate, and the throng of commuters who gather at that spot on that platform every morning edge into the carriage. It's an Inferior Train and James is worried that his day, which started badly, is going to continue in this vein. As he boards the train, he sees a man in a three-piece suit and remembers he has a 10 a.m. catch-up with Sebastian and Duncan from Fisher & Whyman, who have reverted to formal type since the sundowners and shorts of South Africa.

For the second half of the meeting Sebastian and Duncan will bring in Cynthia and Mike from Fisher & Whyman's beauty division to talk to MFDD about a pitch they want James and Dominic to give for a haircare brand. James curses himself for not remembering to dress a little smarter today than his raglan top, jeans and Converse.

The man with the red nose, who always gasps in the last of a John Player Special Blue on his approach to the station, turns right into the carriage and James follows him, despite the lingering smell of nicotine, tar and formaldehyde, because he knows that red nose is good at sniffing out hidden seats on an Inferior Train.

James lowers his backpack off his shoulders so as not to knock anyone, and follows the man towards three remaining seats in a set of five that are squashed together in the middle of the train.

Two seats face forward, three seats face backwards, no table between, just knees trying not to knock other knees. The man with the red nose sits facing forwards in the last seat of the pair. Two of the three seats facing backwards remain. The window seat is already taken by the large woman who chews her nails. James takes the worst of the remaining two, the one in the middle, and slumps in.

Why did I pick the middle seat?

The seat on James's left is free, he weighs up whether it's best to be squished in next to the woman who chews her nails or slide along to the aisle seat where he'll be knocked into by the commuters who are forced to stand.

Before James can properly consider his options, a girl slumps into the last remaining seat next to him and for a second their outer thighs touch, before she quickly pulls her leg away. James tries not to look at her but he already knows that it is the girl with wavy hair and beautiful shoulders. He saw her asleep one time, which afforded him the chance to look up and notice that the curve of her collarbone looked so creamy, dappled with the tiniest sparkles of brown, that he wanted to run his finger along it, but he looked straight back down and carried on reading, hoping she hadn't heard his thoughts.

James opens *The Road* and tries to find the page with the corner folded over neatly. He looks down. Green bows distract him from a reluctant rendezvous with a father and a son in hell. The train snakes slowly, sleepily, expectantly along the track for thirty tense minutes.

'Can I give you this?'

The girl with the wavy hair and the smooth shoulders has risen from her seat and is standing awkwardly on the cusp of five blue faux-velveteen seats. Figures in the aisle wonder what the girl is doing, getting up prematurely to get out of the space she was fortunate to have had, and they stand firm huffily.

We're not stopping yet.

She had a seat.

I'm not moving.

I can't move.

James looks up. The sun shining through the window illuminates brown and orange eyes and he wonders why the girl with the wavy hair is standing looking at him.

What did I do?

'Sorry?' he says.

'Can I just give you this?' Maya says again, this time even more self-consciously; face reddening, pulse quickening, knowing more ears are pricking up this second time around.

James takes buds out of his ears. He thinks he caught what she said this time but is still confused as to why the girl who gets his train is standing over him. Smartly dressed in a green and white silk blouse tucked into grey culottes that stop below her knees, showing slender ankles anchored to the carriage floor by green bows.

'Er, yeah sure,' James says, taking the folded piece of white paper from Maya, hands not touching, not knowing that the paper is slightly less crisp and pristine than it was eleven days ago and that it now it has a horizontal fold cutting through her words.

Maya lets go of the note and turns awkwardly on a pressing heel. Without saying another word, she clutches her bag to her tummy and sees she is blockaded in. She says a few polite but firm 'excuse me's to people reluctant to move out of her way until they are ready to get off.

She had a seat, now she wants to get off before me.

The cheek!

I've got to get out of here.

James unfolds the note and reveals the dimple in his left cheek as he reads, although Maya has already gone, a heart hurting with relief and curiosity. Hoping three sentences and a friendly sign-off will change her life. Later today, she will discover it won't.

'Bloody hell, Millsy, you're a jammy bastard aren't you?'

James blushes and laughs. 'Why does that shit never happen to me?' Dominic is sitting on James's desk, scratching his chin, pudgy brown eyes re-reading the letter. 'Is she fit?'

James thinks of the girl with the wavy hair – Maya Flowers – and the curve of her collarbone leading to her neck.

'I dunno, I hadn't really noticed.'

'Bollocks. She gets your train every day and you hadn't noticed her? So if you're not gonna tell me, then she's either really fit or really butters. And if she was butters you wouldn't have shown me this.' Dominic flaps the note in the air as if it's the golden ticket.

James laughs, a slightly proud laugh, and changes the subject.

'Come on, Duncan and Sebastian are in reception, let's sort our strategy.'

'What are you going to say to her?'

'Who, Cynthia?'

'Not Cynthia. Crazy Train Lady. What will you say to her?'

'That I have a girlfriend, of course.'

'And will you tell Kitty?'

'Of course I will, we have no secrets,' James says as they head to meet the team from Fisher & Whyman, wondering when it would ever come up with Kitty, given they barely communicate at all.

36

It is the morning after, eleven days after Maya's 28th birthday and she is sitting at her desk. On the other side of the two white rectangular computer screens that separate them sits Emma. When Cressida Blaise-Snellman joined FASH yesterday, she requested the window seat from Emma, and Emma's not the sort of girl to say no. Besides, she thinks it will be OK sitting opposite Maya, even though she did like the light of the vast windows overlooking the bustle of Marylebone. Lucy has moved into her own shiny new corner office next to Rich and Rich's offices, and there is a sense of New World Order about the place.

Emma has just finished her trend report for the morning – not much to report. A grumpy-looking cat has done a swimwear shoot and celebrities wearing latex are the only FASH-related talking points, and even those wouldn't be worth a mention.

'Want to grab a coffee?' asks Emma hopefully, even though Maya has only just got into work and is switching on her machine.

Emma doesn't normally suggest they go for a coffee. Emma always drinks and eats at her desk.

'Sure,' says Maya, suspecting Emma just wants to check that she's OK after the double disaster of yesterday.

They get up to weave out, past Cressida as she's coming through the glass doors to head to her new desk – the best-lit desk in the office.

'Morning!' Cressida smiles. A smile that rises no further than her razor-sharp cheekbones as she looks Emma and Maya up and down. Tall, willowy, awkward angles wrapped in a fur gilet and black leather skinnies.

'Morning!' Emma and Maya say in unison as they continue to the canteen.

'Oh ladies,' Cressida turns back over her shoulder. 'New rule: conference at 0930. Without fail. To discuss the fashion talking points of the day and how we translate them to FASH. Should only take a couple of hours.' She looks at her Rado watch. 'See you in five. Meeting room 1.1.'

The door closes.

'Two hours every day? I rarely have two minutes to pee.'

'Oh, Emma!' Maya consoles. Emma really does have the hardest job at FASH. Social media is twenty-four hours, trends update every minute. There is never any downtime and she is a team of one. 'We'd better make this quick, eh?' says Maya, still touched by the fact Emma is checking up on her.

Emma grabs a herbal tea and a croissant, Maya gets a hot chocolate, and they sit at a wooden table for two next to the glass balustrade that overlooks the silver staircase and the reception atrium below.

'So did you see Train Man this morning?'

Maya nods. 'It was so weird, Emma. I thought about getting an earlier train, or a later one…'

'You can't get a later one, Cressida's new regime remember!'

They laugh. Emma peels layers of pastry off her croissant with shaky fingers.

'Well I thought it would be even more embarrassing if I were to get another train and Train Man was hiding on it too, so I just got the same one. I have to face him at some point, don't I?'

'Good for you Maya, you're so brave.'

'I feel stupid, not brave. And I only did it out of duty to Velma. I'm not nearly as brave as she was.'

Emma squeezes Maya's arm. 'You're not stupid! You did a brilliant thing.'

Maya shrugs and takes a sip of hot chocolate for comfort.

'So did you say anything to each other?'

Maya thinks back to an hour ago. Train Man. James Miller. Walked up the platform and came to the same set of doors. Apple green polo shirt with a little penguin on his chest. Strong, lean brown arms bearing the weight of his backpack. Blue jeans and now off-white Converse. An awkward but kind smile revealing a dimple in his left cheek. Maya smiled back and blushed. Embarrassed, defeated, unloved. She didn't avoid him and he didn't avoid her. A small triumph really.

'He said a quiet "hello" and smiled; I said "hi" back. Then it was back to normal. I'm so embarrassed, Emma, so gutted.'

'Oh, Maya. I'm so sorry. At least you know now. You can move on.'

I don't want to move on.

Emma decides not to mention the job situation, that Maya isn't the new site editor, it's irrelevant now, so she tries to put the image of Cressida gleefully sweeping her breakfast pot and belongings across the desk, away from the window seat with a careless arm, to the back of her mind. It won't help Maya to moan about it.

'Girls! Conference!' Cressida barks through the door before disappearing in a flash.

'Erm, are we at school?' Maya frowns. 'And is that fur she's wearing? FASH has an anti-fur policy – I'm not sure Rich and Rich would like that.' Not that Maya cares what Rich and Rich think right now. She doesn't want to be a sore loser, but appointing Cressida over her is only cementing her growing sense of foreboding about the direction FASH is heading.

'Yuck,' says Emma, fairy features frowning.

'That gilet looks like a baby bear clinging onto her for dear life,' says Maya, glancing back at the space from where Cressida hollered. 'It's gross.'

Blue eyes brighten.

'Oh Maya, before we're called back again, I want to tell you before I tell Lucy.'

'What?'

'Well speaking of baby bears...'

Maya looks blank.

'I'm getting one of my own.'

'You'd wear *that*?' Maya is horrified.

'No, Maya. I'm pregnant!'

Maya shakes her head and widens her eyes. 'Oh my GOD, Emma, come here!' Maya wraps her arms around taller shoulders. 'I'm so so happy for you. And Paul. Congratulations!'

'Well we kind of have you to thank for it.'

'Ladies!' calls Cressida again, not caring that the last of the breakfast meetings are still taking place in the canteen and she's shouting over every one of them.

'What *is* she like? We're trying to have a buddy hug here!'

grimaces Maya into Emma's embrace. 'Anyway, what did I have to do with it – you know how the birds and bees work right, Emma?'

'That spa weekend you gave us? Well it seemed to do the magic after a *lot* of false starts. We were getting worried.'

'Wow, well I'm even happier I didn't waste the weekend on me. Amazing news Emma, I'm so pleased for you. When are you due?'

'November.' A cautious smile flutters across Emma's cheeks.

Cressida's impatient angles make a face of disbelief and a hand beckons through the glass door. Emma and Maya release their embrace and hurry to the meeting room, but still all Maya can think is *I have a girlfriend.*

Part Three

37

Maya didn't think she could ever fall in love with someone who didn't know the difference between *your* and *you're*, but she did, almost seven years before she first laid eyes on Train Man. It was the first time she'd ever been in love, other than with Leonardo DiCaprio. Maya had battled with Clara over the *Romeo + Juliet* poster for so long, that when she finally took custody of it from Clara's bedroom at the top of Flowers Towers, and triumphantly flew down three flights of stairs to her bedroom on the ground floor, she chose to ignore the fact that it was torn in the top right-hand corner. Maya was the proud owner of the poster and kissed it goodnight. Every night. Leonardo was Maya's first love.

When love hit Maya for real, it occurred to her that it hadn't happened at first sight like it had when she saw Leo on Verona Beach. It wasn't like that with Jon. Maya's love for Jon grew more steadily.

It started in the university library on the south coast. Maya couldn't concentrate because the tall guy with shaved blond hair, a soft round head like a tennis ball, was parading around the library talking loudly to his friends, Being Charming. It was confidence Maya hadn't seen before, and although her default setting would have been to be annoyed by the distraction, it was an intriguing enough distraction to keep her from *Picasso's Women*. Jon had a cheeky look in his glacial eyes.

Jon enjoyed Being Charming. Charming male friends, charming female friends, charming strangers. Charming the woman who stamped that day's date (3 February, if you must know) wonkily into Jon's books.

Jon walked past Maya and smiled. Later, when Jon told Maya that he fell in love with strangers every day from just a passing look, Maya thought back to their first encounter in the library. She hadn't fallen in love at first sight, not like she had with Leo, not like she would later, on a drizzly train platform. But she wondered whether Jon had fallen for her at that moment, if it was love at first sight for him, or whether he was just Being Charming.

Maya next saw Jon when he turned out to be a friend of her friend, as people are in the small community of a small university, studying Drama & Performance – and oh what a performance. Sitting opposite each other in a curry house, Jon held court with an anecdote about how he had outsmarted a lecturer, earlier in the day, on the language of Christopher Marlowe.

By Easter, Maya had fallen in love. Jon would walk through the library, falling in love with strangers but leaving little notes of declaration only on Maya's desk. It was terribly romantic among the ISBN numbers. They were each other's first love, and Maya wanted Jon to be her last as he stroked her shiny straight hair in his student digs at night, sombrely reciting *Doctor Faustus* as she fell asleep against his torso.

When they graduated and Maya walked straight into the editorial assistant job at Walk In Wardrobe, she couldn't help but feel the prickle of Jon's reaction. Maya had run the entire kilometre from the tube station to their Finsbury Park flat-share *in heels* to tell Jon face to face that she'd just been offered her first proper job – and when Jon's steely smile dropped she couldn't help but notice.

'What's wrong, baby? I thought you'd be pleased.'

'I am,' he said, releasing Maya's arms from around his neck. 'I'm just worried about the audition tomorrow, I can't think of anything else right now.'

And Jon slunk back upstairs to their bedroom to read his script. Deep down, Maya knew he wasn't happy for her but she chose to ignore it. He wasn't that good an actor.

Maya also chose to ignore Jon falling in love with strangers every day in the street while he held Maya's hand a little further away from him, almost hiding her with his swagger. She also chose to ignore Nena's scoffs, that if Jon couldn't get paid work as an actor, perhaps he should get paid work as a barman, a waiter, or in a supermarket so Maya wouldn't have to support them both. Maya thought it was easy for Nena to say, she had landed a job in the West End, and Maya asked Nena to use her contacts to help Jon.

But Maya only had herself to blame for her hair turning wavy. It happened more than two years after their first encounter in the library. Jon needed £5,000 to do a Shakespeare summer school course at RADA, and Maya gave him all the money she had saved for a deposit on a flat. Their flat.

'I know it's a risk but this could seriously be the thing I need to fine-tune my craft and give me the big break. I can feel it around the corner, Maya. And then it'll be a house in Hampstead not a shitty flat-share in Finsbury Park. On me.'

Maya stopped looking at flats for sale and wrote Jon a cheque. She sent him off to summer school with a kiss on his nose and a breakfast muffin wrapped in a piece of kitchen roll with little daisies on it as she went to Walk In Wardrobe.

Maya gradually lost Jon over six weeks of sonnets, monologues and song. As Jon explored the depths of Shakespeare, he discovered the depths of Talia, and when the course ended on a Friday evening in late July, he never came home. Maya cried so hard that the tears ran into her hair and turned it wavy for good. Heartbroken and annoyed that her Seeing The Future skills had failed her. She hadn't truly acknowledged the boy who couldn't be happy for Maya's success. The boy who mistook your and you're. *Your my first love*, said the note in the library.

38

June 2014

James looks at the ticket in his left hand as he waits for the doors to open and notices that it expires today. On Monday he will need a new one, but before that lies a celebratory weekend ahead. Celebrating a win for the new haircare account after he and Dominic gave a brilliant pitch to Cynthia and Mike from Fisher & Whyman; celebrating booking tickets to Jamaica for their September shoot for Femme; celebrating that Jeremy Laws, the chief creative officer of MFDD, has just given his wonder boys another pay rise; and celebrating that tomorrow will be the longest day of the year and he, Kitty, Dominic and Josie will be going to a festival on a farm in Suffolk.

As the doors swing open, James follows the other commuters out of the station. At the off-licence on the station approach James buys a bottle of Pimm's, then nips into the corner shop to buy some cucumber, strawberries and mint and wonders how to tell Kitty about the pay rise. He'll line up two drinks ready for when Kitty gets home and he'll tell her they're celebrating something. She'll be pleased. James has noticed she's been looking at house prices in estate agents' windows recently – perhaps they will buy in Hazelworth after all. They ought to be able to now with their combined salaries.

Kitty usually gets home half an hour later than James, and as he waits to pay at the checkout he contemplates going back into the station to meet her from the train.

Go home. Line up the drinks. Order a takeaway. I can make her happy again.

James walks through the park, across two roads and turns right onto the quiet road with the Victorian terraces. He puts his key in the door.

Shit, I forgot the ice.

The door opens onto the living room and Kitty is already home. Sitting in the armchair in the front room. The television isn't on and their big weekend bag with the birds on it sits on the floor, leaning against a skinny ankle that might snap under the weight of its contents, so bursting is it at the seams.

But we're not going to Suffolk until tomorrow.

Kitty's skin looks paler than ever and the light streaming through the front window makes her eyes shine like uncut diamonds.

James wonders if someone has died and feels panic in the pit of his stomach. The air certainly has a feel of the waiting room at a doctor's surgery, that a death sentence is about to be delivered.

'You're home. Are you OK?'

Kitty looks up at James briefly and then to the Donwood on the wall behind him.

'Kit? What's happened?'

'I'm leaving you,' she says, looking at the wall and then down at her hands. She twists a pale opal ring on her longest finger.

'What the fuck...' James says with a sigh, not a question.

'Don't even speak because then I'll feel too guilty.'

'What?'

'It's definite. It's not me being flighty or moody or whatever you would want to call it.'

'I don't call you anything like that,' James says, feeling a lump rise in his throat.

Silence.

James breaks it first.

'You're my girl; you have been since we were kids. What's happened?'

Kitty looks angry.

'Don't make out like you were happy, James,' she snaps, giving him a brief sideways glance to where he is still standing by the door, blue plastic bag in hand, mint slowly wilting. 'Is *this* really what you want?'

James doesn't say anything.

'Anyway, I've met someone.'

Silence and disbelief hang thick in the joyless air.

'He gets my train. We're moving in together.'

James is sickened by the impossibility of what he's hearing. How could this be happening? Who could she have met on the train?

'What's his name?'

'Does it matter?'

'WHAT'S HIS NAME?'

In the eleven years they have been together, Kitty has never heard James shout in anger. Her eyes widen like a startled bird.

'Simon. He works in Cambridge too. We've got a flat; we picked up the keys today. You won't need to see me, unless we're visiting the kids in Hazelworth, but that won't happen often.' She stares ahead, angry, still. Not a hint of excitement in her voice.

'Kids? What kids?'

Kitty pushes ragged cuticles back with a fingernail.

'Kitty, you never wanted kids!'

James is so baffled, he leans back on his backpack and slides down the inside of the front door until he is sitting on the floor, blue plastic bag still in hand.

'How many kids? How old are they?'

'Stop asking questions, you won't change my mind. I'm in love with him.'

James glazes over, staring into the open doorway to the middle dining room that leads through to the kitchen. He floats up into the air and looks down at his pitiful body slumped against the door, seeing the top of his head, and Kitty's in the armchair.

'What about your stuff? What about our life?'

'I'll come back for more clothes when you're out. And our life? I'm sure your mum and dad will get over it,' Kitty says sarcastically, standing up.

James can't move. He is frozen in disbelief.

'Can I get past, please?'

James leans his head back on the soft support of his grey backpack and closes his eyes. He thinks of the note, still sitting in the front pocket of his backpack, crumpled behind his back against the door. Purposeful, hopeful, kind. The kindest thing a stranger had ever done for him. How he wouldn't even entertain the thought of going for a drink with a girl called Maya who gets his train, when all the while Kitty and a man called Simon were flirting and cheating and fucking and plotting on a train going in the opposite direction.

'Please James, let me go.'

'I am,' he says flatly, standing in defeat to make way for Kitty.

Kitty picks up the weekend holdall and opens the door with her free hand.

A taxi outside waits for her and James wonders if it was there when he sauntered happily down the road, because if it was, he hadn't noticed it.

How many other things haven't I noticed?

James's mind races as Kitty walks down the short terracotta tiled path to the gate and doesn't look back.

'The station,' she says, before a car door closes smoothly and a quiet engine purrs off.

James pushes the front door shut with his forehead. He turns and looks around the small front room and the fragments of their life together. His records. His artwork. A thank you card to James from Albert, the widower who lives next door, for helping him with the garden, sits at one end of the mantelpiece. At the other end of the mantelpiece he sees the invitation to Kitty's mother's 60th birthday party next month. 'To James and Catherine, please do come to my party!' it says, as dancing teapots and cake stands weave in a conga around a large 6 and a large 0. He wonders if Kitty was ever present since they moved to Hazelworth. How long has this relationship been going on for?

James looks down and realises he's still clutching a bottle of Pimm's in a blue plastic bag and throws it towards the front door, sending it smashing against the corner of the room. Glass and Pimm's and mint and strawberries all slide down the wall in a sharp and sticky mess and James slumps into the armchair Kitty had been sitting in. The seat is still warm.

39

Eight people sit around a large oval table, heads turned to face a TV screen at one end of it. Photographs spool. Pictures that Olivia has been in the office searching for since 7 a.m. Celebrities on the red carpet. Celebrities at product launches. Celebrities doing their grocery shopping. All pictures Cressida has asked Olivia to source for the daily two-hour meeting, and today, like most days since she joined FASH, Cressida doesn't seem to like any of them. Everyone is silent, expectant, bored. Waiting for the new site editor to say something directional. Faces on the wall, onto which Cressida had pinned inspirational photos of supermodels and slogans like #iwokeuplikethis, #fashun and #airportswag, also watch, waiting, silent, expectant, uninspired.

Optimistic Alex tries to break the ice with chit-chat.

'Cressida, do you have a sore throat today?'

'What?'

'Well, you're wearing a neck scarf. And a very nice neck scarf it is too.'

Cressida looks at Alex and curls a plump top lip to reveal truculent teeth.

'No. It's just a scarf,' she snaps. 'I work in fashion.'

Liz looks meekly across the table at Maya, who gives her a reassuring smile. Since Cressida started, Liz, who Maya worked so hard to get out of her shell, seems to have crawled back into it.

Cressida studies a supermodel on screen. Lips pout and a finger twists.

'The thing I have trouble with...' she says profoundly, as if she is about to say something full of insight and zeitgeist, 'is when does a dungaree become a jumpsuit?'

When did dungarees become singular? In fact this is something that has crept into the FASH vernacular in recent weeks. A striped trouser. A red lip. A colour-block heel. Maya makes a note to herself to bring back plurals.

No one answers. Maya looks around and wonders when people stopped laughing in their morning meeting. Their team get-togethers used to be joyful.

'OK, move on, next picture.'

Olivia fluffs up her fiery mane and scrolls through.

'I'm not getting anything from these, Olivia. We're meant to feel inspired to translate these looks, but none of these correlate with me. I mean, who even is she? I've never heard of that celebrity.'

Olivia's tired face jolts awake.

'She's in a reality TV show our girls love,' Maya interjects.

'Urgh. So common,' Cressida spits, as she continues to twist thin strands of honey-blonde hair around her forefinger.

Did Cressida just call our customers common?

'Next!'

Maya feels the weight of tension and ill feeling in the room, so she opens her laptop for distraction, to look through today's drop of new clothes for editorial inspiration while the team keep looking through paparazzi pictures on the screen.

Bored, miffed, disgruntled. Maya glances left then right and realises no one either side of her can see her screen, so she types 'James Miller' into Google.

I can't believe I didn't think of this.

A filmmaker, an author, an architect. None of whom are her James Miller. Maya knows from his email that James Miller is Art Director at MFDD, which she googled at the time and saw was an advertising agency, but now she can't find anything else. No Facebook, no Twitter, no Instagram. Clearly not for that James Miller anyway. A few online charity donations that may or may not have been from him but nothing else.

Cressida and Olivia are talking but Maya doesn't listen. She's wondering why she's bothering to look up a guy who's not interested.

Forget about him.

'What was that?' laughs Cressida.

'Mosheeno, the new store opening last night, I've got lots of pics of models there in totally wearable looks,' says Olivia, clinging onto the lifeline as she drags an arrow to a small blue folder on the big screen.

'You mean Moskeeeeeno, right?' Cressida looks disgusted.

Olivia's face burns as red as her hair.

'An easy fashion mistake to make,' says Alex kindly. 'I still think Versace rhymes with face.'

Cressida looks down at her notepad, flabbergasted, and shakes her head.

Maya wonders whether the James Miller and Kitty Jones who donated £50 to Dominic Kennedy's London marathon fundraising page three years ago might be Train Man and his girlfriend.

That's it. He's in love with someone called Kitty Jones and I feel sick.

'Darling, I'm not going to the party, I can't face seeing them. If Catherine is there with that new man of hers I will feel outraged and sick just at the sight of them. What treachery! It's so upsetting. I'm not going. Your father can go on his own if he must.'

James sits at his desk having another hushed conversation. He doesn't think he's spoken to his mum in three years as much as he has in the past three weeks, but it's been surprisingly comforting.

'Mum, it's OK. I'm OK. I'll get through it. Don't take it out on Mary and George. You should go to the party, they're your best friends.'

'Darling, I just can't. Mary is embarrassed enough when she sees me in the street, I don't want to make matters worse.'

'What about Dad? He'd want to go, he'd want *you* to go. All your friends are going, you'd really miss out. None of our mates want much to do with Kitty, don't let any more friendships fall apart because of what happened between us. I'll be fine. Look, I'm going to have to get back to work, I have a meeting in five minutes. I told you about the promotion, yes?'

'Yes you did and I'm so proud of you. Well done darling.'

The plus side of heartbreak is that lately MFDD has seemed like a sanctuary to James. Focusing on products that either wash, condition or remove women's hair suddenly doesn't seem so pointless.

'Well I say go to the party, have fun, and if you see Kitty and… him… just smile politely and talk to someone else. And lace their vol-au-vents with arsenic.'

'Oh sweetheart, you are awful! Well I'll think about it. I'll see what your sisters say. They were meant to be going too.'

'Sisters?'

'Well, Petra is practically your sister too now they're married.'

James laughs. How far his parents have come.

'I have to go. But go to the party, say happy birthday to Mary from me, and tell Dad, Fran and Petra that I'll come home in a few weeks. I just don't really fancy a trip back to Kent right now.'

'I know. I understand. You look after yourself. You are eating, aren't you?'

'Yes, Mum. Got to go.'

'Bye darling. Love you.'

'You too, Mum.'

James hangs up the phone. He doesn't have a meeting. He doesn't have to go. But he is sick of going around in circles and thinking and talking about it. About her. He's sick of sitting at home getting stoned and imagining what Simon looks like. He's sick of wondering whether Simon was in his bed while he was working in South Africa. He's sick of returning home from work and looking in their wardrobe to see if today was the day Kitty came for the rest of her stuff. He's sick of it and just wants to run away from it all.

40

July 2014

At a grand circle bar in an old art deco theatre, Maya hugs her friend.

'He's amazing! You're amazing! Thank you!' she shouts among the muted ferocity emanating from the shy guitarist downstairs and back behind the double doors on stage. Just like the first time Maya ever saw Nena, at a gig across town, she is sparkling with sweat and wearing a black vest tucked into a very colourful, very heavy skirt.

'You know if I never saw you again, this is how I would remember you,' Maya says smiling.

'Oh, don't say that!' frowns Nena, as she pays for two small drinks in two small plastic cups.

'And I still don't know how you jump in that fabric.'

'Hey, I'm glad we could do it!' she says, putting a tipsy arm around Maya's hot shoulder. Both happy to be revisiting a favourite pastime from before Tom, before Nena took a permanent job and became TV talent, before she became a mother, of sorts. Nena downs her rum and Coke in one and decides she can't hold back on her news, even if it is indicative of That Thing That Divides Them.

'Speaking of fabric, I found it Maya, I found the dress!'

'On FASH?' Maya's mouth tingles from the coldness of a dirty gig-bar ice cube.

'Nope, in a little boutique in Islington. It's so pretty. And *very* ladylike. Who knew?' she says, twisting her hair into rope. 'My mum started crying when I tried it on, which *has* to be a good sign – unless she hates Tom – but I don't *think* she hates Tom. Anyway, I'd love you to see it before I make a decision.' Nena is suddenly distracted by the couple behind Maya. A tall man with kind and soulful brown eyes behind black rectangular glasses looks down at a woman with hair as black and shiny as Nena's, bluntly cut at the base of her neck. The woman stands with her back to Maya. The man is listening to her intently. Handsome face, handsome nose, thick dark hair slightly to one side. A thoughtful, listening face. Wide, lovely eyes. Nena drinks in his beautiful features, completely unaware of what it would mean for Maya to see him there.

But Maya doesn't turn around to see who has caught Nena's eye. She's just desperate to see the wedding dress Nena has chosen.

'Cool! Did you take a pic?'

'Not allowed,' Nena says, snapping back in to the conversation. 'In case I copy it, which is a laugh, given I can't sew on a button. Let's go this weekend, yeah?'

'Great!'

'Just tell me if it's too... *womanly*, won't you?'

'Womanly is good,' says Maya, straightening the thin belt on another vintage cotton sundress.

'You can work it, Maya – even at a gig, you look like a fifties maven – I love this style evolution of yours – but I'm not sure I can pull it off.'

Maya thinks back to a year ago when her uniform of jeans and Converse suited her nicely, but she likes feeling a little more polished. Even if it didn't work for James Miller.

'With this hair? Hardly!' Maya says, shaking waves that grew in the mosh pit to Hokusai like proportions. As Maya swats a dismissive hand in the air, she accidentally knocks the girl behind her at the bar.

'Oh sorry!' Maya says, going to turn around as the band strike up the fiery and feral first chords of 'Hotel Yorba'. Nena stops Maya midway through turning as she drags her by the arm, down the stairs and through the double doors into the auditorium, where she jumps with such vigour she almost freezes mid-air. Hair swishing, skirt twirling. The couple upstairs at the circle bar are too embroiled in a heart-to-heart to hear the music.

Maya walks with some urgency up the platform. It is the first day in months that she has felt like there's some unforced buoyancy in her stride – not the bounce she experiences when she goes running, but actual happy feet. It is exactly one year since James Miller waltzed up the platform and into her life, but Maya doesn't know that fact. Today she owes the spring in her step to Nena and to Jack White, whose 'Seven Nation Army' charged her swiftly from her flat to the station in record time in ballerina flats, and whose image plays in her mind as she weaves through familiar faces as the train pulls in.

Last night, as the gig finished and Maya looked up at the ethereal and raucous raconteur standing on the monitor in front of her, holding his guitar aloft in triumph to bid her goodnight, Maya felt fierce and free and strong. And that perhaps there is life without love, because if that moment summed up her life, then she has a very good one.

The Superior Train creaks to a stop and the few Hazelworth workers get off, deliberately slowly to annoy the London-bound commuters in their haste for a seat. In her tardiness, Maya has to jump on the train halfway up, but leaps in, the full skirt of her floral 'twosie' (she coined that, too) just missing the doors as she wafts in and her tummy flashes the carriage under the gentle curve of the crop.

Close.

The train rolls out of the station and Maya keeps walking through from carriage to carriage, using her naked elbow, rather than her fingers, to press the buttons of the interior doors.

Phew, a seat.

Maya slinks into the aisle seat on a set of four with a little table separating the forward-facing two from the rear-facing two.

That was lucky.

Maya puts her new red leather tote, the same shade of red as the roses within her blooming top and skirt, on her lap and sees James Miller across the aisle. Already lost in a book. She takes a sharp intake of breath, which rolls out as a slow, dejected sigh. A girl with Chinese eyes and black hair cut into a blunt bob leans on James's reliable shoulder, and gently scratches her nose as she closes her eyes. She is comfortable, restful, secure in his company. James Miller lowers his glasses and rubs tired eyes.

The theatrical desperation and crunching guitars of 'I Just Don't Know What To Do With Myself' tear through Maya's ears and shoot straight to her heart like electric shock therapy. Suddenly, all the strength and hope she felt since last night pours into the red and green seat she's sitting on and through the carpeted floor onto the tracks. Maya sighs. And wonders without being able to hear anything beyond the music in her ears whether James Miller heard her sigh. Or his girlfriend.

I hate Kitty Jones.

Maya tries not to look but can't help herself from stealing a glance of the woman James Miller loves.

Of course he has a girlfriend, he's beautiful. She's stunning. Why would he have given me a second look?

Maya looks at the doll-like face of the woman in the short fuchsia dress with the tiers of horizontal frills dancing off her smooth light brown skin. Maya pictures the two of them entwined and gets up to walk into the front carriage up ahead.

I can't do this.

A distorted dash of roses in bloom catch James's eye as he rubs the sleep out of the inner corner. He's tired. It was a late night. He's not used to those. He's been staying in and sleeping a lot and watching DVDs and smoking weed and having a glass of red wine and then another and not really wanting to talk to people. Last night was James's first night out since Kitty left him. Dominic came into work with four tickets to a gig and James realised that he'd barely seen anything this year. When they'd finished working on hair you can whip and pubic hair you can whip off, James and Dominic walked up the road to their former agency, the one where Josie is still the receptionist, where they were joined by their 'other single friend' as Josie put it, Phil, before heading to Hammersmith.

James didn't like being put in the 'single friends' bracket. He's never been single. He doesn't know what it's like to not be part of a pair. Even over the years, when Kitty didn't seem to like James much, she was a security blanket of weekends away, arriving at parties together, and signing cards 'lots of love, James and Kitty', even if it was always James who remembered to send them. His new single life feels unfamiliar and uncomfortable. It felt especially uncomfortable sending Mrs Jones a 60th birthday card signed 'lots of love, James', but James did it. And she sent one back saying that she was so very sorry and James would always be part of their family. James knew that wasn't true. He would need to be phased out. Someone else would be going to their Boxing Day parties now. Not that he'd want to; Kitty's the last person he wants to see. By screwing him over and lying to him for most of the time since they moved to Hazelworth, she finally succeeded in making James not like her very much. But he misses her. He misses the security blanket, he misses leaning his leg over her bony hips at night. Having someone to touch, even if she did sometimes flinch.

That's why it's nice to have Josie leaning on him right now as he tries to get lost in a new book. As Josie is lulled to sleep by the wheels on the tracks and lets out that puff of air that only a person in the process of falling asleep can do, James realises Kitty hadn't been that tactile with him in a long time. He thinks back to last night. At the steamy bar upstairs at the Apollo, Josie's delicate doll-like face belied the Essex drawl and obscenities that fell out of little love-heart-shaped lips. Sympathy and kindness darted with expletives.

'I spoke to Kitty, you know,' she said. James looked away. He didn't really want to hear about it. He knows Josie and Kitty have been friends for a long time, but he didn't want to hear about nights out forging new friendships with this Simon guy.

'She wanted to know if we all hated her, whether to cut all ties with the group. Or whether we'd wanna meet Simon one day.'

James downed the rest of his warm beer. Not asking what Josie's response was, although he did want to know.

'I told her "Dominic will always have Millsy's back, he's not bothered about making new mates". I said I'd see her if we have girly nights out, but I don't wanna force anything. Anyway, she lives up in Cambridge now so it won't really happen.'

James looked at Josie and nodded his head in time to the bassline downstairs in the main room.

'She asked how you were.'

'What did you say?' James replied, finally showing interest in Josie's encounter with Kitty before shouting an order for four gin and tonics to the barman.

'I told her you were doing OK, I didn't wanna tell her we hadn't seen you. Get her knickers in a twist with drama. Feel sorry for you. You're better than that, James.' As Josie said his name, she put her tiny hand on his on the bar and squeezed it.

From Josie's tone, James suspected she wouldn't make much effort with Kitty in the future, and he felt a bit bad that it pleased him.

After the show, Phil went back to his flat in Perivale and a drunken Dominic insisted on getting the train back to Hazelworth with James.

'It's miles away, Dom!' Josie bellowed on a pavement in W6.

A ruddy Dominic was cheery to see his friend back out. 'Josie, we're going. Millsy, hail that cab!'

'But Greenwich is way nearer, you loooon!' bellowed Josie.

After one G&T too many and high on garage rock and blues, Dominic thought it would be a good idea to go back to Hazelworth and do a 6 a.m. swim in the local lido to help him train for the triathlon he will never do.

'What about Brockwell?' begged Josie, who wanted to get out of her heels and into her slippers.

'Millsy's not in Brockwell, come on, we're going to Hazelworth, keep him company!'

'Oh, this blinkin' triathlon. When are you gonna do it then, babes?'

The three of them fell into the black cab that took them all the way to the terminal. James tickled by the light-hearted row and the grand gesture of friendship disguised as pursuit of the perfect body – which Dominic often talks about but likes steak, chips and red wine too much to do anything about.

On this train, as her thick black hair sweeps into his olive neck, while the man they both love is swimming (at 8 a.m. not 6 a.m.), stinking of the glue-like toxins he emits when he's hung-over, James thinks about Josie and Dominic. Their vocal rows do disservice to the deep-rooted love and tenderness they have for each other. Warmth, laughter, conversations. And that's something James would love if he ever falls in love again.

Maya stands tall at the front of the classroom, reminding herself to stay strong. The Italian scene on the wall hasn't changed since September: no one has moved. But inside the classroom so much has changed since this cohort first met. Jan and Doug have found a property in the Alpujarras that they now have enough vocabulary to renovate. Gareth ended up sitting his GCSE Spanish while Cecily did her A Levels, and in a month's time he will find out he got an A* and she will have the grades to go to her first choice of university. Glyn is wearing a T-shirt that isn't beige. Housewife Esther seems to have uncovered a passion for flamenco dance, which she's even roped her husband Roger into joining at Hazelworth Leisure Centre on a Thursday night. Doctor Helen now knows how to treat a jellyfish sting in Spanish. Ed is going back to spend the summer in Argentina with his girlfriend Valeria before she moves to London to study politics. Nathaniel made ever such a slight improvement on his Spanish accent, while still managing to speak Castilian as if it's the Queen's English. And even Keith managed to raise a glass and say 'Salud!' after Maya poured everyone a tipple of home-made sangria to drink alongside the polvorones she had baked for the end-of-term party.

The empty chair remains. No one wanted to move Velma's seat, lest it make her death seem permanent. And now it sits there in the centre of the front row under Maya's nose, while her remaining pupils fill in their course evaluation sheets, a little light-headed from the sangria.

Maya pictures Velma boarding a plane to Miami. Being helped up the stairs. Charming the crew. Laughing alongside her fellow passengers. Showing off photos of baby Audrey. Heading to an exciting new chapter in her glorious Technicolor life.

Perhaps it's better if I imagine she's already there.

41

September 2014

'Cheers, Millsy!' says Dominic.

James clinks glasses and downs his dark rum in one.

'Good shit.'

A model drapes a long arm around James's shoulder and raises a fashionably thick eyebrow.

'Wow, you didn't waste time with that, want another?' she says in swishy Dutch tones.

'I'll get them,' says James, going to stand up, before bejewelled fingers press him, urging him to sit down from his crotch. James's rectangular glasses slide down his sun-dappled nose.

A bronzed half-Dutch, half-Peruvian goddess swaggers over to the bar, still wearing the bikini and sheer kaftan from the day's shoot, even though the sun has long since set. Dominic and James couldn't stand another hour in Pez's company, so they left him, his assistant Joe and the hair and make-up girls, back shooting pool and drinking and smoking the local produce in a beach bar on the seven-kilometre stretch of sand that runs up this western corner of Jamaica.

James hoped Lisa and Yoshie would ditch Pez's lecherous looks and clumsy chat-up lines and go and have fun without him, they were better than that, but they didn't, and he couldn't watch it any more. So James made his excuses and jumped in the taxi with Dominic to head back to the hotel on the winding rocky cliffside road away from the party. Just before the taxi door closed, a supermodel slipped in the back seat onto James's lap, even though there was space for her in the front. Two hours and four drinks later, the three of them are among the last guests in the bar at the luxe cliff-edge bolthole.

'You lucky bastard, Millsy. Lena Molina wants to knob you!' Dominic looks like a kid at Christmas, happy that his friend is getting this kind of attention, envious that, just like when they were at uni, when James wasn't the single one, or interested in girls other than Kitty, Dominic is again overlooked for his taller, quieter, less charming buddy. Not that Dominic would ever cheat on Josie. Fiercely loyal to his friend, fiercely loyal to his girlfriend.

James blushes and pushes his glasses back up the bridge of his nose as they both look to the woman standing at the timber and thatched hotel bar. Dip-dyed hair starts brown at Lena's crown and turns gold as it waves down to the middle of her back, finishing like spun sugar on a deliciously pert bottom. Long lean legs that could wrap twice around Dominic's stout frame glisten and reflect the fairy lights that adorn the bar. More jewellery than clothes kiss sun cream and sun-drenched skin. James and Dominic have seen a lot of Lena Molina's body over the past few days shooting the Femme campaign. Dominic can't believe his mate is about to see even more.

Lena saunters back, perched on sky-high wedges, with six

shot glasses teetering in large unsteady hands. She puts them on the wooden table on the edge of an artfully lit cove.

'Here. Let's have some fun!' she says, thrusting two shots into James's hands and nodding at Dominic to help himself *if you must* as she plonks the rest down. An inconvenience at the table.

Dominic knows James has never slept with a supermodel, so he graciously takes Lena's hint and makes his excuses.

'Mate, they're all yours,' he says, nudging the shot glasses back across the table so they all sit temptingly in front of James. Six soldiers leading him to his doom.

Lena smiles, that's exactly what she wanted to happen.

'Night night, Damian,' she says with a dazzling white smile.

Dominic is too embarrassed to correct her, as if he didn't feel insignificant enough already.

Lena slides in closer to James and drapes a long angular arm over his strong tanned shoulder. She's used to getting what she wants.

'Here's an idea,' says Alex, taking a sip of a skinny soy latte. 'I had a meeting with Gina from FASH+ yesterday, and she said sales of plus-size clothes are going through the roof right now – so why don't we do a late summer beach story focusing on big girls?'

Maya bursts into the meeting room, 1.1, carrying a tray of pastries from the canteen.

'Sorry I'm late, breakfast anyone?'

Cressida looks at her Rado watch but doesn't say a thing.

'Don't mind if I do,' says Emma, plucking a pain au raisin out from the basket and enjoying her new curves. They suit her too.

'My *big* big sister is rinsing my staff discount code lately,' pipes up Chloe mid-doodle. 'She says FASH+ is the only big girl's brand that is bang on trend.'

Olivia scratches her chin with a shiny sharp red talon.

'Really?' snarls Cressida.

'Well most twenty-something girls don't take *their* holidays during the school holidays,' continues Alex. 'So a FASH+ holiday wardrobe story on the home page would feel double approximate appropes right now, since kids are back at school and FASH+ is flying,' he says, peering over horn-rimmed glasses at his colleagues around the desk as his idea starts to take hold. Liz gives a deferential nod.

'I guess holiday clothes are harder to cram into a carry-on when there's so much bloody material in FASH+ sizes,' ponders Cressida, click click clicking her FASH branded pen on and off as she looks out of the window.

'I'm off to Ibiza next week,' says Olivia, ignoring Cressida's obvious disgust; excited by Alex's suggestion. 'I would be willing to do a beach edit while I'm away. I could get my mates to style up the pics, put nice filters on it.'

Cressida's face falls. 'Nope. Sorry. I'm all for championing big girls, Olivia, but no matter what filter you use, they just don't look good on the home page.'

Maya does an internal groan and feels upset for Olivia, before her mind wanders to the tiny frame of Kitty Jones, who she hasn't seen since the day after Jack White when she was curled into James Miller's arm. Maya hasn't seen James Miller much either. The odd morning here and there, not at all in the past week. Since seeing him with his girlfriend, Maya vowed to create some distance, to get on at a different carriage, because it hurts too much to see him. But despite knowing that this is the sensible thing to do, she misses Train Man terribly.

James rubs two bleary eyes and tries to focus through the white swathes of mosquito net that surround his four-poster bed. Impaired by short-sightedness and rum, he rolls out of his side of the bed and perches on the edge, focusing on the white flip-flop lines on his bronzed feet beneath him. He looks across at the other side of the bed as he stretches and slinks across the villa to open the cabaña doors that look out to sea. The sun is only just rising and yesterday's flat jade waters have turned grey and moody as waves bubble and foam towards the rocks of the cliff edge and the wooden parasol at the end of his own private promontory. Sea air offers regeneration and James stretches out his arms and inhales the taste of a heavy night. A chest expands, a heart sinks. James looks back into the pristine luxury of the suite he has sullied to see his camera sitting on the bed next to where he slept fitfully. It gives him an idea.

With a wide mouth and a flat finger, James inserts contact lenses that also spent the night fizzing, then throws on faded maroon shorts, a pinstriped T-shirt and a pair of black Havaianas. With care and respect, James lifts his new camera, his first foray into digital photography with the SLR he bought for the trip, loops the strap around his neck, picks up his sunglasses and walks out of his villa. James winds on a limestone path away from the Caribbean Sea, blinking his lenses into place. He passes the infinity pool and meanders through the hotel to the restaurant. Staff are setting the breakfast tables for the early risers.

'You want breakfast, sir?' calls the soft tone of a beautiful Jamaican lilt.

James looks over at the waiter and shakes his head. 'Not

now thanks, Rico, but do you know where I can hire a moped?'

'Sure thing. Take mine,' he says, patting James on the back and rummaging in the pocket of his perfectly pressed white linen trousers for a key. 'No hire, just treat her like you would a beautiful woman, huh?' he smiles knowingly, having worked the late shift behind the bar last night as well as the early one this morning. 'Here, lemme show you.'

Rico leads James out under the fans and thatched roof of the open-sided restaurant to the parking lot beyond reception. Crisp shirt, pristine and white. Teeth so dazzling James remembers he hasn't cleaned his own.

'Take her. She's full. All cool,' he shrugs.

'Thanks mate, I'll be careful,' says James, starting the engine and lowering Wayfarers over his lenses. James feels very English and very uncool, but manages not to wobble as he turns out of the sea-edge sanctuary down the winding road towards the tourist end of town.

As James scoots, his foggy senses are awakened with the tut tut tut of the engine. Past wooden shacks with broken posts, painted in light blues, bright pinks, black gold and emerald green. He sees signs for jerk chicken, patties and Red Stripe, all painted with a thick brush and an unsteady hand. Conch shells sit by the roadside, giving James a satisfactory sense of being half a world away from the solitude of Hazelworth, away from the drudgery of MFDD, away from the shame he has felt since June.

James looks out to sea, witnessing it transform with every revolution of the moped wheel, from grey to royal blue on the horizon. By the bottom of the hill, at the town's one roundabout, the sea is now jade over a still and sandy seabed. James turns left onto the road that runs behind the beachfront hotels, along the back of the tourist strip. A portly man hoses down a hotel entrance. A white woman with dreads carries a trestle table. A moped piled high with crates of ackee overtakes James, a burst of colour peeping out of the slats in the wooden crate, wakening him further. Tourists sleep after a night of rum and reggae, and James leaves them behind as gravel stones jump gaily at his wheels and he zooms on the single lane highway out of town.

The tut tut tut of the engine chugs inland, to a road shaded by a canopy of trees where ropey vines burst down. James sees two boys playing football in the road ahead and slows down cautiously, worried that one of them might run out in front of his bike were the ball to do the same. The smaller of the two boys points at James and laughs.

'Neymar!' he says. The other boy giggles. James stops his bike, lifts his Wayfarers and laughs. In an office on the other side of the world, Maya doesn't know how James's dimples have deepened right now.

James is baffled. Charmed. Wanting to capture the boys' laughter on camera.

'Mind if I take a picture?' he says, raising his camera from around his neck.

'For sure,' says the smallest of the two, giving a little flourish of footwork over the ball as he does. Suddenly James remembers what it felt like to be five and not shy of showcasing your talents.

'You know Messi?' asks the older boy, more serious than his brother.

'Not personally, I'm afraid. I'm from England.'

'Then you Rooney!' laughs the smaller one, losing control of the ball as he giggles.

'Nope, not as rich.'

The boys stop playing football long enough for James to take a few shots. He shows them their pictures on the screen of his digital SLR. Both boys look with pride.

James says thank you and bids them farewell.

'I'll look out for you boys in the Champions League!' he says with a smile.

'Bye Wayne Rooney!' the boys shout in unison cheekily and laugh, clutching their bellies.

James restarts the engine on Rico's bike and heads further on the sun-dappled road under the lush green canopy.

A rumble in his stomach reminds him what time of day it is and that he ought to get back for breakfast, for the final day of shooting Lena Molina for Femme. He drives past a wooden sign painted in thick black brush strokes. It says: Miss Delilah's Great Tasting Patties. The word SECRET bursts out of a red love heart and James knows he has to stop.

He turns off the engine, kicks out the stand, and walks into an open-sided building with a wood and tin roof. A large woman with short grey hair and pendulous breasts sitting atop the waist of a blue cotton skirt walks over to James.

'You wanna eat or just coffee?'

The smell of Blue Mountain coffee and fried plantains in Miss Delilah's own kitchen out the back is too tempting for a rumbling rum-tainted tummy and James senses this is a place without a menu: you eat whatever the chef fancies making.

'Whatever you're cooking, please.'

The woman smiles and walks away.

'Are you Miss Delilah?' James calls out.

'Yah,' she says as she disappears through a multicoloured beaded curtain to start cooking James's breakfast. The room is empty, and James sits on a turquoise wooden chair, silently scrolling through his photos from the trip so far. Maybe digital is better than old-school 35mm film.

Pots and pans clink in the kitchen.

Ten minutes later Miss Delilah walks back through the beaded curtain with a plate bursting with saltfish, ackee, callaloo and fried plantains. An oily sunburst of yellows and greens certain to give James his zing back.

'Thank you, Miss Delilah.'

'You're welcome,' she sings in a smooth voice that dances up and down an octave. She walks away to fetch coffee then returns and pulls up a chair at James's table. 'Where you from?'

'London.'

Miss Delilah takes a sip of what looks like a glass of squash but is mango nectar.

'What's a handsome man like you doin' out here on ya own?'

'I'm here for work. Just having a little wander, taking some photos before we go back to the beach to do a photo shoot.' James feels embarrassed about how easy his life is, given that his office today is a seven kilometre stretch of sand, but then he realises it is for most people who live around here.

'Most boys like you come here on honeymoon but I don't see no ring.'

James blushes. 'Nope, no bride.'

Miss Delilah's lined face crumples in surprise. 'You don't have a girlfriend?' she sings.

James shakes his head.

'My niece Violet lives in London. You should see her – boom – she is beautiful.'

James thinks the way Miss Delilah said all of the syllables of 'beautiful' was beautiful.

'I'm sure she is.'

Miss Delilah watches James eat. Her serene and kindly face makes him feel comfortable, not self-conscious. The lace tablecloth and ramshackle kitchen remind James of his grandmother's house – although geckos don't climb the walls at breakfast in Kent.

'You wanna take a photo of me? Tell the world about Miss Delilah?'

'I'd love to,' James says, tucking into the mysterious scrambled-egg-like texture of a tropical fruit. 'Thanks.'

'Great, when you're done, we'll do it in front of my sign. Take it to Violet, show her I'm healthy.'

'Will do.'

42

'I put myself on the line there, Maya. Being photographed in a size 24 swimsuit isn't something I would do just because I want three million women to see how fat I am...' Olivia jabs at her computer keyboard with a sharp talon as she tries to get her machine to restart. A kaleidoscopic pinwheel of doom enrages her further.

'I know, Olivia. You're a brilliant, beautiful, fierce woman – and Cressida can't handle you. She doesn't know what to do with all that sass of yours. It was a brave suggestion.'

'It was a fucking refreshing suggestion. Good for Alex. If sales of FASH+ clothes are going through the roof, then at some point Cressida is going to have to start acknowledging the fact that big girls are our customers too – and big girls need representing on the home page!'

Maya types in her password and opens up 'Trending Trousers' – the file she had been wanting to work on for the hour and a half she was stuck in the meeting, going round in circles again with Cressida.

'I know. But Cressida's a body fascist, she won't ever get it.'

'But it's dangerous, Maya. I've seen the way she looks at Emma lately, as if having a baby is disgusting.'

Maya couldn't help but notice too – since Emma has been looking pleasingly pregnant, Cressida has made a few comments about her size and how she ought to 'rein in the whole eating for two thing'.

'I'll talk to Lucy,' says Maya, leaning over to press a short-cut on Olivia's keyboard that gets everything working again.

'You're a genius,' Olivia winks. 'What would we do without you, Maya?'

James sits on the beach watching pale gold sand trickle through the gap between his big toe and its neighbour. Once the last of the grains has trickled through he starts all over again, scooping a pile up onto his toes and watching it slide away.

He puts a hand on his brow to his eyes while he gazes out to sea, much calmer than it was at sunrise. Flat, clear, turquoise once more.

Lisa and Yoshie are drinking colourful cocktails as they sit on the seafloor in the shallows, grateful to James and Dominic for giving them the best hair and make-up gig anywhere in the world right now. James is comforted by the distant sound of their laughter but doesn't listen to what they're saying to each other. He hears a familiarly ungainly gait approach from behind.

'He's just left for the airport, the mother of all hissy fits.'

James's gaze is unbroken, he keeps looking out to sea.

'He said he was used to my sniping and bitching, but when you gave him shit, enough was enough. *He's* the talent apparently, and he doesn't like being questioned.'

'Fuck him then, I'll take the photos,' says James, snapping out of a daydream. 'Joe can assist. I was just suggesting a better angle. And if I know you can't shoot a portrait straight into the glaring sun and Pez doesn't, then he's not much of a talent.'

Dominic's little circle of a mouth sits open in shock. He's never heard James be so feisty at work. Or out of it.

'And we're not paying him, he's been nothing but a pain in the arse. He walked out on the job. He didn't fulfil his part of the contract.'

Dominic nods and sits down next to James on the sand. 'Where's Lena Molina?'

James looks back out to sea. 'When Pez stormed off, Lena realised she ought to have a tantrum too, so I guess she's gone to powder her ego.'

'What happened with you two anyway? Why will she only deal with me today? She's barely talked to me all trip. Until now. Although she's still calling me Damian...'

'She couldn't understand why I didn't want to take her back to my cabaña last night.'

'James, why the fuck *didn't* you take her back to your cabaña last night? When will you ever have the chance to sleep with a supermodel again?'

James's soulful chocolate eyes look back down at the trickling sand between his toes.

'I saw her Dominic. It put me off.'

'Saw her? But have you *actually* seen her? She's so fucking beautiful, I'm too intimidated to look her in the eye, let alone tell her I'm not called Damian.'

'No, I *really* saw her. When I'm photographing someone, what I sometimes don't notice in real life I see through the lens.' Sand trickles. 'And when I looked through Pez's lens yesterday to check his shot I... I saw her. And I just didn't like her.'

Dominic exhales exasperatedly and slaps his own forehead with a meaty palm.

'That's why Pez had a strop, you kept checking his shots!'

'I suppose it's why, in eleven years, I didn't take many pictures of Kitty. She was beautiful. She was photogenic. But what I saw through the lens made me sad.'

James drops his Wayfarers from his head onto the bridge of his tanned nose to shield his eyes.

'Mate, you seem quite melancholic still. Are you OK? All this trouble-in-paradise craziness aside... I know we don't really talk about that shit, but are you OK?'

James looks at Dominic in his sun-cream-stained off-white T-shirt and black and white board shorts and smiles. 'Yes mate, totally. I'm going to be all right. It was absolutely for the best.'

'What about that bird on the train who gave you the note?'

James thinks of a gently freckled face. The curve of a smooth collarbone in a carriage full of spring optimism.

'What about her?'

'Does she still get your train?'

'I don't see her so much. Actually I think I saw her standing further back down the platform the other day.'

James's brow furrows as he wonders why Maya Flowers moved now when she hadn't changed carriage before, but he doesn't say it out loud.

'Well she's probably embarrassed. Who wouldn't be? Plus if you're not gonna sleep with a supermodel I'm guessing a stalker on the train might not be up to scratch either.'

James suddenly feels uncomfortable and shifts his position on the sand. 'What about you and Josie anyway? While we're getting all giddy on ourselves and talking about *girls*. How are things with you?'

'Ah, you know she'd love it here,' Dominic says, swerving the question.

James looks at him, expectant. He can see through Dominic; they have played, pitched and swerved together since they were eighteen.

Dominic looks back, knowing he is transparent.

'Well, you know I did want to run something past you but didn't want to bring you down when you're feeling a bit, you know...'

'Go on...'

Dominic scratches his head with a sandy hand. 'I'm thinking of asking Josie to marry me. Is that weird?'

James smiles and stands up, opening his arms. 'This is the part where I give you a manly hug. Don't leave me hanging.'

Dominic stands and loosely pats James on the back before James lifts his stocky friend off the ground.

'Soppy twat,' Dominic scolds.

'I think it's a wonderful idea. Do it.'

Arms relax around each other and James and Dominic laugh.

Lena sashays back across the sand in a white string bikini.

'Knock it off guys, is *this* what your problem is?' she shoots at James.

He looks back at her despairingly and holds his palms up to the sky.

'OK, let's get back to work,' commands Dominic, buoyed by his friend's enthusiasm. 'Joe!' he beckons to the beach bar. 'You're assisting James. Lisa, Yoshie, can you just look at Lena again, give her a quick refresh. We only have a few hours left here, let's make them count.'

43

October 2014

Cressida sits across the long oval table and looks at Olivia, Chloe and Maya on the opposite flank. For some reason, the three of them feel like they're in trouble.

'Hmmm,' Cressida ponders, her index finger tap tapping as she stares at the mood boards. 'It's not really working for me. Chloe, the design is too downmarket. You've taken good still-lifes and made the clothes look like... like... market-stall *clobber*, I think they call it. This treatment isn't working.'

Eager eyes widen in shock.

'And Olivia, these girls you've used, surely FASH didn't shoot them. *Did* FASH shoot them?' she asks in horror.

'Yes, Cress. They're all from the autumn/winter lookbook.' Olivia likes how Cressida winces when people call her Cress.

'Well they look fat. Someone needs to have a word with the model booker.'

Olivia looks down, pulls at her oversized jumper and wonders whether Cressida really is that insensitive.

'I think that's a bit harsh, Cressida,' pipes up Maya, outrage overriding intimidation, knowing that under Maya's direction, Chloe and Olivia have been pulling some serious late nights to get these designs to Cressida on deadline. Chloe and Olivia silently cheer.

'Excuse me?' Cressida's razor-cut cheekbones raise with her hackles. Maya doesn't reply. 'Maya, if this isn't working then I'm not putting my name to it. We have to make FASHmas work harder. In fact I think it's indicative that we need to totally switch FASHmas up this year.'

'Switch FASHmas up?' Maya's freckled nose crinkles. *What does that even mean?*

'I think FASHmas is looking a little tired under your tenure, Maya, so I'm going to be the figurehead for it this year. Freshen it up. Make it sharp. Make it savvy. Make it cool again.'

'"Make it cool again"?' Maya's distaste gives her voice a little wobble, and suddenly she sounds as intimidated as she is outraged.

'You've done it for what, two years? I think it's time to give it a fresh pair of eyes. I've spoken to Lucy, she's already on board.'

'So this is an ambush then, Cressida. If you'd already decided you weren't going to go with Chloe and Olivia's look and my tone of voice, why did you have us working so hard on a concept? That's a lot of wasted hours.'

'Deal with it!' Cressida sings, collecting the mood boards from the centre of the table and dumping them against the little wire bin on her way out.

A door slams.

Chloe starts to cry.

Olivia is incandescent with anger.

'Did she just fucking do what I think she did?' Red hair turns to flames. 'How dare she!'

Maya tries to rally spirits. 'Girls I've seen this before at Walk In Wardrobe. She's a bully. Nothing we would have done would have been good enough. You're both brilliant at your jobs and what you produced wasn't right for Cressida and her designer delusions or Game of Sloane's politics – but it was right for FASH. You did good. But annoyingly it's her call, *she's* the editor. We'll just have to grit our teeth and go along with it. Smile and wave. See what Lucy thinks come New Year.'

'I hope she fucking shoots herself in the fucking Chelsea boot,' says Olivia with a riled smirk.

Maya's calm exterior belies livid anger bubbling beneath.

'Lucy can I have a word please?'

The Ecuadorian cleaner starts to vacuum nearby and Lucy looks jangled from two directions.

'Yeah, I have to leave in five minutes, my nanny is going on a date. Bit selfish...' she jokes.

Maya smiles, light relief from the issue she's about to raise. Everything seems more unnerving in this corner of the building, by the plush offices of Lucy, Rich and Rich.

'Erm, excuse me, can you come back in ten minutes?' Lucy snaps at the cleaner, who meekly wheels her Henry hoover away and turns it off. 'Can't hear myself think,' she says, looking back at her screen and tugging her butter-blonde bob.

Maya waits patiently, nervously, and notices Lucy looks more frazzled than usual.

The office is quiet, and the only other voice Maya can hear is Rich Robinson's muted tones as he goes through his diary with his PA on the other side of another glass wall.

Maya stands gawkily at Lucy's desk.

'I wanted to talk to you about Cressida.'

Lucy looks away from her screen and up at Maya.

'Sit down.' She gestures for Maya to take a chair. 'What did you want to say?'

'She's really causing upset among the team, Lucy. Saying really personal stuff to Olivia, totally diminishing the confidence of the team, coming up with crazy ideas that just aren't on brand... Some of the team have been coming to me saying they're really upset.' Maya feels sweat trickle down the small of her back into the base of her silk blouse.

'"Really upset?"' scoffs Lucy, before round, wise eyes soften a little. 'Maya this isn't high school. This is work. I thought you were bigger than that.'

Maya is silenced. Her moment of boldness quashed. Speaking up for nothing. 'I... I am... I just thought you might want to know...'

'Are you sure you're not just sore about Cressida getting the job?'

'Me? Not at all! I didn't really want the job.'

'It kind of showed, Maya.' Lucy looks back at her screen and doesn't bother to pretend she isn't reading an email.

Maya feels betrayed, by Lucy, by herself.

'Well then you have to believe that I'm not talking from a jealous point of view. I'm just worried for the team. She's ruffled lots of feathers, not just mine.'

Lucy continues to look at her screen while nodding, as if she's listening.

I've blown it now, I may as well go the whole hog.

'It's not just Cressida. Something has changed here. I'm not sure whether it was before the bonuses scandal or after, but people used to be happy. They used to be proud. Even the models on the walls don't look happy any more,' Maya tries to joke.

Lucy stands and packs her phone and her tablet into her bag.

'Oh, please Maya. Don't be so soft. It's business. You didn't get a bonus. You didn't get a job. This is one of the biggest fashion empires in the world. If you're not feeling proud to work here then you can always go back to Walk In Wardrobe. Or I heard Wicked Style were recruiting. I don't have time for this, I need to get home for the nanny.'

Lucy wraps herself in a petrol-blue funnel coat and charges out of the office, down the corridor to the glass double doors by the empty canteen.

Maya is floored. What happened to the best boss she ever had? What happened to the best job she ever had?

Maybe it is *me.*

Maya stands on weak knees and smooths her skirt down as she gathers herself and starts walking back to her desk.

Rich Robinson exits his office with such swagger he overtakes her in his Cuban heels.

'Working late tonight, Matilda?'

'Oh you know... Always dedicated to FASH!' Maya musters and looks at the back of his annoying-shaped head as he skips out.

On the train home Maya opens her dented laptop and starts writing. Words tumble, notes form. Notes about what it's like to work at FASH. Notes on the excitement, the perks, the friendliness, the fun when she first arrived. Notes on how the models used to glide down the stairs in their terry-towel dressing gowns, from the canteen to the studio, proud to be modelling for the world's largest fashion retailer. Notes on how Sam and the tech team seemed like they had the best jobs in the digital world. Notes on how a young designer full of excitement and ideas was made to cry in a meeting, all her effervescence and enthusiasm knocked out of her in one sharp swoop. The countryside outside blackens and words spill onto white rectangles as Maya thinks back and wonders at what point FASH turned from a happy place to somewhere where people can be made to feel so awful.

Maya ponders how a company that makes £68,000 per minute can stop giving staff small bonuses, or at least leave a token bottle of Prosecco on employees' desks at Christmas, many of whom are starting out on a first-job minimum-wage salary. Maya writes down all the Cressida-isms – the cruel things she has said to the team. The negative reactions to people's brave ideas. Her comments about people's body shape. Her disgust and disdain for FASH's own customers, the people who keep them all employed.

As the train jolts and the late workers head homeward-bound, steam emanates from Maya's keyboard, and so consumed is she that she doesn't even notice James watching her from the middle of the carriage.

44

A vacant stool sits in a studio while James tests his flashbulbs against the mottled grey backdrop he rolled down behind it at 6.30 a.m. It's now 8 a.m. and this is James's first booking as a freelance photographer through his agent at Kaye-French. It's not his dream gig – portraits of big cheeses at an asset management firm in the City – but given that fat cats work an earlier day than advertising creatives, it was a booking James could fit in before his day at MFDD starts. A trail of portly men and the occasional woman have steadily passed through the studio, and James is surprised by how many of them he liked through the lens and enjoyed talking to while they sat nervously, out of their comfort zone. The first subject was quite unforgiving when James's digital SLR ran out of battery and he had a 6.45 a.m. conference call to get to, but James was so annoyed with himself, his heartfelt apology meant that headshot #1 (Harold Leaver, Investment Portfolio Manager) cooled a little. James has that effect on people. That's how James has done so well in a career in advertising, despite not being able to talk the talk. Dominic does the bullshit, James backs it up with quiet authority.

Next up on his call sheet is headshot #12, Miriam Wallace, Assistant Vice President.

'Morning,' she says, exactly on time. She walks in, sits on the stool and fidgets.

'Morning,' smiles James, trying to put her at ease.

Miriam has soft beige hair framing a tense, lined face. She undoes a button on an ill-fitting blazer and looks nervously into the lens. She was busting balls in the Frankfurt office via Skype fifteen minutes ago and now she feels vulnerable.

'This won't take long, just try to relax.'

'I don't relax.' Miriam refastens her jacket button and feels the pinch of last night's seven-course dinner hosting her New York counterpart.

'What have you got in store for the rest of the day?' asks James, making chit-chat as he sees some softness through the lens.

'I'm firing someone in Geneva as soon as this is over,' Miriam replies without a hint of irony.

'Oh dear, sorry.'

'I'm not sorry, he's incompetent.'

Saggy lids hang over dispassionate eyes. James doesn't want to take a picture he knows Miriam Wallace will hate every single time she walks past it in reception, however much she would pretend that vanity is beneath her.

The studio goes quiet. James examines Miriam.

'What was the best thing that happened to you all week?'

'What?'

Miriam is taken aback. No one in this building would think or dare to ask her a question like that.

'What was the best thing that happened to you this week?'

Miriam touches soft hair while she thinks.

'My daughter. My daughter got back from Australia on Saturday. She was gone a year.'

Click.

Ever since Velma died, Sundays have made Maya feel somewhat empty. But this Sunday, what feels like it might be the last sunny Sunday of the year, calls for a morning run to get Maya up and out and to stop her feeling lost. Later today, Nena and Tom are finally coming to Hazelworth, so Maya decides to get out early so she can spend the morning baking up a storm for their long-awaited visit.

Maya sits on the black and white chequered tiles of the hallway floor and laces up her trainers. Two rectangles of stained glass let the morning light shine down on her shins and as she flexes her heels to lace up her left trainer she notices definition. A satisfying dip between shin bone and muscle that empowers her.

Maya stands, straightens her running tights up over her waist and pulls a long-sleeved lime green top down over a thin running vest. Beyond the stained glass the sky is tinged with pink hues and sympathy.

Maya runs the short path, turns right, then right again at the end of the road, over the roundabout with the gastro pub with the hanging baskets, that looks like a large selection box of something tasty sitting on the corner. Tired eyes adjust to the light as Maya focuses on the musings she was writing until 1 a.m. on a Saturday night. An Insider's Guide To FASH. As Maya runs down a Roman road with grand houses on one side and tiny terraces on the other, she wonders why she stayed up so late writing it: it's not a style guide, it's not helpful. It's gossipy, it's negative, it's an exposé. But that doesn't matter because it felt cathartic and no one will ever read it. At the end of the Roman road, fuchsia flashes on Maya's trainers as she bears right onto an unspectacular thoroughfare that looks like it could be a through road in any suburban town in this country. Petrol station. Takeaway shops. A grocery store. Houses built in the 1930s, a vet's clinic. But it's a means to a park, where grand gates sweep open to let Maya in.

Tall copper beeches punctuate a path with a white line painted down the middle of it before the path snakes to the left of a large expanse of grass. One side of the path has an illustration of a man wearing a hat, striding with purpose, the other side has a picture of a bicycle. Maya stays on the side with the walking figure on it, even though there aren't any commuters whizzing through the park to the train station at 8 a.m. on a Sunday. Maya starts to find her stride, using the line as a tow to regulate her pace. A dog walker, in the middle of the field, leads an ageing Rottweiler towards the banks, at the far right of the park, against the train track obscured by tall elms. A man wearing a waterproof jacket even though it isn't raining helps a little girl learn to ride without stabilisers. A woman does tricep dips on the bench by the path's edge. The rest of Hazelworth is sensibly still asleep.

Thump, puff, thud. Maya hears the feet of a faster runner coming up the path behind her and obviously moves to one side so the runner can pass her without impediment, or the feeling that Maya is being competitive. One of the unspoken rules in the Running Code that Maya learnt from Herbert Flowers along with Nodding, Never Getting Too Close and Not Spitting, not that she ever did that of course.

The faster runner's pace slows on his or her approach. He or she has chosen not to overtake, which throws Maya because she was adhering to The Code and making it clear that she was Happy To Be Overtaken. As Maya's lungs strengthen and her cadence becomes more confident, she decides to speed up a little to shake off the runner who isn't adhering to The Code. It shouldn't annoy her but it does.

I would have been overtaken. Now I feel under pressure to go faster.

Maya's irked mind flashes to Cressida and she tries to remember the name of the intern Cressida bullied at Walk In Wardrobe, the one who pretended to be run over by a bus rather than come back to work with her. As feet hasten, a name escapes her, but Maya can picture eyes wide with wonder and expectancy on the cusp of a career in fashion. Bullied out by a few off-the-cuff but oh-so-cutting comments that weren't even dwelled upon by their deliverer.

Maybe the intern whose name I can't remember wasn't tough enough to work in fashion either.

Maya speeds up again as she follows the curve of the path, leaving the tree-lined avenue at the entrance of the park and turning into something less defined. A rough track laps around the expanse of grass, heading into hidden nooks and bushes, and a weeping willow by a brook. Maya wonders why her feet chose this route today now that the footsteps following make her feel under duress. Sometimes Maya runs in the countryside, to the hills that frame Hazelworth in its bowl, sometimes through the town itself, zig-zagging the roads that lead off the market square and back again. Sometimes she runs up to Herbert and Dolores's house on the hill, so she can say hello, wave goodbye, then run back down with Hazelworth stretched out before her. Her town. Her home. Her sanctuary.

Why did I run this route today?

Maya needed to run in circles around the park, where she wouldn't need to think about her pace or her route or her surroundings or whether it was too early to wake her parents. She just wanted to think about what she wrote last night. What she was going to bake for Nena and Tom (she's even thinking of some kind of macaron tower as today has a special occasion feel about it) and how she should approach work tomorrow morning. If she's being edged out of FASHmas, is it time to look for a new job?

Still hearing the footsteps behind her, suddenly Maya is aware of how few people are around. That Rottweiler looks hopeless, and the man with the girl is so engrossed in scooping up his daughter after each enthusiastic fall that Maya doesn't think he would even hear her scream. A quick glance back, while adhering to the Eye Contact rule Herbert Flowers taught her: never make eye contact with a male runner if you don't feel one hundred per cent certain that he's not a murderer.

Too fleeting. Maya could only just gauge the height of a slender man with light brown hair. Maya tries to peel away, except now she's on the path that laps the edge of the park by the hidden railway track, there's nowhere to peel away to. The once-kind morning sky has turned grey and gloomy clouds loom. Perhaps the man in the waterproof jacket was onto something.

Go.

Maya's feet are moving faster than her legs can handle and as she revs up her revolutions she trips on a root of the willow tree and tumbles into nettles on one side of the path.

'Owww!'

The runner in pursuit trips on Maya's foot, jutting out onto the path, and falls deeper into the nettles, stinging his arm and scuffing his knees.

'Jesus!' huffs Maya, angrily, dusting off twigs and berries from lime-green sleeves.

'I'm so sorry.' A red face rises. 'I just wanted to know if it was you,' says a man who looks like a boy. A face with more freckles than the spaces between them blushes. 'It *is* you!'

'What?' Maya scowls, bending and flexing her ankle gingerly to see how serious her fall was.

'Maya Flowers? Remember this? Pretty familiar scene, although we used to do it among the silver birches.'

Maya feels stalked and uncomfortable and angry that this man made her feel scared when she usually feels strong when she's running.

'You made me fall over,' she says, still unpicking berries from her clothes.

Maya looks up and sees his face. The face of a boy she used to know. Blue eyes. Light brown hair. Freckles. A checked bomber jacket with a sheepskin collar long since recycled or turned to rags. His hair used to curl over and kiss the sheepskin collar but now it is cropped and short – but Maya can see an eleven-year-old face looking at her with delight.

'Pip? Pip Smith?'

'Maya Flowers. You used to slow down for me in kiss chase – you're faster now,' he laughs.

'That's not funny, you scared me.' Maya's anger turns to relief, and with a little sigh and a whisper of a laugh, the tension flows away like the blood running down Pip's knee.

Pip Smith was the sweetest boy in the playground. Always sticking up for people. Always inventing new games. Always running faster, jumping higher and climbing dizzier heights just to impress Maya. Always drawing pictures for Maya after school, then taking a folded piece of paper out of his pocket the next morning and watching Maya's face as she opened it, to see if she liked the Ninja Turtle or Simba the lion cub or the self-portrait of Pip doing judo. Sometimes Pip used to draw Maya as a princess in Cinderella-esque ball gowns. Maya liked Pip's drawings. And she did secretly slow down for Pip in kiss chase too.

Pip extends a hand to help Maya up. 'I really am very sorry. I didn't mean to scare you. I just saw this flash of familiarity and had to know if it was you. I've been back in Hazelworth for a week and I hadn't recognised anyone until I saw you.'

'Hmmm, that's OK,' says Maya, letting Pip take her weight in his hands as he pulls her up by the arm. 'But a word of advice. Never. Ever. Chase a girl in the park if she's not expecting it. Kiss chase in the silver birches when you're eleven is one thing, but that was just creepy.'

'I'm sorry. Look, why don't we run a circuit or two of the park together – if our legs work.'

Maya looks doubtful.

'I'll protect you from evil Shredder or Uncle Scar,' Pip jokes with a bashful smile.

'Well, OK...' says Maya. Quietly relieved to see a friendly face from the past.

'You made that?'

'Yes!'

'It's beautiful. A work of art. You really ought to sell these, Maya, they look as pretty as Pierre's.' Nena slides her phone out of her pocket to take a photo of a conical tower covered artfully in pale lilac, pale pink and pale yellow circles of lavender, rose and lemon.

'Hmmm, don't look too closely, a few cracked as I stuck

them on,' says Maya, downplaying how pleased she is with her first attempt.

'Can I taste one?'

'Of course! I made them for you guys.'

'I know, but it feels criminal to break into something so beautiful.'

Maya lifts the cone and cautiously moves it along the kitchen counter to place it in front of Nena.

'I think I need to cover the base with some pretty wrapping paper or something, polystyrene doesn't look that tempting, but I ran out of time,' Maya shrugs. 'Google macaron towers and you'll get the idea...' Maya motions to her laptop on the little breakfast counter in the corner where Tom is sitting, and he presses a button to wake the machine.

'Oh my god, amazing!' Nena says with yellow crumbs around her lips and a pale lilac circle of deliciousness in her hand.

'Here, try a rose one too.' Maya watches Nena's face, eagerly awaiting feedback, and both girls go quiet as they eat.

Nena turns to Tom, wondering why her fiancé hasn't said anything about the beauty beholding them in the kitchen. Tom is leaning against the breakfast bar, shoulders up to his ears and chin resting in his palms while he looks at Maya's laptop.

'Did you find a picture?' Maya asks. 'Some of them are just stunning...' Maya notices Tom is lost in something other than Pinterest boards, and she feels a rising panic.

'Hang on!' pounces Maya, embarrassed by what Tom may have read. 'I need to save something,' she lies, sharply turning the laptop away from Tom.

'Maya, did *you* write that?' Tom asks.

Maya's cheeks flush. She's not sure what to say but feels a

little intruded upon by this man she doesn't really know. She doesn't want their visit to turn sour, it took so long for Tom and Nena to leave Islington for the depths of the Shire, so she stays quiet so as not to cause upset. Flustered, embarrassed, exposed.

'It's brilliant! So funny. And shocking. Is that what it's like to work at FASH?'

'What is it?' asks Nena, a rose macaron bursting from raspberry lips.

'What about the taste?' asks Maya, closing the lid of her laptop in order to gloss over its contents. 'I think the lavender flavours could be stronger, no?'

'I'm sorry Maya, I didn't mean to look,' says Tom with a twinkle. 'It was just there on screen. But I saw the hook and was reeled in. Which is testament to how great a piece of writing it is. You should publish that.'

'Publish WHAT?!' shouts Nena, little dot of pink landing on Tom's cream cable-knit jumper.

Maya rolls her eyes and hands Nena the laptop reluctantly. 'Don't judge OK? I don't mean to be bitchy, it's just a private little rant. Well it was meant to be private anyway,' she says, looking at Tom.

'Sorry,' he mouths with a disarming smile.

'Oh I *love* Bitchy Maya!' says Nena, eyes widening with glee as she plonks herself down on Tom's lap. 'I see her so rarely but when I do… she's a tiger!' Nena giggles and turns to Maya's words. Tom wraps his arms around Nena's waist while both of them read.

Maya boils the kettle, wanting the ground to swallow her up.

A few minutes later Nena's face rises. 'I thought you were happy there?'

Maya pours tea into three handless cups with sunbeams on the side.

'I was, but something changed. All the good things about FASH seemed to turn bad. So I just started writing a few notes about it really. Mainly to get it off my chest so I don't bring anyone else down at work.'

'I really think you should publish it. This is brilliant insider intel that loads of people would enjoy,' says Tom, pale eyes looking warm.

'If anyone read that then I'd just look like a bitter employee. Someone who isn't talented enough for promotion. And it's underhand.'

'It's very funny,' counters Tom. 'And you wouldn't have to know it was FASH. There must be a few companies like that, I reckon people would love to know what it's like to work at any of those fashion giants.'

'Come on, Maya, this guy is good at sniffing out talent,' Nena says with a wink. Tom tightens his embrace around Nena's waist and smiles. Proud, besotted, happy.

Tom releases one arm so he can rub his bald head as he thinks. 'I have a friend at the *Standard*, she'd love to read this, I'm sure. She's always asking me about new talent for columns, she wanted a newsreader contact of mine to do one...'

'Which newsreader, baby?' asks Nena, equally proud and besotted and happy.

Tom carries on. 'I think you could write a brilliant column about FASH. From what Nena tells me, it's a crazy place to work. Would you mind if I mentioned you to her?'

Tom's eyes pierce Maya and she finds it hard to say no. Maya gets the feeling that if Tom thinks something will work then it probably will.

'But it's not like anyone has done anything bad – not really bad anyway – it's just office politics,' she counters.

'Yeah, but it's this kind of office politics that fascinates people. A bitchy boss. The fashion vernacular. Models eating fry-ups. It's the little titbits people like to read about and get lost in on their commute. They pay handsomely at the *Standard* too.'

'Hmmm,' ponders Maya, taking the most cracked macaron, a dusty pink one, from the conical tower so no one else has to eat it. 'See what your friend at the paper thinks – but if she wants to discuss it further I'd need anonymity, Tom. It's my job. I need to pay the mortgage.' Maya bites the macaron in her left hand and creates a whirlpool of Earl Grey with the spoon in her right hand. 'Anyway it's Sunday. Can we not talk about work today please? I have funny news.'

'Pip Smith?! The kid in the sheepskin bomber?' Clara's eyes widen. 'I *totally* remember him. He was really cute. Didn't he draw your face on a Ninja Turtle's body or something? Bit weird... But he was a sweet kid. I remember he had a little snub nose and tons of freckles.'

'No! It was my face on *Wonder Woman's* body.'

'Well either way I think you should go for a drink with him. Now *that's* a romantic story. Not a guy you don't know on the train who could be a serial killer.'

'Aunty Maya, another another!' says Oscar, Maya's youngest nephew, tugging at the hem of her tea dress. A scarf hangs around her neck and at each end of it a two-year-old attempts to scale his aunt.

'James Miller is not a serial killer.'

'Aunty Maya! Aunty Maya!' Oscar hangs, pulling Maya towards him from the sofa to the floor.

'Watch out, young man, or the kiss monster will get you!' Maya says, diving down on top of Oscar and nestling into his naked pot belly. Wet giggles tumble out from behind milk teeth.

'Biscuit! I want another Aunty Maya biscuit!' Oscar demands, from the depths of a carpet bundle.

Clara sits on the sofa curled up with a cup of tea. The first one she's had all day that wasn't cold when she started drinking it.

'They're called macarons, Osky. And that's up to your mother.'

Maya popped around to Clara's house to drop off the leftover lilac, pink and yellow macarons, not realising that 6 p.m. on a Sunday evening is probably the worst time you can bestow sugary treats upon three children aged six, four and two.

'One more and that's it!' commands Clara. As soon as the exclamation comes out of her mouth, two slightly larger pairs of feet come pattering into the cosy front room to claim their 'one more' too.

A little blond boy and a slightly bigger brown-haired boy with similar faces stand in front of their mother.

'What do you want, boys?' asks Clara, knowing exactly what they want.

'Aunty Maya's biscuits,' they chime.

'They're macaronnnnnns!' Maya says through the raspberries she's blowing on Oscar's tummy. He laughs so hard Clara is relieved that her baby is still in nappies.

'They're yummy, Aunty Maya,' says Henry, the oldest, matter-of-factly.

'Yes, absolutely yummy, Aunty Maya,' says Jack concurring.

'Thank you,' they chime, and walk out of the room back upstairs to their bedtime game of lining up all their dinosaurs on one side of their bedroom and all of their superheroes on the other side of the room facing them.

'So, Pip Smith. This is encouraging,' says Clara, an expert at drifting from parenting to gossip and back again. 'Is he still cute?'

'Well I only saw him in his running gear, but he looked pretty good. Taller than he was when we were eleven, which is a plus.' Maya blows more raspberries into Oscar, giggling, adoring, hyperventilating on the rug. She breaks away, hovering teasingly over a shattered boy. 'But he's no James Miller.'

'Enough!' shouts Clara.

Maya is startled and picks up Oscar.

'Oh, sorry,' says Maya, straightening Oscar's pyjamas. 'I didn't mean to get him overexcited.'

'Not Oscar. Enough with James Miller. It's a non-starter. He has a girlfriend. You already know that. Gorgeous little Pip Smith is still wanting to play kiss chase with my baby sister and you're wasting your time thinking about someone you don't know, who it can't go anywhere with. Open your eyes, Maya.'

Maya concentrates on keeping her eyes wide open. If she blinks a tear will fall out. She hugs Oscar, for her comfort more than his.

'I know,' Maya whispers, still startled. 'You're right. I've already forgotten about Train Man. I'll call Pip in a couple of days.'

'Who Train Man?' asks Oscar, scuttling out of the room and upstairs to his brothers' bedroom, to see what this new public-transport-based superhero might look like.

45

Maya walks through the glass double doors and rushes to her desk. Since Cressida became site editor, she has had to 'have words' with people about their timekeeping. Not Maya yet, but Maya feels it's coming. Even though Maya often works through lunch and never leaves before 6.30 p.m., if she arrives a minute later than 9.30 a.m. she sees Cressida look at the clock on the top right-hand corner of her screen and is often met with a snide comment.

Maya couldn't even commit to teaching night school at the Hazelworth Collective College this term because of Cressida's office ethos, and she really misses the characters, the jokes, the Italian still life on the wall. When Maya is still at her desk on a Tuesday evening, she often wonders who might have been in her class this year; whether the new conversational Spanish teacher has made a friend like Velma.

Sam looks up. He's on the phone but nods hello as he talks in hushed tones in a now-quiet office. Cressida's diktat for the stereo to be turned off lives on.

'How can you be creative with tinny noise in the back-ground? It's not even good music,' she said with a curl of a full lip, and Maya wondered what type of music Cressida would listen to anyway.

Maya suggested the team could listen through their computer headphones if they wanted to work to music. Cressida banned that too.

'I'm the editor. I need to be heard at all times.'

Maya throws her bag under her desk and slides into her seat. The 8.21 pulled into the station at 8.33, giving Maya twelve minutes when she could have walked up the platform to seek out James Miller but didn't. She waited, halfway down the platform as she has anyway lately, but definitely will do from now on, near where people emerge from running the rattling gauntlet of the underpass. She stood reading her notes from the first of the spring/summer presentations after last month's New York, London, Milan and Paris Fashion Weeks. She didn't even look up when James Miller walked past, so lost was she in roomy denim, one-shoulder dresses and Obi belts.

As she disembarked at the terminal, Maya didn't look around for that familiar, reassuring back of the head that she loved to see walking with purpose ahead of her. She hotfooted it up Euston Road, across the busy intersection, past the Planetarium and left down Baker Street. One minute late.

Cressida, sitting at the best desk in the office, the desk next to the huge window that Emma gave up for her, darts her eyes to the top right-hand corner of her monitor. Maya knows she is checking the time.

9.31. Bite me.

Maya wishes Cressida hadn't made her so petty.

She slips her fluffy pink cocoon coat onto the back of her chair. Maya doesn't love the coat any more, she knows it's time to retire it since it's been hanging on the back of a *lot* of chairs at FASH HQ, but Maya is proud to have coined the term 'cocoon coat' the summer before last. The shape ended up everywhere, and no one knew what to call it until Maya had named it the Cocoon at FASH. Below the knee and wide around the middle like a big fluffy cuddle, it was obvious to Maya.

Sam finishes his phone call, and Maya swings her chair around to see him, tap, click, restarting at his desk.

'Sam,' Maya whispers. 'You going to Emma's lunch today?'

Sam swings around and Maya notices a hole on the shoulder of his Metallica T-shirt.

He nods but doesn't speak.

'I've got a card for everyone to sign. And some vouchers towards a pram. Oh, and some macarons from a tower I made yesterday...' Which reminds Maya to find a photo of it to show Sam, so she starts to scroll through her phone. 'Look, I made this!'

'Very nice,' Sam says flatly, giving Maya's phone a cursory glance.

Maya withdraws with sloping shoulders.

'Conference!' barks Cressida. And seven pairs of hesitant feet stand and shuffle listlessly into the meeting room, notebooks and laptops in hand.

'I'll just nip to the loo,' says Emma, taking her enormous low bump through the double doors and across the canteen for what will be the first of many times today.

'Right, quickly before she comes back, does anyone who hasn't yet put in for Emma's collection want to?' asks Maya, looking around the room but deliberately not at Cressida.

'Oh, I haven't signed the card yet,' says Alex, looking down the table for it through horn-rimmed spectacles. 'May I?'

Maya hands it over and Alex gets the giggles.

'Oh Chloe, that's brilliant!' he says, looking at the sixteen Photoshopped images of Emma's head on pregnant celebs' bodies.

Cressida makes no attempt to even look at the card, let alone sign it.

So mean.

Maya knows Cressida is the only person who didn't tuck a five or ten-pound note into the collection envelope, and as Emma's line manager, she ought to have given the most.

She gave you her all, she gave you her desk!

'Right, we don't have to wait for Emma's little social media update and she doesn't need to hear about FASHmas as she's buggering off anyway, so I'll get us started.' Cressida rubs statuesque hands together. 'Just a quick FASHmas update before we talk about today's celeb pics. But I'm taking over because it means so much to Lucy and the exec team, and I've had some brilliant ideas for this year. I'm presenting them to Lucy at 3 p.m.' She turns to Olivia. 'I want you working on it solidly until then, so Holly, you'll need to do pictures after conference.'

Olivia frowns. 'You're putting me back on FASHmas? You took me off it on Friday.'

'Well, I'm sorry but I didn't take that art degree over the weekend, I need a picture editor.'

Olivia tugs on her jumper and breathes a heavy sigh. 'Well I'm going to Emma's leaving lunch, but I can work on it until 1 p.m.'

'Nope, not going to happen, I'm afraid. I need you to source new images for the mood board. I can get lunch in, if eating is that important to you, but I'm sure you of all people can hold on until 3 p.m.'

Olivia is dumbstruck. Papers stop shuffling. Alex stops writing in the card and looks up.

'Me *of all people*?'

The door clicks open, Emma walks in and Alex tucks the card back under the envelope it was hidden in.

'Me *of all people*?' says Olivia matter-of-factly. 'You mean because I'm so fat I can rely on my reserves to get me through to 3 p.m., Cressida? Or because I could do with skipping a meal? What did you mean, Cressida?'

Cressida blushes, she's not used to being challenged. 'Just a joke, Olivia. Deal with it!' she says defensively, dismissively.

Emma looks at Maya to gauge what just happened. Maya shakes her head softly.

'That is so not on, on so many levels, Cressida,' says Olivia, pointing a glossy royal blue talon towards their boss. 'I will work on the mood board, as I have been for the past few weeks with Maya. But at 1 p.m. I'll go to lunch. Not because I'm greedy, but because I want to be sisterly and to wish Emma well and see her off in style.'

Emma blushes. She doesn't want to get involved. In fact she just wants to get out of the office ASAP and go on maternity leave. Maya feels a roar rising from the pit of her stomach, inflamed by injustice, gaining momentum thanks to Olivia's rebellion, but still stifled by the oppressive regime.

Olivia pushes her laptop towards Holly. 'Can you take the lead on the pictures today, Hols, I can't stomach *that*,' she says, nodding towards Cressida with sass as she stands.

'Oh, if you're going to be so sensitive don't worry about it, Olivia. I'm sure I can find a much more enthusiastic and talented freelance picture editor for FASHmas,' snaps Cressida. 'You're obviously burnt out.'

The door slams.

Cressida's face shows the awkward cocktail of embarrass-ment and defiance. 'Someone's feeling sensitive today!' she says, widening her eyes. 'Pictures please, Holly, before we waste any more time.'

Maya looks across the table at Alex and Emma doodling in their notebooks and opens her laptop. Under the guise of working double time through the morning meeting, she opens her personal mail and emails Tom.

Hi Tom,

Lovely to see you yesterday, thanks for coming. So excited about your wedding!

About your contact at the Standard... if she's interested then I'm game. It's a total joke here.

Mx

Maya presses send and feels discomfort in the pit of her stomach. She doesn't know what she's more disgusted by: what Cressida said or the fact she herself sat back and said nothing.

James stands on the steps of Mayfair Library and looks through his lens. He sees old sweethearts, people who have been in love and lost love a long time ago and fallen back in love again. He sees proud adult children, throwing pastel-coloured paper, cut in to the shapes of hearts and horseshoes and four-leaf clovers, swirling and dancing in the wind. James feels heartened. He wonders how many happy couples have walked down these steps. He is proud to capture this particular couple doing it.

Earlier, when James was standing in a window of their

mews home, taking pictures of the happy couple getting ready, he asked the groom how old he was when he had fallen in love with his bride the first time around.

Startled, a man with thinning hair and a bushy black and white stripy beard stopped tying his tie and looked at James, who dropped his lens for a second.

'How did you know we were sweethearts?'

'I saw it through the lens.'

The man turned back to admire himself in the mirror – ox-like shoulders, thick neck, tiny wise eyes behind rimless spectacles – and finished tying the tie on his Armani suit.

'You've seen her. Can you imagine what a knockout she was back then? She came from Germany on a school exchange, fifty-one years ago. I never should have let her go back.'

James smiled and raised his lens again, taking a side profile of a man who didn't look like he had many regrets.

'But it turned out good. Our families have come together beautifully. You'll meet our grandkids later.' Eyes like currants turned back to look at James. 'She was worth waiting for, son,' he said with a wry smile.

On the steps after the ceremony, James lowers his lens and bends his knees to capture small children with ruddy cheeks in pretty coats. A little girl asks Oma to pick her up. A woman with sleek silver hair, artfully coiffed back to a point at the base of a long tanned neck, picks up her granddaughter. Her new husband nestles in and the little girl snuggles into his badger beard. A shake of his head tickles the little girl and a belly laugh tumbles down the grandeur of South Audley Street on the tail of a wind.

46

'Is this OK?'

Pip Smith cautiously pulls out a little armchair at a table for two, next to a huge arched window looking out onto an Indian summer's evening over Hazelworth.

'Great,' smiles Maya. It is the bar area of the restaurant she spent New Year's Eve with her siblings. If Maya looks over to the noisy restaurant area, lit by stainless-steel pendants and the flares of the sizzling steak pan in the open kitchen, she can see the table where Velma sat with Christopher, Conrad and Madison. Maya's heart drops.

'You want to sit somewhere else?' Pip asks nervously.

'No, it's fine, Pip, really,' says Maya, putting on her happy face. She doesn't want to bring the evening down. And the room is so full of hope this Saturday night.

'What are you having?'

'French Martini, please,' Maya says with a smile, propping herself up in her chair.

'I'll just get them, back in a sec.'

Pip heads eagerly to the bar and Maya looks around. She sees some friends of Jacob and Florian but stays seated and shuffles on the orange armchair. A seat James Miller sat in on New Year's Eve, but Maya doesn't know that.

Pip returns. Pint of cider in one hand, small coupé glass in the other. He is careful not to spill the skilfully shaken raspberry red drink with the pale peach foam on top. Boyish blue eyes concentrate. His tongue pokes out from one corner of his mouth.

'Here you go.'

'Thank you.'

'I have to say you look beautiful, Maya, just how I imagined you would have turned out.'

'Me? What this?' she blushes. Smoothing down the collar on a lemon yellow shirt dress that poufs out at the waist into a circle skirt. It's still October, but a balmy evening demanded a last-clutch-of-summer dress. 'It's from the vintage shop off the square.'

'It's pretty.'

'Well you don't look so bad yourself, Pip. I miss the bomber jacket with the sheepskin collar though. Even my sister remembered that. But the years have been kind to you.'

Pip is wearing a grey T-shirt that's a little bit too tight for him, but deliberately so, Maya thinks, and blue jeans.

'That's running for you,' he winks, then smiles bashfully.

There's a slightly awkward silence for a second and they lock eyes.

'So what do you do when you're not running, Pip Smith?' Maya takes a sip from her coupé glass. 'You do realise I can only call you Pip Smith don't you? The way kids call class-mates by their full names.'

'Lottie Sharman!' laughs Pip.

'Ricky Hill!' counters Maya. She won't mention it now, but Maya's Special Memory skill means she could probably list all of the kids from that class almost twenty years ago.

'Well, Maya Flowers, I'm a personal trainer now. I've

done about four thousand things since leaving school, but this is the only one I've stuck at for more than a year. I love it. I love being the guy to get people up and moving. I love seeing results. I love the feeling of using my body. I guess I loved it ever since I chased you around the silver birches.'

Maya laughs. His enthusiasm is sweet and endearing.

'Sounds brilliant. Although I always thought you'd go into something artistic. You were always giving me drawings, you were really good.'

'Yes, but Ninja Turtle drawings don't pay the rent.'

Maya doesn't tell him she remembered that one. Something holds her back.

'I was a graphic designer for a couple of years, but it was really dull stuff, like posters for estate agent windows and burger bar leaflets. Not exactly the V&A displays I pictured doing. I was working for a really shitty agency in Bracknell. Then I worked in airport parking at Heathrow, then a pet insurance call centre, and then I couldn't stand being so miserable and lazy, so I retrained as a personal trainer.'

'Sweat more, bitch less, huh?'

Pip laughs. The speckled apples of his cheeks rise.

'That's great you do something you love now. Something that makes a difference to people.'

'Well it doesn't really. It's badly paid and most of the time it's a thankless task, I'm the person clients don't want to see at 6 a.m., especially now the mornings are getting darker. Lazy people mostly just want to stay lazy. But when you get a breakthrough and a client says you've changed their life… it's worth it. That's why I moved back here. Tap into commuter clients and mums trying to get back into shape. Bracknell wasn't overly full of people wanting to get fit.'

'Why Bracknell?'

Pip Smith looks sheepish. 'My ex-girlfriend was from there.'

I don't mind.

'Oh, well it sounds more inspirational than what I do,' puffs Maya, the cocktail stick threaded with a blueberry and two raspberries falls from its perch on the side of the thin coupé glass and into her drink.

'What do you do?' asks Pip, taking a sip of cider.

Maya's mind flits to her upcoming meeting on Monday with Tiffanie Doyle from the *London Evening Standard*, and she doesn't want to talk about work.

Pip throws Maya a lifeline. 'In fact, what have you been doing since we were eleven? We must have gone to different secondary schools.'

'We did, silly! You went to the boys' school. I went to Hazelworth High. I didn't ever see you after that.'

'That's weird,' says Pip, sucking cider off his top lip. 'But it's one of those things you don't question when you're eleven. You just let your parents work out your social life for you. But you meant so much to me, I can't believe I didn't push it.'

Maya twists her hair into a side bun fumblingly.

'Well, the summer after I left Hazelworth High I worked in a call centre myself. Saved up some money and booked a one-way ticket to LA, knowing I had a year to get through Central America and back home before uni.'

'Wow, you went alone?'

Maya nods. 'It was the bravest thing I had ever done.'

'"*Had*" done? You did something braver since?'

Maya thinks of him. Wide, lovely, brown eyes. Eyes she misses every morning. 'Have done. It's the bravest thing I *have* ever done.'

'Amazing. Tell me what that was like.'

Maya feels uncomfortable, so she takes an unladylike slurp of a ladylike drink. As the vodka, raspberry and pineapple seep through her tummy and the alcohol to her blood, she feels more relaxed. Pip Smith. He's cute. Their freckles face off. His are more prominent. Hers are vibrant from the last of the summer sun, soon to sink back to just a winter fluttering. Their laughs are warm on a warm autumn night.

'I want to run it in this Thursday's paper, sign for four weeks, then take it from there on a rolling monthly contract. We'll pay eight hundred pounds a column. But my editor will only commit to four for now.'

Tiffanie Doyle sits in the cafe of a health food store on Kensington High Street nursing a carrot, beet and ginger juice – and a hangover. Impatient eyes. Short black hair cut into a severe bob with a high fringe. Her face is so close to Maya's in this intimate corner of a huge energy-promising emporium that Maya can see red lipstick bleeding ever-so-slightly beyond the corners of Tiffanie's mouth. Maya is nervous and intimidated and trying not to show it. She told Cressida she had a doctor's appointment this morning and that she would be late for conference.

Maya is almost lost for words. 'Eight hundred pounds for five hundred words?'

'Yep, we loved it. But we'll play it by ear, yes?'

Tiffanie Doyle says 'yes' a lot at the end of a sentence, even though she's telling, not asking.

'I must be anonymous. I can't lose my job, I'm not even a year into a twenty-five-year mortgage.'

'That's fine. We'll get you a commissioning form that will specify anonymity. We'll come up with a name. In fact have a think over the next couple of days. I'm thinking Belle De Jour meets City Scoop meets Bridget Jones with a fashion twist. And without the sex. For now...'

Maya narrows her eyes suspiciously. 'You want personal stuff in there too?'

'Not right now. The fashion empire stuff is just great. But if the column flies we'd need to know more about what FASH Girl does off duty.'

'You won't mention FASH right?'

'Of course not, dear, we'd be slapped with a libel order faster than you could say sweatshop. Rich Robinson is an old, erm, associate of mine. He wouldn't hold back, I can tell you.'

Maya feels even more nervous. And wonders from the way Tiffanie spat 'associate' what happened between her and the FASH CEO. She also wonders how Tiffanie knows Tom Vernon, but thinks she'd better not ask.

'I'll get our art team to do one of those funny little silhouette drawings of you, doesn't even have to look like you, to use as a byline. But if you can just tighten up column one for me by the end of the day and come up with that handle. I'll be in the office until 11 p.m., file it by then, yes?'

Understood.

Maya looks at her watch and remembers they met at 8.30 a.m.

Wow, I thought FASH days were long.

'Will do.'

With that, Tiffanie stands, signalling the end of their meeting, and swigs the last of her carrot, beet and ginger juice. She winces in the same way she did when she said the word associate.

'I need a fag.'

On the 390 bus from High Street Kensington to Oxford Street, Maya thinks about whether she ought to get involved in treachery and subterfuge and secret meetings with commissioning editors, who must meet people about much more serious issues, like weapons inspections or government whistle-blowers or failing NHS trusts. Then she realises how silly this all is. Four columns. Four weeks. That's £3,200 – potentially more – to spend on windows her flat could really do with. And some light-hearted journalism about life through a fashion lens. See how it goes. It's not as if Cressida isn't giving her enough material lately. After ordering the retouching of all size 8, 5ft 10in FASH models to make them look slimmer (which Lucy and Rich Robinson signed off), she's bullying the fattest girl in the office, and still keeps harping on about that monstrous day she disgusted herself by eating panini for lunch and pizza for dinner: in Cressida Blaise-Snellman's world, double denim = #bigwin; double carbs = #epicfail. Maya knew exactly how her first column should go. She just needs to tweak it tonight.

'You're not up the duff too, are you?' Cressida barks as Maya walks into conference an hour late and slides into her seat around the long oval table.

Holly and Chloe nudge knees under the table, so hoping Maya will bite back when they wouldn't dare.

'Jesus,' sighs Olivia.

Alex pushes his glasses back up his nose and Maya suddenly thinks of James Miller. She is overcome by a boost of empowerment, of boldness, of anger.

'You absolutely can't ever say that to a member of your

team, Cressida,' says Maya. Hot face, clammy fists, shaking knees.

'No, of course you're not,' she says with a half laugh, giving Maya a disdainful look as if to say 'who would impregnate you anyway?! *Jokes!* We've just lost Emma to maternity, we don't want to lose another stalwart.'

'OK, well what have I missed?' Maya asks, getting her laptop out of her bag.

The pen is mightier than the sword.

47

'You can't leave, you shit.'

'I told him the same, but then he's never really listened to me,' Dominic deadpans, briefly raising stubby eyebrows to the ceiling.

James and Dominic are sitting in the office of Jeremy Laws, chief creative officer of MFDD. The room is painted grey from carpet-to-ceiling, apart from the fresco-style canvas rolled out above their heads, a sunny blue skyscape looking down on them to inspire all of Jeremy's blue-sky thinking.

'You bloody bastards are the star partnership here. I've got Fisher & Whyman phoning me up licking my balls over your Femme images from Jamaica, and they want to throw even more business our way. Why would you possibly want to leave? Where the fuck are you going? And why aren't you going too?' Jeremy shoots to Dominic. Jeremy's ginger waves and ginger beard meet at his pockmarked cheeks, his thick neck bursts out of a black V-neck top, red and irritated by the morning's news.

'I wasn't invited,' says Dominic, trying to make light of the thorny atmosphere.

James coughs awkwardly and pushes black rectangles

back up his nose. 'I'm not going to a rival agency. I want to be a photographer.'

'He's been doing freelance shoots on the weekends,' says Dominic, like a proud big brother. Often speaking up for his friend who always takes more time to answer.

'Freelance shoots on the weekend? What, eighty quid plus expenses to shoot a fucking wedding in *Wrexham*? I don't care if you're shooting the Queen's fucking Christmas card, it's not much good to this agency and our clients. You're not going.'

Dominic laughs.

James blushes. He's never been so highly – or so rudely – praised.

This could work to my advantage.

'Give me three months then. Unpaid. If I'm only shooting weddings in Wrexham in three months' time, I'll come back. But I'm aiming for a travel portfolio, reportage, news even...'

'Oh I bet you bloody are. Sauntering off to Barbados for the winter and pretending it's for work. Jesus, Miller.'

The room goes quiet. Dominic, arms folded, looks out of the window at the leaves blowing down Charlotte Street. Jeremy Laws scratches his jaw until red stubble looks like a rash. James sits in the chair facing his desk. Relaxed. Knowing that he is doing the right thing.

'Right, you bastard. You've got my balls in a vice. If I give you three months off, every fucker here is gonna want three months off.'

'Not unpaid. Most of the creatives who work here have families. I'm single. I don't have a mortgage. I have no dependents.'

'Jesus, Miller, didn't you get the memo about growing up?' Jeremy drinks a ristretto from the smallest of paper cups, winces, and makes a grumbling murmur as he smooths back his hair through open fingers. 'Just do it. I hope you enjoy your little A Level art project, but I'll see you back here at the end of January. We'll tell Fisher & Whyman you're owed leave. I'm not telling them you want out.'

'What about me?' asks Dominic, petulantly.

'You can work with Karen. I need to get her off I Should Cocoa. She's not keeping the client sweet.'

'Karen Burns? Thanks Jeremy,' says Dominic flatly, giving James a hard stare.

James supresses his smile so as not to anger Jeremy and Dominic – a smile so small his dimple doesn't dent. He has three months to make a living from photography. It might not happen, but a few months ago a girl on the train showed him that taking a risk for your happiness wasn't such a crazy thing to do.

Sam walks through the glass double doors clutching a newspaper.

'You only just went for lunch!' says Maya, wolfing down a home-made ham and cheese sandwich at her desk. Even the canteen's offering has gone a bit flat lately.

'You have to see this, Maya,' he says, shaking the paper. 'Have you got time for a hot chocolate?'

Actually, since Cressida took FASHmas off her, Maya's workload has been a bit less overwhelming. Maybe she can leave her desk for lunch today, although Sam's urgency is unsettling her. Her first column as Fifi Fashion Insider isn't meant to debut until tomorrow.

'Erm, yeah, what's up?'

'Let's get out of here, I'll show you over the road.'

Maya puts down her half-eaten sandwich, grabs her wallet

and slings her floral bomber over her shoulders. On the walk out it occurs to Maya that Sam hasn't asked her to go for lunch or a hot chocolate or a quick chat at the Venezuelan cafe over the road in a long time. Maybe he stopped asking because she was too busy. Maybe she's upset him. He has seemed less chummy with her in the past few months. Maya embraces the chance to put things right and gives Sam a jokey little nudge with her arm as she ushers him through the open door first.

Sam looks around with a paranoid dart, as if they're doing something they shouldn't. As if she shouldn't have touched him.

'What's the matter?'

'Let's get the hell out of dodge. It'll be all over the place in a few minutes.'

It's Wednesday. I wasn't supposed to feel shady until tomorrow.

'I'll get these,' says Maya at the upstairs coffee counter over the road.

'OK, I'll grab a seat.'

Sam walks down the rickety staircase, heading to the basement seating area. Their favourite sofa is the only available space to sit.

'Boom,' Sam whispers to himself, the drama of what he's just read outweighing the heavy heart he's had for the past few months.

Maya follows with a cappuccino for Sam and a hot chocolate for herself. Two girls wearing lanyards with the FASH logo around their neck, passes dangling between proud breasts, whisper to each other as Maya passes.

'There goes the Christmas party if it *is* someone from FASH,' says the blonde to the redhead.

Shit.

Maya sees Sam on the sofa at the back; he's still clutching his newspaper. It has to be about the column.

Do I tell him? Surely I can trust Sam?

Then Maya remembers they've barely spoken lately, maybe she can't any more.

'Still a cappuccino, right?' Maya says as she hands Sam a low curvaceous cup and saucer.

'That'll do,' he says, he too realising it's been a long time.

'So what's new?' Maya asks casually, brushing a wave of hair from her face as if to act natural.

'This, man. Check it out.' Sam thrusts an already weathered newspaper at Maya even though it's hot off the press. 'Read it. It's got to be about FASH. I reckon that's Cressida they're talking about too.'

Blood rushes to Maya's face in the dark of the subterranean cafe as she pretends to read text she already read a hundred times. A silhouette sits at the top. A black illustration of a faceless girl in a full skirt, one hand on a small waist, pencil and tape measure in another. Wavy hair whisked back in a bun.

She looks a bit like me!

'Shit, Sam.' Maya doesn't know if she's meant to act outraged or amused.

'Who wrote it, Maya? And why have they got it in for FASH?'

Maya measures her face. She wants to remind Sam about Rich Robinson buying a yacht so soon after he cancelled staff bonuses and froze salaries. About the indulgence of the executive board's summer and Christmas parties when warehouse staff are squeezed on minimum wage. About everyone feeling pushed into working longer hours so FASH sells more parkas this year than last. Then Maya realises, if she said it out loud, it would sound petty. That's business. Deep down Maya knows Fifi Fashion Insider is a personal swipe at Cressida, and she's not feeling as proud of herself or as victorious as she thought she might.

'Well some of the points resonate, Sam,' says Maya, teasing the foam of the hot chocolate with her spoon. 'FASH is as ludicrous a place to work as wherever this girl works. Or guy, the picture could be a red herring…'

'Yeah but why go to the papers about it? Who can be that pissed about working here?'

'Oh, I don't know, Sam. If Cressida is the nightmare boss this Fifi Fashion Insider is talking about, she's been rude to lots of people in the past few months, it could be anyone.'

'She's not been rude to me.' Narrow, defensive eyes don't look like they're smiling now.

'Gee, Sam, do you think it might be because you're a guy? It's standard bitch-boss behaviour. Piss on the sisterhood but flatter the guys. It's the only way she got to be site editor. I saw it happen at Walk In Wardrobe.'

'Hang on, My, you didn't write this, did you?' says Sam, eyes breaking into a crinkle as he hits Maya's knee with the rolled-up paper.

'Me? I can only write three or four words at a time, Sam, you know me. "Pastel-poppin prom dresses" and "Jaw-droppin' jeans"? I know my limits…'

'I know, just winding you up.' Sam winks.

Maya inhales hot cocoa and sugar scents, relieved that Sam seems to have thawed.

Three tech guys walk down the stairs and survey the room for a seat. They wave at Sam and raise their newspapers. Sam raises his back.

'Man it is gonna go off.'

Maya needs to change the subject fast. 'Hey, guess what?'

'What?'

'I'm over Train Man.'

'Train Man!' Sam slaps his forehead with an exasperated palm.

Maya looks mock-affronted to cover up the fact she is actually quite affronted.

'Sorry. I know I was boring. But you stopped asking since I gave him the note, just thought I'd give you a little follow-up.'

'I stopped caring, Maya.'

'Oh.' Maya shifts in her seat on the brown leather sofa. 'Well I've started seeing someone, a guy I went to primary school with.'

'That's nice.'

Maya waits for questions that don't come.

'What about you, Sam? Seeing anyone lately?'

Sam runs his hand up the peak of his 45-degree fringe. 'Yeah, I've been seeing someone since the spring actually.'

'Oh. How did I not know that?' Maya feels like a bad friend. 'Anyone I know?'

'You might. Hayley from PR.'

'Oh, wow!'

Sam seems prickly again, Maya feels awkward, and she wonders if it might have been easier to keep talking about Fifi Fashion Insider after all.

Lucy stands tall at the head of the oval table, hands on hips jutting through a black leather pencil skirt. At the opposite end, the monitor usually reserved for looking at pictures of FASH-forward celebrities is switched off. Cressida, Maya,

Alex, Chloe, Holly, Olivia, Liz and Gaby, the new social media manager covering Emma, sit nervously around the table, waiting to hear Lucy's take on Fifi Fashion Insider, who, in four short hours, has become the talk of Baker Street. Maya didn't expect the piece to be picked up on this quickly, and especially not for it to be traceable to this small corner of a fashion empire. She makes a mental note to herself: if she makes it to a second column, throw in a few red herrings to put FASH off the scent.

'Have any of you *not* seen this?' Lucy asks sternly. Razor-sharp butter-coloured bob sitting atop glossy dark eyebrows.

'I haven't,' squeaks Liz, who was probably too busy beavering away at her desk to read it.

Alex slides the newspaper across the table so she can see.

Cressida's cheeks flush obstinately.

Chloe's red lips hang open, quietly and triumphantly, anticipating the reaction on Liz's face when she gets to the bit that must be about Cressida, the 'languid, vacuous, and most unsisterly female boss Fifi Fashion Insider has ever had the displeasure to work with'.

Olivia tosses corkscrew curls like a flamethrower.

'The PR team work so hard to build the FASH brand so that we're relevant and reliable in the eyes of our shoppers. What this does is belittle the company and everything we try to do for fashion-conscious women. Rich is livid.'

Alex shakes his head and the soft whip atop it bounces a little.

'Can I play devil's advocate without it looking like it was me?' he asks with charm only Alex can get away with.

Lucy softens a little and takes her hand off her hip. 'Of course Alex, go ahead.'

'Well couldn't Fifi Fashion Insider be talking about Walk

In Wardrobe? Or Wicked Style? Or Garment Guru? Or any of the fashion big guns who have websites and in-house models and big offices in London?'

Maya tries not to exhale a sigh of relief.

I love you Alex. And I need to speak up fast so I don't look guilty.

'We both worked there, Cressida, it does sound pretty much like Walk In Wardrobe to me,' says Maya, clutching at straws.

Lucy looks at Alex, whose ice cream quiff has wilted a little with the heat of tension.

'It could, Alex, but in this column Fifi Fashion Insider takes the piss out of someone in her office saying, "Once she confessed to having eaten pizza and panini *in the same day* as if such a disgusting feat of greed and gluttony had never been attempted before..."'

'And...?' asks Alex.

A tear rolls down Cressida's chiselled cheek.

Lucy takes the deep breath of someone who knows what they are about to say will sound ridiculous.

'Cressida told me she mentioned to the team that... that *she* once ate pizza and a panini in the same day.'

Olivia tries not to laugh. She doesn't know who wrote the column, but she's bloody glad they did. Her lips stay pursed, her eyes look ignited. She's enjoying every minute of this meeting.

'Well, haven't we all?' says Maya, trying to make light of the situation.

Cressida looks across the table at her with disgust.

Chloe and Holly smirk.

'Well, I'd like you all to keep your eyes and ears open; this kind of treachery needs to be ratted out,' says Cressida.

Lucy interrupts, preferring a gentler approach.

'If there's an insider writing a column for a newspaper, there could just as easily be an insider sending sensitive sales figures, data or strategy plans to our competitors. It's a sackable offence. Rich Robinson will be sending a company-wide email to reiterate that, but I just wanted to talk to you all first, given the link to what Cressida remembers saying. As far as I'm concerned, if you sit within earshot of Cressida, it could have been you.' Lucy looks at Maya and Maya's throat suddenly feels very dry. She did discuss her concerns about Cressida with Lucy only days ago, but she did say that Cressida has ruffled *everyone's* feathers. And Maya knows Lucy doesn't play games. If she thought Maya was Fifi Fashion Insider, she would have spoken to her direct.

Cressida sniffs while Lucy continues.

'I won't be going to Rich with that intel yet, it might be coincidence, let's just hope it was a one-off.'

Gaby looks bewildered, wondering what she's got herself into with this maternity cover.

Holly and Chloe look at each other and put on their best serious faces.

A text flashes up on Maya's phone, which she manages to flip over before she or anyone else could see it.

> Editor loves it. Loads of traction on Twitter,
> more of the same please. TD.

48

November 2014

James looks up at a wall of orange digits rolling, changing, buzzing with the same excitement as the incoming revellers heading out on this Saturday night to theatres, restaurants and parties. The next train to Hazelworth departs in twenty-six minutes, which is almost as long as the longest you ever have to wait for the next train to Hazelworth.

'Shit.'

James really doesn't want to wait around tonight of all nights, but he heads towards the large coffee shop in a glass box in the middle of the station. A girl with a doughy body and a low blonde ponytail looks at James expectantly. A black name badge has Nicola written in white chalk on a low breast.

'Double espresso please.'

'Drink in or take away?'

James looks through the glass up at the clock. Twenty-three minutes.

'Here, please.'

He could do with sitting down.

'Would you like our special mountain blend?'

'What's different about it?'

'It's nuttier than the standard blend and costs just twenty pence more.'

'OK, then.'

'Would you like a muffin or a cake?'

'No thanks, just the coffee.'

'Sandwich or fruit toast?'

'No thanks, just the coffee.'

'Anything else?'

'No thanks, I just want my coffee. Please.' Wide, exasperated eyes.

'That'll be £2.10 please,' Nicola smiles, her perky tone jarring with her worn face and sunken eyes.

Once he's paid, James finds his small white cup and saucer at the end of the counter and seeks a high stool in the corner, where he knows his photographic equipment will be encased safely by his feet and glass walls.

James rubs his eyes with the backs of his hands like a tired toddler. Treacly nutty bitterness bounces on his taste buds. It feels like midnight, not early evening. James was up at 5 a.m. and on the first train from Hazelworth, bright-eyed and excited to be shooting a Paralympian in training for next weekend's Remembrance Day special for *The Observer*. His first newspaper gig, which will do his portfolio the world of good. Weddings and corporate headshots are good money-spinners, but they don't carry the kudos of shooting for one of the UK's most respected Sunday papers. James had to go into London and out again to Windsor to photograph Matty Weatherall swimming in the Thames, riding his specially adapted handbike, then putting on his carbon-fibre blades to do a lap of the track at a local running club. Matty was a Royal Marine Commando who lost both of his legs in a Taliban roadside bomb in Afghanistan. What James saw today made him feel humbled, pampered and lazy.

The day had started tetchily – Matty wasn't overly keen to be tailed by a photographer, but as the hours passed and James quietly and thoughtfully got the pictures he needed without getting in the way of transitions and fuel stops, he won Matty over.

'You know I'm not here to interview you, I'm just taking the pictures,' James said gently, when he saw a scowl through the lens.

'I know mate, it's just I'm not doing it for all this. "The media circus" my mam calls it. I'm doing it for me.'

James put the viewfinder back to his eye and respected Matty even more.

In a pub on the river at the end of the long, draining training session, James bought himself a pale ale and a pint of lime soda for Matty. And then one shy guy asked another just one probing question.

'What got you through it?'

'My missus. I thought about her every day out there. I thought about her every day during my recovery back here. I think about her when I'm pushing the bike or putting these on my stumps.' He looked down and tapped one prosthetic leg with the other, giving a light tinny ring. 'I just wanted a normal life for us. A family. I've wanted to be a dad since I can remember. But as I got fit, I realised I could be better than normal. I always pushed myself, I suppose that's how I got to be a marine, but I didn't realise how far I could go. I'm gonna be a dad next year and Carly is as proud of me as I am of her.'

'Oh congratulations, mate,' said James, savouring his pint

the way Matty savoured his water at every pit stop during his training earlier. 'You should be proud of yourself too.'

'I am. Every day.'

In the glass box, James turns the espresso cup around on its saucer and wonders what Carly looks like. How pregnant she is. How it would have been nice to take her picture too.

James unzips the laptop from its case to have a look at some of the images from today, but then he thinks of *her* and wants to shake off his feeling of laziness and inertia.

When was it?

As James downs his coffee shot he remembers all the furniture of Kitty leaving him. Mid-summer. Long days.

The note was in my backpack that day.

James closes the lid of his laptop as quickly as he opened it and wakens his phone by punching in a code. He goes to the sent items in his email. He can't remember when it was exactly but he remembers her name.

Search: Maya Flowers.

Do I still have her email address?

Sent items show James the email when he told Maya Flowers he had a girlfriend. Last May. Kitty would already have been in a relationship with Simon but this doesn't make James sad. He feels the pang of hope and yearning as his thumb hovers over the screen of his phone, before he looks up at orange digits and realises he needs to pack away his things and head to platform 10.

He zips up the laptop case, puts it in his backpack and slings it onto his back, then closes it. The long thin bags of the tripod and the lighting reflector rise out of the backpack, crossing over above his shoulders like the swords of a ninja.

Camera case in one hand, James lifts his phone off the table with the other. He looks up and sees Maya Flowers through the glass, walking past, heading out for the evening. He is so close, but if he called her name she wouldn't hear him. If he banged on the glass wall that separates them, the man with his arm draped triumphantly around Maya's shoulder probably wouldn't notice either.

James looks back down at his phone and presses the button that sends it to sleep.

Maya gives the clock in the top right-hand corner of her monitor a quick glance: 5.31 p.m.

I'm outta here.

She throws on a belted wool coat and slings her bag over her shoulder. It is Wednesday and all day Maya has been anxious about whether the column will run today, as it did last week, or Thursday as was originally planned. So far today there haven't been any outrageous gasps or whispers in the canteen, or people walking apace through the glass double doors and around the quadrangle of the building towards Rich Robinson's office.

Maybe tomorrow.

Just to be sure, as she heads out of FASH HQ, Maya picks up a paper, from the vendor on the corner of Portman Square. She tucks it into her bag and walks with haste to meet Nena at Liberty. Ankle boots click as Maya thinks about the wedding accessories she's about to help Nena pick out. Hair jewels, purses, shoes, stoles. Maya thinks back to last weekend and how she made a grown man cry. She thinks about what next week's column should be about. Week one was an introduction to a fashion empire and a few key characters, but mostly the Horrible Boss who belittled her own team and said her favourite pastime was to unfollow people on Twitter. Week two is more about the fashion vernacular. The terms Fifi Fashion Insider hears on a daily basis and how, well, fluffy her job is. That took Maya longer to write than she thought it would because she couldn't use any of the terms FASH actually use, or the looks, trends or campaigns she herself created at work, so it was like doing her job twice over. Maya did come up with 'Hell Yeah Partywear' and wished she could nick that in real life. But it made for a more fun, less bitchy column, which Maya enjoyed writing.

As she turns off Oxford Street onto Argyle Street and sees the monochromatic castle in front of her, she decides to hold that thought, maybe ask Nena for column inspiration after they've sorted out her wedding kit and caboodle.

The doors revolve and Maya snakes through the beauty hall to where Nena is sitting in a chair while a make-up artist strokes her face.

'You're having a makeover?' Maya asks, stating the obvious.

'I won't be long, I just realised I need someone to show me how *not* to do my make-up like a clown. I can't get away with red cheeks and glittery green eyes on my wedding day.'

A woman dressed head-to-toe in black smiles politely but carries on putting taupes and beiges and neutral shades over excited eyes.

'This is my friend who works in fashion,' says Nena, as if they've already been talking about Maya. 'She's helping me sort out the rest of my outfit, so I don't end up in my ballet Blochs.'

Maya laughs. 'Do you think your dad will walk you down the aisle en pointe?'

Nena gives a punchy cackle, unsteadying the steady hand of the Laura Mercier girl.

'Sorry.' Nena says through pursed lips.

The make-up artist smiles and swipes a peach gloss over a naturally raspberry pout, then breaks her silence.

'Did you see that thing in the *Standard* last week about the girl who works in fashion?'

'No I didn't,' Nena lies, giving her friend a sideways look from the vice-like grip of brushes and a gloss wand.

'Oh it was proper funny. A girl who works for FASH or Garment Guru or wherever, she was spilling the beans on what it's like to work there. My friend who works at Walk In Wardrobe said it was spot-on. All these models walking around in rollers and thongs while she tries to book a courier. And a really mean boss.'

Maya laughs nervously and deftly changes the subject. 'You must get some real characters walking through here?'

The make-up artist looks away from her canvas for the first time since Maya arrived.

'Oh, definitely. Some good celeb spots too. I've done a few famous faces. Actually you look a bit familiar,' she says, turning back to Nena.

Maya breathes a sigh of relief. She's not sure if she can do this beyond the four weeks Tiffanie Doyle commissioned, it's stressing her out enough as it is.

'What do you think?' Nena asks in the duck-egg and glass grandeur of the second-floor cafe.

'Really?'

'Really.'

Maya hesitates while she chooses her words. She finds it harder than Nena to be candid.

'I don't think you look like... *you*.'

Nena looks disappointed and pouts. 'Oh. But this is the classy, ladylike me. Nena 2.0.'

'But Tom wants to marry the Nena he fell in love with. It's as if that make-up artist took all the natural brightness out of your face and toned it down in a veil of beige.' Maya feels bad. 'Glitter doesn't look ridiculous on you when your blank canvas is so amazing in the first place. It just accentuates an already existing sparkle.'

Nena blushes, mutedly.

'Right, so what did we get?' asks Maya.

'Nothing for me! But I love your hair jewel, and the stole is gorgeous. But I think I need one too. A bride with her baps out does not look cool on a brisk December afternoon.'

'Well here, try the one I bought, if you like it, you have it and I'll find something different.'

'You're so sweet, Maya. But don't be silly, you found it first.'

'You're the bride. Surely the bride gets first dibs.'

Nena clicks her fingers and whips her neck, pretending to be a diva. Hair piled high in a confection-like bun comes undone from its own twist and swooshes into perfect position. Black, straight, shiny.

The girls laugh as a disinterested waiter arrives with two pink lemonades. Happy that the wedding is bringing them closer together.

'Anyway, I need to know, are you bringing a certain "plus one" to the wedding? Tom and I are doing the seating plan tonight. Do we save a place for Kisschase Boy on the top table?'

Maya winces apologetically.

'Just think of the cost saving,' she offers sheepishly through gritted teeth.

'Oh no! What happened?'

'What didn't happen, I think is more accurate.'

'What *didn't* happen?' Nena clasps hands to her face, enormous disappointed eyes waiting above them. Maya sighs. Nena groans. 'But Kisschase Boy sounded so romantic!'

'It *was* romantic. When I was eleven. But he was a bit stuck back there.' Maya stirs her pink lemonade with a stripy straw. 'Stuck in a time of kiss chase and drawing my face on Wonder Woman's body... we didn't really have any spark in the here and now.'

'How did you end it?'

'He brought me to the theatre on Saturday night,' Maya says, nodding in the direction of Covent Garden. '*The Lion King* – which was amazing – but he was watching my face all the way through, the way he did when we watched the film as kids. I dunno, it felt a bit... creepy.'

'Oh, Maya!'

'I know, I know, I feel bad.' She takes her stripy straw and sips through small rounded lips. 'He cried.'

'He *cried*? After what, three dates?'

'Four.'

'Well now I don't feel sorry him. What a pussy! And yeah, that'll save Felipe and Victoria a hundred quid. Go, Maya.'

Maya can't help feeling like she's let the side down. She did really try.

'I haven't told Clara yet – she's going to be really miffed.'

49

Cressida clings to the first edition of today's *Evening Standard*. It must have only hit the newsstand half an hour ago, which means Cressida was poised, waiting, and within just thirty minutes she has devoured Fifi Fashion Insider, become incensed, and called the editorial team back in meeting room 1.1 for another rollicking. This time without Lucy in charge. Maya looks at her watch.

The vanity of the woman! I bet you think this column's about you.

'It's a blatant snub of everyone who works here, which means it's mocking each and every one of you around this table,' she says in a dreary whine. Cressida is wearing a white shirt and mom jeans, with a varsity jacket slung over rangy shoulders. 'Let me read you an excerpt from this trash...' Cressida tucks her hair behind her ear, enjoying the audience: '"Walking up the stairs in summer it's hard not to be hit in the eye by the pendulous bum cleavage in front of you dangling from high-cut high-waisted 90s denim shorts coming up a conveyor belt of polyester and pouts..." – I mean, that sounds like here. We have stairs.'

'Lots of buildings have stairs,' deadpans Olivia.

Cressida's face flushes as red as Olivia's hair. 'Olivia, you're doing a pretty good job of making me think you're the perp here. All this cynicism about fashion, and being mean about models – and people who actually give a shit what they look like.'

'Whoa,' interjects Maya. She sat and watched once, she can't do it again. 'Cressida, let's not go there again.'

Olivia locks eyes with Cressida and smirks, goading Cressida to go that bit further so she can take her to a tribunal. Cressida is silent. Lips poised and pouting, disgusted by treachery.

'Well, I don't know why it's rattled you so much, Cressida,' Olivia snipes. 'Only you would think it's about you.'

'It's not about me, I would *never* wear denim hot pants.'

Olivia throws down her notebook and waves exasperated arms into the air.

'You don't get it though do you? It doesn't matter if Fifi Fashion Insider is you, me, Alex… it's just someone having a laugh at the ridiculousness of this bubble. About the frivolity of fashion. About how humourless some people are. And it's the people who don't have a sense of humour who are getting so rattled by it. Look around you! This is all so fucking lightweight, let's not pretend it's anything but!' Olivia finishes with a laugh, killing any possible accusation of aggression in her efforts to trip Cressida up, to make her cross the line.

'Are you kidding, Olivia?' Cressida spits with a scowl on her pale brow. 'Party season is upon us. Our customers have been planning their wardrobe for months. They come to us to for direction so they know what to wear…'

'"Hell Yeah Partywear" apparently,' pipes up peacemaker Alex, trying to lift the mood. Maya smiles to herself.

Cressida gives Alex a sideways glance and continues.

'Sales go through the roof during party season. But they won't if the very people employed here to move fashion forward and sell as many party dresses as possible think they're above it, that they're *beyond* fashion, and are holding business back. Rich Robinson pays your salary, you work for a fashion retailer. If you don't like it, get out.'

As Cressida says 'out' a tiny bubble of spit shoots from her mouth and onto the illustration of Fifi Fashion Insider on the table in front of her.

Maya's phone pings. She grabs it before anyone sees the screen.

'Well how about that?' Maya says. 'Emma's had a girl! 8lbs 10oz, Lola Felicity. How wonderful!'

Maya rests her head on the inside of the Superior Train window. She's so tired she doesn't even think to use her scarf as a protective shield from the fingerprints and food splatters imprinted onto BS 857-TF kitemarked glass.

Last night, Maya lay on her tummy across the rug on her living-room floor, lit only by the screen of her laptop in the dark, tweeting and retweeting until 1 a.m. from her Fifi Fashion Insider account. Astounded that in just three weeks she has gained 22.4k followers: some prolific, some inspired, some abusive, but all fascinated by Fifi's column and wanting to know her true identity – and for which fashion empire she works.

After the fluffy fashion vernacular of week two, Tiffanie Doyle asked Maya to make the next one feel more 'insider' again, which Maya knew was code for bitchier. And she knew she wasn't being asked, she was being told. So, with a feeling of discomfort, and with Herbert Flowers' disapproving face in her mind's eye, Maya filed a column about body fascism at FASH.

'Body fascism in fashion is nothing new, Fifi,' said Tiffanie Doyle in her reply. Maya wasn't sure if she had got her name wrong deliberately or not. 'But this is hilarious. I love it. We must extend your contract.'

It didn't feel that hilarious to Maya. That Olivia had bravely volunteered herself as a plus-size beach model for a real-life swimwear story and was shot down with a steely glare and the curl of a lip. Of course the details had had to change: Fifi wrote about a 'strappy summer dresses' shoot that an over-weight marketing manager had put herself forward for, not a picture editor, but Maya couldn't help feeling that, with this column, the net might close in on Olivia.

The reaction was immense. Other papers picked up on it. There were debates on *Five Live* and *Woman's Hour*. Everyone reacting to why size was *still* being swept under the carpet for fashion retailers who sell to women who (mostly) aren't supermodels. Everyone speculating about who Fifi Fashion Insider is.

An intern at Wicked Style claimed it was her, but a spokes-person for the *Standard* denied it and the intern lost her job anyway, without the fanfare or notoriety she was hoping would help her segue into a new career in the media.

Heat blasts at Maya's ankles, offsetting the coldness coming through the window against her left temple. Maya was contracted to write four columns, and she filed the fourth yesterday, all about the anticipated excesses of the upcoming office Christmas party based on last year's hedonism. Maya had to be very creative in changing the details of that particular party. The two Riches on the roof of Shoreditch

House with the head of womenswear, five fashion stylists, three naked models and a marmoset could *not* go in.

Maya's lids drop as the train careers towards home, on the fastest stretch of the track. The carriage is quiet. Every seat is taken. But her head is buzzing with questions and subterfuge and how she can continue to cover her back. How only Tom, Nena and Tiffanie Doyle know the real identity of Fifi Fashion Insider, but how with each column she writes she's closer to tripping up and revealing herself. Faintly freckled lids close and Maya thinks of Velma.

What would Velma say?

Maya is walking through a gallery where portraits hang from the walls. Faces of movers, shakers, artists, players. Velma is shuffling along by her side, both women marvelling in slow motion, at the walls, at the bright light above them, at the space around them. Mouths open in wonder. They stop at a photograph of Josephine Baker, standing but reclined, upright but draped. One hand sits on her hip while she extends the other languidly. She dazzles in a silver dress while three men in shiny black bowler hats swoon to catch her fall. Maya can hear the sighs of adoration from the still men's mouths; gasps of appreciation that are drowned by Velma's vivacious laugh. Maya turns to Velma but her face is blurred.

The train thunders down the tracks.

Maya and Velma are climbing a rickety wooden staircase neither of them have summited before. Rising through floors of a department store, *eau de nil* green walls spar with rich red carpet underfoot as the chinks of fine china lure them to a tea salon at the top. Velma leans into Maya for support and Maya realises her friend's frail legs are too unstable to do this alone. Maya extends her arm and invites Velma to hold on; slipper shoes edge up each flight towards a bright celestial light at the top, where the white noise of cheery chatter draws them further up. They rise cautiously, offering each other physical and emotional reassurance and stability, slowing at every landing so Velma can catch her breath, never acknowledging that she needs to. At the top of the stairs, Velma lets out a puff of air. A man in a white suit plays a grand piano with bony fingers and Maya and Velma look on in puzzlement and wonder why they hadn't heard it on their approach, but are delighted to hear 'Tea For Two' tinkling now. On the threshold of the tea salon, staff with white linen draped over their arms carry cake stands and cloches bursting with sandwiches, scones, miniature eclairs and macarons, as they sweep past Maya and Velma like dashing dancers in a golden age Hollywood musical.

The train starts to slow down on its approach, overhead cables spark with urgency.

A waitress glides towards Maya and extends a welcoming arm before asking if she'd like to be seated, her congenial smile beckoning them into the salon. Maya turns to Velma in excitement but she is not there.

The train grinds to a halt and Maya opens her eyes.

I miss her so very much.

Maya drops her keys onto the little console table with a satis-factory clatter as she kicks off her boots. Post lies sprawled on the floor. Maya picks it up and flips through today's offering.

British Gas bill.

Shit.

Pizza delivery leaflet.

I'm hungry.

Roadside recovery offer.

I don't have a car.

Boden catalogue.

I've never even ordered from them.

A letter with a United States Postal Service stamp in the top right corner and Maya's name and address in an unfamiliar handwritten scrawl. Maya decides to open this one first as she walks up the stairs in stockinged feet.

Dear Maya,

I hope this finds you well.

 You made our mother very happy in her final months; she would have wanted you to have this. Do with it what you will, as long as it makes you enormously happy.

Warmest wishes,
Christopher

Three sentences and a friendly sign-off. And a cheque for $100,000 that falls at Maya's feet as she reaches the top of the stairs. She doesn't open any of the other post.

50

Maya is a different woman to the one she was when she first met Tiffanie Doyle in the cafe of the health food megastore, just a few weeks ago. Has the money given her an air of calmness and confidence, or was it the fact that a letter from America and a message from the grave enabled Maya to find a solution, just when she most needed Velma's wisdom?

'Why did you meet me if you're not willing to extend the contract?' snaps Tiffanie, feeling that her time is being wasted. 'We could have just done this by email.'

Her shiny black fringe, shorter and more severe than the last time they met, sits atop her head like the tiny peak of a cap.

'Because I have a suggestion.'

'If it's about money, we can talk about it. My editor doesn't want to lose you. I don't want to lose you. You were the most shared story from our online edition all week.'

'It's not about money, Tiffanie, I have to get out.'

Thin red lips make a small circle as she thinks.

'Why would you do that? You're snowballing, your star is rising.'

'I'm drowning. It doesn't feel right. It's not me. It's unkind.'

'Strange time to get a conscience, Fifi, er, I mean Maya.

Look, this could go far. They were talking about you on *Question Time*.'

'It's too dangerous. At work they're pointing the finger at the wrong person, a person who needs her job more than I need mine right now. Anyway, I'm leaving FASH, I wouldn't be able to write anything sharable about my new life.'

'Well is there anyone else there who would be willing to take over the mantel? A talented writer you're close to? She could be Fifi and no one would ever know.' Tiffanie frantically rummages in her bag for her vape.

'No, I need to kill it, I'm afraid. I'm not very proud of Fifi and I want to leave FASH to do something I am proud of.'

Tiffanie Doyle looks at Maya with the same wince she made when she sipped the carrot, beet and ginger juice the last time they met. Today, good intentions have gone out of the window and she's having a black coffee, but the disdainful expression loiters.

'What I'm suggesting is: why not do the exclusive in your paper? A big reveal of who Fifi Fashion Insider really is.'

'Ahhh, I see what this is about, you want notoriety. Your career won't last more than a day, Maya. It's Fifi and the access she has inside FASH HQ that everyone wants. Not you I'm afraid, dear.'

'I don't want to be famous, I just want it over, otherwise people will be harassing me on social media or pointing the finger at the wrong person until someone else outs me, which would be much worse. Do the reveal in the *Standard* or I'll go to another paper to do it.'

James walks cumbersomely down Carnaby Street, under a sky of multicoloured tubular Christmas lights, illuminated even though it's not yet dark. He turns left onto a small side street of cafes and clothes shops. At the end of the cobbles he sees a stone and glass façade with Kaleidoscope written sleekly above the door, under a big number 11. He looks at the scrunched-up pink Post-it scribbled with an address in his left hand and pushes the door with his right arm as he stumbles and almost falls in to the reception area, slumping his camera case, tripod, lighting and backpack down in front of him.

A tiny receptionist in leopard-print trousers and gold brogues rushes around her desk, switching on answer phones and straightening out magazines on the coffee table.

'You're Kaye-French? I was waiting for you! Come in.'

James has to check himself, he isn't used to being called by his agent's name.

'Yes, James Miller from the Kaye-French picture agency. You have a studio for me, right?'

'Yes, but you're the last booking today and I want to get off Christmas shopping. Have you shot here before? I don't recognise you,' says the receptionist, stopping for a second to look James up and down, as if to say she would have recognised him had they met.

James puts his equipment down on the cream sofa. 'Never.'

'Well I'll give you a quick tour, it's all straightforward.' The receptionist doesn't lift a foot as she pivots from her spot in the centre of the stark white reception area, indicating his limitations. 'The studio you'll be using is there, the kitchen is there, the toilets are there. Help yourself to tea and toast but tidy up after yourself. Are you shooting lots of people, because if so I don't want them all in the kitchen. The cleaner came early so I could get off.'

'One profile. No hair and make-up.'

'Well that shouldn't take long. Here's the key. If you leave before I get back – I will come back to check everything – just lock up with these and put them through the box. I'll come back by five to check everything and set the alarm. You will be done by five, won't you?' The receptionist holds an array of keys up to James like a very small and not terribly imposing jailer.

James looks at the numbered blocks splayed in seeming disarray on the wall behind the desk. A block with hands on it sits in the middle, bringing it all into focus and indicating that the time is just before 3 p.m.

'Yep, five should be fine,' he says.

The girl's rush to get to Oxford Street is calmed by James's smile for just a second before he walks into the studio to prepare for the shoot. He sets up a stool, unrolls the simple backdrop the booker at Kaye-French requested, and looks outside at the ray of sunlight shooting down Newburgh Street and into his workspace. James likes the peace and quiet of prepping a shoot, before the chaos commences.

All the way down Baker Street, Maya prepared her notice letter in her head.

What's the point of a notice letter? If I don't turn up to work they'll know precisely why I've left by lunchtime.

She thought about the wording. She wondered whether to even mention Fifi Fashion Insider in her letter to Lucy. And then she settled on it. She will stick to a polite resignation letter saying she is leaving FASH 'to pursue new opportunities'. She will offer one month's notice, which she knows won't extend beyond the publication of her big unveiling as Fifi Fashion Insider tomorrow. Tiffanie assured Maya that the legal team at the paper had gone over the article and said she wasn't in breach of the law, just her contract of employment, which Rich Robinson would be foolish to punish her for given it would create more bad press for FASH, and Fifi Fashion Insider has become something of an anti-hero.

I don't even care, I just want out.

As Maya stops in the toilets of Café Liberty to touch up her make-up, she examines her reflection. She thinks about Christopher Diamond's big strong arm around her. She thinks about making Velma proud. She thinks about spending the money wisely. One hundred thousand dollars is almost as much as Maya's salary for two whole years, but she doesn't want to become lazy or spoiled. She wants to make this gift count. First, she wants to get rid of the shine on her face caused by rushing out of the office early with a thinly veiled excuse about a doctor's appointment. She wants to look a bit better than she does right now, flushed and frizzy-haired.

These pictures are going to be everywhere and I look awful.

Maya looks from the scrunched-up yellow Post-it in her right hand to the number above the door in front of her.

Eleven. That's it.

A tiny woman in leopard-print trousers bumps into Maya in the doorway, looking backwards to check if she'd left anything on her desk.

'Oh, sorry,' the woman huffs, almost annoyed at Maya for being in her way when she was the one not looking where she was going. 'He's in there.' A small face nods towards the photographer flashing a lightbulb in the light of an open studio.

Maya walks into the airy white room and sees a man. Bending down. The waistband of his underwear rises above slim grey jeans, chasing his green cashmere jumper up his back as he leans into a camera bag, revealing smooth olive skin even in winter. Maya's eyes dart across the studio to the sight of a familiar grey backpack in a far corner, sullied by sitting on the floor of a train carriage. A lightbulb flashes, startling mesmerised eyes and making Maya feel dizzy. He stands and turns around. It is him. Train Man. James Miller. The man Maya loved at first sight last year; who broke her heart this year, now standing in front of her looking baffled and beautiful.

James looks towards the open door at the entrance of the studio. Maya Flowers. The brave and radiant girl who gets his train, whose elegant collarbone he can't see right now.

'It's you. You've come to be shot?'

Maya blushes and laughs nervously.

He's here. This is home.

'I hope not.'

'For the paper I mean, for the *Evening Standard*.'

'Yep, that's me,' Maya shrugs stiffly.

'Wow, small world,' says James, pushing his glasses up his nose and trying not to look flustered. 'Sit down, sit down. Make yourself comfortable.' He scratches his head looking for somewhere more comfortable than the stool in front of the roll-down screen, but there isn't anywhere in the exposed stark brightness of the studio. 'You want a drink or something first?' James asks, wearing the role of photographer as a blanket of confidence. If this wasn't work, he would have choked. Lost for words.

He stands, looking expectantly at Maya, forlorn in the middle of the room, exposed even though she is cocooned in a grey sweater dress that swamps her frame. Pink woollen flowers creep up grey tights, softening the runner's muscle of her shin. Suede black pixie boots ground her.

'Sorry?' she says, unable to say much more. Disbelief that after all the time she spent unable to pluck up the courage to talk to him among the commuters and the crowds on the train, they are finally together, alone, in a studio in Soho. Her heart soars, and then sinks a little when she remembers.

'There are some manky old teabags in the kitchen but there's a coffee shop just out there. I'm going to grab an espresso. Do you want me to get you anything?'

'No, thanks,' says Maya. Confused. Dumbfounded. Embarrassed.

Photographer? I thought he worked in advertising?

'Back in a sec. Make yourself at home. That's where you'll be sitting.' James motions to the stool, stating the obvious, before walking out of the studio and onto the cobbles to a cafe a few doors down. He steadies himself on the other side of the door and leans back against a stone wall before closing his eyes and taking a deep breath. Maya looks around the room before closing her eyes and taking a deep breath.

James waits for his coffee and kicks himself for leaving so soon.

I was totally thrown.

But the fledgling photographer has learned that the first thing he must do to get the best picture possible is to make his subject feel comfortable, and Maya Flowers looked pretty uncomfortable to him.

Be cool.

Fighting an urge to run away, Maya puts her bag on the floor next to James's grey backpack and realises her hands are shaking. She smooths down a wayward wave to calm herself and her hair as he walks back in.

'Right, I got you a hot chocolate anyway in case you changed your mind. It's sunny but it's biting out there,' James says, smiling shyly as he hands Maya a cardboard cup.

Maya sees his dimple and is reassured.

'Actually hot chocolate is perfect. Thank you.'

The warm cup gets to work thawing Maya's nerves.

'If you can just sit there and be yourself, I need to get the lighting right...' James says as he fusses about the studio setting up the shot. 'There will be a few flashes while I sort the positioning, but have a seat and try to relax.'

Maya already has. Despite her embarrassment about what she did last spring, there is something so calming about James's face. Dimples, warmth, kindness. She inhales steam from the sweet syrupy chocolate.

They sit in comfortable silence while James dances around Maya with stands and a silver umbrella.

Maya fidgets a little to straighten her soft wool dress.

They speak at the same time.

'So what's this story...?'

'I didn't know you were a photographer.'

Freckles play peekaboo under a flash of light. 'Oh, you go first.'

James bumbles. 'What's your story then? Why have I been commissioned to photograph you?'

Thick sheepish lashes fall down.

'Fifi Fashion Insider. Have you heard of her?'

James laughs. Dimples get deeper.

'Yeah, she keeps popping up on my Twitter feed.'

'Well I am she. I'm killing her off tomorrow, committing professional suicide too by revealing myself as her in the paper, with your pictures, so I'd better hand in my notice while I'm at it.'

James looks up from where he's positioning the base of the tripod on the floor, mouth open in wonder.

'Wow, that's brave. You're being talked about everywhere. Something of a trailblazer is how I read it.'

Maya's heart races.

'It was stupid really. I should have just left with dignity. Lots of people don't like their job or their boss, they don't create a circus about it. But I didn't mean to.'

'I knew you did something at FASH from your email address when, you know...'

James raises the tripod, stops fussing, and stands still behind his camera facing Maya.

'The note. Yeah I'm sorry about that. I didn't mean to make life awkward for you. It was really rude and presumptuous of me. And ridiculous to think I could fall for someone I didn't know.'

Hearts tighten.

'It wasn't rude. It was the kindest, bravest, boldest thing anyone has ever done for me.' James removes his glasses and leans down to look through the lens before looking back up at Maya. 'It also made me be a bit braver myself.'

Maya stifles a smile.

I made him *braver?*

'How?'

'When you gave me the note I was in a miserable place. In lots of ways. I hated my job...'

Maya can tell he's holding something back.

'I worked in advertising,'

Maya mentally checks her face so it doesn't say '*I know!*'

'I was partnered with my best mate and we were doing OK, but I just wasn't excited about selling cat food or hair removal cream. I wanted to do something more creative.'

'I know how you feel,' Maya half sighs.

'Well your note, it made me think "Fuck it, I'll take a chance, give doing what I love a shot" – and I'm now doing this. Taking pictures for a living. And meeting some really interesting people. Like you. I'm earning half what I was and it's not been easy, but I'm getting there. Thanks to you really...'

Shoulders lower, eyes brighten and Maya relaxes on her perch.

'That's amazing,' she whispers.

James rises from behind the lens and they look at each other. Actual proper eye contact for the first time, without books or distance or commuters to hide behind. Well, the first eye contact since Maya pretended to drop her train ticket, but that didn't count.

James remembers the man with his arm around Maya and breaks away. 'Anyway, I better get these shots of you, the picture desk wants the edit tonight ready to print in tomorrow's first edition.'

James lifts the camera from its anchor and puts his glasses back on his nose.

Ah yes, short-sighted.

I wish I'd worn contacts.

Maya steals a look at James looking at her, the camera a protective shield for them both, and turns away for self-preservation, looking out of the window and up at the Christmas lights above the street outside.

He has a girlfriend.

Maya sighs. The last gasp of sunshine bounces off impressive illuminations outside and orange shards inside and James *sees* Maya. Click. Soft chestnut hair. The profile of her strong dappled nose facing the window to escape the sadness. Click. Still, full, statue-like lips. Click. He can see Maya throwing back her head and laughing from the depths of her core, even though she doesn't move. Click. He sees her on a beach, wet sand matting her wavy hair into twists. Click. He sees the man at the terminal with his arm around Maya's shoulder and a triumphant smile on his face. Click.

'James?'

James and Maya turn in unison towards the door of the studio. A woman with a white-blonde pixie crop stands tall in a black button-down coat.

'Kitty! What are you doing here?'

Kitty? Isn't that his girlfriend's name?

'Can we talk?'

'I'm kind of working.'

'Working?' A familiar flash of puzzlement dashes across thin lips as Kitty's long stiff body leans into the door frame, pleadingly.

'Hang on a sec.'

James removes the loop of the camera lead from his neck and repositions it onto the tripod. He looks at Maya observing him. He now feels as exposed as she did just minutes ago.

'I'll be one second,' James says to Maya with wide, aching eyes.

She doesn't look like Kitty Jones from the train.

The tall woman with the icy blonde hair takes James's hand in hers and leads him out. He neither flinches nor resists.

Maya sits alone on the stool. The sun has gone down. She feels silly and small and embarrassed, even though she already knew this was how the story ended.

In the small clean kitchen behind the reception area, Kitty shuts the door with a firm hand.

'Did your mum tell you?'

'What are you doing here?'

'Did your mum tell you?'

'Tell me what?'

'I've left Simon. It didn't work out.'

'Right. No. No, she didn't.'

'Well it was all wrong, he was such a shit. And I bust a gut for those kids. I'm not ready to be a mum. Those kids are a nightmare. I've been so so miserable, James. I made such a mistake. I'm so sorry.'

James looks at Kitty as she holds both of his hands with each of hers. 'What are you doing here?'

'I was Christmas shopping on Carnaby Street and I saw you coming out of a cafe. I couldn't believe it. I'd even been thinking about you today. I went in and sat there just waiting, getting the courage to come and tell you how I felt. I want us to be together.'

James releases himself from her grasp and runs his hands through his hair. His chest expands and contracts with a puff and a sigh.

'You haven't told me how you feel now, Kitty. Not about us. You've just told me how shit it was with Simon, and you just chanced upon me in Soho. That's not a reason to get back together. That's default. Give me something, give me a reason why.'

Kitty pauses, then takes James's hands again, weaving her long fingers into his like ivy creeping along guttering.

'We spent eleven Christmases together, let's not spend this one apart.'

'That's not a reason, that's just laziness.'

James untangles his fingers and frees himself. 'I have to get back to work. Happy Christmas, Kitty. Give your parents my love.'

He walks out of the kitchen. Kitty follows and turns her heel on a scowl, heading out of the door and back to her Christmas shopping.

James rushes back into the studio, desperate to get back to the girl from his train, the girl who gave him the note, the girl he was commissioned to photograph, who he just *saw* through his lens and wants to know so much more about. The stool in the middle of the studio sits vacant.

Tears roll down Maya's cheeks as she jumps off the number 73 bus and into a puddle. Clouds came with the dark and from nowhere a biblical storm dampened the spirits of commuters and Christmas shoppers. Maya dashes into the shelter of the station and the reverse waterfall suddenly feels like warm comfort in contrast to Euston Road. Waves get wavier. Her boots are ruined.

Maya looks down at the empty hot chocolate cup she's still clutching in her hand. 'James' is scrawled on it in royal blue marker. Holding something he held. Maya suddenly remembers winning the raffle and the trip to Paris with Clara.

I am the unluckiest lucky girl I know.

Her sodden feet squelch through to platform 8. An earlier train home full of optimistic early finishers, excited about getting back to people they love. Maya boards the train and looks left and right and sees a space on a luggage shelf at the back of the Superior Train carriage.

Maya had happily fallen out of the habit of looking for James, but an hour ago he tricked her with a spark of hope. A connection. Flattery. And now she's looking up the carriage for him from the sanctuary of the luggage shelf, even though she knows there is no possible way he could be on this train when he has to pack up the studio. And then probably have dinner in town with his skinny blonde girlfriend. And then probably go home and have amazing sex with her.

Maya wipes spidery mascara from under each eye with the fingertips of both hands. She examines the black mess smudging across whirls, loops and arches, as proof of what just happened.

But I knew he had a girlfriend. I just didn't realise he had two.

By the light of a light box in the attic room of the Victorian terrace, James examines the edit he just sent to the picture desk at the paper. He held one back. The picture he's blown up to have a closer look at. The one where Maya Flowers looks out of the window. A dark brow arches above a long lid where a single freckle leaps gaily away from her nose. Wide glassy pupils are caught in the process of shrinking, adjusting to the changing light, and James can almost hear the sigh of sadness float away from those beautiful lips and into the eaves of the dark room he is standing in. As James pushes his glasses back up his nose and strokes the outline of her lip with his forefinger, he wonders why Maya ran away. She seemed to regret writing the note but they got past that.

She has a boyfriend now.

Why would she run away?

I have to tell her how I feel.

James jumps down the stairs three at a time. Tomorrow Maya will hand in her notice and walk out of her job; he has to find that email address and get a message to her first. Or spend all morning at Hazelworth station waiting for her to pass through for what might be the last time.

Where's she going to when she leaves?

James finds his phone in the pocket of his peacoat, slumped over the sofa in the front room, and sees a missed call from his mum. Which reminds him about Kitty and how this afternoon she managed to wipe away any possible lingering feeling of love and abandonment he might have harboured for her. And then he realises.

She thinks Kitty and I are still together.

Maya Flowers. There she is. There's that email.

James runs back up two flights of stairs, to the attic room, to find his laptop so he can write his message with the composed honesty it deserves after all this time.

51

Maya walks through the imposing façade of FASH HQ for the final time. She got the 7.21 a.m. today, to come in early in the hope of catching Sam and telling him privately first, then clearing her emails and handing in her letter of resignation to Lucy before the paper drops mid-morning. Yesterday's encounter with James is no longer the most important thing on her mind, not while she deals with extracting herself from FASH anyway.

Needles spike through her belly button but she savours each of the lasts she will be doing on this, her shortest day at work. Her last walk through the columns. Her last nod at the receptionist. Her last pain au chocolat. Her last goodbye to Sam, who she still feels the need to clear the air with.

The receptionist with the headpiece that curls around her ear refuses to answer the phone until she puts down her coffee, even though she doesn't need her hands. A private stand-off only Maya is party to as she climbs the stairs to the canteen, nodding a hello as she disappears out of the receptionist's sight. Maya drinks in the images projected on the giant screen that runs from the ground all the way up to the top of the building for one last time. A model with wild hair and killer red lips to match her killer red stilettos. A blonde wrapped up in a khaki parka that Rich Robinson hopes will keep the yacht and its staff running for another year.

Maya stops to pick up a two-day-old pain au chocolat and looks around at the few early risers in the canteen. How many times did Maya sit at those wooden tables next to the glass balustrade that overlooks reception way down below and counsel her teammates? How many times did she and Emma eat falafel and tabbouleh or Asian noodles piled high from the best salad bar in London? How many times did she see young interns climb the stairs wearing the Marnie or the Swift or the Woodstock dress, excited and proud to be working at FASH? That seems so long ago now that getting out feels *right*.

Maya walks through the glass double doors and is surprised to see Lucy and Cressida both standing at Cressida's desk, talking conspiratorially.

'Speak of the devil,' says Cressida with an arched eyebrow, chewing gum clumsily in a way not befitting a Chelsea girl.

This isn't good.

The rest of the office is empty, apart from the background chatter of two tech guys getting watery coffee from a machine with plastic cups in the breakout kitchen further down the quad.

Lucy looks up and gives a measured smile.

'Morning, Maya, you're in early. Can we have a word please?'

Maya nods.

'I think it's best we go to the meeting room. For privacy.' Lucy is clutching a box file, a pen, and her phone.

Maya looks at the empty office around her, they don't need privacy. She has a sick feeling in the pit of her stomach.

This isn't how it was meant to be.

'Sure.'

Before Maya has a chance to remove her coat, she is walking back to the meeting room next to the glass double doors.

Cressida marches with triumph, smiling to herself because she's just handed a mighty juicy apple to the teacher.

'Gorgeous pants, Lucy. Are they Stella?'

Lucy doesn't feel the need to pepper the silence with chit-chat so she just doesn't answer. Instead she stands in the doorway with authority and ushers in Cressida and Maya, closing the door behind her with a seal of doom as Maya sits down, knowing what is coming. She unbelts her coat but doesn't take it off.

'We know it's you, Maya,' says Lucy, in an almost concili-atory tone. A harsh blonde fringe over dark, disappointed eyes.

Before Maya has the chance to ask how, Cressida sits up in her seat like head girl.

'Penelope from Walk In Wardrobe is now fashion assistant at the *Standard*. She saw the layout last night and called me. We need your passwords and login for everything, and you need to clear your desk and go.' A pout projects. 'I just *knew* it was you,' Cressida adds with a hiss.

'You thought it was Olivia.'

Lucy raises her palms to signal silence. 'That doesn't matter. What matters is you have let me down, Maya. You bit the hand that fed you and went behind our backs to spill all those FASH secrets. That's highly sensitive intel.'

'Not to mention highly illegal,' adds Cressida with a shake of her head.

Maya's shoulders shrink into her chair. She feels ridiculous.

To have been caught out; that it isn't going to end the way she planned.

What would Velma do?

'But FASH was never mentioned up to now. And I didn't say anything libellous, lawyers went over everything. Names were changed...'

'It's pretty bloody obvious who you're talking about, Maya,' shouts Lucy.

She'd stand up for herself, that's what.

Maya hears Velma's words ring in her ears.

Just be yourself.

'Only if you work here, and then maybe there's a reason it resonated.'

'Well it's a good job for you that Rich, Rich and Andy are all on the exec board ski trip this week. Going quietly will be less messy and less embarrassing all round. Not that a bloody double-page spread in the *Evening Standard* is going quietly. I'm gutted, Maya.'

Maya looks down and sees her fists clenched tightly on her lap. 'I'm not the bully here, Lucy. And if it's worth anything, I had my resignation letter in my bag, I was going to leave, I just wanted to clear my desk.'

Lucy looks back with round, disappointed eyes as she slides a pendant from side to side on the chain around her neck. 'It's not worth anything, Maya.'

'You don't have the luxury of clearing your desk,' snaps Cressida, sliding a notepad and pen across the table at Maya. 'Passwords!'

Maya scribbles, wanting to cry, but also wanting to laugh at the ridiculousness of it all.

'Where do you think you're going anyway? A career in *newspapers*?'

'I'm leaving to pursue new opportunities,' Maya tries to smile, although her mouth feels too shaky to.

'Good luck with that,' Cressida retorts through a snort.

'Actually, Cressida, I'm leaving to be anywhere but near you. Lucy, you built a brilliant and enthusiastic team, but somewhere in the past year it has turned sour, bitter and mean.' Tiny beads of perspiration dance on faint freckles.

Lucy studies Maya's face and doesn't say anything.

Cressida looks between her and Maya, waiting for a reaction from their boss.

'Oh puh-lease! This is sour grapes because *I* got the job *you* so wanted.'

Maya stands and belts her coat again.

'Ask anyone in the team if they're happy, Lucy. Ask Rich if he thinks this FASHmas is as good as last year. Think about it in January when the sales figures are tallied up.'

Lucy raises an eyebrow as if to say Maya has a point. FASHmas has been panned inside HQ this year. Cressida made it look like the pages of a society magazine. Jutting bones; the few high-end high-fashion pieces FASH stocks; unwearable looks; miserable-looking models. Rich Robinson slammed Lucy last Friday, just before he headed off skiing, because FASHmas this year didn't look very, well, fun. But that's another conversation Lucy will have with Cressida, who already looks aghast.

'And if sales do go through the roof again, which I doubt, be sure to ask Rich to pay his staff their bonus before he upgrades his yacht.'

Maya walks out of the room, closing the door behind her, leaving Lucy and Cressida to their bleak exchange.

Back at her desk, Maya unsticks the photo of Henry, Jack and Oscar from the edge of her monitor, pulls a second coat from the coat stand that she'd discarded on a warm day way back whenever, picks up her notebook and favourite pen, and crawls under her desk to scoop out the three pairs of shoes that have been sitting there with the mice for so long.

They're my things, I'm taking them.

Sam walks in whistling to the music in his ears. He sees Maya scramble out from under her desk.

'My...'

'I'm sorry, Sam,' she says, standing, smoothing soft waves away from her face. 'It was me.'

'Eh?'

'I was Fifi Fashion Insider. I'm sorry I didn't tell you.'

'What?'

Maya bursts into tears, crams her belongings into a spotty FASH delivery bag and walks out, through the glass double doors, as Sam watches her. She heads down the stairs and out of FASH HQ for the final time, without any intention of buying the newspaper on her way back to the train station. She doesn't want to see how stupid she looks from James Miller's point of view.

Cressida hammers letters and numbers at Maya's keyboard under the guise of ratting out further treachery and spilt secrets.

'Ah, here we go. Email.'

As a gleeful finger scrolls down through the inbox, she reads out loud to no one in particular, unselfconscious that people are starting to trickle into work and don't yet know Maya has been told to leave, that *she* was Fifi Fashion Insider. Tact and subtlety were never Cressida's strong points.

'Hmmm, OK. IT support, round robin from womenswear,

work experience request, charity donation request, no-doubt dull email from her mum... Oh hang on. This looks interesting... Subject matter: The Guy From The Train.'

Cressida reads silently, suspecting this might be juicy, licking her lips as she does.

Maya,

I'm so very sorry you left suddenly tonight, I thought the shoot was going well – luckily I got some great pictures, you photograph beautifully.

Although it might not matter to you now, I have to let you know that the girl who came into the studio, she's not my girlfriend – she was, but I hadn't seen her for six months, and I don't want to see her again.

I want to see you, because I saw you properly for the first time today, so if you're still free for that drink, let me know.

If not, I'll leave you in peace and wish you happy travels.

James

x

Three sentences and a friendly sign-off. And a kiss.

Cressida swings around in Maya's chair.

'Sam, do you have Maya's personal email address?' Cressida has no intention of forwarding the message on, but knowing that she could have fills her with smug satisfaction.

'Yeah, why?'

'Urgh, check this out,' she says, gesturing two fingers down her throat.

Sam leans over Cressida's shoulder and reads the email. He ponders for a second, thinking about the girl who was so blind about this idiot from the train, she couldn't even see that Sam had fallen for her; and every time they went for a coffee Maya dug in the knife, throwing his feelings back in his face.

'Fuck it Cressida, I think I lost her personal email the last time I lost my phone.'

'Oh, you are naughty!' Cressida giggles, joyfully leaning into Sam's arm as she glides a small black arrow to a dustbin icon and presses delete.

52

December 2014

Maya tiptoes carefully across a shiny marble floor towards a grand staircase in front of her, laid thick with patterned carpet in a shade of midnight blue. Her silver strappy heels aren't that high, but carrying a conical tower of 148 circles of deliciousness that will bring smiles to 148 faces makes her feel nervous. One slip on the polished foyer floor could see Maya's hard work for the past three days and nights come crashing down around her in a heap of cracked shells and colourful fragments.

It had already been a difficult journey from Hazelworth with a large hatbox packed tightly with macarons in a snail-like spiral. In the kitchen of the grand Westminster venue, while chefs barked at sous-chefs and wedding coordinators shouted at waitresses, Maya quietly threaded macarons onto toothpicks and stacked them two rows at a time in deep purple lavender, bright orange blossom, and fuchsia pink rose before doing it all again, twice over in decreasing circles to the peak. She lifted the light styrofoam cone covered in a sheet of newspaper from one of Felipe Oliveira's vintage copies of

O Globo and placed it delicately on top of the large, circular, flat lemon and lavender cake base, covered in crisp royal icing.

Now Maya is flushed, relieved and pleased that her carnival confection is bigger, brighter and more uniform than the one attempt at a macaron tower she made before. They might not be the pretty pastels of Pierre Hermé but this is the best thing Maya has ever made. And it's so Nena.

I peaked! Maya thinks, before the ball of her right foot slides across marble, further than anticipated, and the entire tower wobbles seemingly in slow motion, first right, then left, in unsteady hands.

'Here!' says a man in a white tuxedo and a black bow tie, as he puts his arms around Maya's, making a frame to prop her up. She steadies the cake, the tower stops leaning.

'Oh god, my heart stopped. Thank you so much, that was so close!' Maya's voice is higher than usual.

'It's OK. It's OK,' the man with sandy blond hair reassures her. 'It would have broken my heart to watch that fall. Let me help.'

Steady hands take over as they head up the blue and gold carpet.

'We're late,' winces Maya through gritted teeth.

'My brother wouldn't expect anything else of me.'

Maya thought this guy looked familiar. Tall and dashing and reassuring and confident, although Tom's brother has more hair, messy and blond.

'Where am I taking this... this... pièce de résistance?'

Maya blushes, but she knows it's true. She is bursting with pride and knows Nena will love it.

'Into the Grand Hall, they want it on display during the ceremony – but we're cutting it fine.'

At the top of the sweeping staircase, double doors are

pulled open by ushers to reveal the wedding venue. High above family and friends, two chandeliers twinkle in excitement, light refracted onto crystal from winter sunshine, through long tall rectangular windows looking out onto Big Ben on the right. Those not whispering expectantly turn around to see who the double doors were swept open for, from their neat rows of chairs across a huge oak-sprung floor. Maya is startled to be stared at, but Tom's brother swaggers towards the front to place the cake and macaron tower on its stand in the right-hand corner of the room. On the left, a woman with brazen hair and curves squeezed defiantly into a little black dress waits for her cue. Between them a table covered in a crisp white tablecloth holds a registrar's folder, and large balls of fuchsia, orange and purple roses bring a Brazilian zing to a stoic city venue. A huge wooden heart-shaped frame spray-painted in silver hangs from the ceiling above the table, a studio prop from Nena's Tiny Dancers show, swinging ever so slightly as it hovers in anticipation.

Tom holds hands with his four-year-old best man while he says hellos to guests and talks to his parents at the front.

'Untle Izaat!'

'Arli!'

Isaac Vernon scoops his nephew up in his arms and together the two of them give Tom a bear hug, Arlo enjoying the novelty of being the same height as his daddy and his uncle.

Maya fusses over the macaron tower and twists it a little to show off its best side.

'Perfect!' she whispers to herself, and looks towards the back for a single chair to sit on. Maya – and Tom's brother apparently – seem to be the only two wedding guests without a plus-one.

Nena's mother beckons Maya to join her at the front.

'Hello darling,' she says, kissing each of Maya's cheeks. Taller, paler-skinned, more fragrant than her daughter, but her taut stomach and lithe legs tell tales of the family trade.

Maya embraces her, clutching the arm of a teal lace dress.

'You look stunning, Victoria.'

'You too, darling!' she says, looking Maya up and down. '"Green is the prime colour of the world and that from which its loveliness arises!"'

Maya's emerald-green dress is more vivid than Victoria's shade of teal, although it is softened by her creamy skin and faint brown freckles. A white faux-fur stole sits on spaghetti straps and soft shoulders. Maya almost wore the Vivienne Westwood she bought with her game show winnings, but something held her back.

She takes the compliment bashfully and goes to run her fingers through rampant hair before remembering it's pinned up in a loose bun on the side. Above it sits a long diamanté jewel, like a whisper above her right ear.

'How's Felipe?' asks Maya in hushed tones.

'Terrified!' Victoria says giddily. 'He thought he'd never have to do this!'

Tom spots the macaron tower atop the cake in the corner and turns to Maya.

'Thank you!' he mouths, clasping his palms together in gratitude.

A lady in a functional suit walks up the aisle, nods to her assistant standing behind the table, then gives the woman in the black dress a smile as if to say 'Go'.

Smoky tones of Bebel Gilberto's 'Samba e Amor' fill the grand room from front to back and guests are transported from Westminster to Nena's father's hometown of Salvador. A small pigeon-chested man walks in with Nena on his arm.

Same height as each other, same bronze skin defying a British winter. The folds of Nena's silk dress flow down her body like freshly poured cream running from shoulder to floor, kissing her breasts to create a plunging space from her collarbone to a sparkling waistband of silver beads and sequins. Matching silver epaulettes sparkle on her shoulders.

The guests gasp. Victoria's mouth wobbles. Maya's eyes fill with tears as she marvels at how beautiful her best friend is. At how, even now, Nena is full of surprise and wonder. Maya would never have picked out that wedding dress for Nena, but in it she dazzles. When they talked about boyfriends or future husbands on those winter walks along the seafront in the sideways rain, Maya imagined the acrobat would run away with the circus and marry a ringmaster in a net dress so cheap and so frilly it was only fit for carnival. But then Nena always managed to surprise, so why is Maya surprised now? She gives Nena a huge beaming smile as she approaches the front.

Nena's enormous, mischievous eyes look humble as she hands bold blooms to her best woman.

Victoria tries to mouth 'Love you' to Nena but her lips are too shaky to make the right shapes. Felipe gives Tom a gracious nod, patting his back as he returns to Victoria. He takes his wife's hand. 'Samba e Amor' comes to a finish and the ceremony begins.

'Sorry I didn't introduce myself – I was so caught up in catching that unbelievable biscuit tower, I forgot to say. I'm Isaac.'

Isaac extends a rough but reliable hand.

'Maya. Pleased to meet you. Again. Oh and they were macarons...'

'Sorry, Macaron Maya,' Isaac laughs.

Maya stands at the bar at the back of the ballroom, mixing the slushed ice of her caipirinha with a flamingo-shaped cocktail stirrer. The chink chink whirl inaudible against the music. Flavours of summer fill Maya's body and the warmth of the room makes her shed her stole and put it on a stool under the bar.

Isaac looks down at the sweetheart neckline of Maya's emerald-green dress. 'Great party, huh?'

'Oh, it's amazing. But Nena always knew how to throw a party.'

'Look at them!' Isaac says, leaning back on the bar with both elbows behind him. 'I'm so chuffed for Tom. After all that shit with Kate, I never thought he'd be in as good a place as this. And so soon. Lucky bastard.'

Maya laughs.

Isaac rubs the sandy stubble of his five o'clock shadow. A black bow tie hangs loose around his open collar.

'Well he deserves it. He's one of the good guys,' Maya smiles. 'And look at Arlo – he is too cute, you must just want to eat him up!'

'God, I love him,' says a proud uncle.

Maya and Isaac survey the scene in front of them. Nena and Tom dance with a sleepy boy slumped over Daddy's shoulder. Victoria and Felipe foxtrot around a sprung floor with panther-like elegance while clumsy guests attempt to glide gracefully around them.

'Wanna dance?' says Isaac, pulling his open bow tie away from his neck and putting it on the bar.

'Why not?' says Maya.

53

'We don't normally book photographers who haven't shot for magazines before,' says the soft voice of a girl with a tiger's face on her sweatshirt.

'Right...' says James, when what he really wants to say is, 'Why did you agree to see me then?'

They are sitting in the cafe of Tate Modern overlooking the river. James's bottom feels cold and bony on the metal chair he's sitting on.

The girl talks with the high quiet voice of a cartoon mouse.

'But my art director and I really liked the shots you emailed us. And I do like your portfolio – this one is ace,' she says, pointing to the elderly groom as she turns the page. 'I really like the way you can almost see what he's thinking, like you're getting into his brain through the light in his eyes.'

James remembers the print in his backpack, equally revealing, more personal. He takes out a tube and unrolls it to show Tammy Newbold, picture editor at *The Passenger*, London's coolest men's lifestyle magazine.

'Oh, I love it. Why's it not in your portfolio?'

'It's recent, I'll put it in soon.'

'Well it's great. I think you're great,' Tammy squeaks. 'If you feel able to handle some of the big celeb egos we shoot then we'd love to give you a go. I'll talk to my art director and get back to you, probably after the Christmas break now, that OK?'

'Yeah that's great. Thanks Tammy,' says James, surprised by the total turnaround in how he thought this meeting was going.

'I'd better get back to the office, it's our Christmas party tonight and we're trying to put the March issue to bed.'

'March, wow,' says James, leaving cash on a small silver circle. 'I'm used to tight newspaper deadlines, turning around portraits in just hours. It would be nice to really put time and thought into a shoot.'

Tammy smiles, and wraps herself protectively under a blanket shawl. 'Off anywhere nice now? I guess you don't have office parties being a freelancer do you?'

'Not any more. But I'm meeting some mates for a few drinks on Charlotte Street. How about your party?'

'Oh, the usual. A club in Old Street. The features' girls will be dodging the creep from accounts. Someone who's normally straight-laced will get wasted and try to dry-hump the MD.'

James laughs quietly, dimples barely reveal themselves, and he slides the cardboard tube back into his backpack, zips up the wallet of his portfolio and says goodbye to Tammy.

'See you in the New Year, James.'

The wintry night beyond the long high windows of the Grand Hall makes the carnival atmosphere inside seem even more sizzling as Nena and former chorus-line colleagues take to the floor in a group samba. The elegant dress from this afternoon has been hitched up to her knickers, showing a brown thigh that reminds Maya of *Princess Tam Tam*.

A flurry of snow starts to flutter under the light of the black lamp posts on the street outside and Maya surveys the scene inside. Happy. Tired. Glowing from the many compliments she received for her lemon and lavender cake and the macaron tower on top.

This is how I want to remember today.

Maya is never the last one standing at a wedding, so she finds her white stole, props her silver clutch under her arm and pushes open one of the huge doors that leads to the sweeping staircase. At the bottom of the stairs, Maya collects the hatbox from a cloakroom attendant and swings it with abandon by its cord handle, relieved it is empty as she heads out into the frozen flurry.

'Taxi!' she calls, into the buzz of Parliament Square.

'You leaving already?' A figure standing in the light of a lamp post puffs on a cigarette. Snow falls onto the shoulders of his white jacket and melts.

'I have to catch my train,' says Maya. 'And really, you don't want to see my lambada.'

'No really, I do!' Isaac laughs.

A taxi drives past without stopping.

'Well, it's always best I leave that to Nena. Taxi!'

Taxis whizz past. Taking politicos back to their constituencies, tourists onto clubs and couples from their office parties to steamy hotel rooms. It is the last Friday before Christmas.

'Here, let me try. TAXI!' Isaac yells, as he throws his cigarette butt into a drain.

A taxi stops. Maya feels slightly disempowered. And very cold.

'Thank you. Again. You had my back earlier with the cake, I appreciate it.'

'No problem. Hey, can I call you sometime, go for a drink?'

Maya looks at Isaac. Tall and dashing with messy sandy blond hair and the same deep-set but twinkling eyes as Tom. She thinks of Tom and Nena and Arlo, who has got a second wind, upstairs on the dance floor in a happy bubble of love.

I want love. I want Train Man, I want James Miller.

'Can I say no?' Maya smiles warmly as she shivers.

'Of course!' laughs Isaac, taken aback by honesty.

'You're lovely, but it's just if today has taught me anything it's to follow my heart. The butterflies and all that stuff. It matters. It hits you. Nena could have anyone at uni, she's never been short of a date since then. But Tom, he just... BOOM, changed everything. And when you know, you know. And when it's forced, well you know that too.' Maya is shivering.

'Are ya comin, love?' shouts the cabbie, trying not to sound riled.

Maya nods and Isaac smiles as his sturdy arm props the taxi door open.

'Well, you know I was only asking you out for a drink, not to marry me, but it's cool, I understand.'

They laugh.

'It was lovely to meet you, Isaac. And I'm sure we will again. Maybe I'll know how to do the lambada by then too.'

Maya slides her hatbox across the seat of the taxi and gets in after it.

'Nice to meet you, Macaron Maya.'

'See you around, Untle Izaat.'

Isaac gives a lackadaisical salute as he closes the door and nods Maya on her way to the train station.

54

Maya rushes across the terminal, under the reverse waterfall, past the wall of orange digits, to her train on platform 8. An Inferior Train. The last train home. Her skipping heart starts to sink a little as she knows that tonight, the last Friday before Christmas, this train will be the vomit comet, full of burger and Cornish pasty smells, sticky floors, and drunken men trying to be funny. In her emerald-green dress to just below very cold knees, Maya feels far too elegant for an icky Inferior Train after midnight.

Why didn't I just book a hotel?

A ten-second high-pitched beep, the ding of doors, and the driver announces that tonight this train will be stopping at all eight stations along the line to Hazelworth, not the usual two.

Her tired arms hug the hatbox as Maya's stole gives little warmth on a train with broken heating. She tries to rest her head on the box but the stiff curve of cardboard and its monochrome stripes make her feel even colder.

Across the aisle a woman with lank brown hair scraped

tight into a straightened ponytail slumps across a man in a leather jacket. A group of teens out of sight but well in earshot cackle about their night at Camden Stables. Maya tries to cling to memories of a beautiful day as she cuddles into her ribs for warmth.

Please just get me home.

The carriage suddenly plunges into darkness and the train brakes to a screeching halt. The woman with the straightened ponytail slips off her boyfriend's lap, sliding down his legs and into the facing seat in front of her. Maya's fall is broken by the hatbox, which bends under the impact.

'Shit,' Maya whispers.

The clock on her phone says 01:31. Panicked passengers go quiet as everyone waits for an announcement. Maya looks at her phone and scrolls through photos of the day to give her a lift. A box flashes up: twenty per cent battery remaining.

Bugger.

Maya switches off her phone to preserve what battery remains and looks out of the window to try to decipher where she is. A freckled nose accidentally touches smeared glass and makes her recoil. It's pitch-black outside, which means they're either in a tunnel or at the part of the track where the train passes through a high grassy verge that must only be as wide as two trains. Maya knows this line. Given the lack of houses and the time on the clock, she thinks – hopes – that she is three quarters of the way home.

A voice crackles faintly from above.

'Sorry about this, there seems to be a problem up ahead. Signals are all fine but we're not sure if someone is messing about on the line. Since I put on the brakes so suddenly we do have a bit of an electrics failure but we'll get them switched back on as soon as possible. We are behind another train and waiting for further information, but as soon as I hear I'll let you know. In the meantime, sorry for the delay and the darkness. I'll update you shortly.'

On the other side of an internal door, Maya hears people shout.

'Turn the heating on, mate!'

Maya shivers, and switches her phone back on for reassurance.

Another box flashes up: ten per cent battery remaining.

Already?

She looks across at the silhouette of the woman with the ponytail as she tries to rouse her boyfriend, still oblivious that they have been plunged into darkness, somewhere on the line. He is dribbling and asleep and smells of beer and sweat and stale leather – but he is there. However useless he is right now, that woman isn't on her own.

At 01:53 the lights come back on. The giggling teens who had started telling ghost stories sound disappointed. Maya is relieved. She looks at her phone once more for company.

Please start moving.

More pictures: Arlo kissing Nena with the soft clumsiness and innocent beauty of a besotted four-year-old; Tom, Nena and Arlo sitting opposite Maya on the circular top table; Victoria rubbing lipstick off Felipe's cheek; close-ups of the macaron tower before it started to look threadbare; university friends; samba dancers; TV presenters; backing singers.

What a shit end to a brilliant day.

Without announcement or fanfare, the train starts to roll slowly out of the darkness of the tunnel or the grassy verge, and Maya sees fields changing colour from the hard dark brown of frozen winter soil to white in the flurry of snow

343

under the moonlight. She now knows exactly where she is, almost three stops from home, slightly heartened by some light and familiarity.

'Sorry about that, someone did jump onto the track in front of the train ahead. That one's stuck but we're going to roll into the next station where this train will be taken out of service.'

The driver pauses for the collective groan he can't hear from his cabin at the front of the train.

'Station staff will advise you on a rail replacement service, or you can find alternative transport.'

Maya's mind races.

Alternative transport? At 2 a.m. in a sleepy village station?

Maya can't wait for hours in the snow for a rail replacement service. Especially not in a strappy green dress, silver sandals and a tiny faux-fur stole.

The pub will be closed.

Maya looks at her phone desperately.

She thinks of Jacob and Florian but knows they'll both have been out drinking tonight. And she can't call Clara and Robbie and wake three exhausted little boys. And Herbert and Dolores will be long asleep, snuggled together in bed in the house on the hill, mobiles left downstairs or switched off.

I have no one.

Maya looks in her silver clutch and scrabbles around for cash. She knew Felipe Oliveira wouldn't let anyone pay for a drink at his daughter's wedding so she didn't take much money with her, only what was in her purse as she rushed to get the hatbox of macarons and its large lemon and lavender base into the taxi that was waiting outside her flat at lunchtime. Maya sees the reassurance of a crisp twenty-pound note.

I hope it's enough. This is a nightmare.

Then Maya remembers to be grateful that she's not stuck on the train in front. Or the person whose soul shot out of their body on impact with the windscreen just three miles up the track. Or that person's family. Or the driver, for whom Christmas will also be ruined.

Get a grip Flowers. Someone just died. You have crossed the Darien Gap on your own, you can get home from Rockfield at two in the morning.

The train rolls slowly and comes to a stop on a quiet village platform. The snow flurry builds, swirling chaotically under the lamps that light the exit. Maya looks at it as she steps off the train, putting an unusually graceful footprint into virgin snow, and it reminds her of the precision and elegance of Felipe and Victoria Oliveira's dance as they moved around the oak-sprung floor hours earlier. She thinks about how they're probably already tucked up in bed, holding each other tight on this momentous day for their only child.

Maya looks to the pub down the steps that lead to the foot of the railway bridge. She has passed that pub every working day of her adult life but has never been inside. The lights are off, the doors are bolted shut. Disgruntled passengers gather outside it in coats and hats and scarves and gloves and Maya hears questions flying across the night sky as disorderly and chaotic and cold as the snow.

'Who would do such a selfish thing?'

'Why isn't the landlord getting out of bed and offering us sanctuary?'

'Where is the bus replacement service?'

'Why aren't there any taxis?'

'Why did I take this train when I meant to come home earlier?'

'Who can I talk to about this?'

'Where are the staff?'

'Why isn't my wife answering the phone?'

'Who's in charge here?'

Maya doesn't feel angry. She feels cold, vulnerable and alone. She looks around. There must be at least 150 frosty, angry, tipsy people, all more appropriately dressed, and she feels utter despair.

A taxi swings into the station, the first to get word of this captive market. A tall man in a fedora and a long, straight coat jumps into the back and says 'Hazelworth,' as if it's a military command: quickly, efficiently, without making eye contact with anyone.

'Hang on a minute, mate!' says a woman with a lot of gold around her neck as she stands to block the door he was about to pull shut. 'There are loads of people 'ere going to Hazelworth. Budge up.'

The man slides along with a sneer while the woman weighed down with gold and her friend squeeze in next to him.

'I may as well too,' says a young man sheepishly, getting in the front passenger seat. The driver doesn't care. More stops, more money.

Standing on the pavement with numb toes painted oxblood red, Maya wishes she had been quicker.

Or just less polite. Pockets of people group together, asking where each other is from. Nortonbury. Leathermore. Peterham. Arguments break out over whose need is greatest. So much for Blitz spirit.

Maya looks at her phone and decides to attempt to wake Herbert on the landline. He would rather get changed out of his nightshirt and come to collect Maya than have her standing in the cold feeling scared. Even at twenty-eight, a girl might need rescuing. Freezing fingers press a button to activate a phone but the screen stays blank, the battery dead.

'You're stuck too?' says a calm voice among the hullaballoo.

Maya turns around and looks up. Tall, safe, comforting Train Man is standing facing her. Or 'photographer: James Miller'. Their names sat side by side in the newspaper, although neither of them opened it to see the finished article, neither could face it. Maya gasps, exhaling breathy relief that rolls out as steam in the cold night.

'It's you.' Maya's blue lips can barely emit words but relief washes over her and suddenly the hostile white night sky seems like a protective blanket swaddling them.

'Big night out?' James says, looking at Maya in her finery. The hair jewel that sat straight above her ear slopes diagonally above a looser, dishevelled side bun. Her green dress shines like a jewel in the darkness.

Maya blushes and gently touches the bun, making sure it's still pinned up at all.

'My best friend's wedding. It was the most wonderful day ever... until now.'

James tries not to look deflated.

'Well, not now,' Maya concedes. 'I must say I'm relieved to see you among all this.' Maya looks around, her brow furrows despairingly at people climbing over each other and shouting, and looks back at James, wrapped in a long cable-knit scarf from the collar of his navy peacoat up to his full and thoughtful lips. Black rectangles frame wide, lovely eyes. Eyes Maya feels she has known all her life. She wants to stand on tiptoes and bury her head in James's scarf, to nestle into his neck, just as she longed to the first day she saw him on the train, but she stops herself as she remembers Kitty Jones, whichever of those two girls she was.

Taxis start to stream into the station approach and disgruntled passengers elbow each other out the way, now in packs, so that this next taxi will be their taxi. Tension cuts through a sleepy village while most of its inhabitants are unaware.

Maya and James hover at the back, facing each other as they lean into the arch of the pub's closed door, framed by hanging baskets, colourful flowers trying to stand up to the snow.

'About what happened in the studio...' James looks down at the floor and sees snow settling on his boots. 'I hope I didn't say something to upset you.' He looks up, dark eyebrows dive in confusion. 'You just disappeared.'

'I'm sorry – you got your shot though, yes? The story went down a storm I hear, and, as expected, it cost me my job.' Maya tries to steer the subject. Embarrassed as she is about being outed as Fifi Fashion Insider, it's less embarrassing than falling for a man who is in love with someone else.

'Did you get my email?'

'THAT'S MY TAXI!' bellows a woman in a Rudolph jumper.

'Look, James, it's all good. I get it. You have a girlfriend. Can't win 'em all!' Maya shrugs, trying to make light of it. 'And some good came of all this weirdness. After what you said about starting all over again with photography, doing something creative, I decided that this should be my new direction.' Maya raises the empty hatbox.

'Millinery?'

'No!' Maya laughs through chattering teeth. 'You said I was brave, but I think you are, you had more to lose giving up something you were doing so well in. So I decided to stop feeling sorry for myself and I've enrolled in a patisserie course. Starts in January. And my friend's wedding cake today – that was my first commission.' Maya beams proudly. 'I'd show you a picture but my phone died.'

'That's brilliant, Maya.'

He said my name.

Maya glows.

James's smile drops.

'She's not my girlfriend, you know.'

'It's none of my business if she is.'

'Well she isn't. She was. For eleven years. But I've been single for six months.'

Maya is confused. About the girl he held hands with at the studio; the one who slept on his shoulder that steamy summer morning after Jack White.

'But what about the Chinese girl, beautiful face…?'

James looks puzzled. '*Josie*? She's one of my best friends.' He breaks into a smile. His dimple deepens in the dark. 'No, Josie's definitely not my girlfriend. But Kitty was,'

Maya thinks of the woman in the studio with the pixie crop of white-blonde hair.

'She wanted to talk to me, she'd changed her mind about an affair she'd had. But she was too late. I'd already seen you.'

Another taxi zooms into the station approach, the driver hoping the four punters he's about to pick up live far away from each other.

'"Seen me"?' quizzes Maya, repositioning her stole over the spaghetti straps of her green dress and wrapping her arms around herself as she shivers.

'Here.'

James slides the straps of his grey backpack off his shoulders and swings it in front of him. The top doesn't quite close due to the long cardboard tube sticking out of it. James draws it out, the way he used to draw inner tubes of wrapping paper out of his waistband when he was playing knights and dragons with Francesca as children.

He hands the tube to Maya, who takes it from the other end and pops open the white stopper.

James removes his coat. 'Here, take this too, you're freezing.'

He carefully rests his thick wool peacoat around Maya's shoulders like a heavy cape. She breathes in the smell of him on the upturned collar that brushes her cheek and looks at him intently. Not wanting to pull away from him to look inside the tube.

Maya slides out a roll of photographic paper and unfurls the scroll. She breaks James's gaze to see a large picture of her in profile. Looking out of a window at the last of the Soho sun bouncing off shards of orange dotted around sad brown irises.

'Gosh.'

'I didn't send that one to the paper, I kept that back. For you. I've been wanting to give it to you but just haven't seen you.'

Maya's not sure if it's the cold or the caipirinhas, but she can't get her head around any of this.

'I don't get the 8.21 anymore,' Maya shrugs in confusion but the weight of James's coat anchors her shoulders, warming her from her tummy out. Suddenly Maya can feel her toes again.

James looks at Maya, she sees defeat in his dark eyes.

'After you ran off I went home and looked at the photos on the light box. This one,' he nods to the picture now curled back together, 'it's the most beautiful photograph I have ever taken.' James says it with such conviction, orange shards drown under tears.

'You can fall for someone you don't know, Maya.'

Maya is so shocked, her mouth hangs open.

'Here, you keep it,' James says, as he hands Maya the tube. He wonders what her boyfriend will think of him giving Maya the picture, knowing he too will agree it's beautiful.

Maya tucks the tube under her arm beneath the navy peacoat cape without taking her eyes off James, locked in the sanctuary of the pub doorway.

The last of the aggrieved passengers bundle into the last taxi and the woman with lank brown hair scraped back into a ponytail bellows out of a rear window.

'Room for one more!'

Her drunken boyfriend slumped on the seat next to her doesn't flinch.

'You take it. You're freezing. I'll wait for the next one,' James says, preparing himself to walk two towns to get home tonight.

Maya looks at the woman. 'No, thanks. I'm staying,' she says, nodding in James's direction.

'Won't your boyfriend wonder where you are?'

Boyfriend?

'I don't have a boyfriend.'

Maya and James lock eyes and laugh nervously.

Cold but content, James holds Maya's face in his hands and wipes a snowflake from her eyelash with his thumb.

'Here, take this,' he says, removing his cable-knit scarf and coiling it around Maya's neck. As James's arm circles above Maya's head and the scarf rises, she thinks of Tom spinning Nena around the dance floor, just hours ago. As she watched, Maya thought it would be a long time before that would ever happen to her. Her Seeing The Future skills have let her down again and she doesn't mind one bit.

Now the world around Maya starts to spin and the street lights and snow and hanging baskets and railway bridge all whir into a blur beyond the comfort of James's winding arm. Tingling feet edge onto tiptoes, silver sandals shine in the moonlight, and Maya reaches up to touch James's lips with hers. He kisses her back. Full of warmth on a cold night. Full of hope for having arrived. Full of excitement for the journey ahead of them. Full of relief to be home.

Epilogue

January 2015

Maya stands on the southbound platform hugging a weighty hardback book. For five minutes she has tried mastering the fundamentals of French pastry, but can't concentrate, her brain whirling like a palmier, wondering where he is. She looks up to the far front end of the platform, shielding her eyes from the cold bright sunshine with her hands.

Maybe if I edge back up there.

Maya looks at the clock. 8.19 a.m. She feels a familiar wrench in the pit of her stomach.

Just see.

She puts the heavy book into a large shopper under her shoulder and feels its weight pulling her down to one side. She looks down at the concrete platform as one patent grey brogue moves in front of the other, advancing under the hem of a chambray skirt and cable-knit tights. A shiny new treat to herself for this shiny new chapter; paying full price for new shoes filled Maya with a comfortable feeling of liberty and abandon.

She advances with trepidation and feels the haunting

sensation of a reassuring palm, gently pressing into the small of her back, urging her along the platform.

'That was close,' says James.

Maya stops in her tracks.

'I thought you were going to miss it!' Relief floods her, and James rubs her back tenderly, encouragingly. 'Did you get your gear?'

'Yep.' James swings the camera case on his right arm and taps the ninja blades of the tripod and lighting parasol rising from his grey backpack. 'Always cutting it fine,' James laughs, as he slides his hand under Maya's jacket and tucks it around her waist. 'I didn't want to miss your first day. Shall I walk you to your building? I have enough time before my shoot.'

'That would be lovely,' Maya says, as she leans into James's arm.

A Superior Train rolls into the station. Doors ding, buttons illuminate, passengers get off. Maya and James allow Inflatable Arms to burst forward in front of them before they board the train in step. James sees one last double seat and leads Maya to it. As they sit, Maya cranes her head into the curve of James's neck and closes her eyes.

Maya thinks about her patisserie course, a new career ahead of her, and feels that strange cocktail of nerves and excitement. She thinks of Velma and Duke Diamond, how they alighted their train together and stayed with each other until his death – and hers too, because there really was no one else. And Maya thinks of her Seeing The Future skills. Perhaps they weren't so wrong after all – Maya *did* see herself with Train Man, together in a happy future.

The train gathers speed and Maya and James sit, facing forwards, this time, holding hands.

Acknowledgements

Heartfelt thanks go to my agent, the amazing Rebecca Ritchie, who is the super-smart romantic to my hopeless one. Thanks for your belief, enthusiasm and energy, I am so grateful we found each other. Big love to the team at Aria and the wider (award-winning, might I add...) Head of Zeus family. Enormous thanks to my editor, Sarah Ritherdon, for heading up the axis of awesomeness and championing *The Note*. And also to the clever designers, sales and production team at Aria, including the brilliant Yasemin Turan and Melanie Price – thanks for your wisdom in helping me guide Maya and James to the right platform.

Thanks also to my book squad: Kathleen, Vicki, Guro, Becky and Liz – all strong and sisterly women, who all kindly offered to read early iterations of my manuscript and fed back with honesty and advice to help me keep moving forward. Thanks also to Rebecca Kelly for helping me jump over the hurdles that kept stacking up along the way; to mentors Helen Placito, Celia Duncan, Melissa Dick; and to Ali Harris, Katy Regan, Marigold Atkey and Ian Critchley for their wisdom and their time along the journey.

To my amazing friends who have held my hand through

this drama from the very start: Esther, Ali, Michelle, Cara, plus Navaz and the whole kickass Cosmeal clan. Also to my Running Bitches: Sarah, Sophie and Guro, putting the world to rights as we put one foot in front of the other.

To my siblings I adore and to my parents: I was very fortunate to be brought up by four wonderful and supportive parents. I'm sorry one of them didn't get to see me achieve this particular dream, but I like to imagine he's looking down from the night sky over Hazelworth.

Above all, thanks to my own Train Man, Mark, whose beauty and kindness inspires me in everything I do: in my heart, in my work and for our sons.